A House Divided

ALSO AVAILABLE BY JONATHAN F. PUTNAM

Lincoln and Speed mysteries

Final Resting Place

Perish from the Earth

These Honored Dead

A House Divided

A Lincoln and Speed Mystery

Jonathan F. Putnam

NEW YORK

This is a work of fiction. All of the names, characters, organizations, places and events portrayed in this novel are either products of the author's imagination or are used fictitiously. Any resemblance to real or actual events, locales, or persons, living or dead, is entirely coincidental.

Copyright © 2019 by Jonathan F. Putnam.

All rights reserved.

Published in the United States by Crooked Lane Books, an imprint of The Quick Brown Fox & Company LLC.

Crooked Lane Books and its logo are trademarks of The Quick Brown Fox & Company LLC.

Library of Congress Catalog-in-Publication data available upon request.

ISBN (hardcover): 978-1-64385-037-5
ISBN (ePub): 978-1-64385-038-2
ISBN (ePDF): 978-1-64385-039-9

Cover design by Melanie Sun
Book design by Jennifer Canzone

Printed in the United States.

www.crookedlanebooks.com

Crooked Lane Books
34 West 27th St., 10th Floor
New York, NY 10001

First Edition: July 2019

10 9 8 7 6 5 4 3 2 1

For my sister, Lara Putnam,
who's been helping me keep my story straight
for nearly fifty years

Chapter 1

A dishonest banker brought me to Chicago, and a pickpocket I met there saved my life.

It was a chilly day in December 1839, and I stood in the drizzle on muddy Water Street. In front of me was the four-story brick block that housed the Chicago branch of the State Bank. At my back was the Chicago River, a sea-green ribbon of tumultuous swells flowing into an endless blue lake under steel-gray skies. Wind whipping off the lake took the water gathered on the brim of my hat and blew it sideways.

I was waiting for a man named Brown. The bank in this tenuous, boom-and-bust city kept running out of hard currency, with disastrous consequences, but no one could figure out why. After several fruitless investigations, the town fathers in Springfield, the state capital, had asked me to look into the mystery. Brown, the cashier of the bank, was my best lead.

After I'd been lingering on the street for an hour, a trim man with a shiny black top hat, fully buttoned vest under his frock-coat, and a walking stick came down the stairs and headed toward the lakefront. I fell into step next to him.

"Brown?" I began.

"If you're looking for a loan, the answer's no," the banker said without breaking stride. His face bore elaborate whiskers and the supercilious expression common to men of his detested profession.

"Quite the opposite. I'm looking for a safe place to keep the funds of my general store, A.Y. Ellis & Co., of Springfield. My name's Speed," I added, extending my hand in greeting.

He gave it a quick, unenthusiastic shake and kept walking. "Why aren't you using the Springfield branch?"

"I'm expanding my business to Chicago," I lied, "and need a local connection."

Brown came to a halt next to an upright wooden windlass that marked one end of the ferry crossing. A bell tinkled, and the rope attached to the crossbar strained as the ferry left the opposite bank and began its journey through the choppy waters toward us.

"We accept paper on Mondays and Thursdays," Brown said. "Come by then, if what you say is true. But we don't take Michigan money. Or canal scrip. All worthless. Only genuine notes issued by the State Bank of Illinois."

The ferry, a flat wooden platform, reached us, and we stood aside as a few men straggled off, bent over against the late-afternoon chill, followed by a double-team of horses pulling a wagon piled high with hog carcasses. The banker stepped aboard and I followed.

The ferryman, a burly man with a blistered face, stopped me and held out a hand riven by scars and calluses. Spray from the river dripped from the bottom of his thick navy pants.

"Across and back," I said.

"That's a halfpenny."

I pulled my leather purse from the pocket of my greatcoat and handed him a bright silver dime. The ferryman sighed loudly and made a show of counting out my change. Three or four other men came aboard, and the ferryman swung his gate shut and started pulling us hand-over-hand into the river. I turned back to Brown and nearly recoiled at the look of unabashed greed in his eyes.

"I've spoken too hastily, Mr. Speed," he said. "I didn't realize you have hard currency to deposit."

"I certainly do."

"That's different than paper. A different situation altogether. Not enough silver or gold in this town to support a tenth of its commerce. You come by my branch anytime."

I touched my hat to acknowledge his newfound amity. The ferry rocked through the swirling river waters. With a jolt, it reached the north bank. One of the other passengers jostled me as we began to disembark. Glancing over, I felt sure I recognized the man as a young laborer from Springfield who came into my store for supplies now and again. I searched my brain but could not come up with a name to fit his features: lanky frame; long, curly hair tossed by the breeze; and a lean face covered by patchy whiskers. I called out a greeting, but the man was already loping away across the landing platform.

"I'll see you soon, friend," Brown was saying. He, too, started to head off.

"Before you go," I said, "can you assure me the rumors aren't true?"

"What rumors?" Brown turned back, annoyed.

"I've been told money flows out of your branch so quickly it's like you've got a hole cut in the bottom of the vault."

"There's no place safer in town to store your hard currency. You have my word."

"Who guards the vault?"

"I have the only key on my person at all times." He patted his pocket with well-kept fingers. "That way I know it's secure."

I felt certain Brown was my man. Now I just had to find the proof.

After taking the ferry back to the south side of the river, I walked a few paces to Chicago's post office. I pushed through the door into a cluttered chamber, lit only by the thin light filtering through two small windows. A middle-aged man with gaudy whiskers straightened as I entered. A handwritten sign resting on the low wooden counter announced, SIDNEY ABELL, POSTMASTER.

"How frequently does the mail pouch depart for Springfield?" I asked.

"It's on the coach for Joliet at two AM daily, Sundays excepted," said Abell in a squeaky voice. "I'm not certain how often Mr. VanHorne sends his coaches south from there towards Springfield, but your letter will arrive in good time."

One of the men who had asked me to investigate the State Bank in Chicago was the fellow I shared lodgings with, a young lawyer and member of the banking committee in the state legislature. I asked Abell for a sheet of writing paper and hastily wrote out a note describing my investigations so far and relating that I hoped to return home within a few days.

I folded the letter, wrote *A. Lincoln, Hoffman's Row, Springfield* on the outside flap, and handed it to Abell.

"Your Mr. Lincoln will pay the postage, of course," he said, "but that'll be a penny for the paper."

I gave the man a sharp look; most postmasters were in the habit of giving away writing materials without charge to promote the business of the mails, and the fact that Abell did not could only be a sign of personal avarice. I reached for my purse, but my hand came away empty. I searched each of the pockets of my greatcoat and then, panic steadily growing, of my waistcoat and pantaloons underneath. The change provided by the ferryman jangled in one pocket; otherwise, I was penniless.

"Don't tell me you've misplaced the thing," said Abell as he watched my search. "How many times do you think I've heard that?"

"I paid the ferryman for passage not thirty minutes ago. I must have lost my purse since then, along the street perhaps. And it contains something much more valuable than money. I've got to find it."

But as I turned to leave, Abell's hand clenched my wrist. "You'll do no such thing," he said, his unfriendly eyes hard on mine. "I want my cent. *Now.*"

Lincoln had better savor his update, I thought as I offered Abell a penny. The postmaster snatched the coin with greedy fingers and promised that my letter would be on the night's stage. Then I rushed out in search of the purse.

That it contained all the money I'd brought on the long trip from Springfield was the least of my worries. The purse contained a priceless possession: the only portrait I had of my youngest sister, Ann, who had passed away last year at the age of eight. I could not bear the thought I'd lost it.

But an hour spent searching the darkening, windswept streets produced no sign of my purse, and I was forced to conclude it was gone. I was crushed. I opened the locket containing Ann's likeness every evening as I prepared for bed. Thinking about my afternoon again, I wondered whether the laborer who had jostled me aboard the ferry had lifted it. If so, at least I'd have a chance of encountering the villain back home in Springfield.

My only other hope was that someone would find the purse and have the decency to restore it to me. The next morning, I paid a visit to the offices of the *Daily Chicago American* and used most of my remaining funds to place a notice describing the lost purse and locket and offering a handsome reward for their return. Then I returned to the streets, my chest aching from the loss of Ann's portrait.

Chicago was a chaotic place. A throng of rootless men in dingy clothes clogged the streets beside me. Several of the principal roads had been graded, with plank sluices set along the edges to carry surface water toward the river, but the rest of the streets were muddy and unimproved. There was a frozen pond lying at the corner of Lake and LaSalle streets; one local told me that, in the summer months, it was full of belching bullfrogs.

Only 350 people had lived in the city a scant seven years ago, but now more than 4,000 called it home. Most had been drawn by the state's promise to build a canal linking Lake Michigan to the Mississippi River and thereby transform Chicago into the essential crossroads of northwestern trade. The Canal Board had encouraged hundreds of Irishmen to migrate here from western New York, where they had recently finished digging the great Erie Canal. But the state's faltering finances amid a nationwide depression had put an indefinite halt to these grand plans. The troubles of the State Bank had been the last straw. The Canal Board was out of funds and deeply in debt. The canal workers hadn't been paid in months. No one knew if or when work on the canal would resume.

That afternoon, I rode my horse Hickory through a coarse growth of oak and underbrush, wet and slushy, to find the canal terminus. I sat astride Hickory on the canal embankment and watched a handful of Irishmen dig away ineffectually at the bottom. After a few desultory minutes the lads stopped working and began arguing with each other over some triviality. Soon the angry words turned to blows and the navvies were rolling around on top of each other, a sorry, muddy mass.

On our way back, Hickory and I came upon a cluster of lean-tos thrown up for the Irish by the Canal Board. The hovels had been erected without much regard for lines, and they perched uncertainly on a hill. Several children, clothed only by filthy rags wound around their midsections, played in the mud in front of their dwelling. One brave little boy, his face hollow and his ribs nearly sticking out of his chest, came over to greet Hickory. The horse dipped her head and let herself be stroked.

"If you please, sir."

I looked up. A thin woman with the hardship of the times etched on her face stood a few feet away. She held a fussing infant in one arm, while her other hand was outstretched, her fingers cupped and trembling.

"If you please, sir," she repeated. She used her forearm to brush a strand of graying hair away from her eyes. "The little ones, they haven't had anything to eat for days."

"The Board doesn't feed you?"

"I haven't seen the Board since last summer."

"Your husband?"

She merely shook her head. The infant in her arms let out a cry, and the woman started humming a lullaby, jiggling the baby up and down. All the while, her desperate eyes never left my face.

The other children who had been playing in the mud were all gathered around Hickory now, encouraged by the first boy's boldness, and the horse whinnied nervously at all of the little hands grabbing at her forelegs.

"Careful they don't get stepped on," I said. I reached into the pocket of my coat and pulled out my three remaining pennies. Bending down, I handed them to the woman. Her palm was ice-cold to the touch. "It's all I have. Truly. I wish I had more."

The woman's eyes flickered from my fine clothing to my well-fed horse and finally to her ragged children on the muddy ground. She turned back silently for the hovel behind her.

"I'll be back with more if I can," I called after her, but the woman gave no sign she'd heard me as she trudged away, her crying infant squirming in her arms.

Chapter 2

As we trotted back toward the forks, the lake was on our right, a vast mirror shimmering in the pale afternoon sun. In front of us, a thin layer of smoke hovered above the rude procession of shanty chimneys and ramshackle structures that comprised Chicago. The field petered out, slowly replaced by small farms and then an irregular street grid. Hickory was a clever, nimble mare, but even she was unable to avoid sinking down with each step along the swampy streets as we proceeded toward Beaubien's Sauganash Tavern, hard along the south fork of the river.

The sleeping quarters at the Sauganash were scarcely deserving of the name. The partitions between rooms consisted of upright studs with bedsheets stretched across them. The inn was crowded with people, both travelers and newly arrived immigrants to the city, who spent their nights sprawled on wood floors, a weary, stinking mass of humanity.

On account of my reputable appearance, Beaubien had graciously allowed me to sleep in his "private chamber," a bare room eight foot square, which I shared with three other men of equal stature. He had also agreed to extend credit and accept payment for my lodging and meals at the end of my stay. Ever since I'd lost my purse, I'd taken every meal at his table. I wasn't looking forward to our conversation on the morning of my departure.

Beaubien's public room was slightly more welcoming. Wood beams ran the length of the low ceiling, drawing visitors toward the bar, where the tavernkeeper presided next to an open barrel of liquor.

"Where'd you go today, Speed?" Beaubien asked as he handed me a clear, brimming glass. The whiskey burned its way down my throat, but it felt warm after the cold day's ride.

"Canalport. Those Irish families are in bad shape."

Beaubien shrugged. "No one made 'em come here. They can sail for home if they don't like it."

"The ones I encountered didn't look strong enough to walk a mile."

There was a pounding at the door, and the innkeeper looked up. The city's waterman had arrived to make his delivery of fresh water from the lake. He backed up his two-wheeled cart, laden with four large hogshead casks and pulled by a beaten-down old nag. Then he extended a leathern hose from the base of one of his casks into a large barrel Beaubien kept just inside his front door. When the barrel was filled, Beaubien handed over a few small slips of paper. The waterman looked up in anger.

"You know I don' accept canal scrip," he said, crumpling the slips and dumping them back into Beaubien's hands. The waterman's face was lined with age and his eyes rheumy. "No telling when the State Bank will get around to redeeming them. If they ever do. I need hard money or you ain't getting water no more."

Beaubien sighed loudly. "Hear now, scrip is all I get from my lodgers these days. Can't pay you what I don't have."

"That's your problem, ain't it?"

The men stared at each other impassively. Finally, a nasty look on his face, Beaubien dug into his pocket and counted out six pennies. The waterman grunted in satisfaction, rolled up his hose, and trudged off down the street, whipping his horse mercilessly as he did.

"Thus, the waterworks of the great city of Chicago," Beaubien said with a grimace, as he saw me studying the transaction. "You should have seen this place a few years back, Speed, before the Panic and everything else that's happened. Men came into town on a Monday, bought up three lots along the canal route on Tuesday, and sold 'em on Thursday for a fifty percent profit. They were heady times."

The next morning, I set out to prove my case against the larcenous bank cashier. Without a purse full of silver coins, there seemed no point in meeting Brown face-to-face. Instead, I blended into the crowd and trailed his progress through the muddy streets. He visited Underhill's slaughterhouse on South Water, Funk's butcher shop on State, Marsh's packing house on Carroll, and then went back again to Underhill's. For a banker, Brown sure spent a lot of time looking at pigs. This gave me an idea.

After waiting until Brown had disappeared down the street, I ventured inside Underhill's, a log cabin near the south bank of the river. A good deal of grunting and an overpowering smell emanated from the livestock pens out back. Underhill looked up when I entered. He was a ruddy Englishman, with a full belly and curly light-brown hair, wearing a blood-splattered apron. Rather than greeting him, however, I made a show of walking around his establishment, inspecting the carcasses hanging from the ceiling and the cut-up meats on his counter, murmuring to myself all the while.

"I'll just have a look out back," I said, moving to walk through the door leading to the pens.

"Who the devil are you?" Underhill demanded, blocking my way.

"Who *I* am is unimportant. What's important is who my employer is. You've heard of Tate Brothers of New York City, of course."

"I'm sure I have," said Underhill, his hands on his hips. If he had, that made one of us.

"Then perhaps you know Tate Brothers is the largest purveyor of pork in five separate eastern states. Six, if you count Vermont. I've been sent to Chicago to search for a new wholesale source. A *huge* source. Someone gave me your name. But—" I looked around critically, clicking my tongue "—I've been misinformed."

"What do you mean, misinformed?"

"I was told Underhill's was a substantial establishment. One that could supply us with a thousand pigs a month." I shook my head and turned to leave. "I guess I'll try Marsh's."

Underhill nearly leapt to restrain me. "Hold on one minute, sir. You were very much *correctly* informed. You've come to the right place. There's no finer slaughterhouse in Chicago. If a thousand a month is what you need, this is the place for you."

"Certainly not. From the look of your pens, you can't have fifty head out there."

"That's because we've recently sent a large shipment off to Toronto. We'll be receiving more stock next week. And we can expand to as much head as we need. We've got unlimited funds."

I laughed harshly. "No one's got unlimited funds these days."

"*We* do. We've got a whole bank's worth of funds. A whole state's worth."

"What?"

Underhill leaned forward and took on a confidential tone. "I wouldn't normally share my particulars, but for Tate Brothers I can make an exception. We're in business with the cashier of the State Bank. Speculation business. Pork speculation, to be specific. Exactly what you're after. We look for opportunities that may arise, and he accommodates us the funds to pursue 'em. Funds from the bank, you see."

"That's a lie," I said.

"No, it ain't." Underhill's face had turned a splotchy red.

"It must be a lie. No bank, especially not the State Bank, would operate that way."

"I swear it's the truth. The cashier was here a little while ago. You just missed him. Sharp fellow, name of Brown. I can introduce you if you'd like." I put up my hand to indicate that wouldn't be necessary, and Underhill continued, his voice rising higher with excitement. "Why, just in the last year, Brown's accommodated me to the amount of twenty thousand dollars." I whistled softly at the figure. "It ain't returned much, not yet, but it's only a matter of time. Especially when Tate Brothers' business is added in."

I shook my head slowly. "If all that's true, we'd be interested. Very interested." I paused. "But when I go back to New York City with this story, they'll never believe me. Especially the older brother, Mr. Benjamin Tate. He doesn't believe anything he can't see with his own eyes. 'Unlimited funds'? Mr. Benjamin Tate won't believe a kite-flying scheme like that. Not for one single second. Nice talking with you, Underhill." I turned again to leave.

"Wait! I can prove it."

"How?"

He hesitated, but only for an instant, his greed getting in the way of whatever common sense he otherwise possessed. "I can give you a copy of the note between myself and Brown, the note spelling out the particulars of our arrangement."

"I suppose," I replied, weighing his words carefully, "if it was an official copy of the official note, and it contained all the particulars . . . maybe, just maybe, that'd be enough to convince Mr. Benjamin Tate."

"Wait here," Underhill shouted, and he scurried away to a side room. Thirty seconds later he hurried back, clutching a piece of parchment covered with cramped, precise writing.

"It's all here," he said. "All the details, right here."

I read it over twice. He was telling the truth. All the details were right there.

"I think that'll do the trick," I said. I rolled up the parchment, slipped it into my pocket, and shook Underhill's hand vigorously. "Congratulations, sir. You're in business with Tate Brothers. You'll be hearing from us in due course." I nearly sprinted out of the slaughterhouse before Underhill could reconsider. Ten minutes later I was back inside the public room at Beaubien's, a broad smile on my face.

"Better day today?" asked Beaubien as he handed me a glass of whiskey.

"Much better. I'll be riding off tomorrow. Home to Springfield at last."

"You've got to tell those godforsaken politicians in that godforsaken town they've got to fix this mess we're in."

"I'll do my best." Springfield had recently become the state capital and seat of government. The change had not helped the town's reputation.

There was a shout of laughter from behind me, and I saw two men sitting with their backs toward me along one of the long tables that lined the room. One of the men was young and thin; the other was older and wider. Their heads were leaned together in close conversation, but there was something familiar about the appearance of the younger figure.

I refilled my glass and moved to sit down a table away from them. From this closer perch, I was sure the younger fellow was, indeed, the pickpocket from the ferry. I strained to hear their conversation above the general din, but the only words I could decipher were "canal route."

Beaubien made my next move for me.

"You two have been taking up those seats for too long," the innkeeper said, approaching the men with a temper. "Pay me for what you've drunk and push off."

"We was just leaving," the younger man said as he struggled to his feet. His voice was a little high-pitched. "I'll pay for the both of us." He reached into the pocket of his shapeless coat and pulled out my leather pouch.

I raced over and spun the man around by his shoulders. A smile burst onto his face. "Mr. Speed," he exclaimed. "What good fortune to see you."

"So you admit knowing me?" I asked, taken aback by his reaction.

"'Course I do." He grabbed my hand with both of his and began pumping it. "Trailor. Archibald Trailor. The carpenter. I've been working on that bookshelf for your friend Mr. Lincoln, for his law offices."

I remembered him now: a nice enough fellow, if a bit slow, to whom I'd sold boards and nails on occasion. Lincoln had told me he was a brilliant carpenter—"good with his hands," Lincoln said. But I was in no mood to appreciate the unintended humor in the statement.

"What are you doing with my purse?" I demanded. "I placed an advertisement seeking its return." I showed him a copy of the *American* I'd kept in my pocket.

Trailor stared at the newspaper briefly, his eyes unfocused, and turned back to me. In a flash, I realized he couldn't read the words on the page.

"I must of missed the notice," he said, "which is why I'm pleased we found each other in the flesh. I uncovered the thing lying in the mud on Kinzie, north of the river. Cleaned it off, had a peek inside, saw your name. So I've been keeping an eye out for you, as I figured you must be about. 'Course I knew I could deliver it to you back in Springfield, if it came to that." He gave a slight bow and placed the purse in my hand.

My heart racing, I undid the drawstring. The locket was there, nestled at the bottom of the pouch. I open it and gazed at Ann's face, and a feeling of peace flooded through my body. Then I recalled the circumstances by which I'd lost the purse and locket in the first place, and I snapped the thing shut and turned back to Trailor.

"Found it in the mud? Nonsense! You lifted it from me. When we encountered each other on the river ferry, a few days back."

"I ought to be offended you'd suggest such a thing," said Trailor mildly. "And we didn't see each other on any ferry, neither. With all respect's due, sir." He gave me a guileless smile and touched his worn cap.

Beaubien coughed. "Are you paying for their drinks, Speed? Somebody's got to."

Trailor looked at me expectantly. "Would you mind? As a reward for my finding your purse and restoring it to you. 'Course, before you count out your coins, I should say I've helped myself already to a *mite* of a reward. Seemed fair. If I hadn't found it, you'd have a total loss." He gave a modest shrug.

"How much did you spend?" I demanded, dumping the remaining coins onto the table and sorting through them.

"Dunno." Trailor nodded at his companion. "Fisher here and I didn't spend a single penny more than our circumstances required, I assure you."

I studied Fisher for the first time. He was old enough to be Trailor's father, though the two men bore no physical resemblance. Fisher appeared to be fifty years of age, with a paunchy midsection and a fleshy face. He had the dark-red hair and red-tinged cheeks of an Irishman. What I had originally taken to be the lean of his head as he spoke in confidence to Trailor appeared to be a permanent defect, as even now he stood with his head cocked over his right shoulder. He was wearing a faded jacket decorated with the insignia of a band of military irregulars and sturdy army-issue boots. On his little finger I noticed the dull shine of a silver ring, on which were inscribed several initials.

"Who's to give me a half dime for their drinks?" Beaubien demanded again.

"I'll take care of it," I said, handing a coin over. Looking at Trailor through narrowed eyes, I added, "I think you've been rewarded more than sufficiently by now."

"I thank you kindly, Mr. Speed. We're square. When are you heading back to Springfield?"

"Tomorrow morning, break of dawn." The answer was out of my mouth before I realized I should have hedged.

"Why, that's quite a coincidence," returned Trailor, breaking into a smile that displayed two rows of crooked teeth. "I myself have precisely the same intention. Perhaps we should ride together."

"I'm not too sure of that." The less time spent with Trailor, I thought, the fuller my wallet would remain upon my return to Springfield. "I've been looking forward to the solitude of the open prairie."

Trailor shrugged. "It's a long journey, especially with winter on her way. And it's said armed thieves roam the prairie these days. But if you'd rather make the ride alone, I shan't disturb you. I'll see you around Springfield, I expect. Let's be off, Fisher. Our run here's over."

Chapter 3

I was out on the riverbank with Hickory an hour before dawn the next morning, the note documenting the banker's illicit pork speculation tucked securely into one of my saddlebags. I wanted to leave well before the time I'd told Trailor. Besides, I hoped to make the entire return journey to Springfield in just two days, a feat that would require early departures and late arrivals at every aspect. Especially with the stop I had to make first.

I let my animal graze on a few blades of grass poking their way through the light dusting of snow that had fallen overnight. It was a cold morning, the temperature right around the freezing point, and the horse's breath streamed through her nostrils like the smoke from a great train engine.

Just as I pulled on Hickory's reins to set her into motion, we heard the *clip-clop* of a horse approaching through the darkness. Archibald Trailor materialized astride a good-sized painted horse.

"Morning, Trailor," I said without enthusiasm.

"Good morning to you," he returned cheerfully. "I didn't expect to encounter you, not this early. I guess it's written that we're to ride together after all."

Archibald leapt down out of his saddle. "Darley here was

displeased with the chill this morning, so I gave him an extra portion. Need to keep the transport happy, don't you know, Mr. Speed?"

"Listen, Trailor, you might as well drop the 'Mister,' if we're to journey together. I'm Speed to my friends. Mr. Speed is my father, at least when he's not 'Judge Speed' on the bench. Anyway, Hickory and I were just about to leave."

The horses did their best to ignore each other. Archibald walked over to Hickory and let her sniff his hand. When she appeared satisfied, he reached up and gently ran his hand over her mane. "She's a beautiful animal," he said. "How long have you had her?"

I could control my impatience no longer. "Let's be on our way. We'll have plenty of time for talk during the ride. Follow me. We'll stop once before we head out to the prairie."

Archibald gave me a look but did not voice his question aloud, and he mounted his painter. I led the way as we rode toward Canalport. The eastern skies were only now starting to brighten, but Hickory was a clever girl, and when I told her we were retracing our steps from several days earlier, she seemed to understand. Sure enough, just as the sun's rays began to flicker off the tallest treetops, we came to the group of Canal Board lean-tos.

"This'll just take a minute," I said to Archibald as I slid off Hickory's back. I walked up to the shanty into which the Irish mother had disappeared and knocked loudly. I could hear movement inside, but no one came to the door.

"Open up," I called. There were sounds of more scurrying around inside, but no one responded. A candle flickered on in a neighboring shanty.

"I say, open up!" Louder this time, and I pounded on the door. There was the sound of muffled discussion, unintelligible, and a voice called out, "Go away! We haven't got it."

"Haven't got what?"

"Whatever debt you're collecting. Go away!"

"I'm not collecting. I have something for you. Open up!"

This time the door opened slowly, and a tall, haggard Irishman, his hair disheveled from sleep, stood in the doorway. I saw the mother I'd spoken to the other day hovering behind him, but when her eyes fell upon me, they widened in surprise and she shook her head violently.

"Who're you, calling at the Lord's hour?" demanded the man through a thick Irish brogue. "What d'you want?"

I reached into my purse and drew out two shiny gold coins, quarter eagles worth two and a half dollars each. "I don't want anything, other than to give these to you."

The man stared at the coins suspiciously. "What're they for?" He swung around and demanded of his wife, "Is this your doing? What've you done?"

"It's nothing to do with her," I said. "I've come on behalf of the Canal Board. They asked me to give them to you. Now take them, or I'll give them to your neighbor. It's of no concern to me. Or maybe I'll keep them myself. I was doing a courtesy for the Board, but if you don't want—"

"I want 'em all right. It's less than half I'm owed. But it's something." The man reached out cautiously, as if still expecting some kind of trick. But when I handed over the coins, his whole body shook, and his wife seemed on the brink of tears.

I left them embracing each other and returned to where Hickory and Archibald were waiting.

"I didn't know you worked for the Canal Board," Archibald said as we rode off.

I smiled. "I don't. I didn't want them to know it was charity."

Archibald thought about this and nodded, and we rode together in silence. Before long we were out into the great prairie. The winter prairie was shades of browns and grays in the slowly rising sun, flecked here and there by the white of snow. The incessant winds had thoroughly rearranged the snow, such that the higher elevations were bare of it while the furrows and swales were piled high. The carriage trail was clear and dry as it rose to meet the hills, icy or slushy in the lower-lying areas. Both horses cantered along with grace, seemingly unmoved by the conditions.

"What brought you to Chicago?" asked Archibald when we stopped to make a noontime meal of hardtack while the horses rested and drank from slushy water.

"I was taking a look into the State Bank. It's been leaking hard currency ever since the Panic set in. No one's getting paid for the canal work they did, and men in Springfield are worried the situation is dire. You?"

"Other side of the same coin. Fisher's pretty desperate himself, with the canal stopped. He holds a contract for a bypass along the route that's hung up. I told him I'd see if I could help him gather information on when work on the canal might resume. Not that we found out much of use. No one seems to know anything."

"Times are tough all over," I said sympathetically.

"Fisher's not quite as bad off as those people you helped back at Canalport, but he ain't far off."

"He could sell his ring, if it came to that." I thought back to the jewelry I'd seen on Fisher's finger. Even in these depressed times, I knew it would bring a good price.

"He couldn't," said Archibald, shaking his head solemnly.

"Why not?"

"It's a mourning ring, to remember his wife and first child. Only child. They died together, at birth. He never takes it off."

We made good time that first day, laying down close to seventy miles before stopping for the night at Perry's tavern at the

Pontiac crossroads, where Archibald and I huddled together to keep warm on a bed of damp straw that stank of gin. Archibald managed to be in the privy at the very moment Perry came to collect his rent, and I shook my head at Archibald's cadging skills and handed over coins for the both of us.

We were back on the trail hours before the sun rose the next morning, and I grew increasingly hopeful we would make it back to Springfield that evening. We took turns riding the point and spoke little, the horses' steady beats and the gusting winds the only sounds to spoil the stillness of the vast land.

Archibald had been leading for several hours, the faint midwinter sun starting to cast lengthening shadows alongside the horses, when he looked over his shoulder.

"How many siblings do you have, Speed?"

"Nine who are living. How about you?"

"Just my two brothers." Archibald's eyes were suddenly cloudy, and he paused before continuing. "But sometimes I can't figure why the Almighty thought two was the best number for me."

I spurred Hickory forward until we were even with Archibald. "How do you mean?"

"It's my lot in life to care for them, whether they want it or not."

"Care for them? How much younger are they?"

Archibald shook his head. "Older, not younger. William, he's twenty years my senior. Owns a concern that was digging part of the canal until the work stopped. And Henry's a few years below William. Henry's a builder. Done some work in Springfield. Then our momma had a whole run of babies who didn't live, not long, anyway, and then she had me and she didn't survive my birth." He blinked. "I didn't know her for more than but a day or two."

"I'm sorry. But meaning no disrespect, Archibald, it sounds

as if each of your brothers is in a position to fend for himself. I don't understand why you need to care for them." If anything, I thought, the reverse was true.

Archibald had pulled up his horse, and the animals were still, the vast prairie stretching to the horizon in every direction.

"My papa made me promise I would," he said.

"When?"

"Last time I ever saw him. I was near on six years of age at the time, I reckon."

I started to object, but Archibald continued, the words tumbling out. "I made him a promise and I've got to keep it. I know I'm not as respectable as either of my brothers. Don't have my own home, or a profession people admire. You see, I didn't have the same chance as a lad to get an education from books like they did. But I make do, find ways to be useful, keep myself fed."

"You're to be admired for that."

Archibald prodded his painter back into action with a gentle slap to the shoulder. "You'll see for yourself, soon enough. I'm thinking we're about ten miles from Henry's homestead. That's where we're sleeping tonight."

It took a moment for his words to sink in. "Hold on," I said. "We're getting to Springfield tonight. At least I hope we are. You'll have to see your brother another time."

"No we ain't," Archibald said over his shoulder as he rode on. "That's why I had us turn east at Holland's crossroads couple hours back. We're heading for Henry's, little ways past Bloomington. We couldn't reach Springfield tonight from here, even if we wanted to."

I gaped at Archibald's back, then stared up at the sky. From the position of the sun, low on the horizon, I saw at once he spoke the truth. The carriage path from Chicago to Springfield was consistently southwest in direction, straight into the winter's afternoon sun. But the sun stood far off to our right; I realized now that the aspect of sunlight in my eyes had changed sometime earlier. Cursing under my breath, I spurred Hickory forward.

Henry Trailor's house sat amid a loosely connected series of farms. It consisted of two modest-sized rooms, and the exterior logs retained the green tinge of having been recently cut. But Trailor had not spared in his use of pitch, and the rooms pleasingly held the heat from the large hearth that dominated the living room. Henry's wife, a tiny, timid girl, served a decent stew, and as I stretched out on a bed of prairie feathers in the corner of the sleeping room, I had nearly forgotten my grievance about Archibald's detour. I was on the edge of sleep when I heard voices, whispered at first but then rising in anger.

"I thought you were going to talk to William about him," Henry was saying as my mind snapped back into consciousness. Henry Trailor was a few inches shorter than his brother Archibald, with a potbelly and—I had discovered as we sat across the cramped dinner table from each other—a permanent scowl. He had the scolding voice of a peevish magpie.

"I'll do it if you insist," Archibald answered in a soft, steady voice. "Though I don't think we're needing to."

Henry grunted. "You don't understand, Archie. You never have. He's all of our concern, as long as he's in this with us. William was the one who burdened us with him in the first place. He should be the one to get rid of him. But if he won't, it's got to be you. Otherwise the riches won't be ours."

Archibald glanced in my direction, and I lay still and pretended to sleep. The tallow candles had been touched out, and the only light came from a few dying embers on the hearth.

"I do understand, Henry," Archibald said, an earnest tone in his low voice. "'Course I do. William told us he had to be part of it. Isn't that good enough?"

There was a small, dismissive noise, and I realized Henry had spat against his own wall. "Still blindly following William, are you?" he said, his voice rising higher by a couple of notes. "I should have thought you'd outgrow that habit. I did long ago, soon as I could think for myself."

Archibald muttered something indistinct in response. Suddenly I felt protective of the simple carpenter, although I had no stake in the argument, nor much interest in their affairs. If the Trailor brothers *hadn't* had some sort of scheme for quick riches, it would have been more of a surprise, given the tenor of the times, where the dream of great wealth hovered all around the impoverished present, like a low cloud floating just out of reach. But feeling sorry for Archibald, I coughed and turned over. As I had hoped, the reminder they were not alone tempered Henry's instinct to bully and browbeat, and the brothers soon fell silent.

Archibald and I left at daybreak. As we were mounting our horses, Henry came to the doorway, wearing nothing but his underclothes.

"Remember what you've promised to talk to William about," Henry called. "See if you can manage to get something right for once." He slammed the door shut before Archibald could respond.

When we were several hundred paces away from Henry's house, I turned to Archibald and said, "He only treats you like that because he knows you're the better man."

Archibald rode for a minute. Then he looked over at me and said simply, "Thank you, Speed." I thought there might be tears in his eyes, but he turned away before I could tell for sure.

We rode on in silence. A cold mist started to hang over us, and I longed for the comfort of my own bed.

It was midafternoon when we first heard the sound. We were in the final stretch of prairie that encircled Springfield; our homes were ten miles away, twelve at most, and both of us, and our horses too, were glad to be nearing the end of the long journey. The prairie was vast and barren, an undulating meadow of lifeless brown grass. There was not a tree in sight, nor a dwelling anywhere.

I began to realize there was a low rumble off in the distance. The sound crept slowly into my consciousness, such that I couldn't have said exactly when I first heard it. All I knew was that it did register, and at that moment I knew it had been there the minute before as well. Whether the minute before that one, I could not say.

It sounded at first like waters flowing together at a distant junction, or thunder just over the horizon. Hickory had noticed it before me, for her ears were alert and twitching, and once or twice she had turned her head to try to look behind us, though I held her reins straight. She was unsettled.

"What's that noise?" I said aloud. It was the first time either of us had spoken in hours.

Archibald pulled up his horse and cocked his head. "I don't hear nothin'."

"I'm certain of it. And look at the horses." Hickory and Darley were both alert and nervous, prancing about on the muddy path.

Archibald squinted through the cold drizzle, which condensed on the brim of his hat and dripped down to the ground. We felt the wind turn suddenly and blow toward the north, only it seemed like it was being sucked there by some powerful force rather than blowing on its own accord. The horses whimpered.

"Whatever it is," I said, "I don't want to wait for it. Let's make haste." I slapped Hickory twice on her hind flank, and though the beast was tired from the trip, she willingly began galloping toward Springfield. Archibald and Darley raced in step with us.

There was no mistaking the noise now, and despite our quickened pace there was no mistaking that it was gaining on us. It was an incessant drumbeat, like a herd of a hundred cattle running across the plain after us, now five hundred cattle, now a thousand, a herd so vast the thundering hooves drowned out all other noise. Archibald looked back over his shoulder and I saw him scream, though no sound reached my ears. I turned to see the cause of his horror and nearly fell from my mount.

A wall of liquid ice swept across the plain towards us, like the leading edge of a freezing waterfall, only it was a waterfall so vast that it stretched from one side of the horizon to the other and so tall that its source was the very heavens themselves. Ahead of the ice storm I felt a powerful chill radiating out, a chill that grabbed hold of my soul and sought to snuff out all hope.

In an instant it was upon us. Pellets the size of walnuts rained down. It was as if we were standing directly under the spigot of a vast, infinitely large barrel of ice. As the cold swept over, the muddy ground seemed to harden in a blink, like molten lead poured from a cask.

I kicked Hickory's ribs and urged her to keep galloping. Perhaps we could outrun it. I sensed Archibald and Darley racing just ahead of us, though the raging storm blocked out all other sight and sound.

Hickory galloped as fast as she could, the ice rattling from her reins, but the storm was faster. The ground was rapidly covering with ice, and Hickory started to lose her footing. At this pace, the safety of Springfield was not more than thirty minutes away. If only we could get there.

All at once, I thought of my younger sister Martha, who lived in Springfield near me. It was a Saturday afternoon, so likely she'd be at home, helping her friend Molly Hutchason prepare the evening meal. But what if she was out on one of her walks through the farms that ringed town? What if she was searching the prairie for one last bunch of wildflowers?

I had to get to Springfield ahead of the storm to warn

Martha. To save her! I kicked Hickory again and again, urging her to go still faster.

Suddenly I felt Hickory's shod hooves skidding on the ice. I hung on as she skidded one way, then was thrown up off the saddle as she reversed field and skidded the other. There was a terrible moment when I realized I had lost touch with the animal, that I was floating in the air above her. Then I crashed awkwardly to the ground, landing on my right foot an instant before my face slammed into a rough sheet of ice. As I skidded to a stop, blood poured from my nose, while my ankle seared with pain.

I looked up in time to see Hickory disappearing into the fog of ice, following Archibald and Darley as they hurtled toward the safety of Springfield. I shouted for help at the top of my lungs, but I could scarcely hear myself, and I knew it was irrational to hold out even the slightest hope that anyone could hear me.

Bracing myself against the ground, I tried to stand. But as soon as I put any weight on my right ankle, I was shot through with pain, and I screamed and collapsed again. I was crippled and alone on the shelterless prairie.

Chapter 4

The ice beat down with unrelenting fury. I gathered up a handful and held it to my nose to stem the bleeding.

"Archibald?" I shouted into the remorseless void. "Hickory? Darley?" I paused, took a deep breath, and then yelled at the top of my lungs, "Help me!"

I listened, but there was nothing but the drumming of the ice. And then, far away in the distance, but gradually coming closer, was the sound of . . . hoofbeats? Could it be Hickory coming back for me?

"Over here!" I screamed. "Over here! Hickory! Come, girl!"

I saw a shadow in the ice ahead of me and screamed Hickory's name again. A few moments later, the shadow dissolved into an actual horse, but it wasn't Hickory. *Darley! Darley with Archibald Trailor still in the saddle!*

"Archibald!" I shouted. "You came back." I felt tears welling up in my eyes, but they froze before they could escape.

The lanky carpenter swung off his horse and strode over to where I was half-lying on the icy ground. His coat, trousers, and boots were caked white with ice, and his hat was rimmed with icicles. He held Darley's reins in his hand, but I could barely make out the horse himself beyond, prancing anxiously about.

"I heard you cry out," Archibald called over the storm, "and then Hickory raced past. I turned back at once, but it took me some time. Couldn't see ten feet in front of me. I'm glad I found you."

"Not half as glad as I am," I replied, grabbing his arm and pulling him next to me so I could speak directly into his ear. Just the touch of another human being gave me a tiny bit of hope.

Trailor pointed at my injured leg, still splayed out on the ice. "Is it broken?"

"I don't think so. But I can't put any weight on it."

Trailor knelt beside me. I threw my arm around his shoulder and he pulled me up. I put my leg down tentatively, started to shift my weight, and then swallowed my scream as my ankle buckled.

All the while, the ice continued to beat down and the wind continued to howl. The ice on the ground was several inches deep already, and it was piling up so quickly I thought I could actually see its level rising.

Trailor shielded his eyes with his hands and looked around. Before the storm had overtaken us, there had been no structure, not even a tree or bush, visible in any direction. His eyes were troubled and I could read his thoughts: there were no good choices.

"You should ride on with Darley," I said. "Springfield can't be far. The two of you have a chance to make it together. You can come back for me when it's over."

I saw in Archibald's eyes the recognition that there'd be no one to come back for after this was over. "I'm not leaving you," he called back, "not after your kindness. Besides, the storm's too strong to outrun. Maybe it'll pass soon." But even as he said the words, I held out no hope they might be true. The storm was, if anything, getting more ferocious by the moment.

"You get up on Darley and I'll lead you out," he said.

I started to protest again that he should ride off, but he shook his head. He helped me place my good foot in the stirrup and then carefully helped me swing my other leg over Darley's back.

It dangled beside the horse's flank; even trying to secure it in the stirrup seemed too painful a prospect.

"Hold tight," Archibald yelled, and he took Darley's reins and started trudging in the direction of Springfield.

For a few minutes, we made decent headway. We were going slowly, very slowly, but at least we were inching toward Springfield.

But as the wind whipped in his face and the ice beat down, Archibald increasingly struggled to find purchase on the icy ground. He slipped and slipped again, once nearly falling before pulling himself up by Darley's reins.

Archibald's head drooped lower and lower, until his chin had fallen all the way to his chest. His curly hair had frozen stiff. His steps became slower and shorter, slower and shorter still. Eventually they stopped altogether. He was still as a statue, leaning precariously into the wind and ice, and for a moment I feared he had frozen to death on his feet.

I maneuvered Darley until I was beside Archibald, and I was relieved to see he was still breathing. His eyes were half closed, his eyelashes white and frozen, and little rivers of ice streamed down his face. Tears or the ice pellets from the heavens. Or a combination of both.

"Archibald?" I called.

His eyelids fluttered slightly.

"Listen, Archibald, let's try to make a shelter. Do you think you can get Darley to lie still on the ground?"

Trailor gave a faint, icy nod.

There was a swale on the trail ahead of us, with a small rise just beyond. I thought there might be a tiny piece of shelter if we positioned the horse's body into the storm and lay down behind it. I pointed to the ground I had in mind, and slowly Archibald managed to trudge over to it, leading Darley.

I slid off Darley, landing carefully on my good foot. Standing on one leg, I handed the reins to Archibald, and he whispered into Darley's ear, scratched his throat, and got him to lay on his side against the rise, such that the wind was hitting his back. With Archibald's help I hobbled over, and together we pressed against the horse's barrel.

"We should use our coats as blankets," suggested Archibald.

So we took off our overcoats and placed them over our heads. We huddled next to each other and against the prone horse and tried to stay as warm as possible as the ice thundered all around. For a moment, the dark produced by our coats provided a tiny bit of peace. Darley was breathing regularly, his chest rising and falling, and I could sense warmth somewhere deep inside his body.

Under our collapsed tent of coats, Archibald's face was three inches from mine. We took turns breathing in and out slowly, trying to conserve energy.

"I've never seen anything like this," I said.

"Me neither," replied Archibald. "Back in '30, I remember we had a deep snow. My brothers told me the roads were blocked for weeks. But never ice like this. And never this quick. We can't be the only ones caught out, with how sudden it came on."

I hoped desperately that Martha would be near shelter when the storm reached her. And Lincoln, too. He might have been anywhere, around town or out in the surrounding farmlands, with the legislature in session.

The sliver of calm and hope provided by our makeshift shelter soon vanished. In its place returned the reality that we were two men, lying against a horse out in the open prairie in the middle of a fierce winter storm, with nothing but coats thrown over our heads to protect us from the falling ice and nothing but traveling clothes to keep us warm. It would not do, not for long.

And the storm refused to relent. The wind was blowing the ice pellets around, and the horse's flank provided little protection. My head felt like it was going to be crushed by the fury of the ice. I was cold beyond the deepest, saddest cold I had ever known. I could no longer feel my toes. And a little while later I could no longer feel anything below my waist.

I lay still, trying without success to move my legs. The storm continued unabated. Time passed; in our makeshift, dark shelter I had no ability to judge how much. Ten minutes? An hour? All I knew is that my soul was withdrawing to a warmer and safer place.

Time continued to pass, and I began to feel I was drifting, drifting on a cloud, drifting . . . away.

I thought about my family whom I would never see again: my sister Martha, the strong, independent young woman who'd been the light of my years in Springfield; my ailing father, the great Judge John Speed, whose lofty expectations I had never had the chance to fulfill; my older brother James, my mentor and confidant, who would never again look at me with his mixture of disappointment and eternal hope. I thought, too, of my mother and my other siblings, and I thought about what a piteous way this was to die and how I hoped they would be spared the details of my final moments. The noise coming from outside our makeshift shelter had receded, and I wondered if I was being drawn down the tunnel of death.

And I thought of Lincoln. Of Lincoln holding forth by the great fireplace at the back of my store and surrounded by our circle of fellows, telling some ridiculous tall tale with a knowing wink of his gray eyes and a boisterous laugh waiting just offstage to make its entrance. Of Lincoln pushing back his chair and finding the courage to stand alone in the well of the courtroom to fight for the lives of his clients. Of Lincoln lying beside me in the bed we shared, night after night, with Hurst and Herndon snoring rhythmically in the other bed, telling one last story as we slipped off to sleep.

His warm, reedy voice, so familiar. It was almost as if I could hear it now.

CHAPTER 5

"*Speed? Speed? Is that you?"*

I was in the twilight stage between wake and sleep, only this time it was between life and death. And just as there comes a moment, each night, when one must let go of the day and surrender to the inevitability of sleep, I had reached the moment of inevitable surrender to death. I let go and felt myself drifting toward the void.

"Speed! We've come for you!"

I was drifting, drifting . . . and then I was being yanked, ungently, by the legs. Or at least I surmised it was by my legs, as I had no feeling below my waist. Either way, suddenly darkness was replaced by light, by the bright light of a brilliant sun. I stared in disbelief.

"There's another poor soul next to him," I heard Lincoln's voice say. "Dunno who, but let's take him, too."

"Is Speed even alive?" asked a second voice, doubtfully. After a moment, I realized it belonged to my friend James Conkling, a young lawyer who had arrived in Springfield from the East within the past year. "He's not—we're too late."

I tried shouting, but no sound emerged. Then I tried moving my arms or legs, only to find they were frozen in place. Finally, I tried blinking as rapidly and demonstratively as I could.

Neither man seemed to notice. I was entombed inside my own body.

"I wager he's alive," Lincoln said. "Just barely, though, and not for much longer. We've got to get him warmed up. They didn't teach you anything at Princeton about making fire in the middle of an ice field, did they, Conkling?"

"I—well—not exactly, but—"

"Of course they didn't." Lincoln barked with laughter. "I know full well you didn't learn anything remotely practical at your famous university. But no time for that now. We've got to get Speed and this other fellow thawed out as quickly as possible. What was that double log cabin we passed on the way out? Zachariah Hillman's, wasn't it? Fetch our horses, Conkling. We'll tie one of them to each of our mounts. Make haste!"

I felt myself being thrown over the back of a horse and felt myself being secured in place by several loops of rope. I occasionally glimpsed Lincoln or Conkling coming into my field of view as they worked.

"Can you hear me, Speed?" Lincoln called out. "As soon as the storm moved out of Springfield, we came searching for you. I guessed you might be on the trail today, based on your letter, and when I heard Hickory had wandered into the stables alone in the midst of the storm, I knew you must be out here. Some advice, though. Next time, stay *on top of* your horse. It's easier that way!" Lincoln chortled at his own joke.

I tried to form the sound *m* with my lips. *M-M-Martha?* But it was useless. I couldn't make a squeak.

"Don't worry about Martha," Lincoln said, looking down at my numbed face with kindly eyes. "She was inside the Hutchason house when it hit. Sitting beside a warm fire the whole time, just like you're about to be."

"It's no use," said Conkling. "He's frozen to death. Ah, well."

"I don't think so," Lincoln said. "There's hope if we can get them to Hillman's hearth. Shouldn't take us more than thirty minutes, I don't think."

The sky above me started to move. It was improbably blue and clear, like a snow-melt stream just after dawn. I caught sight of the sun and tried to will all of its rays to warm my body.

"Say, Lincoln," I heard Conkling remark. "This other fellow? I think I recognize him. Isn't he that carpenter who's always asking for piecework? 'Tailor' or something?"

"Archibald Trailor!" exclaimed Lincoln. "Now that you say it, I do recognize him. I wonder how Speed and he chanced to meet up in the prairie."

Sometime later, we came to a halt. I heard a pounding in the middle distance, and Lincoln's voice shouted, "Throw more logs on the fire, Hillman. All you've got! These two men have nearly frozen."

I felt myself being untied and roughly slung over Lincoln's shoulder like a sack of grain. I bounced up and down helplessly as Lincoln ran toward the house, then ducked through a doorway. Suddenly I was flung down onto a rug not six inches away from a blazing hearth. From my prone position, the raging, towering flames seemed to be licking the rafters of the farmhouse. I felt a tiny flicker of warmth start to penetrate my frozen body. Then, without warning, I got very sleepy.

When I opened my eyes again, the room was dark. I turned my head and saw I was still next to the fire, now reduced to embers that glowed warmly.

"Lincoln?" I called out tentatively. "Conkling?" I heard a rustling noise approaching. "Lincoln, is that you?"

A kindly, moon-shaped face loomed above me. It took me a moment to place it. Hillman's wife. She served Dr. Randall as a midwife on occasion.

"They've gone back to town, dear," Mrs. Hillman said. She rested her hand on my forehead, and her tender touch sent waves of comfort through my body. "Once they saw you were breathing normally, they went to see if they could find anyone else who'd been caught out in the storm. Hillman went with them. Such a terrible day! I cannot bear to think how many lives must have been lost.

"Sit up a second, if you can. A draught of this will do you good." She handed me a flask, and I drank it down eagerly. Stiff brandy. A shot of warmth flooded through me.

"The man I was brought in with. Archibald Trailor. Is he alive?" I started to get up to look around, but Mrs. Hillman gently restrained me.

"He's going to be fine, too," she said, and I let out a breath of relief. "He's still sleeping, just round the other side of the fire."

"That man saved my life," I declared with a force that startled even me. I suddenly felt the urge to proclaim this truth loudly. "I was thrown from my horse and hurt my leg. I was all alone in the middle of the storm. If Archibald hadn't come back to find me, hadn't helped me shelter beside his horse, I would have frozen to death. All alone on the prairie." I felt again the desolateness of the instant before Archibald had reappeared from the storm, and I started to shake uncontrollably.

Mrs. Hillman put her hand on my cheek and held it there until I regained my composure.

"You get your rest," she said soothingly. "Your Mr. Lincoln said he'd send Dr. Randall around in the morning, but I know a thing or two about healing. The both of you will be just fine, once you rest up for a few days."

I relaxed into the warmth of the embers and the compassion of her touch. Once more, I felt myself letting go.

Chapter 6

The next morning, Archibald and I shared a meal around the Hillmans' table. We were, we agreed, exceedingly lucky to be alive.

"In my case, it wasn't just luck," I added, patting the carpenter on the arm. "It was your bravery and friendship, first and foremost."

"You'd have done the same for me," he replied confidently.

I hoped so. That afternoon Archibald headed back to Springfield, on foot, as his horse was still recuperating from its own near-death experience. We shook hands and agreed to gather for a draught sometime. And then he vanished from my life as suddenly as he'd entered it.

Two days later, I felt well enough to return home myself. I told Lincoln and his colleagues about the bank cashier's treachery and showed them the proof. The sheriff was dispatched to Chicago to arrest Brown, but word got out before the sheriff's arrival and the man ended up running for his life one step ahead of an enraged Irish mob, which formed up as soon as they understood that the corrupt banker was a source of their misery.

Meanwhile, back in Springfield, the state made arrangements to replace both the banker and the lost gold. Since there was little hard money left anywhere in the state—or the entire nation, for that matter—the latter task proved especially difficult.

Eventually, Lincoln hit upon the plan for the state to secure a massive loan from foreign bankers. But like a candle flame on a moonless night, the prospect of such concentrated riches in impoverished times quickly attracted insects. Lots of them.

So it was that, several months after my narrow escape from the Sudden Change (as the singular weather event had come to be known), I found myself in the midst of a dazzling throng of persons pressed together in the grand ballroom of the American House.

The businessman Elijah Iles had opened the American House last year in anticipation of the arrival of the state government, now completing its long-awaited move to Springfield from Vandalia. The hotel was the largest in the entire state, with a prime location near the Springfield headquarters of the State Bank and directly across from the new capitol building. With the legislature now in the final stretch of its inaugural session in Springfield, the hotel was jammed with a hundred guests, each happy to pay a steep price to lodge in such close proximity to power.

At the moment, however, all my thoughts were focused on the form of a captivating girl with vivid blue eyes and rose-red lips. I watched while, across the room, Lincoln tried to make her laugh. He stood high above her, his shoulders stooped even more than usual, and he bent down to whisper into her ear. She leaned toward him, brow knitted in concentration to block out the roar of the crowd. Finally, my friend finished his story, a broad smile crinkling across his face, and his companion stepped back and gazed up at him skeptically.

"Oh, Abraham," I thought I could make out her saying. "How can you possibly think *that* funny?"

Moments later he was back at my side. "How'd it go?" I asked in all innocence.

"Not well at all," Lincoln replied mournfully.

"But it looked for all the world as if the fair Mary was in your thrall."

He shook his head. "Miss Todd always seems to take my stories the wrong way. It's as if I'm speaking a foreign tongue to her."

"Perhaps Matilda is better suited for you," I said, nodding toward a pretty girl with cascading ringlets of brown hair who was standing across the room. At her side was her uncle, Ninian Edwards, one of Springfield's leading citizens.

In truth, we'd been having this same conversation for several months. Mary Todd, the younger sister of Ninian's wife Elizabeth, and her cousin Matilda Edwards were two of the most eligible young women in Springfield. Having recently turned thirty-one, Lincoln was among the oldest bachelors in town, and I thought it long past time for him to have settled upon a wife. I had vowed at the outset of the season that I would help him with this task. However, he had proved an uncertain suitor. To make matters more complicated, I had quickly found myself beguiled by Miss Todd's considerable charms.

Meanwhile, it was apparent we weren't the only unmarried men in town with such designs.

"What's Douglas doing?" Lincoln asked sharply.

I saw Stephen Douglas touch Mary's arm and strike up an animated conversation. The peculiar-looking statesman's massive head bobbed back and forth as he gazed up at her. Mary smiled and put a porcelain hand to her lips, as if to stifle a giggle.

"What's his game?" said Lincoln irritably. "Surely she cannot find *him* attractive."

"Who knows what moves these women?" I sighed. "Let's see if we can't throw Douglas onto another scent."

Lincoln and I waded into the boisterous crowd, all the talent, wit, and beauty Springfield could muster mingling together in high glee. Diamonds and jewelry dazzled the eye. Gay revelers tripped happily through intricate mazes of dance to the soft wooing of the lute and harp. But there was a decided imbalance of the sexes tonight: three or four hundred men against not more than fifty ladies, and half of these were married or engaged.

As I followed Lincoln through the crowd, I noticed he was wearing rough Conestoga boots. One of his socks sticking out of them was black and the other a dingy gray. His swallowtail coat was too short and his shabby trousers bore several off-color patches. I walked with a slight limp. My injured leg was better, much better than it had been, but it still gave me trouble on these cold, damp evenings. By the time I caught up with Lincoln, he was already in conversation with Douglas.

"Do you still contend the internal improvements aren't worthwhile, Stephen?" Lincoln was saying. "Why, the canal alone would transform the state, if it's ever finished. Our farmers would have uninterrupted water carriage to ship their yield and animals to the eastern markets. That's why I've resolved to seek this loan. We must restore the State Bank to firm footing as soon as possible. It seems natural that you and your fellow Democrats in the legislature should support the scheme."

Douglas shook his broad face back and forth and snorted. "The improvements may have been a tolerable endeavor back in '37," he said, his deep voice carrying around the room, such that several of the men around us interrupted their own conversations to turn and stare. "But we can hardly afford them now, not in the midst of this depression. You know well, Lincoln, there's no hard currency about in the entire state. And if private capital is absent, we can hardly expect the government to fund the canal. The state should not intrude into the affairs of the people."

I was standing next to Mary, who had been following the discussion between Lincoln and Douglas with a look of frustration spread across her face. Up close I thought her exceptionally beautiful. She had clear blue eyes, long lashes, brown hair with a glint of bronze, and a lovely complexion. She had a strand of pink roses woven into her hair that perfectly matched the pink fan she held in her delicate hands.

"They're talking politics again, Miss Todd?" I said. "Lincoln and Douglas can both be dreadful bores on that topic. It's as if they think of nothing else. I wonder, what are your impressions of the latest novel by Mr. Cooper? Out of character for him, wouldn't you agree?"

Mary's eyes flashed with anger. "It's not that they're boring, Mr. Speed. It's that they're *wrong*. Neither of them understands the true rationale for the canal. It's necessary to avoid the railroad monopoly. *Obviously*." And she strode off in the direction of her cousin, Miss Edwards. Lincoln and Douglas continued jabbering at each other, seemingly oblivious to Miss Todd's departure.

"There you are, Joshua," came a familiar voice from behind me. "I've been looking for you."

My sister Martha and I exchanged a hug, and I stepped back to gaze at her. Martha had moved to Springfield three years ago to escape the strictures of our parents' home, and she had been my constant companion and coconspirator since her arrival. She was almost of twenty years now, with a fresh face and honey-brown hair resting on the shoulders of her handsome silk-and-satin gown. The light-blue dress had a low neck, and it had been everything I could manage at the start of the evening not to insist she cover it with a shawl.

"Did you see Miss Todd unhand Lincoln and Douglas?" I asked.

Martha's eyes twinkled. She and Mary had already become close confidantes since the latter's arrival in Springfield last fall. "If I wasn't related to you," my sister said, "I might have thought *you* were the one unhanded."

"But—"

"*Shhh.* I'm only teasing. But let me ask you this. Do you plan on running for high office someday?"

"Why do you ask?"

"Miss Todd would aspire to be president herself if she could. She can't, of course, so there's only one path for her to the executive mansion in Washington."

"Put in a good word for me, will you?"

"Have you considered Miss Edwards?"

"I was just saying the same thing to Lincoln."

Martha smiled. The young lawyer Conkling materialized at our side. "Did you see Lincoln out on the dance floor earlier?" he asked with a grin. I shook my head.

"It was quite a sight. He looked like old Father Jupiter, bending down from the clouds to see what's going on."

Martha and I laughed heartily. "Will you permit me, Miss Speed?" Conkling said, taking Martha's hand. She allowed him to steer her toward the dance floor. I felt a large hand fall upon my shoulder, and I swung around.

"Simeon!" I shouted.

The newspaper publisher Simeon Francis was breathing heavily, as if he had just completed some sort of race. His untucked shirt strained to cover his bulging stomach, and he rubbed his unshaven chin with a ruddy, freckled hand.

"I don't normally associate you with such fine surroundings," I said, gesturing around the room. Iles had spared no effort in decorating his new palace with expensive furniture, carpeting, and wallpaper, all modeled on the splendor of a Turkish sultanate.

"A fine place for those troubled by a superabundance of silver in their possession, I suppose," allowed Simeon with a frown. "Not my taste, though." He gestured to the man standing next to him. "Have you met Belmont? He's the man who's going to give the state of Illinois the gold it needs to get out of this mess."

"The man whose *bank* is going to *loan* the state gold, if terms can be agreed with the legislature," said Belmont, with a trace of an accent I couldn't immediately place. He was not much older than me, with a jovial appearance, precise mustache, sharp nose, and shiny black top hat. He twirled a silver-handled walking stick at his side.

"How does your bank have any gold left," I asked Belmont, eyeing him with interest, "when no other bank seems to?"

"The Rothschilds always have money," said Simeon.

"You're a Rothschild?" The fame and power of the legendary European banking family was such that mere mention of the name was enough to stop all other conversation.

"A distant relation," said Belmont. "Now I'm afraid I must run. There's another legislator I need to corral. Herding wolves would be simpler." With that, he headed off through the crowd.

"Not a half-bad fellow," said Francis in his wake, high praise from the blustery newspaperman. "I see Weber's here. I'm going to see if I can't go provoke him about his party's candidate. Can you believe it? The Democrats are actually intending to renominate Van Buren. After the hash he's made of the country these past three years? 'Van Ruin' is more like it." Francis snorted with laughter and waddled off in the direction of the publisher of the rival newspaper in town.

I took a step toward where I'd left Lincoln and nearly collided with a young woman in a flowing green gown who was coming in the other direction. "Excuse me," I said, looking up to meet her eyes, liquid pools of green framed by a fair complexion and perfect auburn curls. My breath caught.

"It was I who was clumsy," she said, with the faintest hint of an Irish brogue. She blushed, her color further enhancing a face that was perfection to begin with.

I bowed before her and began, "I'm Joshua—"

"There you are, Rose," said a young man in a smart frockcoat, sweeping in and taking the woman by the arm. "I thought I'd lost you for a moment. There's someone I want you to meet."

The two walked away, arm in arm, and I felt a quick pang of the regret you feel when you pass by a stranger in the street whom you might, in another life, have known, the path on the prairie not taken. Then Lincoln's voice emerged above the din of the crowd and I went to find him.

Lincoln and Douglas had been joined by Ninian Edwards and a fourth man I did not recognize. The stranger was well dressed and compact, with a beak nose, full whiskers, and a gently receding hairline. Even in a gathering of such august personages, he stood with a bearing that suggested he considered himself superior to every man present. I approached the grouping, but since none moved aside, I stood just outside the ring of conversation.

". . . realization of a long-held dream," Edwards was saying portentously. "When my father was appointed the first governor of the Territory of Illinois, he vowed that one day there would be a grand state capitol building in the center of Springfield. I can't help but think of the edifice across the street as a tribute to his legacy."

"The entire state owes your family quite a debt, Edwards," said Lincoln, winking at me.

"Just don't try to collect anytime soon, because the entire state is broke," added Douglas. Lincoln roared with laughter and slapped him on the back, while Edwards looked put out.

The other gentleman cleared his throat and said, "I believe you suggested, Edwards, that Messrs. Lincoln and Douglas might be interested in my expertise."

"Ah, yes." Turning back to the two politicians, Edwards explained, "I told William here that he should speak with you two gentlemen. He has some views on the canal project, I understand."

The stranger launched into a long, detailed recitation. It seemed he sought to convince the legislature to situate the canal in the midst of a particular district as it passed near the settlement of Ottawa. I guessed at once that he hoped to give financial advantage to land he held along the route. Lincoln and Douglas were well used to such special pleading, and they soon lost interest. Each of them scanned the crowd, apparently searching for Miss Todd, although in this contest Lincoln had the definite advantage, being well over a foot taller than his rival. Meanwhile, Edwards finally noticed my presence and grabbed hold of my arm.

"I should introduce the two of you as well," Edwards said. "William Trailor, meet Joshua Speed. And vice versa." Edwards nodded briskly and walked off to greet another guest.

The man stared at me with an intensity that made me uncomfortable. "Which committees do *you* serve on?" he asked.

"None," I said. "I'm not in the legislature at all. I own a general store on the other side of the—" But the man had turned back to Lincoln and Douglas, trying to reclaim their attention.

"Hold on a moment," I exclaimed, as Edwards's introduction finally registered. "William Trailor? Are you the brother of Archibald Trailor?"

He turned back to face me, annoyance clear in his eyes. "'Course I am," he sputtered. "I hope he doesn't owe you money, because I assuredly do not stand behind his debts."

"I am indebted *to* him. Greatly so. During the Sudden Change, he saved my life."

William Trailor took a step back and swallowed. "Oh, you're that Speed, are you? I heard something about that. Nice to meet you, I suppose."

I grabbed Lincoln's arm. "Lincoln," I called, talking loudly against the din of the gathering. "Do you know this fellow is Archibald's brother?"

"Mm-hmm," my friend replied, not taking his eyes off the crowd. "Who's that she's talking to now?" he added to himself. I decided to leave Lincoln to his quest.

"Well, I am very pleased to meet you," I said to Trailor, pumping his hand again and ignoring his disagreeable disposition. While William Trailor did not look like his younger brother, Archibald, there was something very suggestive of Henry Trailor in his forehead and the shape of his eyes. Even Archibald's physical appearance marked him as different from his brothers, I thought.

"I wouldn't be here talking to you were it not for the bravery of your brother," I continued. "Bravery and faithfulness. He came back to find me, in the middle of the storm, and helped us shelter together."

"Is that so?" William Trailor frowned. The notion that Archibald had done something to merit praise seemed difficult for him to accept. "I'm happy for it, I suppose, for your sake. My brother Archibald hasn't done much of consequence in his life. It was your good fortune he chose this one occasion to act."

"It certainly was. He's a fine fellow, very well respected in Springfield." This was hyperbole, but under the circumstances I said it without hesitation. "Are you in town to visit him?"

"More on a matter of business," William replied. His eyes twitched; he seemed to have resigned himself to conversing with me. "I'm here with Archibald and our other brother, Henry. And our business partner, Flynn Fisher, is in town as well. We're working to improve some land up north, and we wanted to favor the legislature with the benefit of our expertise."

Edwards rejoined us, and William abruptly turned his attention back to him. "Are there other members of the assembly I could speak to, Ninian?" he asked. "I'm not sure Mr. Lincoln or Mr. Douglas fully understood the importance of what I was telling them."

"Whatever happened to those two?" Edwards asked, looking past me at the swirling crowd.

"It is possible they went in search of your sister-in-law," I said with a smile. "They both seem rather interested in securing her views. On the canal, I'm sure."

Edwards grinned. "I doubt very much that's what they're after. The full moon tonight may be working its magic. And Mary could make a bishop forget his prayers.

"No matter. Come with me, Trailor. I'll introduce you to a few more of my colleagues, make sure you get a thorough hearing. The whole legislature, near enough, is in the room at this very moment."

They walked away. I spotted the back of Lincoln's head, looming high above the crowd, and I hurried off to join the rivals in their pursuit.

Chapter 7

My general store, A.Y. Ellis & Co., occupied a prime spot near the northwest corner of the capitol square. Some days after the gala, I stood in the doorway and looked out at the capitol building. Although it was now occupied for the first time, construction was not yet complete, and building materials and assorted debris littered the site. As I watched, the Whigs in the legislature assembled for their weekly caucus. Lincoln had left for the meeting a few minutes earlier. As soon as I saw Ninian Edwards walk up the grand marble steps of the building, in close conversation with a few of his colleagues, I left my storefront and made haste to the Edwards house.

The grand, brightly painted home stood on Quality Hill, a sloping elevation with a commanding view of Springfield, where several of the wealthiest men of town had constructed mansions. It required a strenuous climb to reach. When the Edwardses' servant boy, Joseph, answered the door, I asked if the master of the house was in.

Before he could respond, there was a rustling in the hallway and Mary Todd appeared. She was wearing a dress with a vivid yellow-and-navy pattern; the dress fell down to her ankles and its full sleeves covered her wrists. An ivory broach cinched the neck. I told myself to avoid gaping openly at her beauty.

"Mr. Speed, is that you?" she asked, in a voice that sounded like morning birdsong to my ears. "You must have passed my brother-in-law on the way, as he has just this hour left for town."

"That is a great disappointment," I said, holding my expression fixed. "I was hoping to query him on a matter of business."

"Do come in and rest a spell. You must be tired from your walk up the hill."

Mary led me into the front sitting room and motioned that I should take a seat on a three-person horsehair couch against the wall. She gathered her skirts and sat on the opposite end of the same couch. I was surprised, and attracted, by her boldness.

"Mr. Edwards was heading to the capitol," Mary said. "The Whigs are planning their strategy for this year's presidential contest, I believe. Are you interested in the election, Mr. Speed?"

"Most certainly. With Lincoln—with a few of my colleagues—we're publishing a campaign newspaper, *The Old Soldier*, in support of General Harrison."

"I heartily join your cause. President Van Buren has no feel for the real stuff his citizens are made of, certainly not those of us here in the West. The man's a fop. The general is a log cabin–and–hard cider man. I like that, and I daresay the majority of our fellow citizens will as well."

"I'm impressed, Miss Todd. That's quite a full explication of views on the matter of politics."

She frowned. "I don't know why that should come as a surprise. I've been a registered member of the Whig Party since I was nine years old. I assisted my father in his campaign for the Kentucky legislature. And I'll have you know, when President Jackson visited Lexington prior to the election in 1828, I refused to attend a public demonstration in his honor."

I burst out laughing. "Do you think that made a difference to him, the refusal of one little girl to attend his celebration?"

"Perhaps it did, perhaps it didn't," she replied, her tone deadly serious. "How should I know? All I know is that I could not countenance adding myself to his number of supporters."

"Your determination is certainly a credit," I replied with an agreeable nod, and deciding I had better change the topic, I added, "I wonder, how do you find Springfield, now that you've lived among us for several months?"

"I like being free of my father and stepmother. And I like residing with my sister Elizabeth. As for Springfield, I find it tolerable, although there is not always much to do for women of my character. Miss Speed and I have had occasion to discuss the matter."

I glanced at Mary's right hand, lying casually along the top of the couch and stretching out in my direction. It was perfect alabaster; a master sculptor could not have brought into existence a limb more becoming.

This was by far the longest and most intimate conversation I had ever had with her, and I hoped to feed its flame for as long as possible. "And what was it you enjoyed back home in Kentucky?" I asked.

"Teaching school, for one. I was at Ward's in Lexington, working as an apprentice teacher and helping Mrs. Ward with the younger children. I should like very much to teach again, especially younger girls, if a girls' school ever opens in Springfield."

"You yourself had a full course of boarding school education, if I'm not mistaken," I returned. She nodded. "You and I share the view, then, of the importance of a formal education, for boys and girls alike. It is not one all of our neighbors share. Too many are 'self-educated,' to use a term that I think refutes itself, and all too happy to stay that way."

"I cannot imagine you are including your friend Mr. Lincoln in your statement," said she. "Because surely he, though self-educated, would be the first to vote in support of a more developed system of formal education."

"I suppose you're correct." I had been including Lincoln in my condemnation, of course, and it rankled me that Mary had not only declined to join my attempt to denigrate him but had turned my comment into an opportunity to praise him.

"What about you?" she continued. "Do you think you'll follow Mr. Lincoln into the political life?"

"I cannot imagine so." I thought I saw her arm pull back ever so slightly. "I'm busy with the affairs of A.Y. Ellis & Co. The merchant's life suits me."

"My brother-in-law combines matters political with matters of business."

"He does so with great success," I said. "But still, I do not think it's the life for me."

"Stephen fancies he'll be president one day."

It took me a moment to realize that she meant Douglas, and my irritation at the little man's pretensions was surpassed only by my irritation at Miss Todd's evident familiarity with them. Before I could think of a suitable reply, she continued.

"And what of your Mr. Lincoln? What do you think the future holds for him?"

"You'd have to ask him, I suppose." I sensed I had failed to keep the churlishness out of my voice.

"I was recently conversing with Miss Matilda Edwards about you and Lincoln," Mary continued with a confidential tone. "Matilda asked me which I thought the cleverer. I told her I couldn't answer. It's too hard a choice. But she said to her eyes it was you, without question." Mary leaned toward me, and by instinct I reciprocated; our heads were less than a foot apart. I could smell her freshly washed hair. "She called you 'dashing,' Mr. Speed. She really is a very pretty girl."

Mary sat back, a small smile on her face. I remained frozen in place. The implication of her words was unmistakable. Before I could respond, there was a noise in the hallway, and Mary's older sister bustled into the room.

"Mary, whatever are you—Mr. Speed, is that you? What are you doing here? How long has *he* been here, Mary?"

I jumped to my feet, backing away from the couch and straightening my coat, while Mary rose in a composed fashion and said, "Mr. Speed came to call on your husband, Elizabeth. When he found him missing, I insisted he rest a spell before his walk back down to town. He was just saying he would have to leave soon to return to his store." Mary flashed me a quick, sympathetic smile.

Her older sister was not mollified. "I'm glad you showed him such courtesy, Mary, but in the future you are to alert me *at once* when we have visitors. Especially when we have gentleman visitors."

"Of course, dear sister, I shall." Again, Mary smiled at me from behind her sister's back.

"Good day to you, Mr. Speed," said Mrs. Edwards, guiding me firmly toward the entrance hallway.

"Good day, Mrs. Edwards. It's nice to see you again, and Miss Todd as well. I always receive such remarkable hospitality at this house. I'm most sorry for the intrusion."

My thoughts spun with Mary's design to send me in Matilda's direction. Whoever was going to win the contest for Mary's hand, it seemed it would not be me. My excursion had produced exactly the opposite of its intended effect. Deeply distracted, I reached for the handle to the Edwardses' front door, only to find it swinging away from me.

William May, the new mayor of Springfield, stood in the doorway. He was breathing heavily, and beads of sweat encircled his red face. "Is . . . Edwards . . . home?" he gasped.

I was shaken from my ruminations. "Indeed, no. I came to call upon him myself. He's at the capitol, it appears."

"I'll go . . . find him . . . there," May replied, still gaining his breath. "I need his counsel . . . on a matter of great . . . civic . . . importance." He took a deep breath and looked me straight in the eye.

"A man's been murdered."

Chapter 8

May turned and fled down the hill, and after a moment's pause I raced after him. He was an odd-looking man, nearly fifty years of age, with very long, skinny legs and a comparatively squat torso. In his youth he had had a full shock of fiery red hair, and though the little that remained had turned to gray, he was still universally known by his childhood nickname, "Big Red." Other than his hair, Big Red's most remarkable feature was his enormous ears, which splayed out from either side of his head like canvas sails catching a strong wind. Chasing after the man, it appeared as if the breeze captured by his ears was perpetually in danger of lifting him off the ground.

Halfway down the hill I caught up with him and grabbed his arm. He spun around.

"I cannot have even a moment's delay," he shouted, his eyes blinking and his ears hovering. "I must have Edwards's advice, at once."

"You said someone's been murdered. Who is it?"

"I do not know the man." He continued his headlong dash into town, and I trotted alongside him.

"Well, where was the body found?" I asked.

"There is no body."

"Then how do you know there's been a murder?"

In midstride, Big Red turned and stared at me wide-eyed, waving his arms frantically. "Exactly!" he shouted, and he raced ahead.

We had entered the town proper by now, and the mayor's course was taking us in the direction of the capitol building by way of the Post Office Department, which stood on the south side of the capitol square. As the Department came into view, I saw Springfield's postmaster, James Keyes, standing on an overturned crate in front of his office. Though Keyes handed over the mail in packets that ostensibly remained sealed, he had an uncanny ability to anticipate their contents.

Keyes was holding a folded piece of paper, and an unruly crowd was quickly gathering around him, jostling for position. I slowed to a walk as I reached the melee. My bad leg ached from chasing after Big Red.

"Here's the letter some of you have been asking about," Keyes hollered. "The citizens of Springfield are considerably lucky they have a postmaster who keeps such a careful watch on the commonweal."

"What's it say?" yelled a voice from the crowd.

"I am about to relate its contents," said Keyes officiously. He made a great show of reviewing the letter, then cleared his throat. "A Mrs. Joseph Jones from LaSalle writes to her correspondent in Springfield about the recent activities of one William Trailor. The *suspicious* activities of Mr. Trailor, as you'll hear shortly."

I came to a dead stop when I heard Trailor's name. Having met all three brothers, it seemed clear the older two were in the habit of dumping their problems on Archibald. Wherever Keyes was heading, I feared it meant trouble for the carpenter.

Keyes paused, nodding his head as various men shouted questions and demanded additional detail. Finally, the postmaster was stirred to continue.

"Yes, yes, I'm getting to all that. Mrs. Jones writes that

William Trailor is well known to the residents of LaSalle as a skinflint. Lately, however, Trailor has been spreading silver and gold coins all over town, spending with the abandon of a drunken Irishman." The crowd murmured excitedly. It had been growing steadily during Keyes's performance, and thirty or forty men now milled about on the street in front of the Department.

After a pause, Keyes continued. "Apparently, William Trailor has been circulating the story that an acquaintance of his, a Mr. Flynn Fisher, recently passed away and left him one thousand dollars in his will. According to the letter, Mr. Fisher was a respected businessman and town elder in LaSalle." A low gasp went through the crowd, followed by shouts of outrage; the figure was more than most of the men assembled would see in three lifetimes. Many of them were ready to lead William Trailor to the gallows at once, I thought, merely on account of the great sum of money he had accumulated.

The great sum he had *supposedly* accumulated, I corrected myself. Given what Archibald had said about Fisher's financial straits, I was immediately dubious of the story related by the postmaster.

Keyes shook the letter back and forth in order to regain the crowd's attention. "Mrs. Joseph Jones reports to her correspondent, a Mrs. Alfred—er, that part's not important—where was I? Yes, Mrs. Jones reports that the good people of LaSalle are concerned the unfortunate Mr. Fisher was the victim of foul play. And Mrs. Jones relates that when Fisher was last seen alive, he was heading towards Springfield in the company of Mr. Trailor."

Giving a satisfied nod, Keyes folded the letter and put it into his pocket.

"Find the sheriff! Let's get Hutchason!" yelled out one man.

"Where's Big Red?" shouted another. "Isn't it his job to keep us safe?"

Where *was* the mayor? I wondered. Big Red had disappeared

during the postmaster's newsmongering. Looking around, I saw Lincoln's familiar figure coming down the steps of the capitol building. I caught him on the middle of the town green.

"What's the commotion?" Lincoln asked. "Is Keyes airing someone's dirty linen again?"

I quickly recounted Keyes's tale about William Trailor and the apparent death of Flynn Fisher.

"Ah," said Lincoln, "that explains Big Red bursting into our meeting and taking Ninian away."

"What did the mayor want Edwards for?" I asked. "I ran into him at the Edwards mansion; accompanied him back into town, in fact. He was desperate to secure an audience with Ninian."

"You have to remember, Speed, that Big Red's newly elected, just sworn in last month," said Lincoln. "Springfield has never had a mayor before. We've never seen the need for one, until now, with the town grown so big. Many people still think the position's a waste of public funds. Big Red has the office, but he doesn't have the first idea what do to with it. I think he's hoping Ninian will tell him."

Lincoln squinted at me. "What did you say the name was of the fellow who supposedly died?"

"Flynn Fisher. I actually met him, briefly, in Chicago with Archibald, a few days before the Sudden Change. And William Trailor mentioned at the gala that this same Fisher fellow was in town with them."

The throng of men had drifted away from the post office and were scattered about in small groups on the disheveled capitol grounds. More than a few were drinking from flasks. Chicago was not the only town with a substantial population of rootless men these days; Springfield had more than its share as well. They were vagrants and landless farmers, peddlers and hucksters, wearing fraying clothes and angry expressions. There was not enough work and too much time for idle pursuits, and a mob was quick to form over trivial matters. Big Red's concern when faced with the postmaster's gossip was easy to comprehend.

At that moment, the mayor himself, flanked by Ninian Edwards on one side and Sheriff Humble Hutchason on the other, emerged at the top of the capitol steps. Many of the crowd began calling to get his attention. Big Red raised his hands, pleading for order; I was sure I saw his ears twitching.

"Gentlemen," he shouted, "gentlemen, please give me your attention. I have an announcement about the fate of a recent visitor to Springfield, a Mr. Flynn Fisher. Mr. Fisher, as you may have heard, has gone missing. There is reason to fear he has been . . . murdered."

A huge cry went up from the crowd.

"He was a great man!" exclaimed a fellow near us.

"What a loss," murmured another.

Lincoln and I exchanged glances. As far as we knew, not a single person in Springfield was acquainted with Fisher. A certain delusion was taking hold among the crowd.

"Sheriff Hutchason informs me," Big Red continued, nodding at the lawman, who looked on with a disagreeable expression, "that Mr. Fisher was in Springfield with William and Henry Trailor, and that the Trailors lodged at the American House." At this, groups of men began jabbering at each other. A number were ready to charge at once into the hotel, whose steeply pitched rooftop, punctuated by a neat row of chimneys, loomed just beyond the capitol building. Again, Big Red called for order.

"It's no use looking in the American House. Major Iles has confirmed Fisher isn't there. As your mayor, I've ordered an urgent investigation into the fate of Mr. Fisher. My fellow citizens, I need all of you to help with this important mission. We need two search parties. Half of you men, go over there" —he pointed to a newly planted oak tree in the southeast corner of the public square— "and prepare to take orders from the sheriff. The rest of you, wait in place, and I'll be down to lead you. Let's see if we can find Fisher, or his body, by nightfall."

The crowd buzzed with excitement; Big Red had read correctly their desire for action. Edwards whispered into one of the mayor's gigantic ears. Then Big Red walked down the steps, seemingly pulling Hutchason along behind him. Lincoln touched my shoulder.

"Well, Speed, we may rest secure in the knowledge that the mayor has the situation in hand," he said, giving a mischievous smile. "If Big Red's raiding parties don't turn up Fisher, I shouldn't be surprised if they find the Holy Grail, what with the caliber of men he's assembled."

"It's all likely to come to nothing. I certainly hope so, for Archibald Trailor's sake."

"What's Archibald got to do with this?"

"Nothing, I expect." I thought back to the conversation I'd overhead between Archibald and Henry Trailor on the evening before the Sudden Change. "Other than he was with his brothers around the time this Fisher character seems to have disappeared. I hope Archibald would've had the good sense to steer clear of any of his brothers' misadventures."

"I'm not sure how much good sense Archibald possesses," Lincoln said, his tone not unkind.

"That's exactly my worry."

We parted; I headed back to my store, Lincoln to his law offices at Hoffman's Row. I had taken a few steps away when Lincoln called after me.

"Speed, you were up at the Edwards house earlier?"

I knew at once I couldn't deny it. "That's right."

"Whatever were you doing there?"

"Looking for Ninian, of course."

"But you knew he was with me, at the capitol building. We discussed at breakfast this morning that the Whig caucus was meeting." Lincoln peered at me skeptically.

I hoped Lincoln's talent for reading my thoughts would fail him this once. "Indeed," I said. "I discovered I'd journeyed in vain."

Chapter 9

From my post behind the counter of my store, I had a perfect view of the madness that followed. All afternoon, groups of men raced across the capitol lawn, this way and that, in an excited frenzy. Not a small number of them barged into my store, seeking materials for their quest: shovels, rope, ladders, gloves suitable for digging. I readily purveyed the goods in question, as I had no wish to allow my competitors on the square to secure the business. But I watched the scene with growing unease. From the snatches of conversation I overheard, it seemed there was not a potential hiding place within miles of Springfield that was not being ransacked in search of the missing stranger.

Late in the afternoon, Sheriff Hutchason himself lumbered through the doorway. He was a massive man, with the long arms and stocky build of a heavyweight grappler. Hutchason was a popular figure who had first gained prominence during the Winnebago Wars of the early 1830s, and he had served as the sheriff of Sangamon County for nearly a decade. An expression of worry clouded his normally placid demeanor.

"If he's not careful, the fool's going to get someone else killed," Hutchason muttered as he entered the store.

"You aren't talking about our new mayor, are you, Sheriff?

Earlier today on the capitol steps, it looked like the two of you were in perfect concert."

Hutchason grunted. "You'll pardon me if I don't see the humor, Speed. Big Red hasn't the first idea what he's unleashed. He says he was afraid of the townspeople turning into a mob. So instead of waiting for the people to come up with the idea, he's created a mob himself. It would be laughable if it weren't such a risk to the public."

"Any sign of the body?"

"None. Though, based on what I know of the Trailor brothers, can't say I'd be surprised if there's one to be found."

I thought about my debt to Archibald Trailor; I literally owed the man my life. "Whatever turns out to have happened to this Fisher fellow, Sheriff," I said, "I should think Archibald Trailor cannot have had anything to do with it. I daresay he couldn't organize his thoughts sufficiently to plot a crime in the first place."

Hutchason nodded vigorously. "Archibald's never given me a spot of trouble, for all the years I've known him. As for his brothers, we'll have to see if Big Red's search parties turn up anything. Which, come to mention, is the reason I've stopped in. I was looking for a pair of—"

At that moment, there was a great crashing at the door. Three or four men, covered from head to toe with grime, burst into the storeroom. "There you are, Sheriff," shouted one of them. "I thought that was your horse on the hitching post. Come! We've found it. The murder weapon!"

Without another word to me, the sheriff bustled out the door, the men close at his heels.

Lincoln was attending a debate at the Young Men's Lyceum on the coming election that evening, so I dined with Martha in the public room of the Globe Tavern.

The Globe was a noisy, shabby two-story inn around the

corner from our lodgings whose best days, to the extent they had ever existed, were long behind it. As a feeding station for hungry village residents or residence for travelers, it was inferior in every respect to the sparkling new American House. Its only advantage at this point was familiarity, like a pair of shoes that slipped on easily despite worn-away soles.

The Globe's public room buzzed with only one topic: the disappearance and presumed murder of Flynn Fisher. The innkeeper Saunders circulated up and down the long, heavily scarred common table, asking each diner what he had heard or seen and passing along a constantly updated compilation of gossip. By the time we'd taken our last bites of a surprisingly tolerable roast, a rough consensus had formed around the following version of events:

The raiding party led by Mayor May had worked its way from the town center, searching every place a body could have lain overlooked for the past week. Barns, cellars, outhouses, and wells had been ransacked. In his zeal, the mayor had even given the order to dig up freshly dug graves. Fisher's body did not materialize. However, out on the road toward Hickox's millpond, one of the men in the search party found a broken fencepost, the irregular end of which was discolored. Some reports stated confidently that dried blood was found on the post; others said it could have been old paint. Either way, there was no dispute about the most telling discovery: a strand of hair was found sticking out from the jagged edge of the post. The eager search party immediately took the find as proof that the fencepost had been used to bludgeon Fisher.

The brush and a small grove of willow trees, just starting to bud, in the immediate vicinity of the fencepost were searched for Fisher's body, without success. However, the lack of a body seemed a minor detail given the other circumstances. After a quick consultation as the mob surged and shouted all around them, Big Red and Hutchason agreed that William and Henry Trailor should be arrested and questioned for murder.

We tried to ascertain Archibald Trailor's fate. But neither the innkeeper nor the men dining alongside us had heard anything about him, and after a few inquiries I let the matter rest. The town's natural inclination was that Archibald could not have been involved in the affair. Nothing good could come from disturbing that view.

Martha and I were talking over the new developments as I walked her home after dinner. Since she had moved to Springfield, she had lodged in the house of Sheriff Hutchason, as the sheriff's wife, Molly, was an old schoolmate of Martha's from Louisville. It was a chilly evening, the partial moon obscured by gusty clouds, and Martha was shivering under her thin dress. I took off my coat and wrapped it around her shoulders.

"Are you certain Archibald couldn't have had anything to do with the murder, if there was a murder?" my sister asked.

"Positive. The poor fellow doesn't have a mean bone in his body."

"But I thought you told me he lifted your purse on the ferry in Chicago."

"He saw an opportunity and he took it. No one was harmed, especially not when he restored the purse to me several days later. With my portrait of Ann still inside."

"But with several coins missing!" protested my sister. "I think you're being unwise about him."

"Well, I'm certain of this. However bad Archibald might be, his brothers are worse by a factor of ten. I've seen enough of them, and of how they treat Archibald, to know it. My fear is they're going to blame Archibald for something they did."

"He's got to stick up for himself," said Martha. "He shouldn't let his family push him around. I know I wouldn't."

As I returned to my store, ready to head up the back stairs and retire for the evening, I saw a lanky figure lurking in the doorway. At first I was afraid it was a blackguard bent on robbery, but as I neared, the troubled eyes and crooked teeth of Archibald Trailor emerged from behind a black cloak.

"Trailor, what are you doing here?" I exclaimed.

"Waiting for you, Mr. Speed." There was a tremble in his voice. "Can I come inside?"

As I unlocked the door and ushered Archibald in, I was struck by what an odd relationship we had. I had barely known the man prior to the harrowing experience of the Sudden Change, and I hadn't spoken to him more than half a dozen times, and then only in passing, since we'd returned home to Springfield. We'd never met up for that draught we'd discussed. Yet the desperate hours of terror we'd shared sheltering next to his prone horse in the midst of the violent storm had given us an indelible connection many lifelong friends lacked.

He leaned against the counter in the storeroom and gazed at me with a pained expression. "The sheriff's gone for my brothers. He says both of them, Henry and William, are gonna be arrested. He thinks they might have killed Flynn."

"That's what I heard."

"I love my brothers. They're the only family I have."

"I know they are." Having seen how they treated him, I thought neither merited this declaration of loyalty. At the same time, I knew as well as anyone the strength of the bond that family blood commanded.

"What'll happen to them?"

"They'll be taken to jail and questioned, I suppose, and brought in front of Judge Treat. After that, it all depends on what actually happened. Do *you* know what happened to this Fisher character, Archibald?"

He looked up with a frightened face and shook his head.

I spoke as gently as I could. "Does that mean you don't know, or that something bad did happen to him?"

"I . . . I can't talk about it. William made us promise we wouldn't say nothing, and we all agreed. I can't do nothing to hurt them."

My heart sank. This was hardly the declaration of innocence I'd been hoping for. But there was no use in making the poor man even more anxious.

"Quite right of you, Trailor," I said. "It sounds like you should keep it all to yourself for the time being. I know you don't want to see anything bad happen to your brothers, but at least it's them the sheriff's after, not you."

He shook his head again. "The sheriff's gone for Henry and William, but the men that was doing the searching today, I'm afraid they're gonna come to my door next."

"Where do you live?" I realized I had no idea where Archibald made his residence in town.

"At the old boarding house over on Adams. Me and a few of the ostlers from the Globe stables share a room there. The sheriff came by a little while back to tell me he was going to arrest William and Henry. He was civil to me, which he always is. Very civil, the sheriff. He said people might be saying things about me over the next days but I should best ignore them."

"That sounds like good advice." I was pleased to see Hutchason treating Archibald as a victim of his brothers rather than as a potential conspirator.

"But I saw those men charging around town today," Archibald continued. "Running around as if they was deputies of the sheriff. I don't think they're just gonna use words if they fix to come after me."

"Hold on a second." I let myself through the store counter, went to the back of one of the rows of shelves where I stored my goods, and felt along the very top shelf until my fingers touched iron. I took a pistol down from its resting place and, holding the butt end gingerly, laid it on the counter before Archibald.

"Take this. In case the need arises."

He stared at the gun, motionless. "I couldn't never shoot it," he said at last. "I couldn't never hurt another being."

"I know you couldn't. And I'm sure it'll never come to that. But it can't hurt to carry the piece with you, at least until things calm down. And if they ever do come to make trouble, none of those men need to know you wouldn't shoot."

He thought about this and slowly nodded. He picked up the gun and slipped it into his pocket. "Thank you, Mr. Speed," he said as he turned to leave. "You're the only real friend I have."

As I watched him slip out onto the cold streets, I hoped mightily it wasn't true.

Chapter 10

The next morning, Lincoln and I were speaking about the Trailor brothers as we dressed. Our bedroom was a small, second-floor room perched on top of my store. It was dingy and low ceilinged, with two double beds pressed against opposing walls and a narrow opening in between. Since his arrival in Springfield three years ago, Lincoln and I had shared one of the beds. Hurst and Herndon shared the other.

There was a small looking glass on the wall, which I had affixed at a height appropriate for me sometime before Lincoln's arrival. Between the cramped open space in the room, which we crisscrossed to find our garments, and Lincoln's need to bend over periodically to peer into the glass, our dressing routine approximated a two-person quadrille.

"It sounds as if William Trailor, at least, is in a spot," Lincoln was saying as he contorted himself to stare at his reflection while fastening his necktie. "If he's been telling people Fisher died and willed him his fortune . . . well, how can he explain that away?"

"Maybe Fisher died of natural causes. He wasn't the healthiest-looking man." While I had no particular brief for William Trailor, I feared that as long as he was under scrutiny, Archibald would be in peril as well. I nudged Lincoln out of the way and stared at the glass. I frowned at my curling dark hair, which nearly fell onto the top of my shoulders, and at my blue eyes. Something was evidently not to Miss Todd's liking.

"But what about the body?" said Lincoln. Lost in my reflection, it took me a moment to realize he was referring to Fisher's, not my own.

"What about it?"

"If he died a natural death, as you suggest, then where's his body? Where was he buried? William Trailor can hardly plead ignorance of the circumstances of his so-called natural death if he's telling people he inherited money from the man."

"That's a fair objection," I said. "I suppose William Trailor may be another client for A. Lincoln, Esquire. When the sheriff brings him back, he'll need to hire a local lawyer. You'd be a likely choice, would you not?"

"Perhaps in normal times," Lincoln replied, shrugging on his topcoat, "but I've got quite a busy docket at present, between my regular cases and the work of the legislature."

Lincoln thrust a bony elbow into my shoulder and resumed his position, bending down before the glass. He had a high forehead, prominent cheekbones, a heavy jaw, and a blunt nose. But his gray eyes were kind, if a little sad, and I had never once seen his smile fail to light up a room with the power of a hundred candles. He licked his palm and pressed it vigorously onto his scalp, trying to get his shiny black hair to stay in place. Eventually he gave up. "Ah, it's no use. If there's a homelier-looking man in all of Sangamon County, I don't want to meet him."

"You yourself have looked even more homely on occasion," I offered.

"As always, Speed, you know just the thing to put my mood right." He slapped me on the back. "Let's be off."

As I followed him down the winding stairs that led to my storeroom, he glanced over his shoulder. "I was talking to Ninian last night, at the Lyceum."

"Oh?"

"Apparently you and his sister-in-law, Miss Todd, had a long conversation yesterday morning in his parlor. You must have encountered her when you went to call upon him. Even though you knew he would not be present."

"She and I talked for a spell," I acknowledged, straining to keep my face neutral.

"You know my feelings for her, Speed."

"And you know I don't give up without a fight."

Lincoln frowned and then recollected himself. "So, tell me—how was the fair Miss Todd?"

"I wish I could report she succumbed unreservedly to the Speed charms, but my powers of self-deception do not extend so far. It seems for this week, at least, her heart is set upon another."

Lincoln swung around swiftly, almost colliding with me. "Oh?" he said expectantly.

"I tried to talk her out of it. I insisted the man would be too busy with his law practice, to say nothing of his overweening political ambitions, to spare her a moment's thought. But my objections were no use. She appears smitten." I looked up at Lincoln, trying to gauge if the bait had been set. "So, it seems that . . . *Douglas* is the only man she'll have."

Lincoln gave a great shout of laughter. "Ha! That's two for you this morning, Speed."

We proceeded to the common table of the Globe, where we took our breakfast together most mornings. When we arrived, however, there was another man sitting at our usual place: Belmont, the European banker.

"You two know each other?" Lincoln said as we took chairs on opposite sides of the table.

"We met briefly at the American House gala last week," said Belmont. He offered me his hand, manfully, and I shook it. "I gather I have you to thank, Speed, for my assignment in Springfield. Had you not caught the bank cashier at his pork speculation game, I doubt the state would have sought our assistance."

"You're part of the Rothschild dynasty?" I asked. I tried to catch Saunders's eye in hopes of procuring a mug of coffee. Alas, I failed, and no coffee materialized.

"In a manner," said Belmont with a modest smile. He ran his fingers over his immaculate mustache. "I started as an assistant at their main office in the Free City of Frankfurt at the age of fourteen. A few years later they sent me to Naples. Then, when your banks started to have their, er, difficulties—"

"To put it mildly!" snorted Lincoln.

"—we thought," continued Belmont, "perhaps we could be of assistance in this great country, and so I sailed for the New World."

Lincoln had set his stovepipe hat down on the table in front of him. "Without Belmont's assistance," he said, "there will be no money to support any economic activity in the entire northern half of the state. No money to resume work on the canal, for one thing, but it's much more than that. There's no money to pay the Irish navvies for the work they've already done on the canal, which means no one has money to pay farmers for the produce they've grown, which means there's no money to pay the merchants in town for their goods. And so on."

"I witnessed the Irish suffering with my own eyes in Chicago," I said, thinking back to the desperate mother and her pitiful children.

Lincoln nodded gravely. "Unless the legislature votes to make pork legal tender for the payment of all debts—which might not be a bad idea, come to think—the state's in debtors' prison. We'll remain there until we can replenish the bank's store of hard currency. Belmont is helping us make bail. Ah, here we go."

Saunders had finally arrived, placing a mug of coffee and a small, overcooked steak in front of each of us. "We need to eat quickly," continued Lincoln. "We're to meet with the banking committee of the legislature to see if we can finally agree to terms for the loan."

"What's the disagreement?" I asked, chewing patiently. Each bite of Saunders's steak required a great deal of patience before it would slide down the throat.

"Douglas and the Democrats want to line their own pockets with Belmont's gold," said Lincoln between bites. "Keep it locked in iron boxes to be dispensed by the state to favorites of their choosing. I want to make sure it gets out as quickly as possible to the mass of the people, so economic activity can resume. That's the essence of what Douglas and I were arguing over at the gala."

"That, and a certain Miss Todd, it appeared," interjected Belmont. I frowned; it was the sort of observation I might have made, had the banker not imposed himself upon our breakfasting routine.

Lincoln grinned. "At the end of the evening I told Mary I wanted to dance with her in the worst way. Do you know what her response was?" Belmont and I shook our heads.

"She said, 'Having seen you on the floor earlier, Mr. Lincoln, I can confirm you do, indeed, dance in the worst way.'"

Belmont shouted with laughter. "She didn't really say that, did she?" he said, nudging Lincoln in the ribs.

"I swear it's so," replied Lincoln, his eyes twinkling.

I glared at Belmont, who affected not to notice. Even if the future of the state hinged on his gold, I didn't appreciate his interference. Besides, as I thought about it, I spied a problem with the banker's plan.

"Even if the legislature agrees on the terms of the loan," I said, "what are you going to do—write out a draft to the State of Illinois? As if your signature on a mere piece of paper will change the economic situation in a stroke."

Belmont shook his head seriously. "No, it won't be that at all. The State Bank can only resume its banking activities if it has a sufficient store of gold coins physically sitting in its vault. We'll have to move all the specie to Chicago."

"Move it from where? And how?"

"Come now, Speed, you can't expect Belmont to reveal all of his secrets," interjected Lincoln. "Back in '35, when the State Bank at Springfield was first organized, the original bank president personally hauled four huge trunks of silver coins seventy-five miles from Alton to Springfield in the back of his wagon. I imagine we'll come up with something similar."

"Have you ever seen fifty thousand dollars' worth of gold coins?" Belmont asked. His eyes shone at the mere mention of the sum. Both Lincoln and I shook our heads.

"It is a sight both thrilling and disappointing. Thrilling for the power such riches convey to their possessor. And yet disappointing because of the small physical extent of the hoard." He picked up his silver-handled walking stick and sketched a modest rectangular box in the air. "The coins will fit comfortably in a small traveling trunk, one which could barely carry the wardrobe of a gentlemen for a five-day journey. A man cannot be clothed for a week, and yet a government may be financed for years." He shook his head. "The disproportion offends me."

"That shipment will be quite a target," I said.

Lincoln wiped his mouth on the table napkin and pushed his chair back. "That's a problem for another day. First, the legislature has to agree on a sensible plan. Let's be off, Belmont. We need you to explain your terms one more time to my colleagues this morning."

Lincoln settled his stovepipe hat on his head and turned back to me. "I haven't forgotten about your inquiry from earlier, Speed. Are you still concerned about Archibald Trailor's well-being?"

"Very much so."

"Then my advice is to talk to Big Red himself. After speaking with Ninian last night, it's clear to me the mayor's leading the charge against the Trailor brothers. Trying to boost his popularity with the voters, I don't doubt. As long as he's on their trail, your Archibald is going to be in jeopardy."

Chapter 11

I decided to follow Lincoln's suggestion at once. As all of the town's energies in recent times had been focused on attracting and then constructing the state capitol, no one in Springfield had given a moment's thought as to where the functions of the mayor might be conducted. Indeed, no one had given a moment's thought to the idea of *having* a mayor until a year ago, when Big Red May, having been maneuvered out of his seat in Congress by the scheming Douglas, was in need of the stable salary a new political office would provide.

Thus, there was no "town hall," as some of the more established cities in the East now featured, and no plans for one. Instead, Mayor May conducted his business from a cramped room on the ground floor of the new capitol building that had originally been intended as a closet to store the wood necessary to fuel the building's fourteen potbellied heating stoves. I found Big Red in his closet with a case of great distemper.

"No time for you, Speed," he snapped as soon as I appeared in the open doorway. Since the building architect envisioned that clerks would be entering hourly for wood to stoke their fires, he hadn't bothered to provide a door for the room.

"I came at Lincoln's suggestion."

"No time for him, either." Big Red made a show of scrutinizing various books of account spread out on the tall desk in front of him. I had the distinct impression he hadn't even noticed their presence until I arrived.

"I understand you've ordered that William and Henry Trailor be apprehended as possible suspects for murder."

Big Red did not look up, nor did his scowl soften.

"I can't tell you how relieved I am, as a concerned citizen and long-time merchant in the community, that you're taking active steps to protect the public's safety."

This time Big Red was unable to conceal the distinct hint of pleasure in his growl. His enormous ears rose to half-mast. I was getting close to the right key.

"Sheriff Hutchason's a fine man, of course," I continued, warming to the part, "a capable follower of orders. But I don't think he has the foresight you bring to the task."

"The people want action," said Big Red. Then, remembering his distemper, he resumed study of his books.

"I'm sure you're right." I chose my words carefully. "I do think we should make sure there's actually *been* a murder, before we put someone on trial for one. Right now, all we have is the word of one gossip, in that letter Keyes intercepted. For all we know, Flynn Fisher is still alive. Perhaps he's merely indisposed somewhere."

"It's more than the one rumor," Big Red insisted. "There's the matter of William Trailor suddenly having lots of gold to spend."

"All according to an old gossip, who's probably got her facts mixed up. I merely suggest we act judiciously. All those other towns that wanted to have the state capital—Jacksonville, Alton, even Vandalia again—all of them are looking for an excuse to take Springfield down a peg. Neither of us, I'm sure, wants our town to look the fool, not when we've finally had the triumph of opening the new capitol building."

Big Red deigned to meet my gaze this time. "There's been a

murder, Speed, one committed by the Trailor brothers. You may depend on it."

Before I could respond, we heard the sound of several men shouting at once. Soon, four men materialized in the hallway outside the closet, in a tussle, pulling this way and that. As the jostling group pushed past me into the crowded office, I saw a squat, potbellied man in the middle of the melee, his hands bound behind his back. It was Henry Trailor.

"We got him, Big Red!" one of the men shouted jubilantly. Henry Trailor's captors were some of the vagrants from the town green who had formed yesterday's search party.

"Caught him leaving his house in his phaeton," said another. "Had his wife and children loaded up along with three trunks."

"Fleeing the county," said the third. "It's practically an admission of guilt."

Henry Trailor stood defiantly against the back wall of the closet, scowling at Big Red. His gaze had passed over me quickly; it was apparent that in this very different context he didn't recognize me from the single evening I'd spent at his table several months ago.

"I insist you release me," Trailor said in his high-pitched screech. "These men have detained me unlawfully."

"They've detained you on my authority," replied Big Red steadily. "You're under arrest for the murder of Flynn Fisher."

"Utter nonsense!" Trailor shouted, and he took two long strides to flee from the room. But his captors quickly grabbed each arm. After a brief struggle, Trailor was pinned against the wall again. The prisoner contented himself with spitting on the floor near the mayor's feet and unleashing a torrent of epithets.

"Why'd you do it?" asked Big Red, when Trailor's tantrum had subsided. "And what did you do with the body?"

"Like I've been telling these bastards all the way here, I didn't do anything. I demand to see a judge."

"You'll be brought in front of him soon enough," replied Big Red, "but only after you admit what's happened."

"There's nothing to tell. I swear it." Trailor stood erect against the brick wall, his face crimson with indignation.

"Why did you kill Flynn Fisher?"

"I did nothing of the sort!"

"Why'd you kill Fisher?" repeated Big Red, more insistently this time. His ears were flapping, and he jammed a forefinger into Trailor's stomach.

"I'm telling you, no one killed anyone. Flynn Fisher was alive and well the last I saw him."

"Then where is he?"

Trailor tried to gesture, but with his hands still tied behind his back, his body merely twisted unnaturally. "Dunno," he said. "I'm not his keeper, am I?"

"Why did you want Fisher dead?" continued the mayor. "What had the man done to you?"

"He'd done nothing," Henry Trailor replied, "which is why we did nothing to him. When do I get to explain this to the judge?"

"Later. How about your brother, William? What was his role in the deed?"

"Didn't have one. I keep telling you, there was no deed done."

The mayor stared hard at his prisoner and expelled a long breath. He was tiring of the jousting match. "We'll see what William has to say for himself. The sheriff should be arriving with him before the morning is out."

Henry Trailor startled. "You've arrested William too?"

Big Red nodded. "The sheriff and I agreed that my men would roust you while he went to apprehend William. Your brother will be bound next to you before long. Both of you can rot in jail, for all I care, until you admit what you've done. So if you've got something to tell me before your brother gets here, you'd better say it now."

Trailor leaned against the wall; his coal-black eyes narrowed with concentration, as if he was having some sort of internal debate. At last he looked up and exhaled slowly. "Very well," he said, "I suppose I should make a clean breast of it."

He paused, as everyone stared at him expectantly. "Go on," said Big Red.

"Your accusation is correct, in part, sir. Flynn Fisher *was* murdered."

The three men who'd captured Trailor unleashed a shout of excitement. Big Red silenced them and continued to stare intently at his prisoner, who, after a deep breath, continued with his confession.

"But the act was committed by my brothers, William and Archibald. The two of them acted in concert. I had nothing to do with the killing. They murdered Fisher, and then they made me help them hide evidence of the crime."

Big Red gave me a look of supreme triumph.

Chapter 12

"I knew I could get the truth out of this ruffian, if I kept at it," Big Red cried with glee. "Ha! I'll be a hero once the tale is told. You all saw me, didn't you?" He pointed to his motley search party, who dutifully bobbed their heads and assured the mayor they would spread word of his exploit.

"Hold on a moment," I said, looking at Henry Trailor. "Why would Archibald, or William for that matter, kill this Fisher fellow?"

"I'll tell you everything," Henry said, addressing me and the mayor together, "but only if you promise I'll walk free. Like I said, I had nothing to do with the murder itself."

"Of course, of course," said Big Red, his hands and ears flapping in excited symphony. "Tell us the full story of what happened, help us obtain justice for your brothers, and you'll face no jeopardy."

"Can you untie my hands?" Henry asked. The mayor did so quickly, and Henry grunted his thanks and spent a few moments rubbing the red welts that encircled his wrists.

"How about a shot of whiskey? It was a long journey, and your posse weren't too gentle in their methods."

"Get the man some whiskey, Speed," ordered Big Red.

Henry Trailor seemed to have accepted me as a deputy to the

mayor, and I wanted to sustain the illusion. I raced down the corridor to the legislative clerks' room and searched through several drawers until I found an unopened bottle of firewater. When I returned to Big Red's closet, Henry Trailor took a long pull, belched, and handed the bottle to one of his former captors, saying, "No hard feelings, eh, fellows?"

The men accepted the liquor with broad smiles. Big Red ordered one to find Sheriff Hutchason and inform him about Henry's confession so that William and Archibald Trailor could be confined to the jail cell at once. He asked the others to round up the search party and await further instructions. The men agreed and slouched away, passing the whiskey bottle back and forth with enthusiasm.

"Flynn Fisher served alongside my brother William at Detroit, in Mr. Madison's war against Great Britain," Henry Trailor began. "Supposedly, William saved his life in battle by bayonetting a redcoat who was about to shoot him, though if you've ever shared a drink with my brother William, you know there's scarcely any man who served beside him whose life he *didn't* save at least once. In the event, William claimed Fisher was in his debt, and the two remained in contact. They would see each other every few years at Old Soldiers' gatherings."

"Hurry along," said Big Red irritably. "We're not interested in the history. We want to know about the murder."

"I'm getting there," said Henry. "A few years back, Fisher won a contract from the Canal Board to build a bypass on the canal near Ottawa. Fisher happened to see William soon thereafter, and he mentioned his new enterprise. I'll give my brother credit for this: he's faster than any man alive in figuring out how he can enrich himself from any situation. On the spot, William proposed a scheme to Fisher. Before the bypass route was laid out, we would buy up land in the area. Then Fisher would arrange to site the bypass through our freehold, greatly increasing the value of the land. We'd sell it in due course, and Fisher would get one-quarter of our profits.

"Fisher knew a good deal when he saw one. It was a chance for big profit on the side, merely for doing something the Board was already paying him to do. So he agreed, and William, Archibald, and I spent five hundred dollars on a huge tract near Ottawa. It wasn't the best place to put the bypass, but it would do, and it would be easy enough for Fisher to run his section through."

"But your scheme didn't go as planned?" I said. As I listened to Henry, my mind was drawn back to the argument I'd overheard between him and Archibald on the evening before the Sudden Change. They'd been scheming over how to get a rid of a business partner; in light of Henry's explanation, it seemed a fair guess that Fisher was the one.

Henry nodded. "Fisher proved a miserable businessman. Unreliable. He'd disappear for weeks at a time, when he was supposed to be making progress on the canal. Worse, he spent the first three quarterly advances from the Canal Board putting up the best navvy housing those ignorant Irishmen had ever seen. Out of sympathy for his countrymen, I suppose, but a complete waste of money. They might as well sleep in the dirt with their animals, for all the difference it'd make." Henry Trailor spit on the floor again.

"By the time Fisher started laying out his section of the canal, the distributions from the Board had stopped. They'd run out of money. Fisher's crew only cleared a hundred yards of land before they walked off the job for lack of wages. He never got within a mile of our freehold."

"Serves all of you right," said Big Red, "for trying to profit from a public commission."

Henry cackled. "You mean to tell me you've never profited from your office, Mayor? Anyway, the last straw fell here in

Springfield, the day before they killed him. William and I had come to talk to any members of the legislature we could find, to convince them to finish the job Fisher was supposed to do and direct the canal through our land.

"Then Fisher tried to play a card he didn't hold. He asked William for a loan of one hundred dollars. Against his share of the profits, he said. Of course, William told him there were no profits yet, and at the rate we were going there weren't going to be any. But Fisher told William that if he didn't make the loan, he'd tell the Canal Board we'd bribed him in the performance of his official duties."

"You heard this conversation yourself?" I asked.

Henry shook his head. "William spoke to Fisher alone. Archibald and I were putting on a good drunk and exploring some of the amusements available in this town." Henry grinned at the memory.

Trailor's reference was not obscure. The legislature was not the only recently arrived business in Springfield in which a variety of personal services were available if the right price could be agreed upon. A careful student of the economic sciences might conclude it was the appearance of the one that had given rise to the advent of the other.

Henry continued, "Archibald and I met up with William and Fisher afterwards. That's when it happened."

"What happened, exactly?" I asked.

Big Red shot me an angry glance. "This is my interrogation, Speed. Don't go interfering."

"But I know Archibald," I said. Turning to Henry, I repeated, "I know your younger brother. I can't imagine his being involved in something like this."

Henry looked over at Big Red questioningly, and for a moment I was afraid I'd undermined my disguise as an aide to the mayor. But before Henry could challenge me, Big Red said,

"It's going to come out in court soon enough, Trailor. Why don't you tell us the details now?"

"Archibald and I had done our business, and I was about to return to the tavern where I was staying when William found us. He said he needed our help. Told us how Fisher was trying to squeeze us for money and how we'd be ruined if he spilled. He led us to the tavern where Fisher was staying—"

"Which one?" I asked.

"Somewhere on the edge of town. Anyway, he rousted Fisher from his room, and the four of us proceeded out of town. Eventually we got to a clearing, near a grove of birch, and he shoved Fisher to the ground and told him we wouldn't be betrayed."

"What did Fisher say?"

"Denied he'd done anything wrong, but we knew he had. Fisher started to get to his feet, to run away, but Archibald grabbed him by both arms. William told Archibald to bind him to a tree. So Archibald dragged him into the woods, and there was scuffling and shouting. At one point William yelled for them to be quiet, and eventually the sounds faded away. Archibald came back to say he'd tied Fisher to a tree and stuffed a rag down his throat as well, to make sure he couldn't call for help."

Big Red's ears flapped excitedly. "Go on," he prompted.

"We stood in the clearing and debated how to shut up Fisher for good. Then I noticed there were no sounds at all coming from inside the grove, and I went to have a look and . . ." Henry hung his head low. "That's when I saw it."

"Saw what?"

"The first dead man I'd ever seen. Fisher was still tied to the tree, but he wasn't breathing anymore. His body had gone rigid. The rag Archibald had stuffed in his mouth—the poor fool must have stuffed it too deep and it suffocated the man."

Big Red gave a small cry, seemingly of triumph rather than sympathy. "Murder!" he hissed excitedly.

"What happened next?"

"Archibald collapsed onto the ground. Wailing. William tried to get him to stop. And then William told me to take Archibald back to town, put him to bed, and make sure he didn't say anything to anybody, while he took care of the body. He said he'd hide it under a bush."

"How is it possible," asked Big Red, "that this man Fisher had such a weak constitution he could be killed by a rag?"

"On that score I can testify," I said. "He never looked healthy, walking around leaning to the side like he did."

"'Never looked healthy.' That's exactly the way to put it," said Henry. "He had periods when he was lucid, but mostly, he wasn't a strong man. Anyway, William said he'd come back later to dispose of the body. I told him he had to do something. We couldn't just leave the body in the bushes. Before long the wolves would drag it out to have a meal and someone would stumble on the remains."

"What night did all this take place?" Big Red asked.

"Not sure I remember the exact date," Henry said. "A couple weeks back. I know it was on the night of the full moon, because I told William as I was leaving we were lucky no one had seen us."

"The night of the gala at the American House," I exclaimed, recalling Ninian Edwards's remark about the moon's effects on Mary Todd's suitors. "In fact, I talked briefly to your brother William at the affair."

Henry nodded. "He was on his way to some social gathering of the legislature as we went off to our amusements. He must have had his talk with Fisher, where Fisher threatened us, before going to that party. And then, afterwards, he came to roust us. My brothers are quite a pair. One of them can't think straight, and the other never bothers to. They'd be lost without me."

I whistled softly. All the time I'd been talking to William

Trailor that evening of the gala, all the time he'd been petitioning Lincoln and Douglas and the other legislators, he must have been thinking of how he was going to deal with the traitorous Fisher. Not only that, but William had actually mentioned to me he was in town with Fisher. Far from hiding the crime he must have been contemplating at that very moment, he was practically bragging about it. I shook my head, marveling at the man's nerve.

"It'll be an open-and-shut case at trial," said Big Red, rubbing his hands together excitedly. "With your testimony, a murder conviction will be assured. And nothing does more to raise the spirits of the town than a public hanging. Come to think, the only thing better than one hanging is two of them, side by side."

I shivered at the image. But as I thought about Henry's confession, there was an obvious problem. According to his story, William and Archibald had killed Fisher in a bout of panic brought on by Fisher's clumsy attempt at blackmail. But back in Henry's cabin before the Sudden Change, months ago, the brothers had already seemed to be plotting to get rid of the man, and Henry had seemed to be the chief plotter.

"Can you show us where this all took place?" the mayor asked before I could decide whether to challenge Henry. "The fight, the tree Archibald tied him to. The bush William hid the body under."

Henry smiled. "I'll lead you there right now, if you'd like."

Chapter 13

Big Red, Henry Trailor, and I left the mayor's closet and exited through the front door of the capitol building. Across the street to our left was the impressive three-story building, fronted by marble columns and topped by a triangular pediment, that housed the Springfield headquarters of the State Bank. Like the capitol itself, the bank structure was part of a frantic building effort that had swept Springfield in the past eighteen months.

The common rabble of the town, however, were interested in more immediately gratifying matters. An excited crowd waited for us at the bottom of the steps.

"Ahoy, Mayor, is that him?" shouted one of the layabouts as we came down the steps. "Is he the murderer?"

"Afraid I can't say," Big Red replied, slowing his pace. "We're on official business. Off to search for . . . well, I can't say what our business is, neither."

"That's one of the Trailor brothers, ain't he?" said another man, who had been leaning against a hitching post.

"He is," the mayor acknowledged, almost too eagerly. Our little procession, slowed to a crawl, was attracting men from all directions.

"Where're you taking him?" called the first man.

"We deserve an explanation," said another, a tall man with a toothpick jammed into the corner of his mouth, "after all the searching we did for you. I put my knee through my jeans in one of them cellars. We'll follow you, Big Red, wherever you're heading. Ain't no law against it."

The mayor stopped and surveyed the group, which now comprised more than a dozen men, the same collection of miscreants who had participated in the helter-skelter search for Fisher's body the previous day. Big Red climbed up onto a rock.

"Gentlemen," he began, "if you must know, this man is Henry Trailor." A murmur passed through the crowd. "He is not one of the murderers, although I have extracted from him a confession of who the actual murderers are, and you'll not be surprised to learn they're men *very* close to him." The mayor looked around, soaking up the passion of the mob.

"Henry Trailor has promised to lead me to the body of the victim, Fisher." A buzz of excitement swirled about. "As you men have waylaid me, it's only sensible I invite you to join us. The more hands on board, the quicker we'll find the body."

A great *huzzah* went up. Big Red took Henry firmly by the wrist, and the latter pointed the way out of town. By now, the following pack numbered at least twenty men, more than a few stumbling with drink. I followed at a distance. I had no eagerness to associate myself with the rude mob, but at the same time I wanted to be there when the body was recovered. I might spot some detail that would help Archibald with his defense.

After a half hour's procession along a rutted carriage track, the still edge of a millpond came into view through a forest of bare tree trunks. It was the same area where the broken fencepost—the would-be murder weapon, although that story was now discredited by Henry's confession—had been found. The pond was situated in a natural valley, where the dam constructed by Hickox two decades earlier had little trouble filling up a reservoir to provide steady power to the mill wheel. The mill had lost business over time to several operations closer to the center of town. Last year, a Supreme Court justice, who was moving to Springfield with the court, had purchased the property and announced that henceforth the wheel would not turn and the pond would serve as his fishing hole and place of repose.

As we approached within one hundred yards of the pond, Henry Trailor suddenly raised his right arm, and the entire rabble came to an abrupt stop. "It was right . . ." He paused, staring into a particularly dense thicket of trees. "Right . . . there. Archibald tied Fisher to a tree trunk right in there."

The crowd charged into the wood in the direction Henry indicated. I followed behind them, silently cursing my bad leg, but before I could reach the place, excited calls were already echoing back, intermixed with the *thwack* of branches snapping.

"I see it!"

"Look at that branch!"

"And that one over there!"

"Look out!"

"They must of strung 'em up from there!"

"Ooof!"

Big Red was in stride with me, and we came into a clearing where the crowd excitedly milled about in front of a stand of birch trees. A number of the men had climbed up to sit on or swing from lower branches of the trees, and several of the branches had snapped under their weight, sending the men tumbling down. It was a scrum of limbs, human and deciduous, and if evidence had existed that a murder had been committed here, it had just been obliterated.

I was beginning to despair of finding anything of value when a man to the side of the group called out, "Over here! Drag marks."

The mass shifted in his direction, but I managed to get to the front of the pack this time, and I saw he was right. There was an unmistakable path on the ground, roughly the width of a human torso, leading away from the clearing. The trail of bent grasses and scattered twigs led to a nearby thornbush, which was soon surrounded by the crowd.

"That's right," Henry Trailor called out. "That's just where William dragged him. And later, William came back and—"

Before he could finish the sentence, another man called out, "Look, another path!" and the entire mob chased after him as he hurried off in the general direction of the pond. "Here it is . . . and here . . . and over here," he shouted, turning this way and that like a bloodhound on the scent. From my position at the back of the pack, I couldn't tell whether there had been a trail through the brush. Either way, by the time twenty men had followed after one another, there was a pronounced pathway.

We all chased after the bloodhound fellow through the thicket and emerged on the shore of the pond. The mill house and dam stood opposite. The crowd came to a panting halt, men bent over and breathing deeply from exertion and excitement.

There was a moment of perfect stillness. The glimmering surface of the water was quiet as the morning dew. A jay called out from across the pond. And then chaos broke loose.

Three different men, seemingly all at once, had the idea to drain the pond. They shouted and ran toward the dam, and it took only a few moments for the rest of the mob to seize upon their intentions and follow. Soon, all twenty men were crashing through the wood, whooping and hollering like a group of Indians bent on attack. Big Red was caught short, and he gave me a panicked look. Then he hurried after his erstwhile army while I followed close on his footfalls.

When we reached the dam, its destruction was already underway. The dam had been built of irregular rock and brick, with dried mud serving as mortar. The mass of men now covered the slanting face of the structure, digging away at the mud with sticks and stones and bare hands. The mayor shouted to get their attention, but his words were drowned out by the din of the mob's industry.

A few of the men concentrated their efforts on dislodging a large rock near the top of the dam wall that seemed to serve as a keystone for the entire structure. Before long, little rivulets of water started trickling down either side of the rock. The men gave a cheer of excitement and redoubled their efforts.

Just then, there was a large bang from the front door of the mill house, and the millpond's owner strode into view on the other side of the dam.

"What on God's earth are you doing?" he shouted. "Stop this at once! Stop, or I'll have you all hung!"

In their excitement, the men digging away at the dam face were oblivious to the threat. Next to me, Big Red cleared his throat, nervously, and shouted, "Ahoy, Justice Smith. I am trying to prevent—"

Justice Smith's eyes alighted upon the mayor and grew wide with anger. "Red?" he shouted. "This is your doing? I'll run you out of town!"

Justice Theophilus Smith resembled no one so much as Jehovah. He was big and broad shouldered, with a full mane of white, curly hair and a white beard. He shook his mighty fist, and the only evidence that he did not actually control the heavens was that no lightning crashed down upon the men bent on the destruction of his dam.

"But I'm trying to *stop* them, Justice Smith," Big Red called back in a pleading tone. "I wandered up and happened upon this insensible mob, and I've been doing everything in my powers to restrain them."

Smith opened his mouth in reply, but his words were lost, because at that moment the men on the dam face succeeded in dislodging the keystone. Water from the pond poured through the opening, and the force of the sudden current ripped away the remainder of the dam. Most of the men who had been working on the dam face managed to jump to safety just in time, but a few were too slow, and they were carried off amid the water and rubble. The entire dam collapsed in a matter of seconds as, with a great roar, water poured out of the pond.

Justice Smith raged and shouted and shook his fists, but the threats of the modern-day Jehovah proved impotent against the inexorable force of gravity. The surface level of the pond sank quickly, the water streaming out through the large hole in the landscape where the dam had been. In a fury lasting less than a minute, it was all gone.

Some of the crowd had scattered to avoid the judge's wrath, and others who had been swept away were just now struggling to their feet, bruised and soaking wet, from down the spillway. The rest of the mob rushed toward the shoreline of the pond. I pushed my way into the front rank and looked out.

A shallow, barren depression lay in front of us. Scattered clumps of weeds clung to the muddy earth, and dozens of fish flopped about helplessly. All around, men started cursing with disappointment. Next to me, Big Red's forlorn ears drooped.

There was no body.

Chapter 14

I headed immediately to Lincoln's law office. Even without Fisher's dead body, Archibald and William Trailor were going to face murder charges in light of Henry Trailor's confession. Archibald had saved my life. Now his life hung in the balance, and I needed to do everything within my power to help him. Starting with procuring the services of the best trial lawyer in town.

This morning, Lincoln had said he might be too busy to take on William Trailor's case. Now that Archibald was to stand in the dock, however, everything was different. I had to make Lincoln see the importance of defending the simple, illiterate carpenter. But at the back of my mind lurked a concern that Lincoln would try to find an excuse to avoid representing Archibald, perhaps because of festering anger over my refusal to cede Miss Todd's hand to him.

I rehearsed the arguments in Archibald's favor as I reached the handsome row of two-story red brick buildings the landlord Hoffman had built a block north of the square. Among other firms, Hoffman's Row housed the offices of Stuart and Lincoln, Attorneys and Counsellors at Law.

I walked up the familiar stairs to the second floor and burst through the door to No. 4 without knocking. Lincoln was standing beside his cluttered worktable, with the banker Belmont at his side. Both men were bent over and examining some of the papers spread out on the table.

"My friend Archibald Trailor is in grave jeopardy," I exclaimed before either man could greet me.

"I know it," Lincoln said. "Sheriff Hutchason has just been to visit, giving us the latest word."

"You must help with his defense."

"Yes."

"He needs the very best. I demand it."

"I've already said yes, Joshua," said Lincoln. "Do you insist upon not taking yes for an answer?"

"Oh," I said, and I collapsed into an empty chair. The emotion drained out of me as fast as the millpond had emptied. I felt embarrassed for having harbored any doubts about Lincoln.

"I have already arranged," said Lincoln, looking down at me with a bemused expression, "for James Conkling to defend Archibald, and William Trailor, too. I'll stay involved myself, in the background, in case Conkling needs any advice, though I'm sure he'll acquit himself perfectly well."

It took me a moment to realize what Lincoln had said, and then all of my suspicions came rushing to the fore, as if the millpond draining was running in reverse and at triple-speed.

"Conkling?" I jumped to my feet. "You cannot be serious. *Conkling!* He's a good lad, but I wouldn't trust Conkling to look after the smallest commercial matter." Belmont's aristocratic eyebrows arched with surprise and Lincoln held his hand up, but I plowed forward. "I wouldn't trust Conkling to recover a penny from my lowest customer." Lincoln was clutching at his stomach now, almost as if he was laughing, but his posture only fueled my anger. "I wouldn't trust Conkling to prove in court the fact of his *own existence*. And you suggest I should rely upon *him* to defend Archibald's life?" Belmont's eyes were averted to the floor; Lincoln was convulsed with laughter, pounding on the table and gesturing frantically, and finally I came to a stop.

"What?" I demanded.

Suddenly I heard a noise from behind the door I had thrust open moments earlier. "Good day to you, Speed," said James Conkling, coming forward stiffly.

I blanched. "Conkling . . . I didn't realize . . ."

"No," said Conkling. "I don't suppose you did."

There was a heavy silence, which Lincoln finally broke by saying, "You've been unkind, Speed. And you're wrong. Conkling has become an accomplished advocate."

I stared at Conkling. He had arrived in Springfield two years earlier, fresh out of the famous Princeton University in New Jersey, and had promptly joined the bar and hung out his own shingle. Even now, with a slight build, sandy brown hair parted down the middle, and wire eyeglasses, he looked more like a schoolboy than a trial lawyer. There was no doubting Conkling's pure intelligence, but all too often he seemed to have his head in the clouds rather than his feet on the muddy, murky earth where Archibald Trailor's fate would be decided.

"I am truly sorry for the outburst, James," I began, before turning back to Lincoln, "but I do not apologize for my insistence. If you've talked to Hutchason, you know Big Red is determined to see Archibald and William hang. And he's got a willing accomplice in Henry Trailor. Archibald's going to need a tough, experienced lawyer."

I shifted my gaze to Conkling. "Have you ever handled a murder case?"

"Not since I've been admitted to the bar. But at Princeton I read Cicero's *Murder Trials* in the original Latin. Spent all year on a translation. And I've watched Lincoln—"

I held up my hand. "I'm sure you'd try your hardest. I don't intend to demean you, Conkling, but I owe Archibald my life. And he's in no position to protect himself. Certainly not against his domineering brothers, to say nothing of the combined forces of the mayor, the sheriff, and the prosecutor. He needs the very best. And yet apparently Lincoln values his other work more highly than he values our friendship."

Out of the corner of my eye, I could see both Belmont and Conkling shifting uncomfortably.

"I assure you that's not the case, Speed," said Lincoln, his arms spread earnestly. "Has the dead man's body surfaced yet?"

I put aside my indignation long enough to relate the tale of the millpond and Justice Smith's destroyed dam. When I finished, Lincoln was shaking his head. "That *is* unfortunate for Archibald," he said.

"Why? I would have thought a conviction would be harder to secure in the absence of the corpse."

Lincoln waved his hand. "That part, to be sure, may be favorable for Archibald. But the fate of Justice Smith's millpond assuredly is not. The old judge holds a grudge for longer than most."

"But that shouldn't affect Archibald," piped up Conkling. "He's not the one who tore down the dam. Besides, it's Judge Treat who'll be the trial judge for the murder trial. One of his first, I believe, after being appointed to the bench by Governor Carlin. Justice Smith is on the Supreme Court. He would hear an appeal, but only as one of seven justices on the appeals court. He's hardly in a position to harm Archibald or his case."

"I don't think that's the way Smith is going to see things, James," said Lincoln. "In his mind, Archibald and William Trailor will have been the cause of the destruction of his dam, just as sure as if they had torn it down with their own hands. Nor do I think Judge Treat will be unmindful of Justice Smith's grievance."

Lincoln gave me a look that said *I know you're right about*

Conkling, but when he continued speaking, it was not to reverse his position.

"Let's see how Conkling does at the preliminary hearing tomorrow. The judge will be considering bail for William and Archibald at the morning call, and we've already told Hutchason that Conkling will stand for both of them. If things truly appear dire for your Archibald after the bail hearing, Speed, we can revisit my role."

I left Hoffman's Row in a foul mood, and before I reached my store, I convinced myself that Lincoln was acting out of spite because of our competition over Miss Todd. For the first time in the three years of our friendship, I found myself ruing the day Fate had brought Abraham Lincoln into my world.

Chapter 15

The old, dilapidated courthouse on the public square had been demolished to make room for the state capitol, and a new, modern courtroom was due to be constructed inside the capitol building. Like several aspects of the sprawling, much-delayed project, however, the new courtroom had not yet been completed. As a result, the Sangamon County Circuit Court had been forced into temporary quarters. As it happened, the space available was at No. 3 Hoffman's Row, the first floor of the very building that housed Lincoln's law offices at No. 4.

While this arrangement was convenient for Lincoln, who merely had to walk down a single flight of stairs to attend court, it was notably inconvenient for the judge and other lawyers in town. The floor plan that provided a modest office for Lincoln and his law partner Stuart proved an almost unbearably cramped setting in which to conduct the legal business of the county.

The courtroom was already overflowing when I arrived the next morning. The judge's bench, little more than an elevated writing desk with a high-backed chair for the judge to perch upon, was jammed against the far wall. With some small space for counsel and the jury to cram into, there remained room only for two tight rows of spectator benches, while another group of spectators could stand in a kind of semicircle pressed up against the walls. Not least of the problems posed by the overall arrangement was that no one could sneeze or burp or clear his throat without every man present being informed of the details.

When, as this morning, the case being heard excited the town's interest, the public benches were full shortly after dawn, with an excess crowd milling around on the street outside. Judge Treat sought to accommodate the public by throwing open the windows so latecomers could at least hear—and if they were tall, see—the proceedings. But this plan had the unfortunate side effect of welcoming the elements into the courtroom. It was raining lightly this morning, the raindrops running down the brick walls of the building and dripping into the courtroom, where they formed small pools at the base of each window.

Sheriff Hutchason stood in the doorway, blocking it with his massive frame, but when I approached, he nodded and let me squeeze past. I flattened myself into an empty space against the rear wall of the courtroom, doing my best to ignore both the dripping rainwater and the angry grunts of men who were barred by Hutchason from entering.

Lincoln was already on his feet when I arrived, arguing another case to the judge. Though we had both spent the prior night in our chambers, I had managed to avoid speaking to him since I'd left his office. William and Archibald Trailor were also present, their hands bound together and to each other. William was defiant, his eyes darting around the courtroom restlessly, but Archibald's face was placid. He didn't realize the magnitude of what was happening, I thought.

". . . Mr. John Harris had possession of the horse in question, Your Honor," Lincoln was saying, "until his brother Mr. James Harris came along and asserted that the beast had been given to him under their father's will. That's when Mr. *Robert* Harris—"

"Wait a minute, Lincoln," Judge Treat called out in his shrill, nasal voice, setting down his pipe. "I understood there were two brothers Harris in this case. You mean to tell me there're three?"

"Four, actually," Lincoln replied, shuffling through a few pieces of paper in his hand. "I am just coming to the role played by Mr. *Christopher* Harris in regard to the disputed horse."

Judge Samuel Hubbel Treat picked up his pipe and sucked on the stem. He had been appointed the previous year to replace the long-serving Judge Jesse B. Thomas Jr., and in his short time on the bench Judge Treat had quickly become accustomed to the high privileges of the position. He was not quite thirty years of age, with wispy light-brown hair and a nasty expression perpetually pasted to his lips. Of late he had been suffering from a particularly unfortunate attack of acne rosacea, and his nose, forehead, and cheeks were dotted with red, pustular lesions.

Treat blew out a large plume of smoke. "We don't have time for all of them this morning. I'll bind you and the *four* brothers Harris over to the April trial term. If you can't resolve the case before then, we'll hold a quick trial to sort it all out."

Treat looked over at his clerk, my friend James Matheny. "Call the next matter," he commanded.

"The People against Trailor and Trailor," shouted Matheny. "Hearing on the defendants' application for bail."

"Ah, yes," Treat said, gazing out at the crowd, both inside and outside the courtroom, which quieted down at the name of the case. "Today's principal attraction, I believe. Who's standing for the defendants?"

"I am, Your Honor," Conkling called out. The young lawyer had been sitting off to the side, but now he pushed past Lincoln to the small well reserved for counsel. Lincoln, in turn, sat in the chair Conkling had just vacated. I saw Lincoln open his case and start to thumb through a series of folded packets of pleadings, each tied with a red ribbon.

"You're prosecuting this one yourself, General Lamborn?" Treat continued.

"That's right, Your Honor." Josiah Lamborn, the newly elected attorney general of Illinois, rose and stood beside Conkling. He was thick chested and broad shouldered, and next to him Conkling appeared even slighter than usual. Lamborn was also, if you will forgive the redundancy of this description, a Democrat and a drunkard.

"I have some familiarity with the case," Treat began. "I understand both of the Trailors are charged with murder, and moreover that their alleged malfeasance has resulted in the destruction of the property of one of the most esteemed citizens of our community." Treat took a long pull on his pipe and stared at Mayor May, sitting beside Lamborn. May's ears turned the same splotchy red hue as the judge's face.

"I must tell you, Mr. Conkling," the judge continued, "I'm skeptical in the extreme that bail is appropriate in these circumstances. However, you have a right to be heard on the application. You may proceed."

Conkling cleared his throat. "Thank you, Your Honor. As Cicero commenced his famed defense of Gaius Rabirius, also charged unjustly with a murder he did not commit, '*Propenenda ratio videtur esse officii mei.*' That is, let me start by explaining the reason I have undertaken this duty—"

Judge Treat's face had turned even redder, the pustules merging into one angry blotch, and he threw down his pipe. "Mr. Conkling, are you trying to speak *Latin* in my courtroom?" he shouted, his voice rising in disbelief. More than a few spectators started to laugh.

"Not so much *trying* as *reciting*, Your Honor," said Conkling. "You see, when I read Cicero at Princeton, our professor explained—"

The judge jumped to his feet, his head coming perilously

close to the ceiling. "Stop it, Mr. Conkling," he bellowed. "English is the only language to be spoken in my courtroom. I don't want to hear Latin. And I'm not interested in what your Professor Cicero taught you at Princeton. I want your argument for bail, if you have one. In English. So all of us who didn't go to Princeton can understand it."

The crowd was roaring with laughter, and I almost felt sorry for Conkling, who had turned pink as he stared down at his papers and tried to regain his composure. I glanced toward Lincoln and saw that he was already staring at me. I returned his gaze, unblinking and unfriendly, until Conking cleared his throat and started speaking again and Lincoln turned back to watch.

"All . . . all right, Your . . . Your Honor," Conkling said unsteadily. "I'm sorry. I do understand the Court." He paused for a deep breath.

"Your Honor, these men deserve to be freed on bail pending their trial. They are accused solely on account of the words of their brother, words no doubt motivated by some familial grudge. As the Court knows, I think, the sheriff and the mayor have been unable to produce the body of the dead man, despite substantial efforts."

The judge interrupted him. "You're not saying, are you, that there can be no murder prosecution in the absence of the body?"

"At a minimum, it will make it much harder for the People to convict," Conkling returned.

"I think not," said Attorney General Lamborn, claiming the stage. He nudged Conkling to the side, and Conkling fluttered around in the air for a moment, like a leaf caught in a stern autumn breeze, before regaining his feet.

"Your Honor," Lamborn continued, "these defendants murdered the victim, a Mr. Flynn Fisher, as a result of a failed business scheme. Their brother Henry Trailor is an eyewitness to these events and will testify as such. In view of his testimony, the fact that the defendants have thus far managed to conceal the body is no impediment to their trial and conviction. In addition, the defendants present an active threat to the community. When Mr. Archibald Trailor was apprehended at his boarding house by the sheriff, he had a firearm on his person."

This set off a murmur of surprise among the crowd, who craned to stare at Archibald. In a flash, I realized Lamborn must be referring to the gun I had given Archibald. I slumped against the wall, my heart pounding. Not only had I failed to protect the carpenter from arrest or to provide him with an experienced trial lawyer, but I had somehow managed to deepen his peril.

The judge banged his gavel to quiet the crowd. "Do you have any further argument, Mr. Conkling, before I announce my ruling?"

Conkling coughed into the sleeve of his coat and looked over uncertainly at the Trailor brothers. "Your Honor," he began, "Archibald Trailor, in particular, is a longtime resident of this town, and one known for his gentle ways. I would submit that these charges are most out of character for him. He is prepared to prove his innocence, of course, but I suggest there is no reason to keep him confined pending trial. He is an asset, not a threat, to the community."

I was startled to see Conkling's words appear to resonate with the judge, who tipped his chair back and pulled on his pipe, nodding thoughtfully. "I must tell you I am surprised to see Mr. Archibald Trailor in the dock," Treat said. "I do share your view of him, as a general matter. He helped me with some carpentry back when I was in practice. I found him entirely harmless."

Treat pulled on his pipe again. "Let me ask you this, Mr. Conkling. Do you anticipate Archibald and William Trailor will have a uniform defense, or will the two of them be making disparate arguments?"

Conkling shifted uneasily. "I'm not certain of such details,

Your Honor. The Court will appreciate, I hope, that I received the file only yesterday afternoon."

"Do you have any testimonial on behalf of William Trailor, of his character or reputation, similar to what you've provided for Archibald Trailor?"

"Er, not at the present," Conkling replied, glancing at William, who was glowering back at him. "William Trailor lives in LaSalle, Your Honor. He has worked as a contractor on the canal. I have every reason to think he's an honest member of his community, but I cannot tell the Court I know it as a matter of personal expertise."

Treat sucked on his pipe some more. At last, he laid it aside. "Here's what I'm going to order," he said, blowing out a great cloud of smoke. "Bail is denied, of course. In the case of murder charges, bail can only be given in the most exceptional circumstances, and the Court finds none are present. Trial shall be held during the April trial term, two weeks hence.

"However, the Court finds the interests of the two defendants may diverge, such that it would not be proper to permit a single attorney to represent them both simultaneously. Mr. Conkling, henceforth your client shall be Mr. William Trailor and him alone. The Court finds it appropriate to appoint separate counsel for Mr. Archibald Trailor."

Treat gazed around the room. There were a few members of Springfield's crowded legal bar sitting on the side of the room, near Lincoln, and I saw them watching the judge expectantly. For his part, Lincoln was staring intently at some court papers, trying to avoid the judge's eyes.

"Mr. Lincoln?" Treat called.

"Your Honor?" Lincoln looked up.

"Mr. Lincoln, do you have plans for the second week of the April term?"

Lincoln set down his packets and slowly rose to his feet. His head was higher than Treat's, though Treat sat on his elevated platform. "As the Court knows," said Lincoln, "I have a number of cases calendared for the April term, including the Harris brothers and their horse, as just discussed, as well as the O'Fraim assault case."

"It is said there's no tonic for weary men like more work. I hereby appoint you as counsel to Archibald Trailor, to defend him on the charge of murder." The crowd buzzed. I looked at the Trailors. William was scowling, and he leaned over and whispered into Archibald's ear.

"May I be heard on the appointment?" Lincoln said. "Because I would ask the Court—"

"No, you may not," Treat replied, sucking on his pipe stem through curved lips. "You have my order. The clerk shall call the next case." And with that, the judge slammed down his gavel.

Chapter 16

Lincoln and I dined at separate ends of the common table at the Globe Tavern that evening. Two opposing emotions competed inside my head as I chewed on Saunders's overcooked pork and did my best not to glance in my roommate's direction.

I was pleased Lincoln would be defending Archibald after all. I felt sure Lincoln provided the best chance of acquittal, especially after Conkling's unsteady performance in the courtroom. And yet, it rankled that Lincoln would be representing Archibald not out of loyalty to me but rather because he had been ordered to do so by Judge Treat. And ordered to do so against his protestations. As much as I tried to keep my focus on securing Archibald's freedom, I couldn't escape feeling I deserved better from my friend.

I finished my food, pushed away from the table, and made a beeline for the door. Whereupon I ran headlong into the man.

"After you, Speed," said Lincoln, his voice neutral and his eyes focused in the middle distance.

Outside, a cool March wind blew down the dark street. Lincoln turned up the collar of his coat and had taken a few steps away when I called after him, "Wait . . . Lincoln?"

"Yes?" Lincoln turned around, his head cocked crookedly.

"I'm glad you'll be representing Archibald. I'm certain he'll benefit from your counsel."

"I'll do my best. As a matter of fact, I'm on my way to the jail to confer with him. You're welcome to come along, if you wish."

I considered, but only for a second. It was petty to feed a grudge when a man's life was at stake. I fell into step with Lincoln, and we set off for Sheriff Hutchason's house. Though the new capitol building was to include a proper jail in its basement, it, like the new courtroom, was still under construction. For the time being, the only jail cell in town remained a crude, open-air shack in the sheriff's backyard.

"Did you hear," began Lincoln, breaking our silence, "that we rounded up the votes in the legislature to pass the bank plan?"

"That's good," I said without enthusiasm. "Congratulations."

"Douglas and his fellow Democrats decided they couldn't hold out against common sense any longer. Belmont was masterful, it must be said, in explaining for one final time the benefits of the plan he and I have been championing."

I must have made a derisive noise, because Lincoln asked, "Do you have something against Belmont?"

"I don't know him well enough to have an opinion one way or another. You seem to be spending a lot of time with him recently. What do you think?" I realized I sounded petulant but found myself unable to avoid it.

Lincoln looked over as we walked side by side along the dirt streets. "I've spent time with him because I must. This bank rescue is necessary to get the state's economy functioning normally again. It's important for all the poor and working people most especially. Belmont has been a big help in getting my plan through. There's nothing more to it."

"I never said there was."

"Anyway, now it's up to us to accomplish the actual transfer of the gold coins," Lincoln continued. "As you pointed out, that's going to present its own type of challenge. It's a huge fortune in gold to move through the open prairie. Quite a target if any blackguard wanted to get enterprising. There's only so many places Hutchason and the other sheriffs in the state can cover at once."

We were nearing the sheriff's house, and my thoughts turned to the necessity of making Archibald understand that his brothers did not have his interests at heart. I thought back to the way I'd seen Henry Trailor berate Archibald, at Henry's house on the evening before the Sudden Change, and I realized I'd never told Lincoln about the conversation I'd overheard that night. I recounted it for him now.

"Are you saying they were talking about Fisher?" Lincoln asked when I was done.

"They never mentioned his name, but it stands to reason, doesn't it? I mean, they were talking about someone William had brought into a business deal, someone they wanted to get rid of. It matches up pretty exactly with what Henry told Big Red about Fisher."

"The conversation doesn't necessarily prove Archibald's innocent. If anything, it might show the opposite."

"How do you mean?"

"It could go to premeditation. From what you've said, Henry told Big Red that William was enraged by Fisher's attempt to extort money by threatening to turn them over to the sheriff. But if what you're saying now is correct, it means that two months before the killing, Archibald and his brothers were already talking about the need to get rid of Fisher."

"*If* there was a killing."

There was an elaborate, extended howling in the distance, and we came to a stop. Two wolves out on the prairie, perhaps three, were celebrating a meal. "Someone's made a killing," I murmured, and Lincoln nodded.

"In any event, you're quite right," said Lincoln as we resumed walking. "Certainly our first line of defense is there's no proof, other than Henry's naked word, that Fisher was killed by anyone. Either he died a natural death, or perhaps he's alive somewhere and hasn't heard about the search for his mortal remains."

We rounded the corner and came within sight of the sheriff's modest house. There was an elegant, four-wheeled coupe carriage parked in front of the house, the horse grazing on grass in the Hutchasons' yard while a liveried driver slouched on his seat and lazily twirled his whip in the air.

"Isn't that Ninian's carriage?" I said. "I wonder if that means Miss Todd is present." I hastened toward the Hutchason home, but Lincoln with his long legs more than matched me stride for stride.

As our race-walk neared the house, Lincoln now several steps ahead of me, the door swung open and my sister Martha stepped out, holding a colorful carpetbag in her hand. She squinted in wonder at the sight of Lincoln and me hurrying toward her. Then her face brightened with comprehension.

"I've never seen two men so eager to help me into a carriage," she said with a grin. She turned back, said something to an unseen person inside the house, and pulled the door shut. "But I fear your enthusiasm may diminish when you learn I'm alone."

"So Miss Todd . . ."

"Miss Todd is awaiting my arrival on Quality Hill. I've accepted her invitation to visit for a few days. Her cousin Matilda Edwards will be there as well. Miss Todd was kind enough to have her brother-in-law's coupe sent to pick me up. I'll pass along compliments from both of you when I see her."

Edwards's driver had snapped to attention and reached down to open the door of the enclosed carriage. I took Martha's hand and helped her up the step and into the compartment, an elegant, octagonal space, with leather-covered banquettes and windows looking out from the front and sides. She gave me a kiss on the cheek and rapped for the driver to proceed. As she was driven away, we could still see the smile on her face.

"Plainly we haven't lost the capacity to make fools of ourselves," I said.

Lincoln grunted. "Let's talk to Archibald."

We pushed through the gate and approached the jail cell, a metal enclosure that abutted the sheriff's barn. Strips of wood provided a roof to the jail, and the side of the barn formed one wall, but the other sides comprised vertical rows of iron bars, open to the elements. It was a miserable place in which to be confined. The moon was waning and the cloudy skies were dim. We could barely make out two figures lingering inside the jail.

"Archibald?" Lincoln called out.

"Who comes?" came back a firm voice. It was William Trailor, not his brother, who spoke. William strode up to the barred door, his beaklike nose and high forehead reflecting what little light there was in the yard. Archibald remained seated behind him on the simple wooden bench running the length of the cell.

"Evening, Trailor," Lincoln said with a nod. "I'm sorry to see you again in these unfortunate circumstances."

"I'm not sorry to see you," William replied, "as long as you've come to tell me how you plan to get me out of here. This place"— he gestured around— "isn't fit for human habitation for even one evening, certainly not for a man of my stature."

"Judge Treat ordered that I was to represent your brother Archibald," said Lincoln. "Conkling is carrying on as your lawyer. You'll need to talk to him. But you heard the judge make his ruling denying bail. Both of you are confined pending trial."

"Maybe I want you instead," William said. "Maybe Archibald

and I can exchange lawyers. Archibald would be happy to agree. Wouldn't you, Archie?"

Lincoln kept a pleasant expression on his face. "That's not what the judge ordered, and we need to do it his way. Can you come over to the door, Archibald?"

Archibald shuffled forward, and William rested his arm on his brother's shoulder. "Hallo, Mr. Lincoln," Archibald said. "And hallo, Mr. Speed. It's nice to see you two. We was getting a little lonely."

"How are you managing?" Lincoln asked.

"Pretty decent, I suppose," Archibald responded. "Mr. Hutchason said I'd have to stay in this cell for a few weeks, until the jury could decide if I'm innocent. His wife is awfully nice. She's been bringing us a warm meal each morning and each evening."

William Trailor remained at his brother's side. Lincoln cleared his throat and said, "Give us a minute alone, won't you, Trailor. It'll be better that way." William looked as if he was going to object, but he nodded and sat down on the bench immediately behind Archibald.

"Now Archibald," Lincoln continued, "you understand, don't you, that you've been charged with murdering this fellow Fisher."

Archibald nodded.

"And the judge appointed me to be your lawyer," Lincoln continued. "So it's my job to try to set you free."

"All right."

"So anything you know that might help me with your defense, you can tell me now."

Archibald nodded again but remained silent.

"And whatever you tell me is private. No one else has to know. Not even your brother, if you don't want him to."

Archibald cast a quick glance back at William, who was listening without pretense. "All right," Archibald said again.

Lincoln pressed forward. "Now Archibald, you didn't murder this Fisher fellow, did you?"

Archibald swung around to look at William again. "Of course not," William exclaimed, rising and joining his brother. "No one killed nobody."

Lincoln sighed and turned to face William. "Are you saying Fisher's still alive?"

"Could be," William replied. His jaw was thrust forward, and he stood in front of Archibald with his hands on his hips.

My temper surged at the man's interference. "What about the matter of the inheritance?" I asked. "There's a story around town that you were spending all manner of gold coins back in LaSalle, saying you'd inherited a fortune from Fisher."

"Where'd you hear that?" William asked.

"Keyes, our postmaster, has been telling the story to everyone in town who wants to know it, and plenty who don't. I don't think there'll be a man on your jury who hasn't heard it in one form or another."

Lincoln murmured in agreement.

William seemed unmoved, and he shrugged. "I can't very well control what other people think, can I?"

"So the story's untrue?"

"'Course it is. I didn't inherit anything from Fisher."

"And he's alive and well?"

"That's what Lincoln just asked. The answer is, could be."

Lincoln expelled his breath with frustration. "We don't have time to keep spinning in circles. Here's the nub of it. Your brother Henry says the two of you murdered this Fisher. Why would Henry say that if it isn't true?"

William spat on the ground inside the cell and stared at Lincoln. "How many brothers did you grow up beside?" he asked.

"One," said Lincoln, "after my father remarried. My stepbrother, John Johnston."

"Are you close to him today?"

Lincoln shook his head. "The only time I hear from John these days is when he's got my father tangled in another money-losing scheme and they want me to help get them out of it."

William Trailor nodded with satisfaction. "You've answered your own question."

"But surely it's another matter altogether to falsely accuse your brothers of murder," I said. "Surely there's some notion of brotherly love, or brotherly sympathy at the least, that would prevent his putting your lives in jeopardy."

"That hasn't been my experience," William Trailor said.

"What about you, Archibald?" Lincoln asked. Archibald had been standing a half step behind his older brother during the exchange. "Can you think of any reason why Henry would want to malign the two of you?"

Archibald turned to his brother and said, "Do you think it could be because of—"

"Shut up!" I thought I saw William aim a swift kick at his brother's shin. "Mr. Lincoln's not interested in anything along them lines. And we agreed we'd keep it as Trailor family business, didn't we?"

Lincoln took two steps forward so that his face was pressed up against the vertical bars of the cell door. "Look here, Archibald," he said. "This is serious jeopardy you're in. If there's any fact you know that might help me with your defense, I implore you to share it with me. Your brother William will tell you the same thing, assuming he's truly got your interests at heart." Lincoln said this last sentence while glaring at William, but the man returned the stare, unblinking and unyielding. For his part, Archibald was looking down at the dirt floor of the jail cell, refusing to meet Lincoln's gaze.

"We've answered all your questions, the pertinent ones, anyway," William said. "Ever since Cain and Abel, there's been private business between brothers. Now go and get to work so I can get out of this damp, disgusting dungeon."

Lincoln gave one last glare at William and said, "Let's be off, Speed. We've learned all we need to know, at least for this one night."

"Say, Mr. Lincoln," Archibald called as we headed toward Hutchason's gate. "What happens if you can't make the jury understand I'm innocent? How many days will I have to stay here then?"

Lincoln glanced over at me and turned back to Archibald. "Let's take the climb a step at a time. Hopefully it'll never come to that."

Chapter 17

A light rain began falling during the walk back to our lodgings, and the storm had matured into a downpour when I woke the next morning. The pelting rain continued all day and the next one as well. By the morning after that, when the rain finally stopped, the streets surrounding the public square resembled an undrained swamp.

A steady trickle of customers came into my store that morning, each carrying on the soles of their shoes a generous portion of Central Illinois's sticky black loam. Every one of them knocked off his or her boots immediately upon entering. Soon I'd accumulated enough soil inside my doorway that I could have planted my own crop of wheat when the growing season came.

By lunchtime, the sun looked as though it was finally going to reappear, and I decided to take a turn around the square. I pulled on my boots and went out. There was an auspicious March breeze blowing, giving hope Spring was about to make her long-awaited return. I breathed in deeply, trying to ignore the mud clutching at my ankles at every step.

I had reached the far corner of the square and was just turning onto Sixth Street when I glanced in the other direction and saw a bizarre apparition.

Three women—my sister Martha, Mary Todd, and her

cousin Matilda Edwards—stood stock-still directly in the middle of Sixth Street. The women were lined up, one behind another, with Mary in front, and they were all dressed as if for a formal occasion, with long, full dresses in shades of green and blue. Each woman was wearing a white bonnet trimmed with ribbon matching the color of her dress. The bonnets framed cheeks pleasingly colored from mild exertion.

Each young woman wore what looked like the remains of satin slippers, although mud coated their feet, ankles, and the bottom hem of their gowns. Their feet were firmly rooted to the ground even as they swayed back and forth slightly, as if they were trying to maintain their balance on wet rocks while crossing a swiftly flowing stream.

Most puzzling of all, however, was the irregular line of flat stones that trailed away on the road behind them, like the tail of a kite swaying back and forth in the breeze. I certainly didn't remember seeing those stones the last time I had walked down Sixth.

Martha, who was standing a step behind Mary, was the first to notice my approach. "Just in time, Joshua," said my sister. "We could use a little help, I'm afraid."

"Good day. Miss Todd and Miss Edwards." I gave a half bow. "I hope you won't consider it impertinent if I ask what on earth you're doing."

"What does it look like?" asked Mary. I could not gauge whether her tone suggested impatience or pride, or an admixture of the two. "We're out for a walk around town, now that the skies have cleared. No different than you, it appears."

"But surely Ninian's coachman could have driven the three of you down from Quality Hill, if he thought the roads fit for carriages."

Martha laughed and said, "That's what I told Mary, but—"

"I decided it would be much more *interesting* to walk," said Mary. "Besides, I believed we could get all the way to the square without too much trouble as long as we brought along enough shingles."

"Yes, the *shingles*," Miss Edwards repeated, glancing at her mud-entombed feet before collapsing into a gale of laughter.

I looked again at what I had taken to be the irregular trail of flat stones stretching out behind the women and realized it was actually the path they had walked. Then I glanced down at Mary's right hand and saw that she clutched a thin parcel of black, rectangular squares. Shingles, the sort used to cover the sides of more substantial houses. I realized each woman was presently balancing on shingles, one under each foot, in the middle of the muddy street.

"You've walked all the way to town on *those*?" I asked.

Mary smiled. This time, the pride was unmistakable. "We had it all worked out. It's six blocks, give-and-take, from my sister's house to the square. If each block takes us thirty steps, we needed only one hundred eighty shingles to keep our feet out of the muck during the journey. I figured we could hop from one to the next, throwing them in front of ourselves as we went. So I told Ninian's boy Joseph we needed to borrow that many shingles from his stash. He looked at us like he thought us crazy, but he couldn't very well refuse."

"The problem was your arithmetic was faulty," said Martha. "Our strides weren't *nearly* so long as you thought."

"No, they weren't," admitted Mary. "We've been averaging about thirty-five paces per block, with one shingle per step, which leaves us with"—she paused to count the ones remaining in her hand—"six shingles, and one very long block to go. I daresay not even the most heroic series of jumps could get us to the square from here."

"I don't think they've done a particularly good job of protecting your feet, either," I said, pointing to the ground and trying to suppress a smile.

Mary nodded thoughtfully. "That was the other problem, as it turned out. I know Springfield's streets are muddy, but it still seems to me the shingles should have done a better job of protecting our feet."

"I don't wish to sound rude," I said, "but surely there was a more productive use of your time and talents."

"Such as what?" asked Mary, perfectly serious. Next to her, Martha gave me a concentrated look as well.

"I should think—" I stopped. The truth was I had little idea how unmarried women, with no house or family to care for, occupied their time.

Mary must have sensed my thoughts. "It has been five days, I believe, Mr. Speed, since you came up Quality Hill to call upon Ninian and found him absent." I reddened at the memory. "What is it you've done in that time?"

I thought back. Until the rains interceded, it had been a busy few days. "I've been quite preoccupied with the Trailors' saga, I suppose. Took part in questioning Henry Trailor, then participated in the search for the body of his brothers' supposed victim, and then helped out Lincoln with his defense of Archibald Trailor."

"So you've been challenged physically, and intellectually, too," said my sister. She turned to Mary's cousin. "Miss Edwards, what is it *we* did yesterday?"

"Same as we always do, Miss Speed," Miss Edwards returned, an expression of confusion on her face. She seemed not to have been following her sisters' line of argument. "We dressed. We sewed. We wrote an awful lot of letters. Mary, you've been working on that very long letter to your dearest Merce. Then it was suppertime, near about, and we dressed for supper. And after we ate, we worked on our letters some more, before it was time to retire to our rooms for the night."

"And the day before?"

"The same. Surely you remember!"

"And before that? Never mind, there's no need to answer." Mary turned back to me. "Tell me, Mr. Speed, whether you would find yourself satisfied with such a routine?"

I was lost for words. Fortunately, my sister interrupted, saying, "There was one thing out of the ordinary we accomplished yesterday, Miss Todd."

Mary nodded. "That's the other reason for our excursion today. We're coming to see Mr. Lincoln. We think we may have discovered evidence related to his defense of Archibald Trailor."

"We found a stagecoach trunk," added Martha. "In the barn out behind the Edwardses' house."

"A trunk? What's that got to do with Archibald?"

"At the gala at the American House," said Mary, "I overheard William Trailor asking Ninian if he could store a trunk in his barn. Said something about leaving town in the morning, but planning to return in the coming months, and not wanting to have to lug all of his papers and effects away and then back to Springfield on his next visit."

It took me a moment to digest this. Then I shouted, "The hiding spot—" Several men passing by us on the street slowed and turned to stare. I motioned for them to be on their way and continued, in a lower tone, "For the body!"

"That's what I wondered," said Mary. "I tried to remind Ninian the other day about his conversation with William Trailor, when I heard of the draining of the millpond, but he wasn't paying any attention to me. As usual. He thought I was asking for a trunk to store my winter clothes. So he merely sighed grandly and said I should talk to my sister Elizabeth if I *really* felt I needed *another* one." Mary gave me a severe look. "*His* emphases. The possibility I could be talking about something serious, something relevant to public affairs, never occurred to him." Martha laughed at Mary's bold tone, while Miss Edwards looked scandalized.

Mary tossed her head dismissively. "My brother Ninian wouldn't know a clue if it ran headlong into him."

"While we were stuck inside yesterday, with all the rains," Martha said, "Miss Todd told me about the trunk, and I convinced her we should search for it."

"You found the body?"

Martha shook her head. "We did find the trunk, hidden in the hayloft of the barn. But it doesn't appear large enough to have a body inside. Still, we thought Mr. Lincoln would want to know."

"Didn't you open it?"

"It was locked," said Mary, "and I didn't think it proper—"

"Blast proper! A man's life may be at stake. And you're right, Lincoln will be most interested. We've got to force open that trunk at once."

We had been, this whole time, talking in the middle of the street. A number of passersby had stopped to gawk. And we were quite a sight, the three women balancing on their slowly sinking shingles, like statues being pulled down into the deep by an unseen sea monster, while I paced around them in the mud.

At that moment, the drayman Hart turned onto Sixth with his horse and cart. The front of the cart was laden with a few casks, but the back half was empty. "Will you ladies object if I arrange a more conventional mode of transportation to take you home?" I asked.

Mary gazed down at her ruined silk slippers and sighed. "I suppose not."

As the drayman approached, his four wheels churning reluctantly through the mire, I flagged him down.

"This is Mr. Ninian Edwards's sister-in-law," I explained,

"and two of her intimates. They find themselves in need of a ride back to the Edwards house. Can you transport them without delay?"

The old drayman took the cap off his bald head and gave an ungainly nod. "'Course, Mr. Speed," he said. His eyes darted back and forth between the women and the muddy ground, but he had the manners not to voice aloud his curiosity.

"Good man."

Hart swatted his animal, and it pulled the low, flatbed wagon forward a bit, such that the cart's back ledge was even with where Mary stood. The level of the cart was just above her waistline.

"Will you permit me?" I asked.

"If you please," Mary responded, her face composed.

I reached my arms out on either side of Mary's waist. My hands felt her dress and petticoat compress over her firm hips underneath. I smelled the honey in her hair. Mary gave a little hop and I lifted her up and it was over. I placed her down, carefully, on the back of the wagon. Her legs dangled off the edge, and she crossed her muddy feet demurely, as I tried to still my racing heart.

Hart pulled his cart forward, and I helped Martha and Miss Edwards in turn onto the back of the cart as well.

"I'll get Lincoln at once," I said, "and we'll meet you up on Quality Hill to examine the trunk together. Make haste," I shouted to the drayman, rapping the side of his wagon.

Chapter 18

As I pushed open the door to Hoffman's Row, I ran headlong into Big Red May, coming down the stairs from Lincoln's office at full tilt.

"I think you'll be interested—" I began.

But the mayor pushed past me, saying, "No time, I'm afraid," and hurried out into the street. I did not follow. It made sense to see what was in William Trailor's trunk, I figured, before telling the mayor about the development.

Upstairs, Lincoln was seated at the large, square table that dominated the room, scrawling away at some court document. He nodded at my entrance but remained hunched over his pleading. Lincoln's office boy, young Milton Hay, stood next to him, jingling his legs nervously. Belmont sat on Stuart's lounge, wearing an immaculate frockcoat as usual, his legs crossed and his walking stick balanced under one palm. Belmont gave me a half smile as I entered.

"I'm waiting for his attention, too," said the banker. "As was your mayor. We are all in line behind a series of overdue pleadings."

As I waited for Lincoln to look up, the sound of angry shouts floated through the room. I went out into the hallway to investigate, but glancing up and down the dimly lit corridor, I found it empty.

"Who's carrying on?" I asked, ducking back into the office.

"Judge Treat," Lincoln replied, as he dipped his pen into the inkwell. "He's hearing Douglas in the Purkapile case at this hour. I was down there earlier, arguing one of the Wrenwag cases, and His Honor was in a foul mood already."

Lincoln still had not moved his eyes from his pleading. A shout that sounded very much like "hold you in contempt" floated up through the floorboards.

I cleared my throat.

"Yes?" Lincoln prompted, still scrawling away.

"I've come to talk to you about the case."

After a pause, filled only by the sound of Lincoln's nib dashing across the page, he asked, "Which case?"

"Which one could it be?" I said. Finally, Lincoln looked up. His brow was clenched with concentration and his gray eyes were streaked with tiny red lines. He gestured impatiently. "Archibald's, of course," I explained.

"Oh." Lincoln looked down again and resumed his writing. "Because it could have been the Wrenwag cases. Those hearings continue tomorrow morning. Or perhaps the four Harris brothers and their horse. Two of the brothers are due here later to explain their side to me. Or perhaps O'Fraim and his assault trial. He goes into the dock in less than a fortnight, and I have yet to talk to any witness I might call for the defense. And of course that leaves aside Belmont and arrangements for shipping the gold to Chicago."

Lincoln finished his document. He held it up to the light and read it over quickly, his lips moving slightly as he did. He blew on the sheet to dry the ink and handed it to Hay.

"You're to deliver this immediately to Browning. Tell him it's my answer to his motion in the second Wrenwag matter."

Hay bobbed his head up and down, swallowing rapidly. The office boy was of sixteen years, thin as a willow and flighty as a hummingbird. He hoped to read law one day and join the bar himself, but I thought this prospect very dim as I watched him stand nervously in Lincoln's shadow.

Lincoln looked up at the boy, surprised to see him still at his side. "Get going!" Hay gasped and flittered past me. "Remember—the *second* Wrenwag matter," Lincoln called as Hay disappeared through the door. Lincoln pulled out a blank sheet of paper and began scratching away again.

"I hate to interrupt," I said, "but I think you should come at once, Lincoln. With apologies to your suit, Belmont."

"Come where?" asked Lincoln.

"To Mary's—Miss Todd's—house. She and my sister found something important for Archibald's case."

Lincoln's head shot around. He pushed himself rapidly to his feet, and his chair toppled over and clattered to the floor. A shout of "Quiet!" carried through the boards.

"You sought out Miss Todd again?" Lincoln asked. His prominent jaw was clenched and the muscles in his neck bulged.

"Not exactly," I said, taking a step back at the force of Lincoln's challenge. "I was taking a turn around the square when I came upon her. She was with my sister and Miss Matilda Edwards. Quite a sight, actually, the three of them stuck in the mud."

"Tell me what happened," demanded Lincoln, a deep frown creasing his face.

Belmont gathered his walking stick and rose to his feet, giving a little cough. "I've just recalled another appointment," he said unconvincingly. "We'll find another time to resume, Lincoln. Good day, Speed." Neither Lincoln nor I turned his direction as the door closed in his wake.

I explained to Lincoln about the trunk Mary and Martha had found. Scowling, he put on his coat and followed me out the door. We slopped through the muck and mire up to Quality Hill, barely exchanging two words. An angry conversation raged inside my head, where I imagined Lincoln's voice telling me to stay away from Miss Todd while my voice answered that he was being presumptuous in the extreme. There had been no resolution to my internal debate by the time we reached the top of the hill.

We made much faster progress through the mud than could Hart's sturdy draft horse, burdened by his cart and its cargo and passengers, and we reached the curving drive in front of the Edwards home just before Hart did. Lincoln and the ladies exchanged greetings, and Lincoln held out his hand and helped them down in turn from the back of the cart.

"Do you want to change first?" I asked, gesturing at their muddy clothes.

"To the contrary," said Mary, "we're perfectly dressed to go mucking around in a barn." Martha smiled in agreement.

"I've had enough adventure for one day," said Miss Edwards. She lifted her ruined skirts as she headed for the front door.

"Don't tell my sister or brother-in-law we're out here," Mary called. "You can say you turned around first and that Miss Speed and I will be on our way back soon enough."

"Speed told me you'd found a trunk belonging to William Trailor," Lincoln said to Mary. "Can you show us?"

"This way," said Miss Todd. She and Martha linked arms, while Lincoln and I trailed after them, not deigning to look at each other.

The barn was located on the eastern slope of Quality Hill, off to the side of the Edwards house. As the prevailing winds in central Illinois blew from west to east, all men who could constructed their barns to the east of their houses, so that the winds would carry the pungent smells of the barnyard away from their dwelling places. It was a one-story "English barn," a framed, side-gabled structure divided into three bays. It was well made, with regular oak joists, beams, and overhead trusses. The peaked ceiling was open to the rafters. The scent of fresh manure hung in the air.

We entered the center bay, the widest one, which featured double doors at either end to allow carriages to be driven in and out. The Edwardses' coupe carriage, the same one I'd seen picking up Martha at the Hutchason house several days earlier, stood in the middle of the bay. The black paint on the side panels and four wheels shone and the window glass of the enclosed compartment glistened.

"The trunk's up there," said Martha, pointing to a hayloft in one of the side bays.

Lincoln and I hurried after one other and climbed the ladder that had been built into the wall. It was a small, rectangular platform, covered by a broad pile of loose hay several feet deep. Both of us had to stoop to avoid the low, slanted roof.

"Under the hay," called Martha. "We buried it again, after we found it locked." Lincoln and I dug through the hay and soon struck something solid. The trunk was a rectangular box, constructed of polished elm and held together by banded iron straps. It measured about four feet wide and three feet high and deep. A shacklebolt lock hung from its latch.

"It's too small to hold a body," said Lincoln, his voice touched with irritation.

"That's what the women said," I replied, nodding at them, below us on the ground level. "But if it's William Trailor's, there's no telling what might be inside. Something proving his guilt, I don't doubt. And therefore something exonerating Archibald. Let's get it open at once."

But Lincoln took a step back. "I can't be party to breaking into another man's possessions," he said. "Especially one charged with a crime and represented by other counsel. Perhaps if we sought Conkling's blessing—"

"Turn around," I ordered, and after a slight pause Lincoln

complied. I'd seen a loose nail among the hay straws, and I grabbed it and started working on the lock. There was a satisfying click. "Hoy, now! The trunk wasn't locked after all." I threw open the lid. "Let's have a look."

Lincoln and I swore.

"What is it?" shouted Martha and Mary from below.

I reached in and carefully pulled out a bone-handled pistol. There was a box of ammunition of a sort I carried in my store next to the gun, and I grabbed that as well. I held up the weapon so the ladies could see it.

"Is it loaded?" asked Martha.

I shook the pistol and cracked open the barrel. "No." I sniffed the end of the barrel. "But it was discharged not long ago, I'd judge." I opened the ammunition box; five balls rolled around, not the six it was sold with. "And a ball is missing, too."

"So William Trailor shot Fisher with his gun," said Martha. "It practically proves Archibald's innocence!"

"I'm afraid it does no such thing," said Lincoln from behind me. He was still crouched down, sorting through the rest of the trunk. "For one thing, Henry said Fisher was suffocated, not shot. Isn't that right, Speed?"

I allowed that it was.

"For another," continued Lincoln, as he swung the trunk lid shut and relocked the lock, "even if someone was shot with that gun, there's no proving William pulled the trigger." He started to climb down the ladder and motioned that I should follow.

Mary and Martha exchanged disappointed glances, the thrill of finding a useful clue ebbing away. "Still, it's something," I said. "And we have Miss Todd and Miss Speed to thank for its discovery."

"What else was inside the trunk, Mr. Lincoln?" asked Martha.

"What you'd expect from a canal contractor's traveling trunk.

Several changes of work clothes. Maps. A shovel for exploratory digging. And surveyor tools—a compass and chain. I know them all too well myself from my time fighting through the brambles. There's nothing to suggest anything other than the story William Trailor told to Ninian."

Martha's face fell further.

"But the pistol," I said. "Surely that's not a contractor's tool."

"I suspect it is in many parts of the state. You've led us on a wild-goose chase, Speed. A waste of time I didn't have. I'll go inside and give Ninian the weapon and balls for safekeeping. Then I need to return to my office."

Chapter 19

Back inside Hoffman's Row, Lincoln and I confronted each other across his worktable. The argument that had previously existed only inside my head burst out into the open.

"There was no call to criticize me in front of the women," I said. "I wanted to learn at once what was in the trunk they found. I was trying to help you and Archibald. A fine thing, seeing how busy you seem to be with your other obligations." I gestured at the papers and pleadings strewn across his table.

Lincoln was pacing back and forth, agitated. He hadn't said a word on our walk back down the hill, but now he expelled his breath loudly. "You should have come for me as soon as you heard Miss Todd might have learned something of importance."

"I did. And why does it matter, anyway, if I learned it from Miss Todd, as opposed to from any other person in town?"

"Don't take me for a fool, Speed. And don't be one yourself."

I felt emotions welling up inside me. Anger—fury, even. At Lincoln. And then at myself. Why was I letting him speak to me like this? On what basis, exactly, did he purport to inhabit the moral high ground?

"I happened upon Miss Todd on the square," I said deliberately, holding my tone as level as I could. "She told me William

Trailor had asked Ninian for a place to store a trunk. I thought you might think that significant."

"What I find *significant*, Speed," said Lincoln, his eyes boring in on mine, "is that you have the leisure time to engage in so much frivolity and casual conversation. Meanwhile, I am hard at work at my profession, trying to save people's lives. Do you know, I have not had a single conversation with a member of the female sex since the gathering at the American House? I haven't had the time."

"And you blame me for that?" I put my hands on the edge of the table and leaned forward. "You blame me for your unartfulness when it comes to dealing with women?"

"I blame you for a lack of true friendship," Lincoln said, leaning forward himself, so that our faces were only a few feet apart, although the table remained between us. I could hear his fast, shallow breathing. "A true friend would not be pursuing Miss Todd with the zeal you're showing. Would not be pursuing her at all, in point of fact."

I felt the blood pulsating at my temples, and I knew I was losing control of my emotion. "Merely because you command it to be so?" I fairly shouted.

"You know my feelings for her, Joshua. I would have hoped that knowledge would be sufficient for you to stand down." Lincoln's fingers were pressing into the tabletop with such force that his knuckles were turning white.

"But you know I harbor similar interests myself. Surely it's for the lady to make up her own mind."

"Do you 'harbor' them, Speed, or do they merely flit through your mind, as does so much else? Meanwhile, my intentions regarding Miss Todd are steady and true."

"Your intentions? Why should those matter to me? I say to hell with your intentions!" I could barely hear my own shout over the rush of blood in my head.

Lincoln sighed, and he leaned back and spoke in a quieter voice. "Something's changed with you, Joshua. I cannot but think your family would be aggrieved if they could see you now."

For the briefest of moments, Lincoln's words registered, and I knew in that instant that the first of his sentiments certainly was true and that the second one might be as well. But then I lost the capacity for any thought. I launched myself across the table, scattering Lincoln's precious stacks of papers, toppling him onto the floor, and landing on top of him. I could feel his ribs protruding through his miserable, worn coat.

"Don't you dare speak of my family!" I shouted.

Lincoln shouted something in reply, but I could no longer process words. The entire world was emotion. Rage. Hatred. Heartache.

I threw my fists at my friend with as much force as I could muster, striking his face, torso, legs—anything I could reach. At first it seemed Lincoln was merely trying to hold me at bay, but then I felt him striking me in return. He managed to roll over on top of me, such that my back was against the floorboards while he loomed high above and matched me blow for blow.

All the while we were shouting terrible things at each other. Things I doubted could ever be taken back.

There was a loud crash from the side of the room, and we both paused from the struggle. Judge Treat stood in the doorway, breathing heavily, his long black robe billowing behind him and his red face bursting with anger.

"Stop it!" bellowed Treat. "Stop this nonsense at once!"

Lincoln rolled away from me, pushed himself to his feet, and straightened his clothes. His face was bruised, his right eye was starting to turn purple, and a trickle of blood ran from his nose. I imagined I looked about the same.

"I am ever so sorry, Your Honor," said Lincoln. He wiped

the blood off his face with his sleeve. "I hope we haven't disturbed you."

"You're goddamned right, you've disturbed me," Treat hollered. "I am trying to conduct the judicial business of the county, but all we can hear in the courtroom is the din and racket from above. What in the name of the devil himself is going on?"

I lay on the floor, my heart beating wildly. My mind was a conflagration.

"I do apologize, Your Honor," said Lincoln. "I tripped over my own chair, Judge, and I must have called out involuntarily in the course of my fall. Speed here was just helping me to my feet."

The judge stared at Lincoln, looked down at me, and then back at Lincoln. Shaking his head furiously, he slammed the door shut.

Chapter 20

In the week that followed, I learned it is possible to share a room—indeed, a bed—with another man and yet go through life without sharing a single word, or glance, or emotion with that same man. Lincoln and I slept, woke, and dressed side by side, without ever once making a human connection with one another.

By habit, we would head down the back stairs from our bedroom one after the other in the morning and walk in silence to the Globe. But upon entering the public room, I peeled off to sit at a small table near the front door, while Lincoln proceeded to what had been our usual spot at the long common table in back. On the first day this happened, the innkeeper Saunders called out in surprise and nearly dragged me to my normal seat opposite Lincoln. Only Lincoln's gloomy, stony glare alerted him that he should desist. By the third day, Saunders had accepted the new routine without comment.

I spent my days behind the counter of A.Y. Ellis & Co., trying to keep my place in small talk with my customers even though my thoughts were elsewhere. I felt simultaneously hot with anger and cold with sorrow, the hot and cold seeping down into the very marrow of my bones. I replayed the fight endlessly in my mind. At times I was sure Lincoln alone had been to blame: had it not been for his pretense, his imperiousness, punches never would have been thrown. But other times I recognized I had acted shabbily and bore an equal measure of blame. And one evening, as I sat alone on a bench at the Globe and stared at my bowl of cabbage soup until it had gone cold as winter, I convinced myself I had been wholly in the wrong. Certainly, there was no evading the truth that I had struck the first blow.

I considered whether I should apologize to Lincoln, but whenever I had finally decided to do so, my pride took over and argued my intellect out of the decision. After several turns around the same circle inside my mind, I reached an internal truce: I would apologize, just as soon as it was evident Lincoln was willing to make an apology to me. But I saw no sign he was, and that was that.

As far as I knew, Lincoln was busy with his law practice. He dressed for court every morning, sliding his black frockcoat over his bony shoulders. And he came to our bed late at night, several hours after I had retired, as was his habit when the Circuit Court was in session. When he wasn't looking, I tried to discern his sentiment by examining the corners of his eyes, which often gave away his inner mood. But I found I could not read them without facing him directly, and I wasn't about to take that step.

Martha, of course, noticed right away the change that had overtaken us. "Is there something funny between you and Mr. Lincoln?" she asked as she came into the store several days after our fight. Martha and I hadn't seen each other since we'd left the Edwards barn upon examining William Trailor's trunk.

"No. Why do you ask?"

"He came to visit Archibald at the jail cell yesterday evening, to talk about the case. I was surprised you weren't with him."

"I was busy."

"With what?" Martha stared at me intently, hands on her hips.

"With . . . I don't remember. What does it matter?"

"Archibald is suffering in jail and needs all the help he can get. I thought you were committed to his cause."

"You know I am." I paused. "I doubt Lincoln learned much of use from talking to him anyway. I imagine William took over the conversation and turned it to how Lincoln could get him freed, Archibald be damned."

Martha gaped at me with wide eyes. "But surely you know William is no longer in the cell?"

"What!"

She nodded. "It happened the very day we all searched the Edwards barn, although I didn't learn about it until after I returned home. William spent the whole time during the rainstorm screaming at the top of his voice for the sheriff to move him to alternate quarters. It got so bad that a group of the sheriff's neighbors came over to complain."

"So where is he now?"

"After the storm finally passed, the sheriff got together with Mayor May. They decided William could be placed in the new jail cell in the basement of the capitol building until trial. Big Red said it was complete enough to hold William securely for a few weeks. He can't complain about the elements there. And it's way down in the foundation, so William won't bother anyone even if he starts yelling again. Mr. Lincoln told me he was happy to agree to the transfer, as it will let him work with Archibald without interference to prepare for the trial."

I remembered the mayor pushing past me in a hurry as I entered Hoffman's Row in search of Lincoln, and I realized I'd never asked Lincoln what he wanted. I'd been too consumed with my grievance.

Martha must have seen a shadow come over my face, because she asked, "Will you tell me what happened between you and Mr. Lincoln?"

"Nothing happened. I've been busy, and so has he."

"Well, whenever you have some time to spare from your *busy* schedule" —she slowly took in the empty store— "I have an idea for you to pursue. Something that might help Archibald."

"Don't be a ninny. What's your idea?"

"I was thinking about the victim, Mr. Fisher. *Supposed* victim, I should say, because his body hasn't turned up. What if he wasn't killed? What if he merely decided to leave Springfield on his own? We know he got to town by riding in William's carriage. If he wanted to depart on his own, he might have made arrangements with—"

"Frink and Walker," I exclaimed, and Martha nodded. It was the largest stagecoach company in town. As soon as my store clerk Herndon appeared to take his turn at the store counter, I headed over to the line's offices, which were adjacent to the Globe Tavern, whose stables it shared. I arrived at the same instant a new coach pulled up.

The brightly painted stagecoach threw up a slew of mud as it approached, the driver flourishing his long whip from the high box to force his four charges into a gallant dash to the front door. They raced through the gates of the stable yard and came to a masterly stop, the horses panting, the spittle of exertion still dripping from their muzzles. There was a moment of calm. Then the driver blew a single, long note on his horn, and Frink strode forward to greet him.

The next few minutes were a chaotic but carefully planned dance, as some passengers and their trunks left the coach here at the Globe while others embarked for the onward journey. One mail pouch was thrown down from the stage, and a new one was thrown up in its place. Several youthful ostlers from the Globe supervised the changing of the team, four fresh horses brought forward to carry the coach to its next stop.

Seven minutes after the coach had arrived, the yard was

frenetic as a beehive, passengers and trunks and horses flying in every direction at the same time. But one minute thereafter, as if by some magic, everyone and everything had assumed its place. The ostler responsible for the new team had fully secured it, and he was finishing rubbing oil on the harness and applying grease to the wheels. The ostlers in back gave their straps one final tug to make sure the new luggage was secured in place.

The driver was back on his high box, finishing a bottle of liquid refreshment he'd procured inside the tavern. He checked with Frink to ensure everyone was aboard, and he gave another blast on his horn. The driver cracked his whip with a flourish, there was a whirring of wheels, and a great *hurrah* arose from the ostlers as the coach pulled out of the yard. As it disappeared from view, Frink and Saunders of the Globe stood next to each other, watching with expressions of professional satisfaction. Stagecoach competition was intense; only those enterprises that operated with smooth efficiency were likely to remain in business year after year.

I hailed Frink as he turned back toward his offices.

"Decided to travel the sensible way the next time you head to Chicago, Speed?" Frink asked, pointing at my bad leg, which I still held stiffly at my side. "I could have told you nothing good could come of a ride alone over the prairie."

I shook my head. "I'm looking for information. I wonder if you sold a ticket a few weeks back to a man named Flynn Fisher. A ticket out of town, most likely. Fisher's an older man, holds his head to the side."

I started to demonstrate Fisher's habitual lean, but Frink waved off the demonstration. "I know who you mean," he said, "and why you're asking, but I'm afraid I don't have an answer for you about the man's disappearance. He never rode one of our stages. I've checked the records."

I started to turn away, then paused. "*Why* have you checked the records?"

"Because you're not the first person to come around asking about him."

My pulse quickened. "Who else did?"

"The innkeeper, Ransdell. It was a funny conversation. He hadn't heard about Fisher's disappearance, even though the whole town's been up in arms. Didn't know a thing about it. It seems Fisher was lodging with him at the time. Ransdell thought Fisher had skipped out on his bill. Threatened to sue me for abetting his flight. Ransdell's convinced the whole murder trial is an excuse to short him." Frink laughed and walked away, shaking his head.

I realized that Henry Trailor had described the rousting of Fisher from his lodgings on the night of the would-be murder but that we'd never determined where Fisher was staying. Ransdell's made perfect sense. Wharton Ransdell kept a tavern in the western part of town, to which I rarely ventured, as it was twice as far distant from our lodgings as the Globe, and its fare was, if not even less edible, then certainly not superior to the Globe's.

Ransdell was an ill-tempered man, stout, nearly bald, and always ready for a fight. These were qualities that, while seemingly undesirable in an innkeeper, were very much to be treasured in a lawyer's client. He was a mainstay of Lincoln's practice. The man was forever getting into legal disputes with his lodgers and his neighbors, and on some days it appeared as if Lincoln had, and needed, no other client. *Ransdell v. McGee* was followed on the court's docket by *Fleming v. Ransdell*, while *Ransdell v. Vaughn* waited to be heard immediately thereafter.

I headed directly to Ransdell's inn and was greeted by his customary sneer. "Thought you were too good for my fare, Speed. Fall on hard times?"

"I've come to ask about a man who stayed with you a few weeks back. Flynn Fisher."

Ransdell's eyes widened. "So you're the one who helped him

disappear! I should have known he'd pick an equally disreputable confederate."

"Certainly not. I'm looking for him, along with the rest of the town."

"Then *look*. And bring him back to me when you find him. He owes me two dollars fifty for his five nights. Three twenty-five now, with interest. I will not be trifled with."

I suppressed a smile. "I'm not sure if you've heard, but the sheriff thinks Fisher's been killed. William and Archibald Trailor are in jail awaiting trial for his murder."

"Archibald Trailor killed Fisher?" Ransdell said. "That don't make sense."

"Why not?"

"Because the last time I saw the two of them together, it was Archibald who was trying to help Fisher."

I felt a jolt of excitement. "When was this?"

"The very morning Fisher disappeared on me."

"Tell me exactly what you saw." When Ransdell hesitated, I added, "It might help you recover the money you're owed."

"Fisher was in my front room, taking his breakfast—the wife had fried up some eggs that morning, bit of an extravagance—when the carpenter knocked and asked to have a word with Fisher. I said all right, as long as Archibald paid for his meal. I ain't sponsoring a sewing circle, you know."

"Of course not."

"So Archibald handed me a half dime and I let him enter. Fisher had some defect. He was always leaning to the side, you see, and Trailor leaned his own head in and they had a good long conversation. I couldn't hear them too good, but they was talking about some canal somewhere."

"What about the canal?"

Ransdell glowered at me. "I told you I couldn't hear 'em.

Anyways, at the end of a few minutes, Archibald gets up from the table and says something like, 'You take care of yourself, Flynn. You've nothing to worry about. I'll talk to my brother for you.' And they shook hands and Archibald left."

"Do you remember what Fisher was wearing when you last saw him?"

Ransdell cocked his head to the side. "He was always wearing a militia uniform, except it was a jumble. None of the items matched the others. He looked like a jester. All militia issue except one item. On his head he had some kind of fur hat. Definitely not issued by any militia."

"What color was the fur hat?"

"Dirty. And half the fur worn away at that. But it looked like it'd been white originally. Now be on your way. That's more than enough time spent on idle chatter, and not even with a paying customer."

As I turned to go, Ransdell pointed at me with a stubby finger. "And if I discover you helped Fisher dodge his bill, I'll sic my lawyer on you. He's a mean son of a gun, as determined and vicious as they come. You better watch your back."

Chapter 21

Ransdell's tale about a friendly conversation between Archibald Trailor and Fisher on the morning of the latter's disappearance seemed moderately helpful to Archibald's case. But to prove Archibald's innocence, we needed something much more definite.

I decided to pursue Martha's idea that Fisher had departed Springfield on his own accord. Armed with the description from Ransdell of the clothing Fisher had been wearing on his final morning, I spent the next day visiting the three other stagecoach operations in town, along with the four stables where one could rent a horse. But none of those establishments had sold a ticket, or rented a ride, to a man matching Fisher's appearance. He could have walked out of town, I supposed, but the journey back to his home would have taken a week or more on foot, and Fisher hardly seemed vigorous enough to contemplate, let alone complete, such an arduous journey. The only alternative seemed to be that Fisher had never left town, and that left Archibald in jail and facing the very real prospect of the gallows.

I reached this sobering conclusion as I walked along the derelict northern edge of the town square, heading back to my store after visiting the final stables in the greater Springfield area. The north side of the square was known as Chicken Row, and its only two notable residents were the town's rival newspapers, Simeon Francis's *Sangamo Journal* and George Weber's *Illinois Democrat*, placed by Fate in side-by-side dingy, one-story buildings.

On many afternoons the two antagonists, political as well as business enemies, could be seen standing in front of their respective buildings and hurling insults at each other.

This afternoon only Simeon was in evidence. The rotund publisher was lounging in the doorway of his shop, shading his eyes against the sudden appearance of the sun. As I approached, he called out, "What say you, Speed?" Simeon had been particularly careless with the straight razor the last time he'd used it, and an irregular patch of whiskers sprouted on his left cheek, just above his fleshy jaw.

"I've been spending some time investigating Archibald Trailor's case. I wonder if you know how Lincoln plans to defend the man?"

Simeon stared at me with surprise. "Surely Lincoln has told you his thoughts himself. On matters of Lincoln's intent, I've always considered you my first and best source."

I felt myself turning red. "We've spoken, to be sure. But I was thinking perhaps he'd said more to you. When he's been by to work on *The Old Soldier* campaign newspaper, or . . ." As I thought about Simeon's words, I trailed off. It sometimes escaped me just how closely my own personage in Springfield was tied to Lincoln. The realization made me feel proud, and a little sad.

"I only know he's worried about the trial," said the newspaperman, still peering at me with interest. "Lincoln's never had to watch a client swing from the gallows, you know, but he's concerned poor Archibald might be the first—"

He was interrupted by shouts coming from behind him. I saw a large group of men milling about inside the front room of the newspaper office.

"I just received my weekly delivery of the out-of-town papers from the Post Office Department," Simeon explained, beckoning me to follow him inside. "They've got a few of the fellows—more than just the fellows—up in arms."

As my eyes adjusted to the dimly lit interior of the office, I saw that quite a few of the Whig regulars were present. Ninian Edwards was there, and Conkling too, as well as Hurst and Thornton and Browning and a good number of others. Surveying the room, I was relieved to see that Lincoln was not in attendance.

Broadsheets from all around the nation had been flung open and strewn about. The men were pacing the cramped room, reading from long, agate-type columns and excitedly shouting the news back and forth.

"The *Vermont Phoenix* has a detailed account of the defalcations," exclaimed Hurst. "Van Buren's people in New York appointed these Tammany Hall men, Samuel Swartwout and that scoundrel Price, to hold the office of collector of the New York port. Van Buren let them borrow two million on public bonds, when he knew they had no intention of paying it back. Sure enough, having spent the money, the Tammany men retire from office and default on the bonds. Then Van Buren hides the defalcations for long enough for Swartwout to slip off to England with his million and a quarter of the People's money."

"This corrupt dynasty, Jackson and his disciple van Buren, they've plundered the nation with their spoils principle," Conkling cried earnestly. "Is there any doubt that Van Buren will order Tammany to have the Customs House bullies surround the polls this November? They'll only let *reliable* voters pass through their barricades."

"It's an outrage," offered Browning. "How can General Harrison hope to carry New York with the forces set against him?"

"Just as the general will win the rest of the country," said

Edwards. "By exposing the truth about Van Buren. Look here, the *Madisonian* catalogs the People's money that the present administration has wasted decorating the President's House in Washington. One thousand one hundred sixty-five dollars for a dwarf wall between the executive buildings and the President's House. Ten thousand for furniture—Turkey carpets, giant candelabras and mirrors, Oriental indulgences. How much public treasure our grand Locofoco president has squandered!"

"Listen to this," cried Thornton. "The *Daily Chicago American* has a report about threats to the gold shipment scheduled to replenish the State Bank in that city." Several men present, members of the legislature who had been grappling with that very issue, swung around with interest. "Apparently it's scheduled for sometime this week, or perhaps next. It says here there's an organized gang of thieves looking to make raises from stagecoaches in the northern reaches of our state. The 'banditti of the prairies,' it calls them. The article says these banditti are armed with pistols and dirks and bowie knives and that they're on a close lookout for the gold."

Hurst dismissed the story with a swipe of his large hand. "'Banditti of the prairies'? A campfire legend. Here's the story we should take seriously, from the *New York Sun*. 'Mr. St. John, of Peale's Museum, while visiting King Leopold in Belgium, has engaged the services of a modern Goliath. He stands between eight and a half and nine feet in height, well proportioned . . . enormous strength . . . can rise from the floor with three men of ordinary size hanging on to each arm.' Let's see: 'This monster will arrive on the next steam packet crossing the Atlantic and will make his American debut at the Bowery Theatre, where preparations for his reception are already in progress.'"

"What are we waiting for?" called Thornton. "We should all set off for New York at once." Loud guffaws bounced around the room.

"This is no time for humor," shouted a new, high-pitched voice. "We must ensure the People know that Van Buren's own men are deserting him!" It was a woman who had spoken. I swung around and gaped. *Mary.* The banter ceased abruptly, and the men parted as the diminutive Miss Todd stepped forward into the center of the crowded room. She wore a full-length dress, light blue decorated with white lace, and held a notorious Democratic rag in her hands.

"Now, dear sister, I think you may rely upon us to perform that task," Ninian Edwards said, taking Mary's arm as if he meant to escort her out of the building. "The People shall know where their future lies."

But Mary refused to budge. "I know you've stated that intention, dear Ninian, but you'll pardon me if I worry whether the task will be accomplished in a satisfactory manner, if left in its current hands."

A low murmur passed through the room. While Ninian Edwards was a popular subject of derision at gatherings from which he was absent, few of the men present would dare to challenge the famous scion so boldly to his face.

Mary's eyes alighted on me. "Surely *you* agree with me, Mr. Speed. Do you not think the Sangamon Whigs should be doing more to promote General Harrison's cause?"

I felt the gaze of every man present turn to me. "In fairness, Miss Todd, we are doing a good bit. Each edition of our campaign newspaper builds up the general and explains why Van Buren must go. In the last issue, I wrote about the new campaign tune General Harrison is using. The chorus goes, '*For Tippecanoe / and Tyler too.*' Pretty clever. We're publishing two times every month until election day."

"Only two? Why not four times a month?"

Several of the men guffawed.

"I'm not sure there's *that* much popular interest in every last particular of the candidates' positions. Besides, all of us have regular jobs to attend as well."

"But none so important!" cried Mary, to more astonished laughter.

Ninian Edwards took his sister-in-law by the arm again, more firmly this time. "You've said your piece, dear sister. Now, I insist you return home. My wife will be wanting help with the children at this hour, I should think, and surely there is sewing to be done. These men came here to get the news and share their views with each other. They have enough of a woman's hectoring at their own hearths." Mary's face turned crimson as Edwards steered her out the door. He returned, alone, to laughter and no little applause.

When I left the newspaper offices myself a bit later, I was surprised to come upon Miss Todd on the village green. She was striding back and forth with great agitation, her fists clenched into tight balls.

"My brother-in-law is impossible," she cried when she saw me coming. "I tell you, Mr. Speed, I did not move from Lexington to Springfield only to trade the dominion of one man—my father—for another."

"I doubt any man could exercise dominion over you, Miss Todd." The words were through my lips before I realized what I'd said, and I immediately clapped my hand to my mouth, but too late.

Miss Todd stared at me for a moment and collapsed in peals of laughter. "Perhaps," she said, when she regained her bearing, "you know me better than I believed." She paused. "May I confide in you, Mr. Speed?"

"Absolutely."

"My brother-in-law Ninian does not approve of a match between myself and Mr. Lincoln. He thinks Lincoln uncouth. Too rough to be marriageable to a Todd sister. As if marrying one makes him an expert! Pray, what are your views on the subject?"

My head was spinning. How could Mary ask for my advice on her courtship with Lincoln, especially this week of all weeks? And yet . . . I took a deep, steadying breath. I knew there was a compliment lingering inside her question, and I decided to be man enough to accept it. The lady's preferences were clear at this point, and I served no one's interests by falling victim to Iago's green-eyed monster of jealousy.

"We've had our differences on occasion," I said, "but I've never met a finer man. Nor one of such keen intellect. Any woman, of any station, would be lucky to receive his proposal."

Miss Todd nodded happily. "That's just what I think. Thank you for your candor, which I know may come at some personal cost."

"You deserve it," I said frankly, "and so does he."

We exchanged a long glance; it was the truest look I'd ever shared with a member of the fairer sex, though there was no lovemaking to it. It was, I realized after a moment, the start of a new page in our relationship.

"Are you certain, Mr. Speed," asked Mary, breaking into my thoughts, "that you don't have feelings for Miss Matilda Edwards? Such a pretty girl. And I have it on good authority she retains a great interest in you."

I thought about the last time I'd seen Miss Edwards, fleeing inside the Edwards mansion, skirts in hand, to change out of her muddy clothes after the misadventure with the shingles, rather than joining us in search of William Trailor's hidden trunk. It wasn't just Miss Todd's pleasing appearance and high intellect that I valued, I realized, but her readiness for adventure.

"I'm sure she'll make some man a fine wife," I said. "But I don't think it's to be me."

"That's the answer I expected. One day soon," Mary added, "you'll find what you're looking for. Whom you're looking for."

"I appreciate your confidence."

She laughed. "I have one more favor to ask. It's related to the case against Archibald Trailor. Come with me, if you please."

Mary started walking toward the American House, whose long row of chimneys was visible behind the capitol building, and I fell into step with her.

"This business with William Trailor's trunk hidden in our barn has me thinking about the Trailors' case," began Mary. "It's a good deal more interesting than the usual tasks that occupy my time. The other day, Mayor May was over at our house, speaking with Ninian, and I heard him mention that Henry Trailor was being put up at the American House while awaiting the trial."

"Big Red wants to make sure his star witness doesn't go anywhere."

Mary nodded. "I decided to learn what I could about Henry Trailor. As it turned out, Joseph had a good deal of light to shed on the subject."

"Who?"

"Ninian's Negro boy. His bondsman. You're familiar with him from your visits to Quality Hill, are you not?"

I nodded. Slavery had nominally been banished from Illinois since statehood. But the law allowed Negro boys to be held until their twenty-first birthday in contracts of indentured servitude that were slavery in all but name. A number of Springfield's most prominent citizens, including Big Red May himself, joined Edwards in taking full advantage of this oddity of the law.

"Joseph has a cousin who cleans the chambers at the American House. So I asked Joseph if his cousin could keep an eye on Henry's comings and goings."

"What did you learn?"

"He drinks a lot of whiskey, for one thing. More than most travelers staying at the hotel, even. And he's foul tempered and treats the workers at the hotel no better than beasts."

"No surprises there."

"Listen to this," said Mary, as we passed by the imposing front of the State Bank building, directly across from the capitol. She leaned toward me. "Joseph's cousin says Henry has quite a supply of gold coins. Anytime a peddler comes through with something Henry wants, he digs into his pocket and out comes another coin for the purchase. Joseph's cousin hasn't seen that much gold since before the Panic."

"Where does it come from?"

"The cousin doesn't know, but there's one other thing that's very odd. Henry spends a lot of time in the room of another guest at the hotel. In the public areas, Henry and the fellow pretend they're strangers to each other, but more than a few evenings Joseph's cousin has seen Henry near the room of this fellow, either going in or leaving it."

"What's the name of the other fellow?"

We were a few feet from the front door of the American House. Mary came to a stop and smiled. "That's where you come in."

Chapter 22

Five minutes later, Miss Todd and I separately entered the American House. The lobby of the grand hotel was cavernous, with six stately columns holding up a high, intricately carved wood ceiling. An enormous, richly colored Turkey rug covered much of the floor. At the far end of the room was an imposing marble counter, where the hotelkeeper Elijah Iles presided in front of a cabinet lined with cubbyholes filled with keys. I proceeded directly to Iles; out of the corner of my eye, I saw that Mary had settled herself on an Ottoman divan near the doorway.

Iles was a commanding man with wavy, graying hair and powerful whiskers. He was universally known as "Major" from his rank in the regiment raised from Central Illinois in 1832 for the Black Hawk War, during which he had commanded, among other green recruits, one Abraham Lincoln. Iles was also one of the original settlers of Springfield, having opened the settlement's first general store two decades earlier.

"In need of a room, Speed?" Iles asked as I approached his post. "Has Lincoln finally forced you out?"

"What? No, I . . ." I sputtered off, flustered.

Iles laughed heartily. "Believe me, I understand your pain more than most. There were nights in the tent, back when we were chasing after Black Hawk, that I put a sack over his head and smothered him half to death, just to quiet his infernal snore."

"He can be irritating, but that's not the reason for a visit. I'm hoping for a favor, from one old shopkeeper to another."

"Name it."

"I've extended a good deal of credit to one of your guests, so much so that I've started to worry he might run out on the bill."

"What's his name?" asked Iles.

"That's the thing—I've never gotten his name. Most of the time he's dealt with my clerk, Herndon. A fine lad, but not one to trust with such a large account. All I know is: room thirty-two." It was the one identifying detail Mary had been able to glean from Joseph about the mysterious guest in league with Henry Trailor.

Iles's face broke into a broad grin. His bushy eyebrows knit together, and the fine lines under his eyes danced merrily. "I was just about to say, don't tell me it's the fellow in room thirty-two."

"Who is he?"

"Lincoln must truly have driven you out with his snoring if you don't know. Room thirty-two is where the banker August Belmont is staying. He spends most of his days, as you must know, consorting with Lincoln and other members of the legislature. But in the evenings, he spends a good deal of time with—"

"Henry Trailor." My mind was reeling. What business could Belmont possibly have with Trailor?

Major Iles nodded approvingly. "Well done, Speed. I always say a shopkeeper who doesn't know his customers isn't going to be a shopkeeper for long. The same goes double for a hotel-keeper, I've learned."

The lobby had been empty, save for Miss Todd, during our conversation, but we now heard two voices coming down the main staircase off to the right of Iles's desk. Big Red May and Henry Trailor materialized on the bottom steps. They were conferring earnestly.

"Talk of the devil," murmured Iles.

Henry Trailor walked up to the desk and handed a key to Iles. "I'll be back presently," he said. Trailor nodded absently at me, his eyes unfocused, and rejoined Big Red, and the two men walked toward the exit.

"Have the two of them been spending a lot of time together?" I asked Iles quietly.

The hotelkeeper's eyes followed the pair as they walked away. "I'll assume," he said, "that my old subordinate Captain Lincoln has a good reason for wanting to know all of this."

"That's a fair assumption."

"Big Red comes to check in on him every now and again. I don't think he wants his principal witness wandering far. And of course, he's the one paying for Trailor's stay."

"Out of town funds or his own pocket?"

Iles shrugged. "If the town has any funds, I'd certainly like to know it. I was promised a hundred dollars for improving the street outside when I put up this place. I'm still waiting."

Glancing over my shoulder, I saw that Henry Trailor and Big Red had come to a stop not far from the front door and that Mary had managed to reposition herself to be closer to them. "Someone told me Henry Trailor has been spreading gold around," I said. "Doesn't sound like he needs Big Red to pay for him."

"Who declines an offer of free lodging?" said Iles. "Especially at the finest establishment in the state."

"What about Belmont? Could he be the source of Trailor's gold?"

Iles gazed at me a good long time before answering. "I haven't any idea. I'd tell you if I did."

I sensed another guest approaching. I looked up, and my breath caught. It was the auburn-haired, green-eyed young woman whose path I had crossed, ever so briefly, on the evening of the gala.

"May I have my key, Major Iles?" she asked. As Iles turned to search his cubbyholes, the woman glanced toward me, and immediately there was a light of recognition in her eyes.

"We must stop meeting like this," she said, her face relaxing into a mischievous smile.

"And yet we've never properly met at all."

Major Iles, turning his attention back toward us with a key dangling from his hand, said, "Have the two of you never been introduced? Mr. Joshua Speed, of Springfield, may I have the honor of presenting Miss Rose Flannery, of Chicago."

I bowed, and she curtsied. A thought flashed into my mind, wholly formed: *Mary said I'd meet my match. Could this be her, so soon?*

"We may not have met properly before now," Miss Rose Flannery of Chicago was saying, "but I have come to know something about you, Mr. Speed."

"Oh? What's that?" I managed, as my insides tumbled.

"You come from a prosperous family in Kentucky but preferred to make your own way rather than following your father's wishes. You are a thoroughly honest storekeeper but seem happy for most any excuse to abandon your counter."

"How do you know all that?" I asked, astonished.

"I'm not finished. I also know you share lodgings with Mr. Lincoln but don't always share your secrets with him." She gave me a composed look. "We've been lodging at the American House for several weeks. You can learn a lot by lingering in its lobby, if you're paying attention. Thank you for the key, Major. Good day."

She made her way across the lobby and up the sweeping staircase. My heart racing, I watched her receding form.

"My thoughts exactly," murmured Iles beside me.

"Too bad she's spoken for," I replied, thinking with envy of the dashing young man who had interrupted our conversation the evening of the gala.

"What? No, she isn't. At least not that I know of. If you mean the gentleman she's at the hotel with, he's a relation of some sort. A cousin, I believe."

"That's the most encouraging news I've heard in days," I said, my eyes still fixed on the steps Miss Flannery had ascended and my heart beating wildly. "What's their purpose in town?"

"Same as everyone I'm hosting. Business with the legislature."

I forced myself to return to the matter at hand. "Back to my original question. Should I trust Belmont not to run out on his account?"

"You don't trust the Rothschilds?" Iles asked. There was a slight smile on his face. "Before you answer, have I ever told you about the first two years I ran my store here, back when the town was just coming into existence?"

I shook my head. As I continued to face Iles, I held my right hand down at my side with three fingers extended. *Three minutes.* I hoped Miss Todd could make out the signal from where she was positioned at the other end of the lobby.

"I contracted for the building of a log store, sixteen feet square, and set out on horseback for St. Louis to buy goods," the major was saying. "I spent four weeks shopping and brought back fifteen hundred dollars' worth of goods—wrought iron, pot metal, dry goods and groceries. It was July 1821. The Indians were as numerous as the white man around here back then, and I sold to them about equal. Everyone was honest, and I often left my store open for days at a time.

"When my original stock was reduced, I locked the door, gave my key to old Matheny, and left for St. Louis again, in perfect confidence that all would be safe. But upon my return two months later, the store had been robbed. Nearly everything was gone."

"Robbed by whom?"

"I never found out. I heard a rumor that a family called Percifield, living out on the bluffs, was selling my goods out of the back of a two-horse wagon. So I took an officer and searched the wagon. Found goods very much like my own, but the marks had been removed and I couldn't tell for sure. Had to abandon the search. Though a few years later I did hear that the Percifields had been nabbed for another set of robberies. One was hung and the other sent to the penitentiary. At least that's what I heard.

"The Percifields, if that's who it was, did teach me a good lesson." Major Iles looked at me.

"Which was?" I prompted.

"Don't trust nobody. And if someone seems too honest, don't trust them even more."

Right on cue, there was a great wail from the other end of the lobby. Both Iles and I turned to stare. Miss Todd was lying prone on the couch, hands raised above her head, crying out in pain.

"I believe that's Ninian Edwards's sister-in-law," I said to the innkeeper.

But the savvy Iles already knew this, and he left his post and rushed to her aid. In a flash, I reached across the counter and snatched the key out of the cubbyhole marked *32*. Then I raced up the staircase. I didn't look back, but I could still hear Mary carrying on behind me.

I figured I had four minutes, maybe five at most. I reached the third floor and sprinted down the hallway until I found a doorway with a carved wooden *3* and *2* nailed to the door. I turned the key and let myself in. It was dark inside, only tiny slivers of light leaking in through mostly drawn curtains, but I didn't take the time to strike a candle.

The room was richly appointed, like the lobby, with overstuffed chairs and a grand canopied bed. It was immaculately clean. The writing desk was bare and there was not a book in sight. It was easy to picture the fastidious Belmont residing in the place.

The only personal effects in the room seemed to be stored in a traveling trunk that was pushed against the wall, its lid propped open. I rifled through it quickly. There was nothing but the fine clothing, neatly folded, I had seen Belmont wear in his daily perambulations around Springfield: black frockcoats, vests and trousers, and white starched shirts, along with undergarments. Removing these carefully, I felt around the bottom of the trunk. Perhaps he'd hidden a diary or some other type of writing. Nothing. Time was running out.

Despairing that the whole adventure had come to nothing, I was placing the clothing back into the trunk exactly as I had found it when I felt something crinkle inside the pocket of one of the frockcoats. I reached in and felt a tight wad of paper. Without thinking, I grabbed it and jammed it into my pocket. Then I finished putting Belmont's trunk as I had found it, left the room, locked the door behind me, and raced for the staircase.

As I came down the final set of stairs, I saw a crowd of men gathered around Mary. Fortunately, Major Iles was still among them, his distinctive wavy hair and full beard hovering over the stricken woman, and his counter was unattended. I thrust the key back into its slot and hurried to join the fray. Mary was lying on her back and staring at the ceiling, her arms akimbo and her face in great distress, but when I came into view, her eyes suddenly focused.

"I . . . I think it's passed," she announced, starting to sit up, only to be urged back down by several of the men surrounding her.

Iles took notice of me. "What happened to you?" he asked. "You disappeared right after Miss Todd took ill."

"Emergency trip to the backhouse," I murmured, clutching at my stomach, and the innkeeper nodded discreetly.

Miss Todd continued her rapid recovery, and in a few minutes she insisted she felt well enough to be on her way. She squinted at me. "Mr. Speed, is that you? Perhaps you'd be so kind as to escort me back to my house."

"I would be honored, Miss Todd. We'll take it slow."

The crowd parted, and Mary and I walked arm in arm out of the hotel and down the street.

"I hope it was worth it," she said at last, when we were certain that no one who had witnessed the scene at the hotel remained in our vicinity. "The role of damsel in distress is not one that comes naturally."

"And yet you played it with such enthusiasm." I grinned, enjoying our new familiarity. "Let's stop here. I saw Big Red and Henry Trailor talking near you. Did you overhear anything of interest?"

She shook her head. "They were speaking too quietly. All I caught were a few references to 'the trial,' but that's to be expected. How did you make out?"

"The mystery guest in room thirty-two, the one consorting with Henry Trailor, is none other than the banker August Belmont." Mary's eyes widened. "I was only able to search his room for a minute. All I found was this. Let's take a look together."

I took the purloined packet of paper out of my pocket. In the broad daylight, we could see that it was a scrap of newsprint torn from a newspaper, folded over several times and well worn. The newsprint had started to yellow with age, and I unfolded it carefully. One side contained several partial columns from a story about a raid against native tribes in the Iowa Territory. Then I turned the fragment over. Together we read a notice on the other side, printed in large type that spread the width of two normal columns:

BEWARE OF COUNTERFEITER!

On or about the 12th day of August, a man giving his name as August Belmont and his birthplace as the Free City of Frankfurt was arrested near Dubuque for having in his possession fifty pages of blank bank notes from the Miners' Bank. It was believed that Belmont intended to fill out the notes himself and put them into circulation, passing them off as genuine.

The following day, Belmont was brought before the presiding magistrate. He claimed that he was a banker, with connections to a famous European banking family, and that he had come into possession of the notes in the honorable practice of his profession. A vice president of Miners' Bank appeared and testified that neither he nor any other officer of the bank had had any dealings with Belmont and that the blank notes were to be considered stolen property. The magistrate found cause to bind Belmont over for trial at the next sitting of the circuit court.

Belmont gave bail for his appearance at the next term in the sum of eight hundred dollars and left the county. He has not been seen again, and the notes comprising his bail were later determined to be made out on false paper. The public would do well to be on the lookout, as a master thief is in our midst.

—Iowa Territorial Gazette

"What does it mean?" asked Mary, her mouth parted.

My blood was rushing; my dislike for Belmont had been vindicated. "It means," I said, "that the banker is actually a bandit."

Chapter 23

"I confess I've always had a bit of wonder about that man," said Mary as she read over the article one more time.

"Oh?"

"Something about him doesn't feel right. My father served several years as president of the Kentucky State Bank, back home in Lexington. He came into contact with European bankers in the course of his work, and I insisted that he take me with him to several meetings." Mary smiled. "Mr. Belmont's manner is very different than what I've seen in that class of men."

"I've been telling Lincoln all along he's a suspicious character."

"Then we must show him at once what you've found."

I began to make an excuse as to why this wasn't possible, but I stopped myself before the words left my mouth. Everything was different now, I realized in a flash. Just as my frank conversation with Mary had definitively turned the page and opened the way for a new, more satisfying, relationship between me and her, it had also changed my dealings with Lincoln. If we were no longer romantic rivals, then there was no reason for me to cling to my grievance. The clouds parted, and all at once I felt a rush of happiness.

"Yes, let's," I said. I lent her my arm and she took it. We

shared a happy smile, the two of us feeling flush with the success of having puzzled out together a mystery, even if the greater mystery of Fisher's murder remained, for the time being, unsolved. And good fortune continued to smile upon us, for there was Lincoln himself on the road ahead, striding towards us in great haste.

"Lincoln," I shouted.

"Speed! I heard a report that Miss Todd took ill. Have you seen—" Lincoln belatedly noticed Mary at my side. He came to a sudden halt. His facial muscles contorted with rage, and he exploded with an anger I had never seen before.

"How dare you! Both of you! After all we've—"

Both Mary and I were motioning frantically to get Lincoln to stop his rant, but our coordinated actions only seemed to fan his fire.

"—been through. An outrage! An affront! I thought I knew—"

"Stop, Lincoln!" I shouted.

"Please, Abraham," pleaded Mary.

Lincoln finally paused for breath.

"It's not what you think," I said. "Everything's changed."

"I'll say everything's changed," said Lincoln, pointing at our linked arms, his breaths still coming fast and furious.

"Will you please listen for a second?" said Mary. "Just for one second."

Something about her urgent, earnest tone connected with the man. Lincoln stopped his tirade and took a deep breath to gather himself. He nodded.

"First of all," I said, "I need to apologize for the way I acted. I think, in fairness, we owe one to each other, but since I threw the first punch, I'll speak first. I am very sorry for how I've behaved, Lincoln, when we fought and for the past week, too. I'd like to think I'm a better man."

I held out my hand, but Lincoln only looked at it warily. "And this?" he said, nodding at Mary and me, standing side by side.

"*This*," said Mary, "is because Mr. Speed and I have successfully completed some investigating together. Investigating on behalf of your client, I hasten to add. I don't know all the details of whatever disagreements you've had" —she gave a small smile, making clear she knew exactly what, or rather who, had been the object of the same— "but Mr. Speed has taken the honorable step of apologizing first. Now, there's only one way for you to respond."

"Yes, of course," said Lincoln after a moment. He reached out and clasped my outstretched arm. His palm was warm, his fingers strong, and we held the clasp for a second longer than normal. "I'm sorry, too, Speed. You're a better man than you've shown, and so am I. Let's resolve, both of us, to put such matters in the past."

"Agreed."

"And now that's settled," said Mary, nodding approvingly, "let us tell you what we've discovered." She described the information about Henry Trailor and Belmont and the scene at the American House, and I showed Lincoln the newspaper article, which he read over, twice, the skin around his eyes drawing tight as he took it in. When he had finished and handed the article back to me, I related the results of my interviews with the stage and stable men and my conversation with Ransdell. Both Lincoln and Mary laughed as I recounted Ransdell's threats to come after me with his ruthless lawyer.

"Toothless, more like it," said Lincoln, grinning.

"Hardly," said Mary, grasping his arm and gazing up at him with admiration. I felt a pang of jealousy, but just as quickly I tried to chase the feeling away.

"What about Belmont?" I said instead. "I told you you shouldn't trust him."

"I can't believe he's a counterfeiter," said Lincoln. "He's been honest and forthright in all our dealings."

"It's here in black and white," I protested, waving the article in my hand.

Lincoln sighed. "There's nothing to do but ask him. He's at Hoffman's Row right now. We were just working out the final details for the gold transfer when I received word Miss Todd had taken ill. Give me the article and I'll ask him about it."

"I'm coming too," I said. "I've never trusted him."

Lincoln looked like he was going to object, but then he relented, and after exchanging promises with Miss Todd that we would see each other soon, the two of us headed for his office at Hoffman's Row.

"I'm glad we're back in league together," said Lincoln as we walked. "And this shows the value of the unsent letter."

"What are you talking about?"

"It's a trick a friend taught me when I lived in New Salem. When I'm angry with someone, I mean really furious, I'll write a letter to the person detailing all the ways they've wronged me. Every chapter and verse. Then I put the letter into a drawer and never send it. Writing it gets the anger out of my mind, most of it anyway, and there's no benefit in confronting the other person again. These things usually die away."

"I'd like to see the letter you wrote me sometime," I said, smiling. "I bet it'd make for good reading."

"No, you wouldn't," said Lincoln seriously. "Anyway, I burnt it a few days ago, once I realized our feud would end before long."

It appeared a winter blizzard had swept through Lincoln's law office. The writing table in the center of the room was littered with pleadings and loose scraps of paper. A patina of papers had fallen off the table and lay on the floor, tracing the outline of the table like snow surrounding the base of a soaring pine. The reclining lounge of Lincoln's law partner Stuart, who was back east in Washington doing his duty in Congress, was covered by another impending avalanche of papers.

Belmont sat beside Lincoln's table, perusing one stack of papers among the many on the desk. "How is Miss Todd?" he asked as we entered.

"Never better," said Lincoln. "It was a false alarm."

Without preamble, I threw the newspaper article about Belmont's arrest for forgery onto the table. "How do you explain this?" I demanded.

Belmont's eyes flicked over to Lincoln. "Has Speed shown you?" Lincoln nodded.

Belmont picked up the article, folded it, and slipped it into his pocket. "I had assumed," he said slowly, "that a man's private belongings were treated with respect in this town."

"How do you explain it?" I repeated.

Belmont swallowed, collected himself. "It's simple. You see, I planted the article myself."

"What?"

"When I first ventured to the western expanse of your vast nation, I realized at once the peculiar challenges of running a money-lending operation in this territory. There are, I soon learned, bandits and bankers, and it's often impossible to tell the one from the other. The one often *is* the other."

"You'll get no argument from me," I said. "But how does it explain the crime that's detailed in the newspaper?"

Belmont gave one of his elegant shrugs. If my discovery of the incriminating article had momentarily thrown him off stride, he had regained his balance with the utmost rapidity. "There are times when I must operate amongst respectable men, such as Mr. Lincoln and his colleagues in the state legislature. For those occasions, I naturally have my uniform." He gestured at his immaculate frockcoat and trousers. "And there are other times when I must operate amongst thieves. For those occasions, likewise,

I must have the proper trappings." He indicated the pocket into which he had placed the newspaper article.

"What are you saying?"

"Just as persons like Mr. Lincoln have certain expectations about their partners in business, so do bandits have such expectations. In the latter case, the expectation is that their business partners be thoroughly *dis*reputable. So I wrote up the article, took it to a printing office, and had it struck off upon a piece of newspaper which was printed on the opposite side. And then I trimmed the edges to give it the appearance of having been cut from a newspaper. Ever since, I have carried it on my person, to use as circumstances may require."

I stared at the man, dumbfounded. It was the least plausible explanation for abject criminality I had ever heard in my life. It was so obviously false, I thought, that it could almost be true. And yet, it was inconceivable that the tale was true.

"You don't believe him, do you, Lincoln?" I asked the man.

Lincoln was silent. He was slouched against the back of his chair, his long legs splayed outward and his unshaven chin resting on tented fingers.

"There's another thing," I said to Belmont. "I've heard you've been spending a lot of time at the American House with Henry Trailor. The low-lived person who's accused his brothers of murder. Do you deny it?"

"I admit it," said Belmont. "Henry and I have become well acquainted."

"What explanation do you have for that?"

"Do you intend to justify for me every one of your acquaintances?" For the first time, there was a hint of anger in Belmont's voice, but it quickly receded. "It is no matter. I've learned to hold my potential enemies near to me. As near as possible. It is another type of protection."

"But why is Henry Trailor your enemy?"

"Until the gold shipment is securely in place, everyone is a potential enemy."

"There was an article in the *Daily Chicago American*," I said, "speculating about the exact date and path of the shipment. What is it?"

Belmont and Lincoln exchanged glances. I thought I saw Lincoln give a tiny nod. "We're keeping the details secret," said Belmont, "but I suppose there's no harm telling you. The gold's coming from St. Louis. I've arranged for my bank to make a withdrawal from the federal reserve depot there."

"And what's the plan to get the shipment from St. Louis to Chicago?"

"The trunk will be leaving St. Louis tomorrow," said Belmont. "It will come by packet steamer from St. Louis upriver as far as Peoria Lake, and overland by stagecoach from there to Chicago." Belmont paused. "Only a few men know the final route we decided on. As you've noted, it could prove a tempting target, if anyone with bad intentions got wind of the plan."

"And you have the trunk carefully protected?"

Belmont nodded. "I've taken care of the details myself. I have two men, my very best, guarding it at all times."

I must have looked skeptical, because Lincoln added, "It's *his* gold, Speed. We've agreed to borrow money *from* Belmont. You can't be suggesting he's planning to steal his own gold."

I hadn't thought about this, but an answer immediately occurred to me. "Why not? He just admitted he's made all the arrangements for the protection of the shipment himself. So he arranges with some banditti confederates to steal the gold, and then he comes back to you and the legislature and demands you honor the terms of the loan. Forces you to pay him back. And he doubles his money, just like that. There's nothing in your agreement that discharges the state's debt if the shipment gets stolen, is there?"

Lincoln shook his head.

"It's the perfect plan." I turned to Belmont. "Do you deny it?"

"Of course I deny it," said the banker. "It's ridiculous."

"I think it's plausible," I said. "Very plausible. You should have your own form of protection of the shipment, Lincoln."

"I already do," replied Lincoln, but when I gestured for him to continue, he did not elaborate.

Belmont used his walking stick to push himself to his feet. He bowed formally in turn to me and to Lincoln. "It has come time to wish each of you a good afternoon. As always, I have found our conversations most enlightening."

"Who are you?" I blurted out.

"I am August Belmont of the Free City of Frankfurt."

"Are you banker or bandit?"

Belmont smiled the smile of a man leaving the chessboard after executing an elegant checkmate. "I am August Belmont of the Free City of Frankfurt." And he turned on his heels and strode from the room.

Chapter 24

The newspapers in the following days were alive with speculation about the gold shipment. If Lincoln and Belmont were trying to keep the details of the transfer a secret, they were doing a poor job of it. By the middle of the week, the general outlines of the plan conveyed to me in confidence by Belmont were practically a matter of public knowledge. My suspicions that Belmont somehow planned to steal his own gold grew steadily, but whenever I raised the idea, Lincoln dismissed it out of hand.

Meanwhile, I continued to search for evidence exonerating Archibald. It had been a full moon on the night of the American House gala. Surely someone had seen something. I asked everyone who came into my store if he or she had been anywhere near the millpond on the evening in question. None had. I repeated the same question up and down the common table at the Globe Tavern, morning and evening, with a similar lack of results. I even stopped by the offices of the town's two biggest professional gossips, the newspaperman Simeon Francis and the postmaster James Keyes. But neither man had heard anything of relevance.

That evening, I decided to continue my investigations at Torrey's Temperance Hotel, the shabbiest public room in town and the place where, the name notwithstanding, it was easiest to achieve a cheap drunk. The moon-faced Torrey scowled when I entered, but he otherwise left me alone as I circulated through the dark, dank room, asking the men present whether they had seen anything by the millpond on the night of the full moon. Again my questions came up empty, but I was offered a number of full glasses, which I was too polite to decline.

A few hours and more than a few drinks later, I was back out on the gently rolling streets, weaving my way toward our lodgings. It was a cool, clear night, and the waxing moon and a full firmament of stars lit my path. My serpentine route took me past the grand entrance of the American House. As I passed, the front door suddenly swung open and a rush of feminine energy swept down the steps, accompanied by flowing auburn hair and translucent green eyes. I gulped.

"What good fortune to encounter you, Mr. Speed," came a breathy voice that made my insides melt. "I had just resolved I would have to set off in search of you in the morning."

"Miss Flannery." I attempted a deep bow, although I may have wobbled in the execution. The lady smiled.

"As I recall," she said, "the last time we spoke, I told you some of what I knew about you, but you did not reciprocate. Have you learned anything about me since then?"

"Er . . . not much, I'm afraid."

"What an appalling lack of curiosity." Her eyes glimmered.

It really was, I thought. Miss Flannery was wearing the same light-green dress she had worn when I'd first seen her at the gala, without any overcoat. At that moment, she shivered. Perhaps a breeze had blown through.

"May we step inside?" she asked.

"Of course."

The hotel lobby was brilliantly lit by several chandeliers laden with blazing candles, and it was thronged with persons, men and women in fine dress coming or going from one social occasion or another. The legislature had just wrapped up its annual proceedings, and there was a boisterous, festive sense in the air. Miss Flannery gestured to an empty space along the wall, near a small palm tree growing in a blue pot. I joined her, standing as close to her as decorum permitted. Perhaps even a little closer.

"I'll give you another chance," she said. "What do you know about me?"

"Much less than I wish. You are from Chicago, I believe, and you're in town with your cousin. Other than that . . ." I spread out my arms helplessly.

"It's an appalling deficit," I continued, "one I must address at once. Were you born in America?"

She shook her head. "County Kerry. My father sailed for this country when I was four. He found work, digging the canal in New York, and then he sent for me and my mother." She paused. "But I never saw him alive again. He died in an accident, two weeks before we arrived. Another navvy hit him in the head with a shovel while they were working beside each other."

"I'm sorry."

"I wish I'd seen him just one more time. He called me his 'Róisín.'" She pronounced the word *RO-sheen*. "It means 'little rose' in our language."

"How did your mother endure on her own?"

"It was hard, but we managed. Her brother came over from County Kerry, too. He's Patrick's father—that's my cousin, who's in town with me. They worked hard, and they made a decent life for themselves. Like my people do. Now my uncle's running his own crew up north, for the Illinois and Michigan Canal, with my mother's help."

"That's all most impressive. What brought you to Springfield this season?"

"The legislature, naturally. Our family's interests along the canal route are greatly affected by issues being debated by your

Mr. Lincoln and his colleagues. Patrick's father sent him, and they thought it would be advantageous for me to accompany him."

"Speaking selfishly, I concur wholeheartedly."

She smiled demurely. At that moment, Belmont passed through the lobby not far from where we were standing. I didn't think he saw me, but I turned away nonetheless. The last thing I wanted was for him to intrude upon my conversation with Miss Flannery.

The lady had seen the man and my reaction, however. "He is not a friend of yours," she said. A statement, not a question.

"I don't think so."

"Decidedly not. I overheard something he said of you the other day . . . Unequivocally not a friend."

"What did he say?"

She leaned closer still to me. I breathed in her intoxicating scent. "Mr. Belmont is nothing to us. What I wish to speak with you about this evening is something different. Something confidential." She glanced around at several couples standing nearby and whispered, "Only for your ears."

"Perhaps we can find a quiet corner?" I looked around for one.

Miss Flannery shook her head. "Even the corners in this room have ears. Perhaps we should repair to my chamber. My cousin is out on the town. He won't be back until late." My cheeks must have colored at her boldness, because she added, "Unless you have some objection to my chamber."

"Not at all. Lead the way."

And I followed after her, my head still a little foggy but my blood surging with desire. It had been several years since I'd been with a woman. We passed near Major Iles, standing at his counter and directing traffic, and he managed to catch my eye. He winked.

Miss Flannery led me higher and higher until we had reached the very top landing of the staircase. I stepped into the hallway, feeling dizzy. Either the hotel was spinning or my head was. I followed Miss Flannery to the end of the hallway. She reached into her dress, pulled out a key, and opened the door.

"Come inside," she offered, striking a match.

I followed her wordlessly. The room was smaller than Belmont's chamber, and she lit a single candle sitting on a side table. There was nowhere to sit in the room except for the double bed. She turned to face me.

"I believe you and Mr. Lincoln are searching for someone who might have seen something relating to the murder that took place on the night of the gala at the hotel."

My eyes widened. "How do you know that?" I considered. "Knowledge gleaned from the hotel lobby, I suppose."

"Normally, I wouldn't go anywhere near a court case, but when I heard you were involved, I decided I should tell you what I saw."

"I'm very glad you did." I winced twice, trying to clear my head.

"Will I have to testify?"

"It would be up to Lincoln. He's representing Archibald Trailor in the murder case. But I can tell you Archibald is a good man, a friend of mine, and if you've got any information that could help him avoid an unjust fate, then I'd urge you to share it."

"You sound very loyal to him."

"I'm loyal to all my friends."

"I like that."

Suddenly, Miss Flannery took two steps forward, grabbed my frockcoat, and pulled me toward her. Her face was less than a foot from mine; I could smell the rosewater in her hair and feel the warmth of her body. The lust coursing through my body felt uncontrollable.

"Perhaps we can use our newfound friendship to mutual advantage, Mr. Speed," she said quietly. Her palms were on my chest, and I felt sure she could feel the beating of my heart. My gaze was locked on her ruby lips.

"What did you have in mind?" I managed.

"An exchange . . ." she breathed.

"Yes?"

"Of information."

"Yes." I would have said yes to an exchange of anything in the moment.

She moved even closer, her lips now inches from mine. "Can I trust you?"

I was breathing too quickly to think straight. To think at all. "Most certainly."

"Good. I'll go first, because I want you to know you can trust me."

She leaned forward and brushed her lips against mine. My heart surged; my head pounded. But then, before I could return her kiss, she leaned back to look directly into my eyes.

"Here's what I know. Late the night of the gala, in the small hours after midnight, I saw William and Henry Trailor working in concert. It was not at all like they'd had a falling out, as Henry is saying. Do you understand?"

I nodded, wordlessly.

"They drove up in a large, enclosed carriage," she continued, "with Henry on the high box and William inside the carriage. They went inside the hotel together and came out again carrying several pieces of baggage. They loaded the carriage together and drove off. The whole time they were dead silent. Moving stealthily. They definitely didn't want to be seen or heard by anyone."

She leaned forward again and pressed into me, and I closed my eyes, expecting another kiss. But it never came. Instead she said, in her most breathy voice, "Now it's your turn."

I opened my eyes and let out a long breath. "Of course. Anything."

She nodded over her shoulder at the bed. "Do you think we'll be more comfortable sitting there?"

"Definitely."

She took my hand, led me over to the bed, and settled herself onto its edge. I sat beside her, hoping she couldn't hear my pounding heart.

"My cousin and I need to know when work on the canal is going to start again. When will the new funding from the legislature arrive? Knowing the exact date will give us an advantage over the other crews, you see." She gave my hand a squeeze, for encouragement.

My heart sank. "I wish I could help you, Miss Flannery. I truly do. But I'm afraid I know no more about the workings of the legislature than you do. Less, almost certainly."

"I think you know more than you're admitting." She took her other hand and started running it along the top of mine.

"I can't tell you how much I wish I could help you. Anything in the world."

She smiled. "You know the legislature has been working out the terms of a loan from the banker," she said.

"That's right."

"There's going to be a shipment of gold to Chicago?"

Based on what had been reported in the newspapers, I figured this was more or less well known to everyone already. "Yes."

"And the shipment's underway?"

I couldn't remember whether this was public knowledge, and as I felt her body so close to mine, I couldn't remember why I should care. "I believe they were planning to leave St. Louis a day or two ago."

She leaned forward and gave me a soft kiss. "By stagecoach or steamer?"

"Packet steamer from St. Louis."

Another small kiss. My body was on fire. "Up the Mississippi?"

"Yes."

"And then?"

"And then up the Illinois as far as she can navigate. Peoria Lake."

Another kiss. I was mad with desire. "And then the shipment of gold will go overland from there to Chicago?"

"Yes."

"How?"

"I think they're planning to take a regular stagecoach."

"With all the gold?"

"Yes."

"All the way home?"

"Yes."

"Until all that hard currency has entered the bank vault?"

"Yes."

"Good idea," she breathed, and she lay back onto the bed and pulled me on top of her.

Chapter 25

I woke early the next morning in my own bed, my head pounding. I thought perhaps I had dreamed the encounter with Miss Flannery, but then I felt by my cheek her lace handkerchief, which she'd given me as we parted. And I sighed contentedly and turned over and fell back asleep.

When I woke again, it was to a hard, unrelenting rain. I foreswore the morning walk to the Globe and breakfasted instead on stale biscuits I took from the store's shelves. The rain had driven most of Springfield's populace inside, and so when I heard the door creaking open a few minutes after ten, I expected our first customer of the day. Instead, it was Sheriff Hutchason, water dripping from every limb.

"Awfully wet morning for your rounds, Humble," I said.

"Without the downpour, I doubt I would have found him."

My pulse quickened. "Found whom?"

"Fisher. At last. I need shovels and a burlap bag, for collecting the remains. If you want, saddle up your horse and come see for yourself."

After fetching the supplies for the sheriff, I threw on my greatcoat and grabbed an old straw hat that was already ruined for proper occasions. Then I hustled around the corner to the Globe stables and got Hickory ready as quickly as I could. She never minded the weather, and as it had been several days since I had taken her out for exercise, she was jangly and eager to set off.

The sheriff called out impatiently from the yard, and I jumped aboard Hickory and we took off, the mud flying up from both horses' hooves. Sometime later we came to an abrupt halt, and I blinked through the rain to gauge our location. After a moment, I realized we were about a quarter mile distant from Hickox's millpond, only on the side opposite where Henry Trailor had led Big Red and his search party.

In front of us was a low bank, about four feet high. Rainwater streamed down the bank, and there was a muddy pool at its base. Parts of two weathered military boots stuck out, soles first, from the sloping surface.

"That's him," Hutchason said. He was bareheaded and his scalp was wet and glistening. "What remains of him, anyway."

"How do you know it's Fisher?" I had to shout to be heard over the din of the pounding rain.

"When he first turned up missing, I got a description from Ransdell of what he was wearing on his last day. Keeps a close eye on anyone who owes him money. Ransdell told me about the boots, and the jacket and hat, too." Hutchason pointed, and I saw a tattered half-coat caught in some brambles a few feet from the boots. The coat bore a pattern that, while faded, I recognized as the insignia of a band of military irregulars. And a few feet away, impaled on the end of a bare branch, was a discolored fur hat, with part worn away. It was exactly what Ransdell had told me, too, of Fisher's final outfit.

"Is any of his flesh and bones still there?" I asked. A steady stream of water was pouring off the brim of my hat, and I had to squint to make out Hutchason.

"There're a few bones scattered about. I'll walk around carefully to recover what I can, but I don't think much is left. The wolves must of eaten him. There's not much else for them to eat this time of year."

"How do you think he got here?"

"Dunno." The sheriff shrugged. "Maybe this is where the Trailor brothers buried him, until the rains eroded away the bank and put him to the surface again. Or maybe they left him on the other side of the pond, where Henry indicated, and the wolves dragged him over here to have their meal."

We sat atop our horses quietly for a minute or two, while the rain pounded down on the lonely remains of Flynn Fisher. It was a gloomy scene, befitting the sorry end to Fisher's life.

"How did you come to look for him here?" I asked, breaking the silence.

"That's the funny part," said the sheriff. "This morning, when I went to check on William Trailor in his cell in the capitol basement, he asked me if Fisher's body had been found yet. I said it hadn't, and he said why don't you search again, on the far side of the pond. Indeed, he gave me pretty decent directions to this exact spot."

I gazed up in confusion. "But why would William want you to find the body? Surely it's better for his defense if it never surfaced."

The sheriff shook his head, flinging a jet of water off his scalp.

"Perhaps it's some kind of trick," I said, trying to answer my own question. "Perhaps William arranged for another set of remains to be placed here, suggesting it was Fisher, and then in the middle of the trial he's going to prove it's not him, in order to discredit the prosecution's case."

"Beyond the clothing, I'm not sure how anyone could prove for certain whose bones these are," said Hutchason. "Unless the wolves left his skull, but I don't see anything that large. Not intact, anyway."

I had a sudden inspiration. "Did you spot a mourning ring among the remains?" I related what Archibald had told me about the ring commemorating Fisher's dead wife and child.

"Haven't seen anything of the sort."

"Let's keep an eye out for it as we collect what's left," I said, swinging off Hickory. "Here, I'll help you."

We dug and poked around in the mud for the better part of an hour. We bagged the clothing and the bones we could find. They were human bones, no doubt, although they added up to considerably less than a full skeleton. The wolves had scattered, or eaten, the rest.

We were nearly finished with our work when I thrust my spade into the muddy ground one more time and heard a sort of *clink*. Excitedly, I dropped to all fours and dug. Finally, I was able to scoop the object up, and I held it in my cupped hands. As the sheriff watched beside me, the falling rain washed away the mud, gradually revealing a silver ring with intertwined initials.

"The very one I saw on Fisher's finger in Chicago," I said. "It's him, all right."

As we parted, Hutchason asked me to tell Lincoln about our discovery of the body, but when I called at Hoffman's Row, he was absent. Hay told me he was closeted with Belmont and Big Red, overseeing the final details of the gold shipment. In fact, Lincoln was gone all day, and when I awoke the next morning, his side of the bed had not been disturbed.

Later that morning, Herndon and I were behind the counter of my store, sorting through a newly arrived shipment of fashionable hats from New York City, when my sister Martha burst in. Her face was flushed, her hair dripping, and she was gasping for breath. She waved her arms frantically.

"What is it?" I said, coming through the gap in the counter at once.

"Joshua . . . I need you," she panted. "Come with me to the

sheriff's house . . . at once. Archibald Trailor's future may depend on it."

"Of course—but why?"

"He's about to confess to something he didn't do. You've got to stop him."

I shouted to Herndon to find Lincoln, wherever he was, and send him to the jail cell immediately. Then I took Martha's arm and we hurried through the door.

Outside, it was a chilly spring morning. It was raining again, though more gently than the day before, and the streets were sloppy and slippery. Martha's shoes and stockings were already coated, but she paid them no heed as we splashed through the muck.

"Tell me what happened," I said, holding my hand to my brow to keep the rainwater from running into my eyes.

Martha's chest was still heaving with agitation. "I was having a conversation with Archibald this morning out back at the cell. Henry Trailor came into the backyard and said he'd arranged for Big Red to be by shortly, and Archibald nodded and said something like, 'It's set, then.' And Henry told me Archibald was going to confess that he and he alone was responsible for Fisher's murder."

"What?"

"I know," said Martha, bobbing her head. "I pleaded for Archibald to talk to Lincoln first, but Henry started arguing back and wouldn't let Archibald say another word for himself. I knew I had to enlist your help. Oh, we've got to hurry!" She gathered her skirts in her hands and splashed ahead through the mud.

"Did you hear the sheriff found Fisher's remains yesterday, right where William told him to look?" I asked as I caught up with her.

Martha nodded. "Humble started to describe the scene at suppertime last night, until Molly shushed him and told him it was no business for the baby's ears. But I got the gist of the story. I know it's looking grim for Archibald. We've got to stop him before he makes it worse."

We soon reached Sheriff Hutchason's house, but as we raced through the gate toward the cell in the rear yard, we saw the jail door standing open and Archibald Trailor being led out by the sheriff himself, with Henry Trailor walking behind his brother. The prisoner's hands were tied behind his back.

"What's this?" I said as I hurried to intercept the little procession.

"Speed? I should have known your sister would go for you." Hutchason frowned. "You'll have to step aside. I've been told Mr. Archibald Trailor has a statement to make, and as a service to him, in view of the weather, I've agreed he can make it inside the house. Big Red's waiting for them near the hearth." He indicated over my shoulder to his house, and I could just make out the mayor's distinctive profile, watching us through the window.

"But why's he coming?" Martha asked, pointing at Henry Trailor, who returned a glare full of daggers aimed squarely at her.

The sheriff sighed. "Archibald asked that his brother be present, too, for his statement. Now, I must ask both of you Speeds to step aside. You can't interfere. This is legal business."

I went up to Archibald and put my hand on his shoulder. The carpenter's face was puffy and his eyes were bloodshot, as if he hadn't gotten a full night's sleep in days. "What are you doing?" I asked in a quiet voice.

"No more than I must," he returned.

"This isn't still about your five-year-old self telling your father you'd protect your brothers, is it? You've got to protect yourself, first and foremost. Your life could be at stake, Archibald. Your father would tell you the same, if he were here."

"I made a promise." It was barely a whisper.

"I urge you to refrain from saying anything. At least until

you've had a chance to consult with Lincoln. *He* has your interests at heart. None of these other men do. Not the sheriff or the mayor. And definitely not your brothers. I've been around Lincoln long enough to know he's going to tell you to stay silent."

"Stand aside, Speed," said Hutchason. "This doesn't concern you."

"It concerns Lincoln, at a minimum, and he's on his way at this very moment," I replied, hoping mightily it was true. The fact that Big Red had returned to town gave me a glimmer of optimism that Lincoln was about as well. Hopefully Herndon would track him down.

"What's the delay, Sheriff?" came Henry's screeching voice. He was only a few feet from us, close enough to have heard the entire exchange. "I was under the impression you are the principal lawman in this county. And that ordinary citizens do not have the power to subvert the interests of the law. Meanwhile we're all standing in the rain, getting wetter and wetter."

I turned and said hurriedly to Martha, "Go inside. Now! You'll know what to do." Martha nodded and rushed toward the sheriff's back door. The sheriff watched her without comment; I figured he wouldn't bar her from entering the house she'd called home for several years.

Turning back to Henry, I said, "It seems to me it's you who's subverting the interests of the law."

"This is your last warning, Speed," said Hutchason in an angry voice. "Stand aside voluntarily, or I'll have no choice but to lock you up yourself." He pointed toward the jail cell.

I raised my hands in the air and moved a few feet away. But as both Trailors passed, I fell into step behind them. The sheriff opened his back door and ushered them inside. I was a step behind Henry, and I managed to block the door with my foot just as the sheriff was pulling it shut. "I won't say one word," I told Hutchason. "I promise."

He stared at me for a moment, calculating. "A single word and I'm jailing you for a week," he finally replied, standing aside to let me pass.

The Trailor brothers had taken seats next to each other around Hutchason's hearth. Big Red May sat across from them, his hands folded on his lap and his enormous ears flapping with excitement. Henry frowned as he saw me enter the room, but he kept his tongue.

Martha, standing in the far corner, avoided catching my eye.

"Why don't you untie my brother, Sheriff, now that we're inside," said Henry. "He's no risk of flight in here."

Sheriff Hutchason agreed, and Archibald rubbed his wrists and stretched his arms once the sheriff removed the bindings. I stared through the window, willing Lincoln to appear before Archibald inflicted permanent damage on his case. The rain had picked up and was coming down in steady sheets.

"Go ahead and warm yourself," said the mayor, pointing toward the hearth. Inside a proper building for the first time in days, Archibald gratefully extended his hands toward the fire.

"Now Archibald," began May, honing in on his target, "you and I have known each other for quite some time, haven't we? Going on ten years at this point."

"I reckon you're about right, Big Red," replied Archibald peaceably. He rotated his wrists back and forth in front of the smoldering logs.

"And we've had good relations during that time?"

Archibald nodded.

"Now, Archibald, this trial for you and William is going to begin in three days."

Another nod.

"You understand, don't you, that the sheriff found the remains of Mr. Fisher yesterday, found them out by the millpond."

"That's what I heard."

"I've got to tell you, Archibald, you and William don't got much of a chance, not between the testimony of Henry and now the body turning up. I'm just being honest with you, all right? The men of this town want justice. They're going to hear the evidence of what you've done, and a picture's going to come into their minds of you and William swinging from a pair of gallows set up on the green beside the state capitol, and they're going to think that's justice. You understand what I'm saying?"

Martha stiffened. Archibald said, "I understand." A hint of tension had begun to creep into his temples.

"I don't want that to happen, Archibald. Truly I don't. But if it's you and William together on trial, I'm telling you, that's what's going to happen." Big Red stole a glance at the sheriff. "Now, if it was just you on trial, Archibald, you by yourself, it'd be a different matter. A different trial altogether. I imagine your lawyer Mr. Lincoln could put on all manner of evidence about your character. About what a credit you've been to the town of Springfield all these years. About how many folks you've leant a helping hand to. How many you've done good, honest carpentry for. I'm telling you, Archibald, if that's what the trial is, I don't think anyone's going to be swinging from the gallows, not William, and certainly not you, either."

Again Archibald nodded. Henry was watching him intently.

"So, Archibald, tell me what really happened between you and this Fisher fellow."

There was a pause, during which everyone but Archibald leaned forward with anticipation. If the man himself was experiencing inner turmoil, it was hard to tell. He cleared his throat.

"It began when—"

"Wolves!" screamed my sister. "Two wolves out by the barn. The chickens and milk cow are about to get eaten!"

"Are you sure, Miss Speed?" The sheriff turned to her with a suspicious look.

"Positive. Two shadows creeping past the jail cell. They slipped between the boards into the barn."

The sheriff lumbered through his door, after first grabbing a shotgun from atop the door frame. The rest of us sat in awkward silence. A few minutes later the sheriff came back inside, dripping wet.

"There were no wolves," he said, glowering.

"You must have chased them off," said Martha, her face steady. "What a relief."

"Now Archibald—" began Big Red again.

"Don't say anything!" cried Martha.

Everyone turned to look at her again. Both Big Red and Henry Trailor shouted angrily. Sheriff Hutchason took several steps toward her. The expression on his broad face was somewhere between resignation and fury. I stepped in front of Martha to shield her from the approaching lawman.

There was a bang behind us. A soaking-wet Lincoln crashed through the door and into the home. He took in the scene as water dripped from his stovepipe hat and started to form a puddle on the sheriff's floor. Then he marched up to Archibald Trailor, grabbed him by the scruff of his work shirt, and pulled him to his feet. "Close your mouth and come with me," commanded Lincoln.

The words unleashed an uproar. Everyone started speaking at once. Everyone, that is, except Archibald.

"He's in my custody," said Hutchason. "You can't take him."

"This is my interrogation," said Big Red. "You can't interrupt him."

"He was about to confess," said Henry Trailor. "You can't stop him."

"I can do all those things," responded Lincoln coolly. "This interrogation is over."

CHAPTER 26

An hour later, Archibald was back in the jail cell behind the sheriff's house while Lincoln, Martha, and I huddled close to him on the other side of the bars, trying to stay dry against the spitting rain. After a heated discussion, the sheriff and Big Red had agreed not to question him further in Lincoln's absence. And Henry Trailor had been instructed to desist from further contact with his brother as well.

Archibald himself proved the more challenging problem. He stood silently as Lincoln berated him for planning to incriminate himself. "I can't defend you," said Lincoln, with great exasperation, "if you won't defend yourself. Why would you take the blame for something you didn't do?"

Archibald's eyes were full of grief. "That night, I did something I shouldn't have. I did wrong to Flynn."

"But Fisher was your friend, wasn't he?" said Lincoln. "You never wanted to hurt him."

"Of course I didn't."

"And, whatever happened to Fisher, your brothers were there, too, weren't they? You wouldn't have done anything to him on your own."

"That's true."

I expelled my breath in frustration. "Just tell us exactly what you did, Archibald, and exactly what your brothers did. At the least, tell Lincoln. That way, he'll be best positioned to defend you in court."

Archibald shook his head. "I've told you before, Speed, I can't. I promised my brothers."

"But your brothers are the ones trying to make you take all the blame!" cried Martha from the other side of our little gathering. There were tears of frustration in her eyes, and for a moment I wondered why she had become so devoted to Archibald's cause.

"I was only doing what I thought best," mumbled Archibald, his eyes downcast. He seemed to be trying to avoid Martha's gaze in particular.

"Will you assure me you won't do it again?" said Lincoln. "Don't make any statements about what happened the night Fisher disappeared. Not to anyone. Not even your brothers."

Archibald stood mutely. Some seconds passed. Then he said, quietly, "Very well. I'll do as you say, Mr. Lincoln."

Lincoln, Martha, and I headed back toward the square. I told Lincoln about my excursion with Hutchason the prior day and our grim discovery of Fisher's remains.

When I was finished, Lincoln shook his head. "As a human being, I've been holding out hope Fisher was still alive," he said. "As an advocate, I had been hoping his body—if there was a body—wouldn't materialize before trial. It definitely added an argument for us to make. But I guess there's finality now for his family, if he has one." Lincoln paused and stroked his smooth chin with his thumb and forefinger. "Perhaps Conkling encouraged William to tell the sheriff where the body was."

"But why would Mr. Conkling think it good strategy to have the body found?" asked Martha.

"It's certainly not the one I would have chosen. But if you were Conkling, defending William, and you couldn't argue Fisher was still alive because you knew he'd been killed, what would you argue instead?"

"If I were Conkling," I said, "I'd probably be translating Cicero from the original Latin and Plato from the ancient Greek rather than working on the Trailor case."

"You're underestimating him again," said Lincoln with a smile. "He's gotten to be a much better advocate. He's going to be forceful in William's defense. You'll see."

"In that case," Martha offered, "perhaps he'll argue it was all Archibald's doing. Or Archibald and Henry together, I suppose."

"Very good," said Lincoln, nodding. "It could be Conkling thinks that having the body emerge will enhance his argument. Maybe there's a mark on the body of some sort. We'll have to see what Hutchason finds when he has a proper chance to examine the remains."

"But Conkling's hurting your case," I protested.

"There's nothing much I can do about that. William and Archibald are charged jointly with killing Fisher, and they'll be tried in the same trial. But that's no guarantee they'll pursue the same defense, or even defenses aligning with one another. One potential hazard of the joint trial is that I'll advance one argument on Archibald's behalf and Conkling will advance a contradictory one on William's behalf. So it's not just the proofs of Attorney General Lamborn I'll need to worry about at trial. It's my co-counsel's as well."

"That's not fair," protested Martha.

Lincoln shrugged. "This sort of situation happens in trials from time to time. Remember, the whole reason Judge Treat appointed me as separate counsel for Archibald is that he decided the two brothers' positions in the case might diverge. So I can hardly complain now that Conkling might make arguments not in Archibald's best interests."

"Perhaps," said Martha, "William directed the sheriff to Fisher's remains because he knew Archibald was going to confess. William thought he was about to be in the clear."

"But how would William know what Archibald was planning to do?" I asked. "They've been jailed separately for weeks now."

"William must have conveyed a message to him," said Martha, "a direction that he confess. An order. Passed along by Henry, I imagine."

"Has Henry come by to visit Archibald at the jail cell before today?" I asked Martha.

"I haven't noticed."

"Still, what you're saying makes sense." I turned to Lincoln. "Go tell William to leave Archibald alone. Big Red and the sheriff agreed not to question Archibald further, and you warned Henry away. But Martha's right—William's the one in charge."

"I suppose I can speak with Conkling about it," said Lincoln doubtfully.

"But you just said yourself that Conkling's trying to put the blame on Archibald. He's not going to help. You need to warn off William yourself."

"I can't," said Lincoln. "He has his own counsel. It would be against the court rules for me to speak with him directly."

"But surely those rules don't prevent you from protecting your own client," I said, frustrated with Lincoln's rigid stance.

"They're the rules. As a member of the bar, I'm pledged to follow them." Lincoln looked into my eyes for a moment. "It's hard not to admire Archibald's loyalty to his older brothers, for all they mistreat him. But the fact is something took place among the three Trailor brothers and Fisher the night of the gala at the American House. Fisher isn't around to tell us what happened, and none of the Trailors are going to tell us the truth, at least not the whole truth. If the two of you want to help Archibald, you'll try to find me a witness who saw what actually happened that night."

I realized I hadn't told Lincoln about Miss Flannery's tale of seeing William and Henry Trailor working in concert on the night of the murder. I did so now, although I left out the circumstances in which she had related the story to me.

"And who was the witness who told you all this?" Lincoln asked when I had finished.

"A woman named Rose Flannery. She's staying at the American House, with her cousin, during the legislative term."

"Would she make a credible witness in front of the jury?"

"I find her most stirring."

Martha chortled. I gave her an elbow to the ribs.

"It could be a very helpful story," said Lincoln, "depending on how the prosecution's evidence comes in. Can you tell her to be ready to testify on Tuesday? That's when I'd want to call her."

"Absolutely," I said, happy to have an excuse to call upon Miss Flannery again so soon.

We had reached the edge of the capitol square, and we were about to part when we saw the bulky figure of Simeon Francis hurrying toward us across the muddy construction site and waving his arms frantically. He was shouting something at Lincoln, the same phrase over and over again. Eventually I understood the words: "Is it true?"

"Is what true?" asked Lincoln, smiling, when Simeon finally reached us.

"That you've moved the gold *here.* To the Springfield State Bank." Simeon pointed at the ornate front of the bank building, opposite us.

Lincoln grinned.

"What?" I exclaimed.

"You were right on one account the other day, Speed," he said. "I needed an insurance policy. This was it."

"But the papers have been filled with stories about the shipment to Chicago," said Martha.

"You misled me, Lincoln," said Simeon, looking aggrieved.

"And me too," I added.

"I didn't have a choice," said Lincoln unapologetically. "Only a small handful of men could know the truth. That shipment was always going to be a huge target for thieves. We decided early on we'd put out the word it was heading to Chicago. Even told the other members of the legislature it was the plan."

"Three separate stagecoaches along the Chicago road were attacked yesterday by banditti," said Simeon. "Several travelers have arrived here in town this morning with similar reports."

Lincoln nodded. "But no one was injured. We gave instructions to all the stage drivers that they should consent freely to boarding and a search." He turned to me. "That's why I was out of town yesterday. I wanted to oversee that aspect myself."

"It was all a ruse?"

"Exactly," said Lincoln. "We told enough people 'in confidence' that we felt certain word would spread about the gold being on the Chicago road yesterday. Meanwhile, early yesterday morning, Belmont's men loaded the trunk carrying the gold into a stage across the river from St. Louis in Alton. They traveled dressed like merchants, ready-made shoe salesman. And atop the gold in the trunk was a layer of ready-made shoes, just in case anyone forced them to open it. The stage arrived in Springfield as scheduled in the middle of the night, and the men took the trunk and moved it into the bank's vault. Where it safely rests."

"Amazing," said Martha, her eyes wide.

"And now, the State Bank can resume its activity," continued Lincoln. "I'm going to persuade the committee in the legislature to get work on the canal restarted right away. That's the only path to long-term prosperity for the state."

"You could have trusted me," I said to Lincoln, feeling a little hard done by.

"We didn't trust anyone," said Lincoln. "And the events on

the Chicago road yesterday prove we were right not to. If you'll excuse me, I'm due to meet up with Belmont and the banking committee at this very hour. We've got to explain to them what happened. They're going to be madder than a nest of hornets, but I'll make no apology. I was charged with fixing the banking crisis, and it's just what we've done." And he walked off, a lop-sided smile of satisfaction spread wide across his face.

Chapter 27

As I lay in bed that evening, I thought again about the deception Lincoln and Belmont had pulled off regarding the gold shipment. I felt irked with Lincoln; he should have trusted me with their true plans. But as I turned the situation over in my mind, I realized I had been part of spreading the false story. I didn't have a perfect memory of the evening with Rose, but she'd said something about needing to know about the shipment for her family's contracting business. She'd get the good word, along with the rest of the state, that the gold had arrived safely and that canal work would soon be resuming.

In the middle of the night, I awoke with a start and sat up straight in bed. What if Miss Flannery's interest in the shipment was nefarious? I wondered. What if she was allied with one of the banditti gangs intent on its theft? Beside me in our bed, Lincoln gave a loud snore and turned over, mumbling to himself. I lay back down, resolving to seek out Miss Flannery first thing in the morning.

I took breakfast at sunrise and proceeded directly to the American House. Major Iles was at his usual stand.

"Is Miss Flannery still in residence?" I asked straightaway.

"Afraid she was running off without leaving her address?"

"I have a message to convey, from Lincoln. Will you send up my compliments?"

Iles handed my card to his boy, who hurried with it up the staircase. Then I waited, increasingly impatient, trying to avoid Iles's knowing, growing grin.

Ten minutes later, Rose swept down the stairs, looking more beautiful than ever. My heart did a flip, and I came forward to give her my hand.

"This is early, Mr. Speed," she began.

I flushed. "Normally I would have waited a few days after . . . a few days after our previous visit, but I had a matter of some importance to discuss."

"I meant it was early in the morning for a visit," Rose countered, light playing behind her eyes. Behind me, Iles chortled. "I was barely finished with my toilet." She indicated her freshly scrubbed face and carefully brushed hair.

I drew Rose a couple of steps away, where we could speak in confidence. She gestured for me to continue, but suddenly I was at a loss for how to proceed. "Yes?" she prompted, after an uncomfortable moment.

"I wanted to see if you were true," I blurted out.

She took a half step back. "What kind of question is that?"

"Er—that wasn't what I meant to say. I wanted to see if what you *said* was true. About observing the Trailor brothers that night. But of course it was true. Why would you have told me otherwise? What I meant was, I wanted to see if you would be willing to say it in court. I've talked to Mr. Lincoln, and he says your testimony could be very important in getting Archibald free. Which is very important to me. So that's what I came to ask you about."

"It must be very important to you to come by before breakfast."

"I've already had breakfast, but yes, it is."

She giggled. I colored deeply.

"I'm usually more articulate, but around you, Miss Flannery, I seem to lose myself."

"You're very earnest," she said.

"Is that bad? As far as you're concerned, I mean."

"It doesn't suit most men." She paused and contemplated me frankly. "But it does you."

I took a deep breath. "I'm glad to hear it. And you'll be glad to know, I think, that the bank rescue plan worked. Lincoln and Belmont transferred the gold successfully the other night. To the bank here in Springfield, not the Chicago branch. Which was a complete surprise to me, like everyone else. But at least it's there safely, and now the canal work can resume. I believed you'd want to know, at once."

"I heard the news last night."

I tried but failed to read her expression.

"What is it?" she asked, catching me.

"Were you glad to hear it? That the gold transfer had been successful."

"I was very happy to hear the canal work would be resuming, of course. But at the same time a little bit disappointed."

"Oh?"

"Because it means we'll be leaving Springfield soon." She stared deeply into my eyes, and my heart surged.

"But not before you testify at the trial," I said.

"But not before the trial." She took my hands in hers and squeezed them. "Now if you'll excuse me, Patrick and I have a few matters to attend this morning."

I could still feel the warm, electric touch of her hands on mine as she walked away. I veritably skipped out of the hotel. I was most of the way back to my store when I glanced over at the capitol and thought about William Trailor, awaiting trial in its basement. I still believed William had been behind Archibald's attempt to confess to sole responsibility yesterday and that he might try again. But Lincoln had said we couldn't warn him off without involving his lawyer Conkling.

A moment later, I corrected myself. Lincoln had said *he* couldn't contact him. And he'd said so with a peculiar look on his face. I turned on my heels and headed straight for the capitol steps, nearly colliding with Big Red May, who was walking through the debris-strewn construction site surrounding the new building.

Inside, I wandered around until I found stairs leading down to the basement. The lower level, dank and musty, consisted of a warren of dark storage areas. There were occasional windows cut high into the walls that allowed slivers of light from outside to filter in. The jail cell was not immediately in evidence.

"Hello?" I shouted. "Trailor?"

"Who comes?" returned a weak voice.

Following the sound, I wound through several passageways and ultimately came upon a modest-sized space cut into an outer corner of the basement. It was plain at once that the room hadn't been completed. The stone-and-dirt sides of the room were jagged and unfinished. The rest of the room was enclosed by crude wooden walls and a set of iron bars running from floor to ceiling.

William Trailor squinted out through the bars in the dim light. His appearance was much changed from the haughty figure he'd previously cut. His face was smeared with dirt and grime. Instead of an immaculate frockcoat, he wore a stained work smock and jeans with worn and wrinkled knees. His fingers were similarly crusted with dirt.

"Oh, it's you, Speed," Trailor said as he belatedly recognized me. "What do you want?"

"To see a mole's life, for one." I gazed around his cell. "You should have stayed in the sheriff's backyard. At least you had fresh air to breathe there. And well water for washing." I glanced again at his unclean hands, and he quickly thrust them behind his back, not wanting me to dwell on his miserable condition.

"I've complained to the sheriff and mayor, but they've refused to move me. And they've had an easy time ignoring me, stashed away down here." He kicked at a pile of loose dirt on the floor. "Soon enough, though, I'll have the chance to prove my innocence. Tell me, is it Saturday?"

"That's right."

"Good. Two days until trial starts. Which means no more than five until I'm finally freed from this pit of hell."

"You're awfully confident in the outcome of the trial."

Trailor managed a grin.

"Which is the other thing I've come about. Stay away from your brother Archibald."

He gave a harsh laugh and gestured at the bars between us. "As if I have a choice."

I shook my head. "I'm sure you have a way of getting messages to him. I imagine you heard he tried to confess yesterday, before Lincoln and I stopped him. I know you put him up to it. Don't do it again."

William Trailor's face displayed neither surprise nor anger. Instead he said, in his usual supercilious tone, "You've no right to tell me what to do."

"I have every right to protect Archibald. You know better than anyone, he's got no ability to protect himself from you."

"That's what makes him an ideal younger brother," said Trailor with a sneer.

"Stay clear of him."

"I'll win in the end."

"I wouldn't be so confident."

"I always win," he repeated. "Now, leave. I've business to attend to, and the least you can do is afford me privacy while I do it." Trailor gestured over his shoulder at a crude metal chamber pot pushed against the wall. I was about to leave when I saw what was next to the pot: the trunk from the Edwards hayloft.

"How'd you get that in here?" I asked, pointing.

"Not that it's any of your concern," he replied, "but the mayor finally agreed to let me have it. So I would have appropriate clothes during my period of confinement in this hole." He gestured at his dirt-covered uniform. "I have my smart clothes stored inside for safekeeping. I want to look my best when I'm a free man next week. Now, I insist on privacy." He turned his back on me and walked stiffly toward the chamber pot, and I left him to it.

Back outside, I blinked against the bright sun. I couldn't last two hours in such dark, depressing conditions, I thought, to say nothing of the two weeks William Trailor would have endured by the time trial arrived. He was strong-willed; I would give the man that.

"Joshua!"

My sister was striding toward me across the green. At her side was a small, slight boy, surely not more than eight or nine years of age, his little face all but obscured by a mass of curly brown hair. Martha's fresh face was alive with excitement.

"I've found a witness for Archibald!"

"Where?"

"Right here." She patted the boy's head, and he rewarded her with a shy smile. "I'm bringing him to Mr. Lincoln right now. Come along. You won't want to miss what he has to say."

Inside Hoffman's Row, we found Lincoln at his table, scrawling away. He looked up and saw the boy at Martha's side. "Who's this?"

"This," said Martha, "is the witness you've been looking for. Wait till you hear what he saw on the night of the gala." She gave the boy a gentle push on his back, and he started walking uncertainly toward the lawyer.

Lincoln got down on one knee and beckoned the boy over. Even kneeling, Lincoln towered over the child.

"What's your name, son?" Lincoln asked, a kindly expression on his face.

"Bill."

"I'm Abe. Nice to meet you." Lincoln reached out his right hand, and the boy rested both of his on it. "Do you have a last name?"

The boy nodded.

"Well, what is it, son?"

"Davidson." The boy drew out his surname carefully, pronouncing each separate syllable as if it were its own word.

"I knew I recognized you!" exclaimed Lincoln. "You're one of Caleb Davidson's boys."

The boy nodded again.

"Now, what is it you told Miss Speed?"

"I ain't in trouble?" the boy asked. He glanced anxiously over his shoulder at Martha.

"Not at all," said Martha. "Just tell these men what you told me earlier. They're trying to help a good, kind person who is in a spot of trouble. He needs our help."

The boy nodded seriously. "All right."

"What'd you tell Miss Speed earlier?" prompted Lincoln softly.

"I was herding my pa's cattle, like I always do. He calls me his 'chief herdsman.'" Bill pronounced this last phrase carefully, as if it had been the subject of much practice, and he gave a tentative smile. Lincoln broke into a broad grin.

"Does your pa have a large drove of cattle?" asked Lincoln.

"Near on thirty head," said the boy. "I knowed every animal in his drove. Knowed who Pa bought 'em from and when they joined the herd. And I give them each names, my own names, cuz I wanna make sure I don't lose none of them. That would make Pa angry."

"Who helps you with the herding?" I asked.

"No one. Just me."

"And how do you herd such a large drove all by yourself?" I asked.

"By riding old Ned." The boy looked at me like I was slow.

"But you can't possibly be large enough to even climb aboard a horse by yourself."

The boy bobbed his head. "I ain't. My pa, he sits me up on top of old Ned every morning. And he ties me to the saddle, so I won't go nowhere. And my ma puts my dinner in my pocket and then Pa slaps Ned on the rear and off we go. I ain't got no reason to get down till the end of the day."

"You sound like quite a capable young man," said Lincoln.

The boy nodded seriously again.

"You were telling me, Bill," said Martha, "about what you saw out by the millpond, on the evening of the full moon."

"Yes, ma'am." He turned back to Lincoln and waited.

"Go ahead, son."

"The sun was going down, and Ned and I was herding our cattle. It was time for 'em to get back inside our paddock so Pa could water 'em. Ned, he's a good herder, always darting after any of our herd that bolts. Ned darts so quick, can't nobody else stay atop him. But it ain't hard for me. I just lean forward and grab ahold of his neck and we dart together, see?"

Lincoln looked up briefly at me, amusement playing in his eyes, and then back at Bill. "Go on," he prompted.

"The sun was going down and we're getting the drove near to the paddock, and suddenly Bessie, she makes a run for it. She's a naughty girl, always making trouble for Ma in the mornings when it's milking time. She thought Ned and I ain't paying attention to her, and so she goes and takes off. But I notice right away, and Ned notices right after me, and so once we make sure we got the rest of 'em inside, we turn and dart after Bessie."

The boy swallowed, and Lincoln nodded gently for him to continue.

"She got a head start, but we're on the chase, and 'course we can run much faster than her. She's heading to the old millpond for some reason. Bessie gets crazy ideas into her head. So she's most of the way to the millpond when we finally catch up to her, and Ned rounds on her and gets her walking back toward our pasture. It's nearly dusk now, so we gotta hurry." He paused. "And that's when I seen 'em."

"Seen whom?" asked Lincoln.

"There were three of them. Three men, in a clearing. They was fighting with each other. Only, they wasn't fighting with each other."

"What do you mean?"

"They was fighting, but they wasn't."

"You're not making any sense," I protested.

"Joshua!" said my sister sharply. "Let Bill tell his story. You're doing great, honey," she added, coming forward and running her fingers through his unruly hair. "Do you have older brothers or sisters who give you trouble?"

"My big brother Jack's an ass," said Bill. "At least, that's what Pa says."

"Exactly! My big brother can be an ass, too. You just ignore him and go ahead and tell Mr. Lincoln what you saw."

Bill looked again at Lincoln. "They was fighting," he said slowly, his jaw tight, his eyes squinted, and his fists clenched, visibly straining to make the lawyer grasp his meaning. "Only, they wasn't fighting. Not really. Do you understand?"

"Are you saying they were only *pretending* to fight?" asked Lincoln.

The boy's face relaxed all at once, and he blew his hair out of his eyes. "Right!"

"And you told me," said Martha, "you specifically remembered this was on the night of the full moon, isn't that right?"

The boy nodded. "I gotta keep track of the moon, cuz the herd acts different with different moons. Specially with a full moon. That might of been what made Bessie go wild to begin with."

Lincoln and Martha exchanged glances.

"Now, these three men you saw," said Lincoln. "What did they look like?"

"Dunno. They were 'bout as old as my pa, but with more hair on their head. Pa ain't got any."

"I reckon he doesn't," said Lincoln, smiling. "Did they look like one another? Like they could be brothers?"

The boy shrugged. "I s'pose." He considered. "Two of them, definitely, could have been brothers. I don't know about the other one, though."

"William, Henry, and Archibald Trailor," said my sister with conviction. "With Archibald being much younger, so he doesn't look as much like his older brothers. It has to be them. And the fact they were pretending to fight in the clearing at dusk means they never intended to hurt Fisher. It was all going to be some sort of joke."

"The one who didn't look like the other two," said Lincoln, turning back to Bill, "was he younger than them?"

Bill screwed up his face with concentration. "Dunno. Maybe. He was kinda funny-looking."

"Funny-looking how?"

"Just . . . funny-looking."

"Flynn Fisher!" said my sister. "Fisher, with his head leaning to the side. It was William and Henry and Fisher. Out by the millpond. Archibald had nothing to do with it. I told you it proved his innocence."

"It could mean a hundred other things," I said. "Besides, how would Lincoln prove it, even if it's what you say? Surely our friend here is too young to testify from the witness chair."

Martha started to speak in Bill's defense, but Lincoln, still kneeling in front of the boy, held up his hand. "Do you think, Bill," said Lincoln, "you could tell me your story again in a couple of days? There'd be a few more people listening, but all you'd have to do is tell me the same story, like you have just now."

The boy considered this at some length and asked, "Where? Here?"

"Downstairs. Come with me and we'll take a look."

Lincoln stood up, leaned over far sideways, and took the boy by the hand. We could hear them conversing amiably as they walked down the stairs to the temporary courtroom on the first floor beneath us.

"How did you find him?" I asked Martha.

"It took a lot of effort," she said, smiling with pride. "Lincoln said we needed to find a witness who saw what happened the night of the murder. So I walked the route from Ransdell's out to the millpond, to see what the Trailor brothers would have seen on the way out and, more to the point, who might have seen them. I passed by a few farms and I inquired at each one, but I couldn't find anyone who had seen anything that night. Finally, late in the afternoon, I spotted Bill on his horse, wrangling his herd, just like he described. He's quite amazing at it for such a young boy.

"Anyway, I waved at him, but he was so intent on his task that he wouldn't stop to talk. I followed him, keeping up as best I could, and when he got his drove to his family's paddock, I helped him swing the gate shut after them. Only then would he answer my questions." She smiled at the memory.

Lincoln and Bill were coming down the hallway back to the office. "We've decided," said Lincoln, "that Bill is willing to tell me his story again, even if there're a few more people around to hear it. Isn't that right, son?"

Bill nodded seriously.

"Let's shake on it." Lincoln bent down and took Bill's right hand in his own, and they shook hands vigorously.

Lincoln straightened up and glanced at Martha. "Very well done, Miss Speed. Can I ask you to take Bill back home before his ma starts to worry? And see if you can't convince Mr. Davidson to spare his son for a few hours on Tuesday. You tell him I haven't forgotten the service I did him a few years back, when he had a calf that got itself crippled. Tell him we'll be square if he lets me borrow his chief herdsman."

Chapter 28

Before I had even left my bedroom on Monday morning, I could tell from the noise rising from the street that the crowds for the first day of trial would be immense. Perched on the edge of the frontier with its 2,500 residents, Springfield harbored none of the diversions that larger, more established cities featured. There were no museums, no theater halls, no traveling circuses. There were, to be sure, a wide variety of taverns and groceries, happy to dispense harsh alcohol to anyone with a few pennies in his pocket. But citizens hoping to find entertainment that did not arrive in a bottle or cask were destined to be disappointed. Except when the circuit court was in session to adjudicate the county's legal disputes. Then, the entire human condition, comedy and tragedy alike, was on display and free for all to watch.

Lincoln had departed before the crack of dawn, so I dressed alone in our bedroom and headed down the back stairs. Fifth Street was thronged with people as I pushed my way toward Hoffman's Row. Several enterprising tavernkeepers had already put out their stalls, selling food and liquid refreshment from pull carts, and they were doing a brisk business. Between transactions, the competing sellers hawked their wares at the tops of their voices, their call-and-response shouts mingling with the excited chattering of the ordinary citizens streaming toward the courtroom to produce a great swell of noise and excitement.

I walked past several of the vagrants who had taken part in the search for Flynn Fisher when he'd first been reported missing. The subsequent events had turned these men into something approaching legends, at least in their own minds, and I heard two or three declaiming on their heroic quests with a grandiosity that would have made the poet Homer proud.

As I walked through the carnival-like atmosphere, I realized the fact that Fisher had been a virtual unknown before his murder made the trial of his accused killers an especially satisfying entertainment. Fisher had no weeping relatives on whom one had to expend pity. No one needed to pretend to be sorry for Fisher's demise. Instead, it was possible to revel in the excitement of the trial, to speculate on the motives of the Trailor brothers for turning on one another, without misgiving. Fisher's sorry life and untimely death amounted to nothing more than the handful of couplets comprising the Prologue in *Romeo and Juliet*, to be pronounced by the Chorus as the audience settled into position. It was mere prelude to the actual drama everyone had come to watch.

Sheriff Hutchason stood at the door to the courtroom, and he nodded as I approached. "How early did you arrive?" I asked.

"Stoke of seven. There must have been fifty people gathered already to get one of the seats. When I told them there was space only for thirty inside, I thought fistfights were going to break out. One actually did. Lincoln asked me to save a few seats. Go on in. There's room for you in the back."

Once I squeezed past Hutchason's bulky frame, I saw Martha waving me over from the last row of the gallery. Walking toward her, I passed Mary Todd and Matilda Edwards, sitting next to each other on the other side of the room. Miss Todd and I shared a warm exchange, and I found myself pleased with our newfound ease.

A few steps further along, I squeezed past Big Red May.

When he saw me, he grabbed my arm. "I told you the people were eager to see justice done."

"Too eager."

Big Red shook his head vigorously. "The Trailor brothers are getting their day in court." He gestured around the crowded room, alive with excited conversation. "It's all they're due. And the people know they have a mayor working hard to protect them. Again, what they're due."

He smiled sanctimoniously, and I shook free of him and went to join my sister.

"How's Lincoln feeling about Archibald's case?" Martha asked as I settled in beside her.

"Anxious. The little boy you found will help, and Lincoln has a few other lead balls to shoot. But Henry's confession and accusation against his brothers is damning. It's hard to get around, if the jury believes him. So the cross-examination of Henry is going to be crucial. That's what Lincoln spent most of the weekend preparing for."

The court clerk Matheny shouted for order as Judge Treat ascended the low platform serving as his bench in the temporary courtroom. To his left was a jumble of six chairs, currently empty, on which the twelve gentlemen of the jury would squeeze, two to a chair. Pulling coolly on his pipe, the judge gazed out at the packed courtroom and the jostling crowd on the street, which was waiting impatiently to observe the proceedings through the wide-open windows.

Archibald and William Trailor were led into the courtroom by Sheriff Hutchason. Each brother's hands were bound in front of him, but the similarity of appearance ended there. William had cleaned up for trial. He'd exchanged the dirty work shirt and jeans I'd last seen him in for his usual shiny frockcoat and trousers. His face was newly shaven, his hands washed, and his hair was combed back slickly from his high-peaked forehead.

Archibald, meanwhile, looked like the lanky, scruffy carpenter he'd been before Fisher's disappearance had thrust him unwillingly into the center of the stage. His smock was dirty and his face fringed by untamed whiskers.

Henry Trailor was absent. As a witness, he was not permitted to attend the proceedings until his time to testify.

Archibald looked around the gallery as he walked to the front of the courtroom, and when he spied Martha and me, he gave a little wave, which both of us returned. I remembered the sight of his face when he'd ridden back to find me, crippled, in the midst of the Sudden Change, and a renewed feeling of gratitude flooded my body. I could only hope Lincoln's efforts on his behalf would help repay the debt I owed him.

A hush fell over the crowd as the defendants took their seats and the judge commanded counsel to stand. Lincoln, Conkling, and Lamborn all rose. In the close quarters of the crowded courtroom, they made for an odd trio, the towering Lincoln sandwiched between the slight Conkling and the thick-chested Lamborn.

"The case is the People against Trailor and Trailor," announced the judge. "Each defendant is charged with murder with malice aforethought. Does counsel have any remarks before we select the jury?"

To my surprise, it was Conkling who spoke in his boyish squeak. "On behalf of the defendant William Trailor, Your Honor, we have a few preliminary motions."

"Will you be presenting the motions in Latin or English, Mr. Conkling?" asked the judge, sucking on his pipe with a cruel sneer. Those members of the audience who had witnessed Conkling's misadventures during the bail hearing laughed knowingly.

Conkling colored. "Your Honor, I—"

"There's no need to reply, Conkling. Get on with it."

Conkling proceeded to raise a series of objections to various pieces of evidence he expected the prosecution to use. The objections quickly came to follow a common path: Conkling stood and laid out the objection, gesticulating wildly with his arms to punctuate his argument; Lamborn rose and forcefully refuted the objection; and then the judge denied the objection with a few terse remarks. But there was always another one on the tip of Conkling's tongue. The gallery began to rustle impatiently.

"What's Conkling doing?" Martha whispered to me as the Princeton-educated lawyer rose to present his fifth argument, seemingly undaunted by the summary denial of his first four. "It's as if he's trying to stall. Maybe he didn't have time to finish his preparation."

"He's had several weeks." I peered through the crowd to glimpse the expression on William Trailor's face. William was watching his lawyer with a scowl and hardened eyes. But I thought I detected a note of satisfaction behind his mask. "I wager he's doing it to convince William he's going to be aggressive in pleading his case. And it may be working, at least as far as his client is concerned."

A fundamental change had come over Conkling. The hesitant, prim schoolboy had disappeared and he'd been replaced, if not by a silver-tongued advocate, then at least by a lean, wiry grappler willing to go down flailing.

Finally, after a half-dozen rejected motions, Conkling sensed he had exhausted the judge's patience, and he desisted from further argument. William Trailor patted his shoulder as he returned to his side.

The judge turned to Lincoln. "Do you have any motions for the Court's consideration, Mr. Lincoln, before we dig into the jury box?"

"I don't think there's any left after Brother Conkling's performance," replied Lincoln from his seat. "We can all agree his Professor Cicero would be proud." The judge put down his pipe and burst out laughing.

A large wooden box containing the names of eligible jurors was perched on the edge of the judge's table. The clerk Matheny drew the names of the veniremen one by one, and each was located by a series of shouts that spread through the thronging crowd. The three lawyers followed the pattern they had previously adopted: Conkling was spirited and long-winded in questioning the potential jurors for bias; Lamborn was curt and forceful; and Lincoln was good-humored, almost casual.

"Don't you think Mr. Lincoln should be more active in querying the jurors?" Martha asked after Lincoln, leaning back in his chair, had acquiesced to the seating of a juror with a casual wave of his hand, saying merely, "I reckon he'll do just fine."

"I'm not sure how much more there is to ask, not with the way Conkling is going after each of them," I replied.

Martha frowned. While she often lent a hand with Lincoln's more puzzling cases, she seemed particularly invested in Archibald's cause. I scrutinized her face but could not divine her thoughts.

At length the jury was seated, and Lamborn called the prosecution's first witness. Sheriff Hutchason lumbered to the witness chair.

"You are the sheriff of Sangamon County?" began Lamborn.

"I am."

"And it was your somber duty to recover the remains of the deceased?"

"It was."

"Tell the gentlemen what you found."

Hutchason turned to the jury and began his narration. He kept it short and to the point, leaving out the many false starts that had characterized the search for Flynn Fisher, including the wild pillaging of every cellar and outbuilding instigated by Big Red, as well as the mob's frenzied search near Hickox's millpond and the destruction of Justice Smith's precious dam. Instead, Hutchason picked up his story on the rainy morning I had accompanied him on horseback to the other side of the millpond.

Hutchason inventoried his finds that day for the jury: a tattered half-coat with a military insignia, a pair of weathered military boots, a dirty fur hat, the mourning ring, and assorted bones. Hutchason opened a case and drew out the clothing and ring for inspection by the jury. Several men in the gallery rose partway to their feet to try to inspect the relics; in turn, angry voices from the street outside shouted for them to sit down so as not to obstruct the view.

The court called for order. Eventually it was restored, and Hutchason testified that the innkeeper Ransdell and three other persons had identified the clothing as that worn by Fisher when he'd last been seen. The sheriff explained that he had reburied the physical remains as a mark of decency.

With that, Lamborn thanked the witness and sat. The judge called for cross-examination. Lincoln and Conkling rose simultaneously and then looked askance at each other.

"You forgot to agree on an order of examination?" said the judge, his eyebrows raised. "That's an inauspicious start for the defense." Martha squirmed beside me. "Perhaps the clerk can supply lots to draw."

"There's no need," said Conkling. "Brother Lincoln can have the first go at the sheriff. I'll take the initial turn next time."

"Good morning, Sheriff," began Lincoln, his angular figure topped by his stovepipe hat towering over the hushed courtroom like a church steeple against a flat plain.

"Morning."

"You have identified the deceased in this case as a Mr. Flynn Fisher, is that right?"

"Correct."

"Did you ever encounter Fisher during the course of his life?"

"I don't believe so."

"And the remains you found amounted to some scattered bones and several articles of clothing?"

"That's right. I reckon the wolves ate the rest. It was a harsh winter for them, between the Sudden Change and the long frost."

Several of the farmers on the jury nodded at this. There had been more reports than usual over the past winter of livestock falling victim to the fearsome predators. The legislature had, at its most recent session, approved an increase of the bounty payment for hunters turning in wolf scalps, but the animals had largely outwitted their human pursuers. No one had any real idea how many wolves still prowled the prairies surrounding Springfield; estimates ranged from dozens to tens of thousands.

"I need to ask about the bones you found," Lincoln was continuing. "Which bones were they? Did you find the skull?"

"I did not."

"Legs? Arms? Ribs?" A few of the ladies present in the courtroom stifled gasps at Lincoln's indelicate questioning.

"None of those—not intact, anyway. I think perhaps one or two were ribs, and there was part of a leg bone; lower leg, if I'm not mistaken."

"Well, what was the largest bone you found?"

"It was" —the sheriff cast his mind back—"not larger than a foot, I'd say. Maybe not longer than nine inches. A fragment."

"Was it actually a foot? I mean, that part of the body, not the unit of measure?"

"I don't think so."

"Then what part of the body did it belong to?"

"One of the legs would be my best guess. The wolves had greatly ravaged the remains, I'm afraid."

"So for all you know, the bones you found could have been those of a horse or cow, or even a large feral hog, rather than human bones?"

"I've never seen a horse wearing these," replied the sheriff, holding up Fisher's boots. "Have you?"

Lincoln joined in the laughter sweeping through the room.

When it had died away, the sheriff added, "No, I'm quite certain the bones I found were human." Having seen them myself that gloomy morning, so was I. Lincoln was doing his job by trying to sow doubt with the jury, but I was skeptical the argument that Fisher hadn't been killed would, in the end, prove to be a winning one.

"Have I ever told you, Sheriff," continued Lincoln, "about the man who couldn't shoot a squirrel from ten feet?"

A faint smile came to Hutchason's lips. Like many of the men present, he'd heard his share of Lincoln's fairy tales. I glanced over at Lamborn, but the prosecutor showed no sign of objecting. Even in the midst of a trial, there was little choice but to play along. Lincoln would be determined to make his point one way or another.

"I don't think so," the sheriff replied.

"I heard it a good while ago," continued Lincoln, nodding happily to himself. "Back when I lived in New Salem. I wager it's true. If it's not, well, shame on me. It'll serve either way." Casting a glance around the rapt courtroom, Lincoln nodded to himself, crossed his arms, and gave a crooked smile. A weaver of stories, fully in his element.

"It goes like this. A man is walking along in the woods, hunting varmint. He's been at it all day with no luck. Nothing to shoot. Finally, he sees a squirrel on a tree trunk, maybe thirty, forty feet distant. At last! So he shoulders his rifle, aims, and *bang*, the gun goes off. The man's knocked back a bit by the force of the gunpowder, but when he recovers his balance, he looks and the squirrel is still there."

Lincoln glanced at the sheriff. "Are you with me so far?"

Hutchason nodded.

"Good. So my hunter, he walks a little closer, loads in a new wad and a new ball, takes aim again, and fires. *Bang.* Looks up and it's still there. Again gets closer. He fancies himself a good shot, and he's getting angry. Can't be more than fifteen feet away now. No way he can miss. *Bang.* It's still there. Closer still, within ten feet. *Bang.* He can't believe it. The squirrel is still there on the tree trunk, right in front of him."

The gallery and the jury alike were alive with whispered speculation about how the tale would end.

"By now," Lincoln continued, "the man is right next to the tree. Can't even shoulder his gun to shoot it because the barrel would knock into the trunk. The squirrel's right there in front of him on the tree trunk, and the man reaches out his hand to touch the critter, because it ain't moving more than an inch or two as he looks at it, even with him being so close. He reaches for it, and—" Lincoln came to a dramatic pause. "It's not there.

"Now, Sheriff, what do you reckon was going on?"

Hutchason shook his head. From the back corner of the courtroom, a voice shouted, "A louse!"

Lincoln swung around with a smile. "I guess I told *you* this one before, Jeb. I'm mighty grateful you didn't spoil it before now." He turned back to Hutchason.

"The man drops his gun and feels all around the tree with both hands, but he can't touch the squirrel. He still sees it, right there in front of him, but he can't touch it. He begins to fear he's going mad. Eventually he draws back his hands and rubs his eyes. In the process, he dislodges the louse that had crawled out of his hair and attached itself to his eyelashes. *And the squirrel disappears.*"

Shouts of laughter bounced around the room. "Sometimes," Lincoln said over the outcry, "we see things as we want to see them, rather than things as they are. Would you agree with that, Sheriff?"

Lincoln resumed his seat before the lawman could answer.

CHAPTER 29

Conkling's examination was unmemorable by comparison, and the sheriff was soon excused from the witness chair. The judge called for lunch, and the crowd scattered on the village green to eat and drink and swap opinions about the morning's proceedings. Then the clerk bellowed that court was resuming, and the gallery resumed their places.

"For our next witness," announced Lamborn, as the spectators were still quieting down, "the People call Henry Trailor."

The entire crowd took in its breath and stared as the accusing brother entered the courtroom and wound his way through the cluttered gallery. Henry Trailor wore a blue-jeans suit and a broad scowl. If he felt any remorse at the prospect of condemning his brothers to the gallows, neither his face nor his bearing gave any sign of it.

Henry settled into the witness chair. His coal-black eyes roamed the courtroom, looking at everyone except his brothers, who, in the cramped surroundings, were staring at him intently from a distance of less than five feet. The room was utterly silent. It was as if everyone had stopped breathing at the sudden arrival of the long-awaited fraternal confrontation.

"State your name, please," began Lamborn.

Henry straightened his back and thrust his potbelly forward. "Henry Trailor."

"Your occupation."

"Farmer. And builder."

"And you are the brother of the accused, William and Archibald Trailor?" Lamborn gestured at each defendant as he called their names, but Henry Trailor's gaze remained fixed on his questioner.

"I am."

"Did you know a man named Flynn Fisher?"

"Yes."

"Who was he?"

"An acquaintance of my older brother William's. They'd served together near Detroit in the late war against Great Britain. In the past couple of years, Fisher had begun to work as a contractor on the canal. William suggested we all go into business together. He explained his idea to me, and it sounded like a good one."

"What happened to your business venture?"

"Our plan didn't come out like we hoped." Henry turned to the jury and added, "Once the Canal Board ran out of money, nothing seemed to move forward." Many of the jurors bobbed their heads with comprehension. The failure of the state's internal improvements scheme and its widespread effects were well known to everyone present.

Attorney General Lamborn deftly took Henry Trailor through the story I'd heard him confess to Big Red: Fisher's request to borrow 100 dollars from William before their scheme had realized any profits; his threats when William refused the loan; William finding Archibald and Henry on the night of the gala at the American House to tell them that something had to be done.

"What happened then?" asked Lamborn. The gallery was quiet, listening carefully.

"William said we should teach Fisher a lesson for trying to betray us, and Archibald agreed right away. So we all went to the inn where Fisher was staying and said we wanted a word. He was getting ready for bed, but he finally agreed to come outside."

"Did the four of you talk outside the inn?"

"We started to, but there were a few persons about, and William was nervous they might be listening. He suggested we all head out of town, towards an old millpond, where we could talk without being overheard."

"Before we go further down that path, can you explain the relationship between William and Archibald?"

"William's the oldest. He's used to being in charge. And Archibald is used to doing what he's told. He's illit—he's less educated, less schooled, than we are."

There was a murmuring in the courtroom, over which Lamborn said, "What happened when you got to the millpond?"

"William told Fisher we wouldn't stand for his treachery. Fisher said he'd done nothing wrong. They went back and forth like that for a good long while."

"And then?"

"At some point Fisher said he'd had enough, and he started walking back towards town. William told Archibald to stop him. Archibald and Fisher struggled, and then Archibald got a good hold of him. There was a discarded length of rope near us on the ground, and William told Archibald to tie Fisher to a tree, with his hands behind his back, to make sure he didn't go nowhere."

The jury and the gallery were listening to Henry Trailor's narrative with rapt attention. I strained to take the measure of his brothers. William was glaring at Henry defiantly. But Archibald had slumped down in his seat, his chin tucked to his chest and his cheeks hollow. It was almost as if he was giving up the fight to defend himself. I wished I could rush forward and give him courage, just as he had given me courage in the middle of the Sudden Change.

"What happened next?" Lamborn was asking.

"We walked a bit aways, to discuss what to do next. I suggested we let Fisher go. We'd given him a good scare. I thought that was enough. But William said we needed to do more. Said we had to shut him up for good."

"Henry's got to be lying," Martha whispered from beside me. "I'll bet he was right in the middle of the assault on Fisher."

"Maybe so," I replied, "but that's not going to help Archibald one wit. *His* guilt or innocence is at stake, not Henry's. If the jury concludes Archibald was involved in Fisher's death, the fact that his brothers were also involved doesn't lessen Archibald's guilt."

"And then?" prompted Lamborn.

"Fisher was still making noise, crying out, and William told Archibald to go make sure he couldn't shout for help. William gave Archibald a rag and told him to gag him with it. Archibald did as he was told and came back, and the three of us argued about what to do next. That's when it happened."

"What happened?"

"After Archibald had gone to gag Fisher, the noise quieted down. Soon, there was no noise at all. William went to check on him, and he came back to us, his face white as paper. 'He's dead,' is all he said."

"Dead how?"

"Suffocated. William said Archibald had pushed the rag in Fisher's mouth too far, prevented him from breathing. I went to see for myself. It was awful. His body was slumped against the trunk. Limp. Eyes goggled and face red. Like he'd been trying to get rid of the gag but failed."

A swell of emotion rushed through the courtroom and the street outside. There were angry shouts and jeers. Several men muttered loudly that the gallows would be too gentle a punishment for the Trailors, that only drawing and quartering would serve the demands of justice. Sheriff Hutchason took a protective step toward his prisoners, and he stared out at the crowd with clenched fists and a warning gaze. The judge shouted for order.

"What happened next?" continued Lamborn over the simmering crowd.

"We wanted to get out of the area as soon as we could, so we left the body under a bush there. William said he'd come back later and take care of it. Bury it somewhere, I assumed."

"Did he?"

"I don't know. I took off for my home near Bloomington that very night. I didn't want to stick around the scene of the murder, or my brothers, any longer than I had to."

My heart started beating faster. This testimony was directly contradicted by what Miss Flannery had seen: Henry and William slipping out of town together later that same night. That would make her a crucial witness, possibly enough to start the unraveling of Henry's entire tale. I tried to catch Lincoln's eye, but he was still focused on the witness.

"Finally, Mr. Trailor," Lamborn was continuing, "let me ask you this. Do you feel any remorse being here today and testifying against your brothers?"

Henry paused, and the gallery leaned forward expectantly. It was exactly what many of them would have asked had they been given the chance.

"Of course I do," Henry responded at last. "I grew up alongside William. Always idolized him as my older brother. And when Arch came along . . . William and I near as anything raised him ourselves." He swallowed and looked Lamborn straight in the eye. "But I witnessed my brothers kill a man. I didn't want to testify against them. I don't want to be here today. But when you and the mayor told me I had to . . . what else could I do?"

The crowd murmured sympathetically, and the gentlemen of the jury whispered among themselves as Lamborn took his seat. It was, I thought, an effective end to the examination. Even with the one contradiction I had spotted, I feared Henry's testimony would have a devastating effect. Archibald was in serious jeopardy.

The judge called for a short recess to allow the jury to stretch its legs. Looking around the courtroom, I saw Belmont leaning against the back wall. He nodded at me. Why was the banker still in town, I wondered, now that the gold transfer had been completed? Before I could head over to ask him, James Conkling rose for his cross-examination.

Conkling cleared his throat and adjusted his wire-rimmed glasses. "Mr. Trailor, I represent your brother William Trailor."

Henry screwed up his eyes and stared at Conkling, taking his measure. Henry nodded to himself. I guessed he'd concluded the slightly built lawyer posed little threat.

"Your testimony, I believe, is that when you all got out to the area by the millpond, Mr. Archibald Trailor restrained Mr. Fisher against a tree. Correct?"

"Yes."

"How, exactly, did he restrain him?"

"He tied his hands together behind his back, then pressed him against a tree trunk and secured him with several loops of the rope."

"And Archibald's actions prevented Mr. Fisher from moving?"

"That's right."

"If Archibald hadn't secured Fisher in place, Fisher could have simply gotten to his feet and run away, isn't that the case?"

Martha tugged at my arm and hissed, "But he testified William was the one who told Archibald to tie him up!" Lincoln had the same thought, because he shot Conkling an aggrieved glance and rose to his feet, saying, "Objection, Your Honor, I believe the testimony—"

"This is my examination," said Conkling curtly.

"Your brother counsel is right, Mr. Lincoln," said the judge, putting down his pipe. "Any questions you have, you're free to raise during your cross-questioning. The objection is overruled."

"Let me ask the question again," said Conkling. "But for the restraint imposed by Archibald, Fisher could have gotten to his feet and run, correct?"

"Correct."

"And if he had run away, he'd still be alive to this day, correct?"

"I imagine so, yes."

"Now," continued Conkling, after he'd paused to allow the testimony to sink in, "I believe your evidence is that William came to find you and Archibald on the night in question to tell you about Fisher's treachery."

"Yes," said Henry.

"At what time, in the evening, was this?"

Henry rubbed his belly while he thought. "About ten at night, I reckon. Maybe a bit later."

"Are you aware of what Archibald had been doing, earlier that same evening, before William came to get the two of you?"

"Yes, he was—"

"Objection!" shouted Lincoln, jumping to his feet. "Objection. Lack of relevance. And prejudice."

"Your Honor," replied Conkling, "the testimony is highly relevant to the facts in dispute. I intend to prove—"

"Your Honor!" cried Lincoln, glowering at Conkling. "May I be heard? In private. Before my brother spills out the subject matter under advisement."

The judge pulled on his pipe and contemplated counsel, while the gallery whispered excitedly about what fact Lincoln could be trying to keep from the jury. "Counsel may approach the bench," the judge said at last. He looked doubtfully at the tiny open space beside his perch and then at the first row of the gallery, crowded nearby. It was hard to see how the lawyers could argue the point without being overheard.

"May I suggest," said Lincoln, "that the court and counsel go upstairs to my chambers? We can have a private bench conference there."

"You truly believe the issue is of such importance, Mr. Lincoln, as to require an interruption of the proceedings?" asked the judge.

Lincoln affirmed it was. The judge reluctantly consented, and the three lawyers and the judge threaded their way through the gallery and out the door. We could hear the stairs creaking as they retired upstairs to No. 4. In the meantime, the gallery's speculation about the nature of the objection grew to a fevered roar.

"This isn't good," said Martha, taking in the scene.

"It certainly isn't. I'm sure the last thing Lincoln wanted to do was to give the evidence added attention by creating a fuss. But Conkling's maneuvered him into it." I shook my head. "And to think I believed Conkling was too passive to give Archibald an effective defense. I misjudged him severely."

"Do you know where Archibald was earlier in that evening?" Martha asked.

I nodded.

"Where?"

I shifted uncomfortably. "I don't think I should . . ."

Martha punched me in the arm. "You can say the words 'lewd house' to me, Joshua. I'm not a child. I haven't been for a long time."

Before I could respond, we heard the litigants coming back down the stairs. From the expression on Lincoln's face, less aggrieved than it'd been when the group walked out, I guessed he'd achieved at least a partial victory. The chattering crowd fell silent.

"You may proceed, Mr. Conkling," said the judge, once he'd resumed the bench, "consistent with my ruling."

Conkling cleared his throat. "To your knowledge, Mr. Trailor, had your brother Archibald been drinking alcohol that evening?"

Henry nodded. "They served us as much whiskey as we wanted. It's all part of the same price."

A number of men in the crowd chuckled knowingly. Lincoln started to rise up to object, but the judge motioned him down and said to the witness, "Please try to answer the question posed and nothing more, Mr. Trailor. The question is, had Archibald been drinking?"

"Yes, he had."

I let out my breath. This couldn't have been going worse for Archibald if it had all been plotted out ahead of time.

"And have you been around your brother Archibald, in the past, on occasions on which he'd become intoxicated?" continued Conkling.

"Yes."

"In your judgment, was Archibald intoxicated on the night of Fisher's murder?"

"Very." A course of low laughter ran through the audience. In the front of the room, Archibald's head hung low. The judge called for order.

"Now I've heard it said, Mr. Trailor, that your brother Archibald has a reputation for peacefulness in some quarters. In your experience—"

"Does he?" interrupted Henry, his surprise apparently genuine. "That hasn't been my experience of him." Several members of the crowd laughed nervously at the naked animosity on display.

"Be that as it may," continued Conkling, "in your experience, does Archibald become more docile or more aggressive when he's intoxicated?"

"Certainly more aggressive."

Martha and I exchanged downcast glances. The beating Archibald was taking was worse than any the brothers could have administered to Fisher.

Conkling proceeded to take Henry through his testimony about the scene by the millpond. For each step in the sequence, he carefully asked only about Archibald's action or reaction, deliberately leaving his own client, William, out of the scene. For an observer not paying close attention, it would have been easy to believe Archibald alone had conducted the attack. This was precisely Conkling's intent, of course, and I found myself both surprised and irritated by his deft touch.

After a while, Conkling came to the end of the sequence. "And when first William and then you went to check on Fisher, you realized he'd been killed, suffocated, by Archibald's rag, is that right?"

"Correct."

"And what did Archibald say at that point?"

"I don't think I recall his exact words."

"Did he appear to be happy? Triumphant?"

"Objection," interposed Lincoln. "Calls for speculation."

"Sustained," said the judge.

"What was the expression on Archibald's face in that moment?"

"Same objection," said Lincoln.

The judge shook his head. "Overruled."

"Satisfied, I would say," said Henry. "Like he'd accomplished something. For once."

Conkling took his seat, having landed one last blow. I would never underestimate him again, I thought. Lincoln shuffled through the papers on his lap and started to rise, but the judge said, "It's getting late, Mr. Lincoln. Why don't I give you a fresh start in the morning."

"If it pleases, Your Honor," said Lincoln, springing to his feet quickly, "I'd very much like to begin my examination at once. Without delay."

"I think the gentlemen have had a full day," said the judge, glancing over at the jury, who did indeed appear eager to be released.

"But—"

"That's my ruling." Turning to the jury, he added, "Mr. Lincoln desires to commence his examination because he thinks he has contrary evidence on behalf of his client to adduce from the witness. He may or he may not. We'll see in the morning. I instruct you to keep an open mind until you've heard all of the evidence. Today you've only heard one portion of the evidence. Do you understand?"

The jury affirmed that they did, and the judge brought down his gavel and dismissed them for the day. The courtroom exploded with noise.

Chapter 30

Lincoln remained motionless in his chair as the sheriff took custody of William and Archibald and led them off to their respective cells. The rest of the crowd started filtering away, talking excitedly about the day's evidence. Few seemed to harbor any doubt about Archibald's guilt. Mary Todd was one of the only people to stay behind. She went up to Lincoln, rested her hand lightly on his shoulder, and offered him soft words of encouragement. Martha and Matilda Edwards waited for her to finish, and then the three young women went out arm in arm, consoling one another in hushed tones.

Lincoln finally rose and made to go upstairs to his chambers. He did not object as I followed alongside.

"Challenging day," I offered once we'd entered his office and closed the door.

"I've had better," replied Lincoln quietly.

"Conkling was brutal this afternoon. Remorseless."

"He was doing his job as William's counsel. I can't complain."

"You'll get your chance tomorrow."

"If it's not too late." Lincoln wearily lowered himself into his chair. He took off his stovepipe hat, set it on the floor, and arranged his buffalo-skin cloak around his shoulders. He sat in silence, his head tilted to the side and resting on one hand, occasionally jotting a note on a loose sheet of foolscap lying on the table in front of him.

"I'll leave you to your preparations," I said after a while.

He nodded. "Your Miss Flannery will be ready to go tomorrow?"

"She is. Her testimony contradicts what Henry said about—"

"I realize it. She could be crucial for us. Make sure she's ready in the morning." Lincoln fell silent, and after waiting a few moments to see if he had anything else to say, I walked back somberly to our chambers.

The next morning, I awoke as the first light was starting to creep through our window. I felt the bed beside me, but it was empty and the bedclothes were undisturbed. Lincoln had spent all night at his office.

I dressed quickly and set out for the American House. I crossed the town green, silent and dew covered, and skirted around the capitol building, whose limestone foundations were starting to glow pink in the gathering morning light.

The lobby of the grand hotel was empty. Major Iles was not yet at his usual post. I thought about rousing him, but I reconsidered, given the early hour. So I went back outside to the town green, determined to wait thirty minutes and renew my suit. Around me on the edges of the green, a few people moved about sleepily. The town was starting to stir.

"Excuse me, sir," came a weak voice.

I turned around. A tiny, wizened old man, with a large nose and wild wisps of white hair, stood near. He must have been at least seventy years old, perhaps seventy-five, and he could not have weighed even one hundred pounds. He was wearing an ancient traveling cloak, mud-splattered boots, and an anxious expression.

"Can you tell me where the main square of Vandalia is?

I thought I'd arrived there, but this doesn't look familiar. Not at all."

"Vandalia? Why, you are seventy miles distant from Vandalia. Do you believe yourself to be in Vandalia?"

"I thought so," the man said. "But now I'm not sure." His voice trailed off and he scratched his cheek. His brown eyes, beneath thick, tangled eyebrows, were clear enough and seemed unaffected by drink. "Perhaps it was Vandalia I set out from. Tell me: where am I?"

"You've arrived in Springfield, friend," I said. "Pray tell, how did you get here? Perhaps your driver can remind you of your business."

The man's eyes lit up. "Springfield—yes, exactly. Springfield! I *am* heading to Springfield. From Vandalia to the courthouse in Springfield. I was told it stood in the middle of the town square." He stared uncertainly at the massive capitol building behind me. "But that doesn't look like any courthouse I've ever seen."

"That's the new state capitol," I said. "The courthouse used to stand in the same spot, but it was torn down a few years ago. Your informant was out of date. But the current courthouse isn't far away. I can easily direct you."

"I didn't have a driver, nothing that fancy," the man said. I stared at him in wonder, but then realized he was answering a question I had posed a few moments earlier. It was a shame, I thought, when men outlived the proper functioning of their own minds.

"I drove us in my cart," he continued. "Drove all day and all night to get here. But the cart broke down and I came the final miles on foot. I need to talk to the judge."

"You must have important legal business, indeed. I'm Joshua Speed," I added, extending my right hand to him.

"Garrett Gilmore," said the man, giving me a faint shake. His skin felt as insubstantial as a fallen leaf. "Physician. At your service."

"It is nice to meet you, Dr. Gilmore. You'll find the courthouse in that row of red-brick buildings over there. It's closed now."

"But I must see the judge at once," Gilmore cried. "It's a matter of life and death."

"The courthouse should reopen at nine this morning. The judge, Judge Treat, is conducting a murder trial today, but I suppose it's possible he'll see you before court begins if you truly have urgent business."

"Nine days?" said Gilmore. "I cannot possibly wait nine days."

"No, friend, I said 'nine in the morning,'" I said, talking loudly and slowly. "I'm sure the judge may see you then, if you explain your urgency, whatever it is." I turned to leave.

"The murder trial's just the thing," said Gilmore. "I need to see the judge about the murder trial. Because the victim of the murder is under my professional supervision at this very moment."

I swung around quickly. "What did you say?"

"I said, I am treating the victim of the murder," Gilmore repeated. "Perhaps you have an obstruction in your ears, young man? I could take a look if you like."

"I heard you perfectly. What do you mean, the murder victim? You don't mean Flynn Fisher, do you?"

"That's right," Gilmore replied, brightening. "Do you know him? A fine fellow. Not in the best of health, not even in good times, but certainly still alive and breathing. At least, he was when I left him in my cart. It broke down on the road and I walked the rest of the way here."

"Flynn Fisher is alive?" I shouted.

"That's what I'm trying to tell you," said Gilmore, shaking his head with frustration. "That's why I need to talk to the judge at once."

"Why, my good friend is the lawyer for one of the defendants in the murder trial," I said. I realized my heart was pounding. "Telling him is as good as telling the judge. Come, let's go see him right now. He'll want to hear your tale from your own mouth."

I took Gilmore by the arm and marched him along. A few persons were starting to materialize near the entrance to Hoffman's Row, hoping to secure a spot at the front of the line to get seated inside the courtroom. They stared at the odd-looking man at my side, but I ignored them as we made our slow progress. When we reached the staircase to No. 4, Gilmore paused and gazed uncertainly up the fourteen steps. Then, very slowly and taking them one step at a time, we managed the climb together. I pushed open Lincoln's door.

"I hope that's you, Speed," said Lincoln, without turning to face us. He was in his usual posture, writing pen in hand and hunched over at his table. The candle at his side had burned all the way down to the nub. His hair was disheveled and his shirt was unbuttoned carelessly. "And I hope you've brought breakfast. My stomach is complaining something fierce."

"I've brought you something much better than food," I said, with a smile that was lost on him.

Still immersed in his legal notes, Lincoln said, "I cannot possibly think of anything I desire more at this precise moment than food."

"Then you are suffering from a condemnable lack of imagination. Lincoln, may I present Dr. Garrett Gilmore."

Lincoln finally looked up, squinting.

"Dr. Gilmore," I continued, "please tell Mr. Lincoln who it is you have in your care."

Gilmore had been following the exchange between Lincoln and me with a puzzled expression, and it took him a moment to realize I'd asked him to speak. When he finally did, he cleared his throat and said, "I've treated a good number of souls in my time. Well into the thousands. And that's not counting all the men who stop me on the street and ask my advice."

"But who's the one you just told me about, when we met outside on the green?"

"You mean Flynn Fisher?"

Lincoln jumped to his feet, nearly knocking over the frail doctor, who staggered backward until I caught him. "You've treated Flynn Fisher?" exclaimed Lincoln.

"I *am treating* Flynn Fisher," replied Gilmore with unusual—though useful—precision.

"When did you last see him?"

"I read an article in the *State Register,*" Gilmore said. "It said two brothers were going on trial for murdering Fisher. Which struck me as odd, because Fisher was at that moment in my lying-in room. I decided to adjourn to Springfield at once to call a halt to the proceedings."

"I knew it!" shouted Lincoln. He pounded his worktable with his fist. Turning back to the doctor, he added in a more measured voice, "How did Flynn Fisher come to be in your care? Everyone in Springfield is convinced he was murdered."

"Fisher suffered a lamentable head wound. During the war. Shouldn't have survived it, but he did. He's suffered from aberrations of the brain ever since. I've been treating him for years. He'll spend a few months in my house, and then he'll vanish without a word. I don't think even he knows where he is some of the time."

"Your arrival could not have been better timed," said Lincoln. He was gathering up the papers in front of him. "Fisher's murder trial started yesterday. The Trailor brothers are facing great jeopardy. At least, they were until you showed up."

"I last saw Fisher after midnight," said Gilmore. "When my cart broke down. Middle of the prairie."

I motioned my friend over. "I think the poor fellow's mind is starting to go," I whispered. "His answers are sometimes out of sequence to the questions being asked."

"I don't think that'll make a difference," Lincoln replied. "If there's been no murder, that's the end of the matter." He turned back to Gilmore and said, in a loud voice, "Where did you leave Fisher?"

"The Trailor brothers are facing jeopardy?"

"William and Archibald are. They've been accused of Fisher's murder. That's why I want to know where you left him."

"Fisher was in the back of my cart. The axle cracked and I couldn't fix it, not in the dark. He's in no condition to walk. So I left him and came by foot."

"Which direction were you coming from?" asked Lincoln.

"LaSalle?" said Gilmore, more a question than a statement.

"I thought you said you were coming from Vandalia," I said. The two towns were in directly opposite directions from Springfield.

"I said I was going *to* Vandalia. Er, going *to* Springfield *from* Vandalia. Er . . ." He looked between Lincoln and me, and his face colored. Old pride died a slow, unsightly death. "I'm not sure where I was coming from," he said, scratching his cheek again. "Or going to."

"No matter," said Lincoln. "You've arrived in precisely the right place at precisely the right time." To me, he added, "We need to send out two men to find Fisher, in case Dr. Gilmore's testimony alone proves insufficient to get the judge to dismiss the case. Can you spare Herndon for the day?"

"For this I can."

"Good. You send Herndon north, on the road towards LaSalle. I'll send Hay south on the Vandalia road. One of them should run across Fisher. Hopefully he'll still be in Dr. Gilmore's cart. Sounds like the man has a habit of wandering off."

Turning back to Gilmore, Lincoln added, "Will you accompany me to court this morning, sir? The judge is going to want to hear from you as soon as possible."

"Now that you mention breakfast, I wouldn't say no to a spot," said Gilmore. "I've been traveling for several days." He yawned and put a heavily veined hand to his mouth. "Could you point me towards the public house here in Vandalia?"

"I'll come along with you," Lincoln replied heartily. "Could use a bite myself. And then we'll go to court together." Before further confusion could ensue, Lincoln took Gilmore by the arm and ushered him out the door.

CHAPTER 31

An hour later, Martha settled into the seat beside me at the back of the gathering gallery. "I could barely sleep," she whispered. "I'm so worried about what might happen to Archibald."

"You'll sleep better tonight, I predict."

She stared at me. "What makes you think that?"

"You'll see."

Before she could reply, the clerk called the courtroom to order. Henry Trailor had been standing off to the side, arms folded, his eyes darting about the crowded courtroom. The judge motioned that he should resume the empty witness chair at the front of the room. Lincoln rose.

"I have a witness to take out of turn, Your Honor," he said. Both Lamborn and Conkling swung around in surprise.

"In the middle of the People's case?" asked Judge Treat, sucking on his pipe stem. "In the middle of the cross-questioning of Mr. Trailor? I don't think—"

"I discovered definitive proof overnight that there's been no murder. I'd ask Dr. Garrett Gilmore to come forward."

The courtroom was alive with excited speculation. Lincoln strode over to Gilmore and helped him to his feet. The elderly doctor walked slowly to the witness chair. Martha turned to me, her mouth open and her eyes wide with hope. Down the row of spectators, I saw Big Red May gaping at Lincoln and Gilmore, his ears flapping wildly. Henry Trailor looked around confusedly, but when no one gave him guidance, eventually he wandered off to the side. William Trailor was glaring at him. Archibald Trailor, meanwhile, squinted at Lincoln, more confused than ever.

"I object, Your Honor," said Lamborn, rising to his feet uncertainly. "It's highly improper, in the middle of my case—"

"You don't have a case," replied Lincoln. "And, for your own sake, you're best off realizing it without delay. Have a seat, Doctor," he added, helping the old man lower himself into the witness chair. Gilmore gazed out at the crowded courtroom and the bustling street beyond and blinked several times.

Lamborn glared at Lincoln suspiciously, but all he said was, "I reserve the right to move to strike the witness. And to cross-question."

"Of course," replied Lincoln mildly. "Can you please state your name, Doctor?"

"Garrett Gilmore."

"You are a medical man?"

Gilmore nodded.

"And where do you reside?"

I felt myself tensing. Given Gilmore's chronic confusion regarding location, I hoped Lincoln had been over this question with him several times during the course of their breakfast.

"Near to LaSalle."

"Can you tell us whom you currently have in your care?"

Gilmore looked uncertainly at Lincoln. "I've cared for many thousands of men—"

"We don't have time for all of them, Doctor. I'm asking about a particular man."

"Which one?"

Lamborn started to rise to object, then thought better of it. I felt my heart sinking. If Gilmore didn't come through for us now, after Lincoln had made a fuss about calling him out of turn, Archibald's death warrant was as good as signed.

"Dr. Gilmore, do you have a man named Flynn Fisher in your care?"

This time Lamborn shot up. "Objection, leading the witness!"

"Sustained," said the judge, pulling on his pipe. "Mr. Lincoln, I've given you the benefit of the doubt, but the benefit is very close to expiring."

Lincoln nodded, the skin around his eyes drawn tight. "Do you know a man named Flynn Fisher, Doctor?"

"Yes."

"Describe him, so we know we're talking about the right fellow."

"About fifty years of age, fleshy, dark red hair."

"Have you cared for him?"

"Ever since I've known him, he's leaned his head over his right shoulder." Gilmore demonstrated briefly.

"Very well. And have you cared for him?" Lincoln tried again.

"For many years."

"For what malady?"

In a burst of lucidity, Gilmore explained about Fisher's war wound, his unlikely survival, and his intermittent need for treatment ever since. From time to time, Gilmore added, Fisher would without warning turn up on his doorstep in need of care, like a homing pigeon returning to his roost.

"When did Fisher most recently appear at your home?" asked Lincoln.

"The first time was more than a decade ago. I recall, I was in the middle of treating an invalid named—"

"If I may, Doctor," broke in Lincoln, "I want us to focus on Fisher."

Gilmore looked somewhat put out. "All right," he said. "Flynn Fisher."

"Which other one could it be?" he demanded irritably. "Do you know another Fisher?"

"I don't," replied Lincoln, to a few titters around the courtroom. Judge Treat sucked madly on the stem of his pipe. I caught sight of Big Red, his ears stiff at attention. "When was the *last* time—the *most recent* time—Fisher showed up at your house in need of care?"

"About a month ago."

"Henry Trailor testified yesterday," said Lincoln, "that Fisher disappeared from Springfield on the night of the most recent full moon. Do you recall when, in relation to that, Fisher appeared at your house near LaSalle?"

At Lincoln's reference to Henry, I glanced over at where he had been lingering along the wall, but he was no longer there. Gazing around the courtroom, I could not spot him anywhere.

"I recall that moon," Gilmore was saying. "It was a beautiful one. Low and round and orange. I said to Maude, I said—"

"Dr. Gilmore, if I may, these gentlemen" —Lincoln gestured to the jury— "are interested in one very specific thing, and that's the fate of Flynn Fisher. My only question about the full moon is whether you can tell us when in relation to that moon Fisher appeared on your doorstep?"

"It was a few days afterwards."

"So *subsequent* to the day Fisher was supposedly murdered in Springfield, he showed up at your home near LaSalle, is that what you're saying?"

"Right."

The crowd murmured excitedly. Archibald Trailor looked perplexed; his mouth hung open. His brother William, next to him, seemed consumed with anger.

"Did he show up under his own power?"

"No. He was carried to my door."

"He was?" asked Lincoln, genuinely surprised. I was surprised too; Gilmore hadn't mentioned this to me either. "By whom?"

"Why, by that man." Gilmore reached out an unsteady finger. He seemed to be pointing to William Trailor. The crowd was roiling. William glared at the witness. Conkling leaned over toward his client, and the two men began whispering back and forth furiously.

"By Mr. William Trailor?" asked Lincoln, moving to stand directly beside the man.

"Right."

"Did William Trailor say anything to you, when he deposited Mr. Fisher at your doorstep?"

"Yes."

"What did he say?"

Gilmore appeared agitated. "I've already told you. He was brought to my door by that man." Again he pointed, but this time his wavering finger appeared to be aimed at Archibald Trailor, next to William. Archibald looked up with a confused expression on his face. He wasn't the only one.

Lincoln moved to stand between the two brothers. "This is an important point, Dr. Gilmore, so I want to make sure your testimony is clear. Mr. Fisher was deposited on your doorstep by someone, correct?"

"Several days after the full moon. It was a beautiful one. Low and round and orange. I said to Maude, I said—"

A few members of the audience started to laugh. Martha and I exchanged worried glances.

"Yes, sir," said Lincoln, straining to remain composed. "When Mr. Fisher was deposited at your home, was he brought by this man" —he pointed to his left, to Archibald— "or this man?" He pointed right, to William.

"That one." Gilmore pointed to William again.

"And what, if anything, did William Trailor say to you at that time."

"He said, 'Flynn's gone ill again. Take care of him. Make sure he stays alive.' I remember that last part, because he repeated it several times. 'Make sure he stays alive.'"

"So William gave Fisher to you, saying, 'Make sure he stays alive'?"

"Right."

The crowd was alive with excited speculation.

"And where has Fisher been since that day?" Lincoln asked.

"In my lying-in room. Under my care. He complains every day about missing his wife and child."

"Oh?" said Lincoln. "Is he married?"

"His wife died years ago. And they never had any children. I think his mind's a muddle."

"This doctor's a muddle," hissed a man near us in the gallery.

But I realized at once what the testimony meant. "Fisher's complaining about missing his *ring*," I whispered to Martha. "The mourning ring for his wife and child. Someone must have taken it from him and buried it for us to find."

"Now, how did you happen to be here in this courtroom today?" Lincoln was asking his witness.

"Mostly I keep the curtains drawn, no candles alight, and keep a damp rag on his forehead. It seems to help assure his mind."

"That's your treatment, you're saying?" tried Lincoln.

"That's what you asked, isn't it?"

"The question, Dr. Gilmore, is what brings you to this courtroom today?"

"I read an article about this trial, realized you thought—" the doctor gestured at the judge behind him—"Fisher had been killed, and I loaded us in my cart right away and started driving. Been driving without stopping."

"I'm very glad of it," said Lincoln. "And so are the defendants." Glancing over at him, I saw William Trailor's red face alive with emotions. "Glad" did not appear to be among them. "Where is Mr. Fisher now?"

"My cart broke down on the way, and I had to leave him."

"*Of course it did!*" muttered Lamborn under his breath, though loud enough for everyone inside the small courtroom to hear. Several of the jurors sniggered.

"When did your cart break down?" continued Lincoln, ignoring the interruption.

"Somewhere on the road to Springfield, I suppose."

"No, 'when.' *When* did you leave Fisher in your cart?"

"Last night, of course."

"And was he alive when you last saw him, last night?"

Gilmore peered at Lincoln and grabbed at his few remaining strands of white hair. "What are you suggesting? That I killed him?" Several men in the courtroom laughed. I heard one remark sneeringly that the doctor had obviously lost his mind.

Lincoln lifted his stovepipe hat and ran a hand through his hair. "Certainly not, Doctor. I merely want you to confirm for the jury that Mr. Fisher is, in fact, alive."

Lamborn rose, saying, "Objection, leading the witness."

"Let me rephrase," said Lincoln, as Lamborn remained standing at his side, his arms folded across his thick chest. "Dr. Gilmore, was Mr. Flynn Fisher alive the last time you saw him, sometime yesterday evening?"

"Yes. Yes, of course he was."

Lincoln turned to Judge Treat. "We ask you to dismiss the charges, Your Honor. There's been no murder."

"Wait, wait, wait!" shouted Lamborn, as the crowd called out with approval and derision in equal measure. "Lincoln's proven nothing of the sort. Dr. Gilmore, you say you left Fisher in a cart?"

"Right?"

"Where?"

Gilmore shrugged. "I don't know. Middle of the prairie . . ." His pause lasted an uncomfortable length. Then he added, in an apologetic tone, "You see, I'm not too good with directions these days."

"Your mind's not quite what it used to be?" asked Lamborn with feigned sympathy.

"I'm afraid not."

Lamborn nodded and glanced over at the judge to make sure he was following along. Judge Treat was working his pipe with short, quick pulls.

"Is Fisher there right now?"

"Where right now?"

"Wherever you left him."

"But I don't know where I left him."

"So where is he now?"

"So where is who now?" Gilmore looked over at Lincoln and back at Lamborn. "I'm confused."

"Exactly!" shouted Lamborn. A flick of spittle flew out of Lamborn's mouth and landed on Gilmore's scalp. Neither man seemed to notice. Several men in the audience laughed. Martha and I exchanged nervous glances again.

"The truth, Dr. Gilmore," continued Lamborn, "is that this is all a ploy. A trick. Did Archibald Trailor put you up to this?"

"Who?"

"Archibald Trailor. This man right here." Lamborn pointed at Archibald.

"I've never seen that man before in my life—"

"Are you certain—"

"—but *him*, I know." Gilmore pointed at William Trailor.

"So William Trailor put you up to this?"

"Up to what?"

"To testifying in court. To claiming that Fisher is still alive."

"Fisher is still alive," repeated Gilmore. It was hard to tell if Gilmore's response was a question or a statement, and he balled up his hands and rubbed his eyes. The old man was getting tired, I thought. And even I was starting to wonder if his tale was true. It was all so improbable.

"William Trailor put you up to this," repeated Lamborn. An accusation, not a question.

"He asked me to take care of Fisher," replied the witness.

"So you and William agreed you would come into court and testify Fisher was actually alive?"

Lincoln struggled to his feet, evidently deciding he needed to come to his witness's rescue. "Your Honor," he began, "I fear Attorney General Lamborn is confusing the witness with his questioning."

"The witness is confused, all right," parried Lamborn. "Hopelessly confused. He admitted it himself. Not my doing."

"The objection is overruled," said the judge. "I'm going to give the People every latitude and leeway."

"You and William spoke at your house?" Lamborn said to the witness.

"Right."

"And did you agree to come into court and testify Fisher was actually alive?"

"Did I agree with him about that? No, that's what Mr. Lincoln asked."

"So Lincoln put you up to this!" roared Lamborn, to cries of excitement from the crowd out on the street. He punched the air with his fist. "What did Lincoln promise you in return?"

Gilmore looked at the attorney uncertainly. "Breakfast."

Laughter swept the courtroom.

"He promised you breakfast if you testified?"

"Didn't promise it. Bought it for me. I was powerful hungry."

"So Mr. Lincoln gave you financial favors in exchange for your agreement to testify. Is that what you're telling us, Dr. Gilmore?"

"It was ten cents' worth of coffee and eggs," called Lincoln calmly from his chair. "Saunders's finest at the Globe. I daresay Dr. Gilmore's honesty can't be bought so cheaply."

"I'm not testifying for breakfast," said Gilmore. "I'm testifying because I saw the article about this legal case, and—"

"You're testifying because William Trailor asked you to take care of Fisher," said Lamborn forcefully.

"Eggs and coffee," replied Gilmore.

"So you *are* testifying for eggs and coffee?"

Before Gilmore could reply, the spectators in the courtroom became aware of a great swell of noise coming through the open windows. It seemed to originate from the very back of the crowd on the street and quickly streaked forward, gaining intensity like the whine of an approaching cannonball. It was a mixture of cheers and jeers, applause and catcalls, whoops and loud groans. Just when the commotion had reached a fevered pitch, it was punctuated by the door to the courtroom being thrown open.

My clerk Herndon stood in the doorway, his face red and perspiring, his hat askew and his riding coat smeared with dirt. Dragging along by his side, his arm thrown over Herndon's shoulders for support, was a limp figure. His head was tilted unnaturally to the side. The figure was unwell, infirm, feeble. But the figure was, unmistakably, Flynn Fisher. And, just as unmistakably, he was alive.

CHAPTER 32

The courtroom erupted. Some of the spectators looked quizzical, some melancholy, and some were furiously angry. One man whom I recognized as having led the wild hunt for Fisher's body near the millpond announced loudly that he'd always known the man was alive and that he was glad he hadn't stirred an inch to search for him.

Martha threw her arms around my neck and squeezed me tight. Large tears of relief rolled down her rosy cheeks. I could see Mary Todd and Matilda Edwards on the other side of the courtroom sharing a joyous embrace.

Big Red May looked stricken by panic, no doubt wondering how he could possibly explain his miscalculation to the voters at the next election.

"It's too damn bad!" exclaimed one man sitting near us to his neighbor. "All this trouble we went through, and no hanging after all."

Archibald Trailor had adopted an appearance of stoical indifference through most of the trial, as if to signal he was prepared to calmly endure the worst. But when the man he was accused of murdering was led into his presence, he broke down in a flood of tears, which were followed by uncontrollable fits of sobbing and moaning.

William Trailor's face had gone purple. He pulled Conkling toward him and unleashed a long string of invective. He did not immediately give the appearance of a man happy to be vindicated for a murder he had not committed.

Henry Trailor was nowhere to be seen.

Some minutes later, Martha, Lincoln, Archibald, and I went upstairs to No. 4, Hoffman's Row, to try to figure out what had happened. All of us were in a bit of shock. Judge Treat had dismissed the People's case with prejudice. Lamborn protested that if not murder, the defendants must be guilty of some other crime, but the judge shook his head and said he would not hold them any longer on such speculation. Sheriff Hutchason duly removed their restraints and the brothers stood and awkwardly embraced, free men. In turn, Lincoln directed Herndon to take Dr. Gilmore and Flynn Fisher over to the American House, with instructions to find suitable accommodations for the two travelers to rest from their arduous journey. Each of them looked desperately in need of a bed.

"I don't understand," Archibald was saying now, teardrops of relief still shining on his face and whiskers. "I don't understand."

"Damnedest thing I ever saw," said Lincoln, shaking his head. "The dead man shows up at his own murder trial."

"All you need to understand," said Martha, giving Archibald's arm a squeeze, "is that you're free. You can go back to living your life. Nothing else matters." He gave her a radiant smile. Not for the first time, I wondered, and worried, about their relationship.

"Did you notice Henry Trailor disappeared in the middle of Dr. Gilmore's testimony?" I asked Lincoln. "It's no wonder, I suppose, given that his entire story turned out to be false."

"Hasn't he committed perjury?" said Martha. "Surely he deserves to be thrown in jail."

Lincoln started to agree, but Archibald broke in, saying, "Henry didn't lie."

All of us stared at him. "How can you say that?" exclaimed Martha.

"Because everything he said in court was true."

"No, it wasn't! Fisher's alive. We all saw him just now. That's why the judge dismissed your case."

But Archibald shook his head stubbornly. "Everything happened just the way he said. Where he and I had been earlier that evening; William sending for us, saying Fisher had betrayed us; rousing Fisher from his hotel; taking him to the grove by the millpond; me tying him to a tree and gagging him because William told me to. I saw it with my own eyes. I did it with my own hands."

"Only Fisher didn't die," repeated Martha.

"That's what I don't understand."

"Perhaps your memory of the evening is impaired," I suggested, "by drink."

"I was drunk rotten, there's no denying, but I'm certain it all happened. I'd swear on the Good Book. I've thought about that evening every day and every night since."

"But you personally never saw a dead body, did you?" asked Lincoln, cutting to the heart of the matter.

Archibald considered this. "I didn't want to, after William told me I'd killed him. I couldn't bear what I'd done to Flynn. He was a good fellow, always nice to me."

"But don't you see?" I said. "You didn't kill him. William told you that to make you think you were guilty. To trick you."

Archibald was unpersuaded. "Henry went and looked, as soon as William told us he was dead. Henry saw him, too."

"They're *both* lying to you," said Martha, nearly at a shout, tears of frustration welling in her eyes. "They have been, from the very beginning."

"I don't think they'd do that," said Archibald, but with less conviction this time. The awful truth about his brothers' betrayal began to seep into his features.

"Remember what Bill, the little chief herdsman, told us," said Martha. "He saw three men in the clearing near the millpond *pretending* to fight. So maybe, when William assaulted Fisher, he was merely pretending to do so, only Archibald wasn't able to perceive the difference, because of his condition."

"But that was at dusk," I said. "Bill was trying to get his herd home before dark." I turned to Archibald. "Was it dusk when you and your brothers confronted Fisher out by the millpond?"

"No, much later. Well after ten, just like Henry testified."

"And had you been out at the millpond earlier that afternoon, or evening, with your brothers?"

Archibald shook his head.

"So that pretend fight didn't involve Archibald." I turned back to Martha. "Maybe they were practicing for something that would later deceive Archibald. Remember, Bill said two of the men he saw had the appearance of brothers. So it was William and Henry and—"

"Fisher!" said Martha. "He was part of the plot, too."

"But that would mean Fisher agreed to stage his own death and trick Archibald in the process. Why would he do that?" I turned back to Archibald. "Did Fisher have a grudge against you?"

"Not that I know." The carpenter shook his head blankly.

Lincoln had been striding back and forth around the office. He rounded on us and said, "You're getting far afield. William's the key to the mystery."

"How do you figure?"

"Archibald thinks Henry was telling the truth when he testified. Shoot, I wouldn't be completely astounded if Henry himself thought he was telling the truth. Probably not, but it's possible. But William must have known it was a lie. Because he subsequently brought Fisher to Dr. Gilmore. That's what Gilmore testified to, and while he was confused on any number of matters, I doubt he's mistaken on that one."

"But if William knew the murder victim wasn't actually murdered, what's he been doing sitting in jail all this time, rather than telling Conkling, telling the world, where Fisher is?" I said. "It makes no sense."

"And on top of that," said Martha, "William is the one who directed the sheriff to Fisher's supposed remains on the other side of the pond. Far from protesting his innocence, he's been deepening his own guilt."

Lincoln turned to Archibald. "Did William ever suggest to you, while the two of you were in the jail cell together, that Fisher was alive?"

Archibald shook his head. "All he would say was, 'Do what I say, and everything will turn out right.' So that's what I did. I've been used to doing what he says for a long time," he added, almost apologetically, glancing around at us. "If you think of it, in the end, he was correct."

"How can you say that!" cried Martha, as I gaped at Archibald, astounded by his continuing loyalty to his undeserving brothers.

"Let's see if Conkling can tell us what William was thinking," said Lincoln. Hay had returned to town, empty-handed, shortly after Herndon had appeared with the prize, and Lincoln sent him off in search of Conkling. The slight, Princeton lawyer appeared about thirty minutes later, a broad smile still etched across his youthful face.

"What a victory!" said Conkling, striding toward Lincoln with his hand outstretched. "Even Cicero would hesitate to write such a history. They'll be talking about this trial for years."

"Perhaps they will," returned Lincoln. "But I don't understand why William didn't tell you at the very outset of the case that Fisher was alive and under Dr. Gilmore's care."

"He didn't know," insisted Conkling.

Lincoln explained the logic behind our conclusion that he must have. When he'd finished, Conkling shrugged and said, "He never said a word of it to me. Gilmore was confused in his recitation, most likely. You saw and heard him yourselves. I'm grateful he appeared when he did, of course, but the poor fellow barely knew where he was. Besides, why would a man possibly stay in jail, at risk of the gallows, if he knew he could prove his innocence?"

"Go ask him now," I suggested.

Conkling shook his head. "He's gone. As soon as we got out of the courtroom, he was in a hurry to leave town. Paid me a little extra above the usual fee and asked me to help him carry up his heavy trunk from the basement of the capitol and put it into a carriage. And off he rode. Heading home, he said, no wish to remain in Sangamon County after the ordeal he went though. Can't say I blame him."

"But if Mr. Lincoln's right," said Martha, "he put himself through the ordeal."

"If men always acted rationally," said Conkling with a laugh, "there'd be much less need for lawyers, eh, Lincoln?" Conkling slapped his fellow counselor on the back, said he needed to get back to his law office, and took his leave. In his wake, the rest of us stood there silently, trying to make sense of William Trailor's strange behavior.

"I wonder . . ." began Archibald, before drifting off and shaking his head.

"You wonder what?" asked Martha.

"About the note William gave me for Henry."

"What note?" said Lincoln sharply. "When?"

"After court yesterday, William and I were led out together by the sheriff. First we went down into the basement of the capitol building, where the sheriff locked William back into his cell, and then the sheriff took me to my cell, behind his house. But as we were parting, William made a remark about Trailor family business and slipped a note into my pocket. For Henry. Sure enough, last night, Henry stopped by my cell and asked me if William had given me anything for him."

All of us were looking at Archibald dumbfounded. "This was all last night?" Lincoln asked.

"That's right."

"But why didn't you tell Lincoln?" I said.

"Trailor family business. Besides, I didn't have the chance, not with the doctor appearing so early this morning."

"Do you still have the note?"

Archibald shook his head. "I gave it to Henry, just like William said."

"What did it say?" Martha asked, her eyes shining brightly.

"Martha, if he doesn't have the note anymore, it's no use," I said. I added, in a hushed voice, "You know he can't read."

"Yes, he can."

"What?"

"What do you think Archibald and I have been doing, all the time I've been spending out at the jail cell with him?" The pride in her voice was unmistakable.

"Miss Martha's been teaching me how to read," added Archibald, giving a loose, toothy grin. "And I've been making some advance. I got a ways to go, but I've been doing some learning. More than I ever did before."

Each of us shouted, more or less simultaneously, some version of, "What did the note say?"

"I'm about to tell you. I can't be certain. I guess I need more lessons." He gave Martha a bashful smile. "But I reckon it said . . . 'The . . . shop . . . mint . . . is . . . ours.'" He pronounced the words deliberately, as if sounding them out from a page of writing in front of him.

"What's 'ours'?" I said. "The 'shop mint'? But that's gibberish."

"I reckon that's what William wrote down." Archibald surveyed our faces and, sensing our confusion, looked away. "I'm sorry, Miss Martha. I wish I learned your lessons more."

Lincoln, though, was gazing at the man with dawning comprehension. He had taken out a piece of paper and scribbled down Archibald's words. "Not the 'shop mint,'" said Lincoln. "The 'shipment.' 'The shipment is ours.'"

"'The shipment,'" repeated Martha. "But what could that mean?"

Lincoln had already turned to Hay. "Go find Belmont. Sheriff Hutchason, too. Right away! Tell them to meet us at the State Bank building. Tell them it's urgent."

He looked back at us. "I think the Trailors were planning to steal the gold."

Chapter 33

We clambered down the stairs of Hoffman's Row, close on Hay's heels, and made a direct line for the bank building. The streets outside were still laden with spectators from the trial, and a number of them muttered epithets as we pushed through. It was apparent the crowd was still angry at Lincoln for having produced the victim alive.

"We should hang 'em anyway, just because," said one man, nodding at Archibald as we hurried past.

Martha wrapped her hands protectively around Archibald's arm.

We crossed the green, looped around the capitol, and came to the grand bank building just opposite. As we mounted the steps, Sheriff Hutchason raced up from the other direction. Mayor May was trailing right behind him.

"Hay said it was urgent, Lincoln," said the sheriff.

"I was with the sheriff when your boy came up," explained Big Red. "If there's a threat to the city, I need to know. There's plenty of anger out there already about the way the trial ended. If we're not careful, a mob's going to form up."

"Funny that you're concerned with that now," I said, unable to hold my tongue. "This man"—I put my hand on Archibald's shoulder—"was at risk for his life because you *catered* to the mob."

"I did what I thought was right to protect the citizens of the town," replied Big Red, "and I shan't apologize for that."

"You owe Archibald an apology," said Lincoln, "but there's no time for that now. Ah, Belmont, just in time. Or perhaps too late, I fear." The banker had hurried up to join us at the top of the steps, Lincoln's boy Hay at his side.

"What's happened?" Belmont demanded, his usual cool absent for once.

Lincoln put his hand on one of the marble columns standing like sentries at the bank front. "The Trailor trial came to an abrupt end this morning. The victim wasn't a victim—there was no murder after all. Even more surprisingly, it seems inescapable that one of the defendants, William Trailor, knew from the start he could prove his innocence, yet did nothing to do so."

Belmont, who hadn't been in court this morning, whistled in surprise. As Lincoln detailed what had happened, an expression of worry clouded the banker's face. "But why?" asked Belmont when Lincoln had finished.

"That's exactly the question. It would appear William, and perhaps Henry Trailor, too, instigated the whole thing as some sort of ruse. To what end? Let's proceed inside. I fear we're about to find out."

"I don't understand," said Big Red. "Explain your thinking to us again?"

"There's no time," said Lincoln. "We'll see for ourselves soon enough. Follow me."

Lincoln led the way through the bank's doors. The cashier of the Springfield bank was a man named Roy, a nervous fellow who kept to himself and always looked behind him as he walked, as if in constant fear of bodily assault. He was the kind of person who locked the door after he entered a room and then checked the lock three times to make sure it was set. In short, he was the perfect man to serve as cashier. Or so it had always seemed.

Roy came forward to meet the large group as it entered his sanctuary.

"What's all this?" he demanded.

"We need to examine the vault," said Lincoln.

"Why?"

"Because we have reason to believe the gold shipment is missing."

"Impossible! Ever since Belmont's men arrived with it, it's been sitting in the vault. The day it arrived, I carefully counted out every last coin. Fifty thousand dollars, on the button. And I've checked the box twice every day since, once in the morning and again in the evening. I checked on it not two hours ago, upon my arrival this morning, and it was sitting undisturbed."

"Nonetheless," said Lincoln, "we must see for ourselves."

Lincoln made toward a staircase leading down from the ground floor of the bank. Roy started to block his way, but upon seeing the menacing Sheriff Hutchason following immediately behind Lincoln, he desisted. After the sheriff went Belmont, who was absently twirling his walking stick and looking more and more alarmed, and then the rest of our little search party.

The basement level of the bank resembled the basement of the capitol building, a mostly unfinished space with narrow, horizontal windows cut into the tops of the walls to allow outside light to filter in. I remarked upon the similarity to Big Red as we followed the procession along.

"No surprise," said he. "The same firm worked on both buildings."

At the front of the line, Lincoln came to a halt beside a locked iron door.

"Open it, if you please, Roy," he said.

The cashier looked around warily at the large crowd. He shook his head.

"We're not going to rob you, man," said Lincoln. "We have

the sheriff and mayor here, not to mention myself, from the banking committee in the legislature. We'd be robbing from ourselves if we did."

Hesitantly, Roy reached inside his shirt and pulled out a chain he wore around his neck. A key dangled from the chain. Roy bent over and fiddled with the lock until it clicked. He swung the door open to a small, cubical chamber, perhaps eight feet on each side.

"Right there, just where it should be," said Roy. I stood on my tiptoes and peered over the men in front of me. There was a small wooden trunk, apparently undisturbed, sitting in the middle of the room.

"That's it, all right," said Belmont, giving a relieved sigh. "Looks like you need a different theory to explain the strange ending to your case, Lincoln."

"Open the trunk," commanded Lincoln.

"This is all irregular," said Roy, shaking his head wildly. "Highly, highly irregular."

"Open it!"

Grumbling to himself, Roy knelt in front of the trunk and inserted a key. "See," he said, swinging open the lid, "just as I—" He broke off, then shouted, "Good God!"

"What is it?"

"I—I—I . . ." The bank cashier bent over, hands to his knees, and was sick.

Lincoln and the other fellows in the front rank rushed forward to examine the trunk. They reached in and pawed about furiously. A hail of shouted epithets followed.

"Nothing but clothing," cried the sheriff, holding a dirty smock above his head.

"Gone, all gone," wailed Big Red.

Lincoln was silent. I'd never seen him at a loss for words. He shook his head back and forth, mutely pulling one dingy garment after another out of the trunk, as if hoping by some alchemy to change cloth into gold.

After all, I thought, some strange alchemy had turned the gold into cloth in the first place.

"What have you done, Roy?" demanded Sheriff Hutchason.

"It wasn't me," insisted the cashier. "I swear, it wasn't."

"But you just finished telling us that you were the only one with access to this room," said Big Red, his ears flapping uncontrollably, pointing with an accusing finger.

The cashier, the mayor, and the sheriff argued back and forth, their voices rising into an angry cacophony.

Belmont had been strangely subdued during the entire search of the basement vault. Now and then, he used his walking stick to rap upon the floor absently, as if he was making some point of argument to himself. Unlike the others, his demeanor was not that of a man who'd suffered a great loss. I turned on him.

"This was your doing," I said.

It took a moment for Belmont to realize I was speaking to him. Belatedly, he responded, "What did you say?"

"You've been in league with the Trailors from the outset. It should have been obvious to all of us long ago. This was your doing."

"It's my gold. I above anyone else would want to protect it."

"It's the people of Illinois's gold," I shot back. "It has been, ever since it entered the vault. And now it's gone. You've admitted to spending lots of time with Henry Trailor, over at the American House. Now we know what you were conspiring about."

"Preposterous!"

Martha had finally worked herself to a position near the trunk, and she pulled on my arm. "Isn't that William's trunk? It is! It's the exact trunk we saw in the barn behind Mary's house."

I turned back to Belmont. "Is that the same trunk your men brought from St. Louis with the gold?"

Belmont's face was red with fury. He managed a nod.

"No, it's the trunk we saw in the hayloft," said Martha, as the tumult continued all around us. "The one William hid there. I'd swear to it on little Ann's grave."

There was a sharp intake of breath next to me. I turned to see Archibald, looking paler and more agitated than I'd seen him since the evening I'd found him huddled at my storefront all those days ago.

"What is it?" I asked.

He mumbled something, but it was inaudible with all the hue and cry around us. "Say that again," I prompted.

"I made two for him."

"Two of what? For whom?"

"For William. I made him two identical trunks."

"What?" shouted Martha from beside me.

Archibald nodded. "I made him one last year. Gave it to him on his birthday, and he was very pleased. So pleased that he asked me, a few months ago, to make him another. 'Identical in every respect,' he said. I'd never seen him so happy with my carpentry."

I turned to share this revelation with Lincoln, when a piercing whistle cut through the tumult. Everyone was silent at once, gazing around to find the source of the noise. To my shock, I saw that it was young Hay, standing near one of the exterior walls of the room and gesticulating wildly. Hay was afraid of his own shadow; I'd never known him to make any noise at all in a gathering this large.

Everyone in the room was staring at him now. The sudden attention seemed to surprise the slight boy, and he stood there, dumb.

"What is it, Hay?"

Hay opened his mouth, but no words emerged.

"Speak up, boy," demanded Lincoln.

"There's a hole in the wall," the boy said, his voice cracking. "Right here. I think it's a tunnel."

Chapter 34

Hay pointed to a void in the wall at about knee height. A large stone, which Hay had evidently dislodged, stood beside him at the base of the wall. The boy knelt down beside the hole and disappeared into the void.

Big Red turned to Lincoln. The mayor's enormous ears were waggling back and forth frantically. "What's in that direction?"

"The basement of the capitol," said Lincoln, his face lighted with somber comprehension.

"William Trailor's cell," said the sheriff. He added a word I'd never heard him use before. Martha, standing beside me, blushed.

"Arrest him!" shouted Roy.

"William Trailor rode out of town right after the trial ended," replied Lincoln. He looked at me. "Conkling told us he'd helped him carry up his trunk from his basement cell." Lincoln reconsidered, his face pained. "Helped him carry up *our* trunk, that is.

"We'll ride after him at once," Lincoln added, turning to the sheriff. "We'll be much faster, on horseback, than he'll be in a carriage with that heavy trunk. With luck, we should be able to track him down in a few hours."

Hay's face popped out of the hole in the wall, and the rest of his body followed shortly thereafter, his entire set of clothing now covered with dirt. "Leads right to the jail cell in the capitol," he said. "And look what I found there, under a pile of stones." Hay held up a shovel. I remembered that Lincoln had found a shovel at the bottom of William Trailor's trunk when we searched it in Edwards's hayloft.

"We know his game," said Lincoln, nodding grimly. "Our only hope is that we've caught him out in time. Come, Sheriff. Let's ride off after him."

"I'll go as well," said Belmont.

I eyed the banker suspiciously. All the time he'd spent with Henry Trailor, as well as the fact that he'd remained in town after the gold transfer had been completed, made sense now. I felt certain Belmont was part of the robbery plot. Very likely, he was the ringleader. "And I'm coming along," I said.

"Me, too," said Martha with excitement in her voice.

"Certainly not," I replied. "I forbid it." Martha glowered at me.

"Let's meet in five minutes," said Lincoln, "ten at most, at the Globe stables. In the meantime, Hay, go see if you can find someone who saw William Trailor leaving town, so we know which direction to head. Start with Conkling. He must have some idea, given that he helped him load the trunk. Conkling's practically an accessory. And good work on finding the tunnel."

Hay stood rooted to the spot, beaming with pride at the unaccustomed compliment.

"Get going!" shouted Lincoln, and giving a start, the boy scattered.

Exactly eight minutes later, Hutchason, Lincoln, and I sat atop our mounts in the courtyard beside the Globe stables, waiting for Belmont to join us. Hickory pranced around beneath me excitedly. She had the sense we were about to head off on a chase.

Martha and I had argued the whole way over to the Globe. She was persistent in her desire to ride with us, not even stopping her pleading when I ducked into my store and, reaching up on one of the top shelves, brought down a pistol and box of ammunition. But I was just as persistent that a posse was no place for a young woman. By the time we reached the stables, Martha realized her cause was lost, and she strode into the tavern in a huff, not even wishing us good speed on our journey.

Belmont rode up. He had arrived in town aboard a magnificent Arabian, but now he was perched atop a plain, chestnut-colored Morgan. Belmont was dressed like a ragged stablehand, with a shabby cloth vest over a wrinkled riding shirt. Unlike the other three of us, he was bareheaded. The only sign of his usual affectation was his well-loved walking stick, which poked out of one of the saddlebags slung across his mount.

"Why the costume?" I asked.

"I've told you before, Speed, although you did not want to listen. In my position, I must be prepared at all times to be either banker or bandit. We venture into the den of thieves. We must appear as if we have come to partake in the meal, not to be served on the platter. You three . . ." He trailed off and gestured despairingly at us. "Ach! You three are unlikely to apprehend the thieves. Whatever you are wearing will not matter in the end."

"And where's your Arab?"

"No bandito worth his name would mount an Arab. It's much too conspicuous on the prairie."

I nodded. The banker did make sense on occasion.

"What's taking Hay so long?" asked Lincoln irritably, glancing at the sun, which was nearing its highest point. "We need to track down William by sunset if we're to have a real hope of recapturing the gold."

We were about to leave a minute later when we heard shouts coming from the street. Soon thereafter, Hay himself materialized, running as fast as his spindly legs would carry him and gasping frantically for breath.

"No . . . one . . . saw . . . him . . . leave," he panted. His dirt-covered clothing was rent through with sweat.

"Impossible," said the sheriff. "It was broad daylight. Someone must have seen which direction he went."

"What did Conkling say?" asked Lincoln.

"Couldn't find . . . him," replied Hay, still catching his breath.

Lincoln looked over at me. "What do you think, Speed? We could spend more time canvassing the area around the capitol building. The sheriff's right: someone must have seen something. But there's no guarantee we'd find the person in an hour, or even two."

"We haven't got the time," I said. "It's most likely William headed west, towards Jacksonville. It's the least-traveled road, the one where he's least likely to excite notice." I looked around. "Two of us could take that road. And then one the road south towards Vandalia, and the fourth on the road north towards Peoria." These were the three principal carriage roads leaving Springfield. If William Trailor was driving a carriage sturdy enough to haul the trunk full of gold, he'd have to be taking one of the three routes.

"But you're just guessing," protested Hutchason.

"Guessing is the best hope we've got at this point," I replied.

"Unless you want to ask the man who rented them their carriage," came a feminine voice from behind us. We swung around to see Martha walking toward us from the door of the Globe, the tavernkeeper Saunders at her side.

"What?"

"Tell my witless brother and the rest of this group what happened earlier, Mr. Saunders, if you please," prompted Martha.

"Potbellied fellow came by this morning, in a real hurry, asking if he could rent out a horse and carriage," said Saunders.

"Henry Trailor!" I shouted. "He disappeared from the courtroom soon after Dr. Gilmore showed up. I knew the two brothers were in it together. Henry must have realized at once they'd be needing a quick escape."

"Go on, Saunders," said Lincoln.

"The fellow said they was driving north, towards Peoria Lake, but they'd return the lot in a month's time, when they were back this way. I don't usually allow my rides to be taken out that long, but he gave me a good price, all up front, very nearly the full price of the horse and conveyance together. It's all profit to me when they come back."

"Perhaps he merely said he was going towards Peoria as a ruse," said Belmont.

"Just listen, if you please," said Martha. She gestured at Saunders to continue.

The tavernkeeper pointed toward the capitol square. "He drove off that way—"

"To collect William and the trunk," exclaimed the sheriff.

"And then, not thirty minutes later," continued the tavernkeeper, "I see the carriage driving back the other way, out towards the Peoria road, driving fast enough to scare a clan of badgers."

"What horse and carriage did you give him?" asked the sheriff.

"He said he wanted to go as fast as possible. So I let him have Daisy. She's the fastest Morgan I've got. And I gave him my best phaeton. Didn't have time to wash it down, as he wanted to drive it out of the yard at once. But it's painted dark blue under all the dust."

"Appreciate the information, Saunders," said Lincoln, as the four of us turned our mounts and prepared to ride out of the yard. "And thank you, Miss Speed, for thinking to ask Saunders what he knew. Your quick thinking, as always, has been invaluable."

My sister trained a triumphant glare in my direction. "Enough!" I shouted, when she would not blink. "Now wish us luck, and we'll be off."

"Good luck, Mr. Lincoln," said Martha. "And to you, too, Sheriff. And Mr. Belmont."

Shaking my head, I followed the others out of the yard, all of us riding at a smart canter. Within minutes we had left the town and surrounding farms behind and were out into the open prairie.

The last time I had ridden through the prairie had been the day of the Sudden Change. But now, the frigid grays and whites of that winter's day had been replaced by an explosion of brilliant color. There seemed to be no edge to the land. The prairie rolled on forever, like the back of an enormous animal that might at any moment get up and run.

Riding down the center of the two-tracked carriage path, we passed beside tall green grasses giving off a sweet, dry smell and up and down gentle hillsides covered with purple and blue and rose-colored flowers. Giant sunflowers broke through the glassy surface of the grasslands, their heads a swirl of gold, tawny brown and coppery green. Tiny yellow-breasted birds perched on top of tall, lime-green weeds that swayed in the breeze.

We were a thousand miles from the sea but the land rolled like the sea, and the gentle winds blew the grasses back and forth like churning waves. The shadows of the clouds raced us up and down the grassy slopes. And every now and then we would catch sight of a dark stand of timber off on the horizon, like an uncharted island waiting to be explored.

After we'd been riding for about an hour, we came to a fork in the road. One after another, we pulled up to contemplate it.

"Peoria Lake is that way," said the sheriff, pointing to the right-hand branch of the fork.

"And the quickest way to the Illinois River is that way," said Lincoln, pointing left. "If they're planning to make a water escape."

As we contemplated the fork, the horses ducked their heads

and drank from a small stream that gurgled through the grasses. Nearby, a pair of hummingbirds fed on the red blooms of an Indian paintbrush stalk.

Sheriff Hutchason swung off his horse and examined the rutted carriage tracks, along with the surrounding grasses. He walked back and forth, then got down on his knees to stare at a stalk of tall grass that had sprouted between the two tracks. "The most recent carriage to come through went right," he announced. "Makes sense. They want to get back to their home area as quickly as possible. Know the territory better. Know the hiding places."

Hutchason swung back atop his horse and started toward the right fork. Lincoln moved to follow behind him.

"I think I'll go left," said Belmont. "Just in case. If I reach the river without finding them, I'll tack back towards you."

I eyed him with suspicion. "And I'll go with Belmont," I said. "Divide our resources evenly. Let's be off."

Without further discussion, we parted. Belmont and I rode swiftly along the rutted carriage path. A flock of wild geese flew far overhead, squawking at each other like a group of truant schoolchildren. I spent a good deal of time contemplating the man riding expertly by my side. The question I had asked him in Lincoln's office echoed in my head. *Are you banker or bandit?* I still had no idea.

At one point, Belmont caught me staring. "You don't trust me," he said, a statement, not a question.

"No." I considered. "Not yet."

"I imagine that caution has served you well throughout your life," he replied. "But you'd do best to forget it for the rest of this journey."

"Why's that?"

"When the fight comes, it will favor the bold. To hesitate is to lose." He kicked his horse and rode on ahead, before turning back to add over his shoulder, "And I don't plan on losing."

A little while later, we approached a gentle rise in the road. But as we started to ride up it, Belmont suddenly put up his hand and reined his horse to a quick stop. I did likewise. "What is it?" I asked.

"Listen."

I did so, then shook my head, but Belmont nodded. "Up ahead. Somewhere over the rise. Someone's shouting. Maybe two voices."

I listened again, intently. Nothing.

"I'm certain of it," said Belmont. "Here, let's tie our horses to that bush over there. They'll hear us approaching on horseback. Might have already. But we'll be much quieter on foot."

I shot Belmont a gaze, openly suspicious. If he meant to take me, here was the perfect opportunity, alone in the prairie, off my trusty Hickory. The bandit banker read my thoughts precisely.

"Look, do you want to regain the gold and apprehend the Trailors?"

"Very much."

"Then get off the damned horse and follow me."

There's no glory for cowards, I thought as I brushed my hand against the pistol in my pocket. I jumped down and led Hickory over to the bush and secured her. Belmont did the same with his ride. "Follow me," he said.

We waded into the long grasses bordering the carriage path and crept forward, up the rise and down again. Every few minutes Belmont would stop, wait, and listen. Then he'd nod to himself and proceed. On the third stop, I thought I heard a noise on the breeze, and on the fourth I was sure of it. Just like Belmont had said: two voices.

We crept closer. The voices became louder, more distinct. The men appeared to be stationary, rather than moving away from us. During one of our periodic stops, I knelt in the grass and loaded my pistol, jamming the wad down the barrel, tearing off the top of the powder package with my teeth and pouring in the fine grains, ramming the ball into place.

Belmont watched me intently. He was apparently unarmed himself, and he displayed not the slightest concern about this fact. Once I'd finished loading my weapon, Belmont crept forward again, gesturing for me to follow.

The next time we stopped, I felt sure I recognized one of the voices as the high-pitched whine of Henry Trailor. And on the next stop, I concluded the other voice was his brother William. Quietly, I told Belmont. He nodded, as if he'd come to the same conclusion long ago.

"But why are they stopped in the prairie?" I asked.

We were at the top of another ridge now, looking down. A hawk flew in broad circles above us. The voices were coming from somewhere in the plain before us. But there was no vehicle in sight.

"And where's their carriage? They can't possibly be walking with that heavy trunk."

"Perhaps they've already passed it to a confederate," said Belmont.

Soon the voices were loud enough that we were almost on top of the brothers. And still we could not see them. I raised my gun and crept forward. Belmont was a few steps ahead of me. Suddenly he rose up to his full height.

"Good afternoon, gentlemen," he said.

I rushed forward to join him. There, in the grass in front of us, sat William and Henry Trailor. They were bound by thick rope, back to back, on the side of the carriage track. Their faces were badly bruised, as if they'd been on the receiving end of more than a few blows. Henry spit half-heartedly in our direction.

Neither their carriage nor the trunk was anywhere in evidence.

"We was robbed," said Henry.

William adopted something approaching his usual haughty tone. "At last! Untie us, if you please. And I insist you send word to your sheriff at once. Not only did I have to endure trial for a crime which I did not commit, but now I've been assaulted. My treatment has been nothing short of outrageous."

"What happened?" asked Belmont.

"We were attacked by two banditti on horseback. They followed our carriage for several miles, riding back and forth in front of our path, then set upon us from behind, from separate directions. We tried to fight them off, but they were too nimble for us. And well practiced at their thievery. They stole the carriage right out from under us, left us here to starve."

"You'll not starve anytime soon," said Belmont unsympathetically. "Where's your belongings?"

"They stole everything," said William. "Even my traveler's trunk. Of course, it was only carrying clothing and my contractor tools, but still, it's a loss to me. Some of those tools carry my sentiment."

"We found the tunnel into the bank vault," I said. "We know exactly what was in that trunk."

Henry winced, but William did an admirable job of keeping his face straight. "I have no idea what you're talking about," he said. "Besides, you'll never be able to prove what was in there." He nodded at the area around him. "It's gone. Now set us free."

I laughed. "You're fine right where you are. The sheriff will be by soon enough. We'll send him your way." I turned to Belmont. "Let's be off. Our real quarry remains ahead, it appears."

"What did the banditti look like?" Belmont asked.

"That was the worst part," wailed Henry.

"I can't believe you let them take us," said William, looking over at his brother for the first time.

"Me? You're the one who had the best chance to fight them off."

William shook his head and muttered, “You’ve failed us again. We had it all figured and you failed us.”

“What did the two men look like?” I repeated.

Henry glared at me sullenly. He appeared so defeated that, for a moment, I almost pitied him. Then he spoke. “They ain’t two men. One of them was a girl.”

CHAPTER 35

Belmont and I were back atop our horses, charging along the carriage path. My head was swimming.

"You are familiar," he said, as the cries of the Trailor brothers faded away behind us, "with a young woman who was staying at the American House with her cousin. A certain Miss Flannery."

I don't bother asking how he knew. "Yes. Though I never properly met the cousin."

"I became acquainted with both of them. They were very interested in my business. Too interested. Their intentions were clear to me." He rapped his animal with his walking stick, urging him to race ahead still faster. "But I underestimated them. To thieve from the thieves . . . this takes a good amount of preparation. And skill."

"It doesn't have to be them," I said, talking loudly over the horses' clattering hooves. "The prairies are thick with banditti. It could have been anyone. And perhaps the woman was actually a slight man, in disguise, in order to throw us off the trail."

"If you wish to think that, I shan't be the one to correct you. Such hopeful thinking is perfectly understandable for a man in your position." Belmont managed to make one of his elegant shrugs while riding at full tilt; I'd never been more infuriated at him. "I have already told you that you won't be the one to catch them, so what you choose to believe is not of consequence."

He rode ahead without a backward glance. I spurred Hickory to keep pace. I was determined to prove Belmont wrong, whatever that meant for Rose.

A few miles later, Belmont turned back toward me. "Was she worth it?"

"Who?"

"You know who. The Irish lass."

"No—yes—ask me after we've caught them."

Belmont whipped his horse again and rode ahead. For an instant I thought he'd murmured in his wake, "*I* thought she was," but no: surely it had only been the wind.

An hour after we'd left the Trailors behind, we came upon Sugar Creek, a meander of water flanked on both sides by giant sycamores, some more than a dozen feet in diameter, as well as cottonwoods, hickories, and oaks. For most of the year it was a modest stream that emptied lazily into the Sangamon River. Now, however, fed by the spring rains, it was a swiftly moving current some fifty feet across. Belmont and I pulled up on a bluff and gazed across; the horses snorted warily. Two muskrats chased each other in the shallows along the far bank, which was straited with bands of red and yellow ochre.

There were the unmistakable fresh tracks of a carriage in the mud on our side of the bank leading into the river and on the opposite side leading out. I pointed them out to Belmont, and he nodded.

"How deep, do you reckon?" asked Belmont.

I squinted into the swirling waters. "Could be six feet. Maybe more, this time of spring. There must be a ferryman near. I suppose that's how they got across. Let's call him."

I reached into my saddlebag and drew out a small horn. Wetting the mouthpiece, I gave three quick blasts. We listened intently.

No response. The afternoon sun filtered through the latticework of vines clinging to the treetops and danced on the ground in front of us.

"Try again," suggested Belmont. I did, and again we listened. Hickory cocked her ears attentively. There was no reply.

"I know a man," I said, "who waited three days at a river trying to summon a ferryman. Three straight days, he blew his horn at regular intervals, day and night. Finally, on the afternoon of the third, the ferryman floated on up. Said he'd heard him all along but he'd been too damn lazy to answer the call. But when he kept at it, the ferryman figured he'd better answer so he could finally get some sleep."

"Waited three days?" repeated Belmont, incredulity in his voice.

"That's right."

"I've never." He gave a great shout of "Alala!" and hit his horse on the rump with his walking stick. They charged down the bank and into the waters. The horse pranced through the river until the waters were up to its barrel; then it tossed its head and Belmont slid off, holding his saddlebags and the horse's lead high above his head with one hand while he swam with the other. Side by side they paddled through the deepest part. When the horse found his footing again, Belmont floated over and threw his leg over its back. He rode him out of the shallows and up the bank on the other side. When they reached the top of the opposite bluff, Belmont swung his horse around and gave another "Alala," this time triumphantly.

"There's your three days!" he shouted. "I'll give you three minutes; then we're going."

"Let's go, girl," I whispered into Hickory's ear. It had been a while, but we'd used to swim together back home at Farmington, in the man-made lake my father had created. Hickory carefully stepped down the bank and into the creek while I held on tight, and we swam through the waters together, just like old times. A minute later, Hickory was striding up the bank to take her place next to Belmont's horse, as I scratched behind her ear and whispered words of thanks.

"I told you you'd have to abandon caution," said Belmont, as if taking credit for Hickory's feat.

We resumed our ride through the vast, empty land. The sun and the breeze soon dried our wet clothing. We had seen only a handful of other riders out on the prairie all day. We had passed only one or two private dwellings and no inns or public houses at all.

"We'll come to the inn at Holland's crossroads soon," I said. "And the Illinois River is about twenty miles west from there. If we don't catch them before we reach the river . . ." I didn't voice the rest of the sentence aloud: *I'll never see Rose again.*

"We'll find her, don't worry," said Belmont.

The sun was starting to climb down the sky to our left. We surmounted a hillock, and looking far into the distance, we could see a structure with a thin line of smoke leaking from its chimney. A well-marked road in front of the building crossed the path we'd been following at a right angle.

"That'll be Holland's," I said. "We should ask if Holland has seen them."

Before long we were riding into the yard. We tied up the horses next to the trough, and Belmont started to head for the tavern. Before following him, I studied the yard. There was a dusty phaeton parked tight against the side of the barn. A fine Morgan was tied up nearby, grazing lazily from a pile of hay.

"Look—over there!"

My gun drawn, I hurried toward the carriage. It was empty. I climbed up onto the step and searched inside. No traveling trunk full of gold. Nothing.

"I don't see any owner's markings," said Belmont skeptically.

"It's just as Saunders described. The horse, too. And look." I wetted my forefinger and traced it through the dusty sidewall of the carriage, revealing dark-blue paint underneath.

"Something's not right," replied Belmont, shaking his head.

I eyed him suspiciously. "We've caught up with them. I don't see what's not right. They must have figured they'd escaped by now, and they've taken a room inside the inn. Come, I'm friendly with Holland from the merchant circuit. He'll tell us everything we need to know."

Inside, the public room carried a comforting, faintly sweet smell from the many pints of beer that had been spilled over the years. But the ready grin and wild side-whiskers of Holland were nowhere to be seen. Instead, we were greeted by a stranger, a stout man with thinning hair and thick fingers. He wore a bow tie and a fully buttoned black vest decorated with white swirls. The room was otherwise empty.

"Where's Holland?" I asked.

"His wife's bedridden," the man answered. "I've agreed to stand for him this week. Are you needing lodging or just a meal?"

Holland was a confirmed bachelor. But before I could signal Belmont, he charged ahead. "Do you have a pair staying here who drove up within the past few hours in the phaeton parked outside?"

"Perhaps," said the man.

Belmont repeated the question, this time sliding a golden eagle across the counter.

"Certainly do," said the man, nodding. "Told me they could pay in hard currency, and showed me the coins to prove it."

"Take us to their room." Belmont dumped a few more golden eagles onto the counter.

The innkeeper didn't hesitate. "Follow me."

He led us out of the public room, past the kitchen, and through a warren of hallways until we reached a closed door at the end of a corridor. The innkeeper looked at Belmont, standing at my side. "Ready?"

Belmont nodded. My hand tightened on my pistol; my heart beat rapidly. My eyes were fixed on the innkeeper's left hand, poised next to the door handle.

An enormous force crashed down on my head. And all was dark.

Chapter 36

When I awoke, I was lying on my side in a cold, damp room. I'd been stripped of my coat, and my shirt was soaked with sweat. When I tried to straighten up, I discovered my arms were tied together at the wrists and my legs tied together at the ankles. I strained against the ropes, but they were tight and did not budge. Looking through the sole window in the room, I could see that it was almost twilight outside. I'd been unconscious for several hours.

"Belmont?" I called out.

"Right here," came a voice from behind me.

I wriggled into a sitting position against the wall. Belmont was leaning against the opposite wall, bound in a similar manner. He, too, was missing his coat and personal effects. There was a cut on his forehead, covered with dried blood.

"He got you too?" I asked.

He nodded. "Right after you. I thought you said the innkeeper was a friend of yours."

"That fellow was an imposter."

"What?"

I stared at Belmont, thinking about the look that had passed between him and the false innkeeper the moment before I was struck. I still didn't trust the bandit banker.

Belmont saw my expression. "Surely you can't think I'm responsible for having us both assaulted."

"All I know is that you led us into an ambush. And that I've missed whatever's transpired for the past few hours. Whatever plans you and the banditti have made."

"Don't be ridiculous. I'm a victim, too. I've suffered just as much as you." He indicated the cut on his forehead.

"That doesn't mean—"

The door was flung open and two persons walked in: Rose and her cousin, Patrick, both clothed in dusty traveling cloaks. The cousin wore a battered straw hat pulled low across his face. They were carrying our belongings, and they tossed them at us. I wriggled toward my coat and started feeling around for the pistol.

"Don't bother," Patrick growled, and he showed me where he'd lodged my gun in his own coat pocket.

"Rose—" I began.

"Don't say a word, Speed," she said, her tone flat. "It will be better for both of us."

She had the same lovely face: two deep green pools for eyes and perfect auburn curls spilling out from beneath a cloth traveling cap. But her expression was wary, and her eyes were missing their usual shine. She was, I reflected, at once an intimate acquaintance and an absolute stranger.

Her cousin was focused on Belmont. "I thought you told us you were a banker—cousin to the Rothschilds and all that," he spat.

"That's right."

"You've been lying all along."

"Have I?" Belmont's voice was neutral, betraying neither fear nor surprise.

Patrick waved a torn piece of newsprint. "It says here you're a counterfeiter."

"Certain authorities believe me to be," said Belmont, with the hint of a smirk coming into his features.

"Is it true?"

Belmont shrugged. "I am informed that the newspapers in this country print the truth. Or at least they do sometimes."

"So you're saying it is true?"

"What do you think?"

Patrick considered this, then: "Are you a good one?"

"If I am one, I've never met anyone better."

"Who's he?" The bandito nodded toward me.

Belmont spit on the floor in my direction. "A sucker." Rose stiffened.

"What're you doing keeping company with a sucker?"

"I find it useful, on occasion, to have one around."

"He's not a friend of yours?"

"Certainly not."

"You mind if I shoot him with his own pistol?"

"Mind?" Belmont gave a short laugh. "I'd be grateful. He's grown tiresome. And there's little worse than a tiresome sucker."

Until now I'd been willing to believe Belmont's talk was all part of his act, but my confidence began to drain away as the bandito took out my pistol and checked to make sure a ball was loaded.

"Help me, Rose," I said.

"Do what he says," she replied, her face tense, "and no one will get hurt."

"Your name's Speed?" Patrick said, waving my pistol in front of my face.

I flinched. "That's right."

"Is this fellow telling us the truth? He's a counterfeiter and you're his sucker?"

I decided I had little choice but to follow Belmont's lead. "It's news to me," I said, doing my best to appear vexed, "but I suppose it must be so." I sighed, perhaps too grandly, but fortunately the bandito did not appear to be a particularly astute student of the human condition. He seemed, instead, pleased that he had mastered the situation.

"Well, I'll be," he said, nudging Rose in the ribs. "I'll be." Rose's expression hardened further.

"Where's the gold shipment you stole?" I said. "If it doesn't get returned to the State Bank, this economic depression is never going to end."

The bandito waved my gun in front of my face again. "It's our gold now," he sneered.

"The State of Illinois needs that gold."

"*We* need the gold," broke in Rose in an urgent tone.

"You don't, Rose. No one does. Not a whole trunk's worth. Take a few coins, if you must, and leave the rest."

Patrick laughed harshly, but the features of Rose's face had sprung to life. "Don't you understand, Joshua? It's not for the two of us. It's the rightful property of our kin. All our kin. None of us have been paid for months for the work we've done on your canal. Our fathers can't keep their children safe. Our mothers can't keep their children's bellies full." Her eyes shone with determination. "We didn't take the gold for ourselves. We claimed it for the people."

"Lincoln and the legislature are going to make sure your countrymen get paid. But they need the gold back to do it."

Patrick shook his head. "We saw the way your legislature works, staying there at the hotel across the street for the past month. The rich get paid. The politicians get paid. But the people don't. Especially not the Irish."

"It'll be different this time," I said. Turning to her, I added, "Rose, I swear it. This time will be different. You have my word."

"And you're going to make it so?" sneered her cousin. "*You*, Speed? You're a shopkeeper. You're nobody."

"Lincoln will make it so," I said.

Belmont laughed harshly. I turned to him, angry. "What are you laughing at?"

"I don't know which of you is more pathetic," he said. "The gold shipment. Ha! All of you are wasting your time."

Patrick started to challenge Belmont, but Rose put her hand on his arm. "Why do you say that?" she asked.

"Most of the coins in the trunk you stole are fake. Cheap metal painted to look like gold. You read the newspaper article. You think I'd give the State Bank actual gold coins?" Belmont sneered. "You picked the wrong ticket. But you know what's a whole lot more valuable than fake gold coins? Paper! Now there's the right ticket."

"What's valuable about paper?"

"There's a stage passing along the road outside any minute carrying a pouch stuffed full of blank bank notes." Belmont looked Patrick square in the eyes. "Do you know how much blank bank notes are worth?"

"How much?"

"Tell me what number to fill in. Any number. Five dollars a note? A hundred? Times thousands of blank notes. That's how much they're worth."

The cousin turned to Rose, perhaps intrigued by Belmont's offer, or perhaps confused by the math problem he'd served up. In any event, their attention left him for a moment. In a flash, Belmont grabbed at his walking stick, which the cousin had thrown at his feet. Belmont twisted the stick and one end slid off like a scabbard, and he was left holding a long knife, a sword in effect, rapier-sharp.

With two quick movements Belmont slashed through the ropes binding him. He leapt to his feet and slashed the bandito's hand. The man cried out in pain, blood gushing from his wrist, as my gun clattered to the floor.

"Untie me!" I shouted at Belmont.

But Rose's cousin soon regained his wits and he raised his arms into a fighting position, fists clenched, ready for combat, even as blood continued to leak from his wound. The two men circled each other warily.

"Help me, Rose!" I cried.

Rose knelt on the floor near me and stared directly into my eyes. My breath caught, and I felt the same frisson of excitement I'd felt when we'd been alone in her room at the American House.

"Help me," I said again, more quietly.

"I can't," she mouthed.

Rose picked up my gun from the floor. Then she stood and, gathering her skirts, ran from the room.

Chapter 37

Belmont and Rose's cousin fought, hand to hand, while I watched helplessly from the floor. Belmont had the advantage of being armed with his walking stick–turned–knife, but Patrick was tall and broad shouldered and, it soon became clear, an experienced grappler. They crashed into each other and into the walls of the bare room, neither party obtaining the upper hand.

"Untie me," I shouted at Belmont, "and I'll help you."

The banker bandit gave no sign he'd heard my plea amid the tumult, but some moments later a well-aimed kick from the bandito sent Belmont sprawling onto the floor near me. Without taking his eyes off his opponent, he reached out his knife and sliced through the ropes binding me. Then he leapt to his feet to confront his prey again.

I rose to my feet, stiff legged, and shook out my numb hands.

"Get to his right," said Belmont, "while I come at him from the other side. We can corner him together."

I considered. "You have the situation in hand, or will soon. I'm going after the gold." *And Rose.* I dashed out the door.

Figuring that the false innkeeper might still be holding sway in the public room, I proceeded through the inn cautiously, seeking a back exit. It took a while, and I tried several doors only to find them locked. Finally, I found one that opened onto the stable yard. I pushed through and shut it securely behind me, breathing deeply of the fresh night air.

The twilight skies were dark purple. The air was heavy with moisture. I searched the yard. The phaeton and horse that Rose and Patrick had stolen from the Trailors were gone. I gazed out at the crossroads just beyond the inn. Four directions to travel. I had one chance in four of guessing right. And if I guessed wrong, I'd never find her.

"Who's there?" shouted a high-pitched voice.

I turned, my fists clenched, fearing the false innkeeper had spotted me. But I saw instead that the words came from a slight stablehand, a boy of fifteen or sixteen years, with a patchy growth sprouting from his chin. He was advancing toward me with an iron bar clutched in his hands.

"I'm a friend of Holland's," I said. I tried to remember what Holland had said when we'd spoken the previous fall. "You must be his nephew. He told me, last time I was around, you were coming to work for him. Your name's . . ." I cast my mind back again. "Everson."

The young ostler relaxed his grip on the bar. "That's right."

I stuck out my hand. "I'm Speed. There was a phaeton parked over there." I pointed. "Did you see who left with it?"

"A *lady*, that's who." The boy grinned widely; several teeth were missing.

"Did you see which direction she went?"

"I can't say. She made me promise not to tell no one."

I reached into my pocket and pulled out several gold coins. "I can make it worthwhile for you."

"She gave me more, from the trunk she asked me and the boys to help her load before she rode off. She sure had a lot of gold in there." He whistled.

"But it's very important I find her," I said. "A matter of great public urgency. If you asked your uncle, he'd tell you to tell me."

The boy shook his head earnestly. "I gave the lady my word. And she said, 'Don't tell no one who don't know the secret word.'"

"The secret word?"

He grinned his gap-toothed grin again. "I reckon she was having me on. But she said, she told me a funny word I ain't never heard before and she said, 'If a fella comes along who knows the secret word, why you can tell *him* where I'm heading.'" He gazed at me again and shrugged. "Obviously you ain't him."

A thrill shot through my body. "Róisín!" I shouted.

The boy's mouth dropped open.

"Róisín!" I repeated. "It means 'little rose' in—oh, never mind. All that matters is that's the word. She told you to tell the man who said to you, 'Róisín.'"

The boy nodded dumbly.

"So which way did she go? Tell me at once! Which way?"

Belatedly, the boy pointed. North. "Towards Chicago. She said she was driving her trunk all the way to Chicago. I told her she'd do best to wait till dawn, no telling who might be riding the prairie at night, especially against a girl on her own, but she said she ain't scared. And off she rode."

I thanked the stablehand and jumped aboard Hickory. My heart pounding with excitement, we followed the stage road north as the last vestiges of light slipped from the corners of the sky.

Despite the prize that lay ahead, I went at a cautious pace. A single misplaced shoe from Hickory could easily result in a broken ankle, and that would be the end of the chase. I was wary, too, of coming upon other banditti without warning, alone in the midst of the boundless prairie. Every turn in the road, every little rise of the prairie, might reveal a clutch of deadly and determined men, ready to hazard their own lives and reckless to mine.

We passed on in silence. The only sounds came from the horse's hooves and her steady breathing. Every minute of that electric, dangerous night felt like an hour of ordinary existence.

The moon rose, and the broad meadows were lit by the pure and holy calm of the moon's soft light. At length I judged it must be after midnight. We had not passed any stagecoaches nor any lone riders during our resumed ride. It was just me and Hickory—and my churning thoughts.

Where is Rose? Ahead, somewhere in the vast land. And, more to the point, I realized, as I thought about it further, what would she do when I caught up with her? Kiss me? Shoot me? Either seemed possible.

Plainly, she had wanted me to follow after her, and eventually, since she knew I could ride Hickory faster and longer than she could drive her carriage, to catch up with her. But why? *What will she do?* I couldn't fathom. And then a new thought hit me. Hit me with such force that I nearly fell off Hickory. *What will* I *do?*

What will I do?

I rode through the night. The moon set. Thicker and thicker layers of clouds covered the firmament of stars until they were extinguished. I had to slow Hickory to a walk; the horse could barely see the ground beneath her. Then the rain started, a drizzle at first, making the prairie grass hiss like steam escaping from a hearth that's just been damped. The drizzle matured into a steady rain. In my haste to escape the inn, I'd left my hat, and the rain soaked my bare head and ran down into my eyes. I squinted around for any trees under which to take temporary shelter, but I could make out nothing but the rolling fields. So I kept a tight grip on Hickory and we trudged forward.

We had ridden for many hours when I saw a dark shadow looming in the tall prairie grasses to the side of the road. At first, I figured my sleep-deprived eyes were playing tricks, but there it was again. We rode toward it for several minutes before I knew for sure. A carriage. I steered Hickory over.

Rose was sitting on the exposed driver's seat of the phaeton, her cap and traveling cloak slick with rain, watching me approach.

Her horse, still harnessed to the conveyance, nosed around on the ground. The trunk from the bank vault rested at her side.

Her right hand held my pistol. It was aimed directly at me.

"Took you a good while," she said as I pulled up, breathing deeply with exertion, about ten feet away from her.

"Figured you were waiting so I could take my time."

"I'd just about concluded you weren't coming. That you didn't want to catch me after all."

I smiled. "I doubt you ever thought that."

"I could shoot you right now, and no one would ever be the wiser."

"Probably could," I agreed. "If you're going to, I wish you'd hurry up and get it over with." I looked at her, and she met my gaze. "But I don't think that's what you want."

She feigned deep consideration, but only for a moment. "No." Then, after a pause: "Do you suppose anyone knows where we are?"

"I doubt it. That stablehand is determined to guard your secret word." A thought suddenly occurred to me. "You didn't tell Belmont about your father's nickname for you, did you?"

"Belmont? Of course not. I've never had a private moment with the man in my life."

I chose to believe her. "Good. Then he won't be on his way. And I imagine he'll have gotten the better of your cousin, so he won't be coming after you, either."

"As far as Patrick knows, the plan was to drive west and disappear down the river." She thought about my words. "You didn't stay around to help Belmont fight him?"

I shook my head. "I didn't want to waste a second in pursuit of you."

She smiled and said, softly, "So here we are . . ." She did not continue. I did not say a word. We stared at each other. I felt longing, desire. What did she feel?

The rain had fizzled away to a dense fog. Now the fog started to dissipate, a sign that daybreak could not be far away.

Rose rested her arm on the trunk beside her. "Do you believe what Belmont said back at the tavern? About most of the gold coins in here being counterfeit?"

Belmont's actions at the crossroads had resolved my doubts. He was an interesting, complex fellow, to be sure. But at bottom he was a banker, not a bandit. "He was trying to confuse the situation, and it worked. But I don't believe he would have swindled Lincoln. I wager it's all real. Fifty thousand in gold coins."

She nodded. "I think so, too. Fifty thousand dollars. It's enough to pay all the wages our men are due and have a fair sum left over. There's more than enough for a person to disappear into the streets of Chicago, or the far reaches of the Wisconsin Territory, and make quite a life for themself." She looked up and stared into my soul. "More than enough for two persons to disappear and make quite a life for themselves together."

"Yes."

Here was the moment I had expected. Hoped for. Feared.

What will I do?

Her eyes were still intent on mine. "Speed?"

"Róisín?"

"What do you think?"

A kaleidoscope of images swirled through my mind. I thought about the downtrodden Irish mother in Canalport, unable to feed her children. About Lincoln and the countless hours he'd worked to secure the money to pay off the navvies and restart the state's economy. About Mary Todd and her prophesy that I would soon encounter a woman to spend the rest of my life with. About Belmont and his injunction that I throw aside my natural caution in pursuit of the prize. About Martha and her shining determination that, whatever the cost, justice be done.

I turned back to Rose and gave her my answer.

Chapter 38

The journey took three days and three nights. I soon learned that taking possession of a trunk containing a vast fortune in gold coins was much easier than moving it safely through the endless open prairie. I sent word for men to come help guard the shipment, and we took to sheltering by day and traveling by night. Finally, just as the third night was ebbing away toward dawn, we reached our destination.

Hickory and I rode into Springfield with the gold-laden carriage as the first hint of light came into the crepuscular skies. Sheriff Hutchason himself accompanied us on the final miles of the journey. Lincoln, Belmont, Mayor May, and the Springfield bank cashier all awaited our arrival on the front steps of the State Bank. They clapped as I pulled up and, with a flourish of my arms, presented them with the chest full of gold.

A small portion of the treasure was missing, I told them, coins that had been lost during the struggle in which I'd reclaimed the trunk. Then, ignoring their questions, I went to my room above the store and fell fast asleep.

When I awoke, it was nearly nighttime again. There was a note from Lincoln on the dressing table, suggesting that I join him and the mayor for a celebratory dinner at the American House.

It did not take long to find Lincoln. A peal of his laughter reached my ears as soon as I stepped through the front door of the grand hotel. I followed the noise and found my friend at a small table in the gentlemen's dining room, sitting opposite Big Red. Both men exclaimed as they saw me approach, and Lincoln gripped my arm and pulled up another chair.

"We're eager to hear how you recovered the gold," said Lincoln. "Tell us what happened."

I did, in a fashion, although I left out several key moments. Major Iles appeared in the middle of my story, and Lincoln ordered a round of whiskey. When the liquor arrived, I gulped it down and asked for another, while Big Red sipped steadily at his. Lincoln, who professed to be a teetotaler—although I knew better—mostly swirled the clear liquid in his glass. He appeared to be in an unusually good mood.

When I finished my tale, I fixed a serious stare on Lincoln. "You must assure me that now that we've recovered it, the money will go to the Irish workers."

Lincoln arched his eyebrows. "Belmont told me you'd recently been converted to their cause."

"There's nothing recent about it. I've cared about them ever since I saw the dire conditions at Canalport, on my trip to Chicago before the Sudden Change."

Lincoln nodded. "I'm teasing you, Speed. You have my word. Indeed, I spent the better part of today, while you were sleeping, working with the bank and my committee in the legislature to make sure the money goes where it's needed at once. Work on the canal is scheduled to resume next month, with the navvies getting paid everything they're past due."

"I'm glad to hear it," I said. "Makes all our efforts over these past weeks worthwhile."

"I agree." Lincoln turned to the mayor. "Don't you think so, Big Red?"

"What?" The mayor had been contemplating the contents of his whiskey glass.

"Don't you think it swell that work on the canal can proceed, now that Speed has recovered the gold for the state?"

"I'm sure I do." Big Red's enormous ears hung limply. In stark contrast to Lincoln's good cheer, the mayor appeared positively glum this evening.

"What happened to the Trailor brothers?" I asked. I realized that, in my exhausted state earlier, I'd neglected to inquire about them.

"The sheriff picked William and Henry up on the trail, right where you and Belmont said we could find them," said Lincoln. "In view of William's proven ability to escape, Judge Treat sent them directly to the Alton penitentiary. There's no escaping from there."

I shivered. A previous case with Lincoln had taken me to the new state prison in Alton, a wretched block perched on windswept bluffs high above the Mississippi River. It was a residence I wouldn't have wished on my worst enemy.

"And Archibald?" I asked.

"Archibald's become something of a notorious figure in the past few days. Infamous and famous in equal measure. People are slowly coming to understand he was one of the heroes of the whole affair."

"His true character revealed itself to me long ago."

"What about you, Big Red?" Lincoln turned to the man, a grin dancing on the edges of his wide lips. "You must admit surprise for how things ended up for Archibald, given how you spent weeks professing certainty he was guilty of a heinous crime."

The mayor cleared his throat and took a gulp from his whiskey glass. "I'm sure I do," he said again.

"Is something the matter?" I asked the mayor, peering at him.

"Throat's dry."

"Perhaps some more whiskey," Lincoln suggested to Major Iles, who passed by our table at that moment. "We're going to be here for a while."

As he marched away, Lincoln turned back to me. "In the past few days, I've had plenty of time to contemplate the Fisher murder-that-wasn't-a-murder. I keep coming back to one aspect. Do you know what I find the most telling part of the whole thing?"

"Beyond William Trailor sitting in jail for weeks for a crime he could prove he didn't commit, you mean?"

Lincoln smiled crookedly. "Yes, beyond that. It's the bones."

"What bones?" I asked, surprised by Lincoln's answer.

"Fisher's bones. The ones you and the sheriff found that morning in the rain, out on the other side of the millpond. Only we know now that they weren't Fisher's bones."

"So where did they come from?" I asked.

"Exactly."

I considered my question. "You suggested in your cross-examination of the sheriff that they might have been animal bones, but I tell you, they weren't. They were human bones. I'm certain of it."

Lincoln nodded. "I spoke to the sheriff, the day after the trial ended, about exactly that point. He dug the bones up from where he buried them, and we examined them together. Human bones, all right. Do you have any idea, Big Red, where they might have originated?" he added, turning to the man.

"None, I'm afraid," the mayor said sourly.

"I didn't either," continued Lincoln, "until I thought about it some more and realized that there's only one place in town, logically, where bones could come from."

He looked at me expectantly, and I felt the levers in my mind clicking into place. "Higgins Burying Ground!"

"Exactly." Once the private burial plot for the family of the town's cabinetmaker turned undertaker, it now served as the final resting place for all of Springfield's departed citizens.

"Did you ask Higgins if he's had any robberies? It might shed light on the Trailors', er, plot. Excuse the pun."

Lincoln grinned, his whole lantern jaw lighting up. "Very good, Speed. I did ask him. He's had no graves robbed. Other than, of course, the first day of the frantic search for Fisher's body. As you'll recall, a number of plots were dug up that day. On the orders of—"

"Big Red!" I exclaimed. Lincoln nodded.

The mayor had just swallowed a big gulp of whiskey, and he almost spit it out. "You're mistaken, both of you," he sputtered, once his coughing fit had subsided. "No one was giving orders to the rude mob that day. Certainly not me."

"My memory's different," said Lincoln. Turning back to me, he added, "And then I started thinking about why the search for Fisher was instigated in the first place."

"It began with the letter Postmaster Keyes intercepted," I said, thinking back, "relating that William had been spending gold coins he claimed to have inherited from Fisher."

"That's not quite right," said Lincoln. "The letter did surface, and it whipped up popular excitement. But who was the first person you actually heard say Fisher had been murdered?"

I tried to reconstruct the events of that day. I recalled listening to the postmaster read the letter from the top of an overturned crate. My leg twinged at the memory, and I recollected it had hurt as I stood listening to Keyes, hurt because upon terminating my failed attempt to court Mary Todd, I had rushed down Quality Hill in pursuit of . . .

I gazed across the table. "It was you, Big Red."

"What was me?"

"*You* were the one who told me Fisher'd been murdered. You

showed up, at the Edwards home, looking for Ninian, and you told me there'd been a murder."

He shrugged. "Maybe I did." To Lincoln, he said, "Don't know why you're bothering to dredge up all these trivialities. The gold's recovered and the Trailors are in the penitentiary. The affair's over and happily, too."

As he said this, Big Red did not appear happy.

"First answer me this, Red," said Lincoln. "Who told *you* there'd been a murder?"

Lincoln was leaning forward now, and while he remained seated, he had taken on the cadences and demeanor he used in the courtroom while cross-examining a reluctant witness. The exchanges never ended well for the witness.

"I . . . I don't recall," sputtered Big Red.

"You don't? As the mayor of Springfield, you organized a search party for the body of a man who was said to have been murdered, and you don't recall how you learned he'd been murdered?"

"I suppose Keyes must have told me. From the letter he intercepted."

"There was nothing about murder in the letter," I said. "I'm sure of it."

"Speed's right," said Lincoln. "I had the idea to retrieve the letter from Keyes last week, in the midst of the trial, when I was still working on Archibald's defense." He tapped the pocket of his coat. "It says nothing about murder."

"I was being cautious," said May. His ears had turned a splotchy reddish-pink. "The letter suggested foul play. I thought we ought to search for Fisher, in case something had happened to him."

"A lot of solicitude for a stranger you'd never met," I said.

"Here's another thing I've been wondering about," said

Lincoln. "Who first had the idea to arrest William and Henry Trailor for the supposed crime?"

"Sheriff Hutchason insisted upon it," said Big Red at once.

I shook my head. "The sheriff was opposed to the search from the beginning. Skeptical that there was anything or anyone to look for. Big Red was the one who gave the order to have the two men arrested." I turned to the mayor. "Gave the order that resulted in William Trailor being placed in jail in the first place."

"But since there was no physical evidence that Fisher was murdered, because of course he *wasn't* murdered," continued Lincoln, "the key to the scheme was Henry's confession. That evidence seemed ironclad, and it gave everyone a basis for believing William and Archibald had committed murder."

"I was there when Henry confessed!" I exclaimed. A few nearby diners turned to stare, and Lincoln motioned for me to lower my voice. "I was there, in the storeroom of the capitol building, as Big Red interrogated him until he confessed to having seen his brothers murder Fisher. But . . ." The full realization took a moment to sink in. "But it was a ruse. It was all made up to advance the scheme."

A failed attempt at a smile remained frozen on Big Red's face. He raised his whiskey glass and took a large gulp. His hands were trembling.

"And who," continued Lincoln, his eyes fixed on Big Red, "gave the order for William to be moved to the unfinished jail cell in the basement of the capitol, where he could dig his tunnel to the bank vault without being observed?"

"Tell me this," I broke in, turning to Lincoln. "Who knew that the actual destination of the gold was the vault at the Springfield bank, opposite the capitol jail, rather than Chicago?"

"Only three people," said Lincoln. "The plan depended on absolute secrecy. Myself. Belmont. And Big Red."

"You're . . . you're mistaken," said the mayor, trying to rally.

"Can't you see? I was always doing my job, defending the public's safety. Besides, the money's been recovered. No one is harmed in the end."

"It was recovered thanks to Speed and Belmont," said Lincoln. "No thanks to you."

"But you did recover the money," the mayor said urgently. "You recovered it, and I helped you do it. You see, I never wanted anything for myself. Never wanted harm to befall anyone."

"Do you remember him helping us?" Lincoln asked me.

I shook my head. "I remember Big Red showing up, uninvited, when we went to search the bank vault, wanting to learn what we knew and what we would uncover. In fact, he tried to slow us down from our searching. To give the Trailors more time to get away."

"That's precisely what happened," said Lincoln.

Big Red hung his head.

"I don't think you're a bad person, Red," continued Lincoln, now nearly in a whisper. "In fact, since Douglas caused you to lose your seat in Congress, we share a very prominent common enemy. That almost makes us friends." Lincoln smiled; Big Red did not. He took out his handkerchief and mopped his face.

"But, friend or not, justice must be done. Ah, just in time. Good evening, Humble."

Sheriff Hutchason had materialized beside our table. He put a meaty paw on Big Red's shoulder.

Chapter 39

The wedding took place on the grounds of Ninian and Elizabeth Edwards's mansion on Quality Hill, on the first Sunday in August. It was, people agreed, generous of the Edwardses to agree to host the affair, given everything that had happened. And yet, they never wavered in their commitment to host the happy celebration.

I was awoken early by the summer light coming through our window, and as I rolled over in bed, I saw that Lincoln was already awake, staring up at the ceiling. It was hard to tell which of us was more anxious.

"Have you decided yet what you're going to say?" I asked.

He shook his head back and forth on the pillow. "I'm hoping something will occur, when the moment arrives."

We dressed together, elbowing each other out of the way to take our turn in front of the small looking glass.

"I thought this day would never come," I said.

"Nor I."

"But they seem a happy couple, don't you think?"

"I must say," replied Lincoln, "I'm skeptical matrimony could make any man happy, but if there's anyone who can make it work, it'll be Archibald."

I was shocked when Archibald Trailor had delivered the news

the prior month; I'd never seen it coming. And certainly he hadn't seen his bride-to-be coming.

"You're not upset, are you?" Lincoln continued.

"At what?"

"That he's marrying *her.* I know you had strong feelings on the subject."

"Passing feelings, I assure you. No, I'm pleased with how it ended up."

We walked together along the dusty streets, joining others who were headed up the hill for the affair. By the time we reached the curving drive of the grand house, I was sweating beneath my black frockcoat. I saw tiny droplets of perspiration gathering at the crown of Lincoln's stovepipe hat.

Edwards had erected a large white tent to shield his guests from the sun. There were several unoccupied seats as we entered, but Lincoln suggested we sit in the back row, so he wouldn't obscure anyone else's view. We saved seats between us for the two ladies, once they'd finished their duties as the bride's attendants.

Eventually the hour of reckoning arrived. Martha and Mary, each dressed in her Sunday finest, stepped out of the Edwardses' front door and began processing toward the tent. Between them was Martha's cousin Matilda Edwards, wearing a blue calico dress. Matilda blushed deeply when she saw her groom waiting nervously for her at the front of the aisle.

Their duties completed, Martha and Mary came back to the seats we'd reserved for them. We all exchanged congratulations on the happy day. The couple was, we agreed, well suited. Two persons who enjoyed the simple pleasures in life without thinking too deeply about them. And Miss Edwards, it must be said, appeared to enjoy the whiff of adventure that had followed Archibald after his trial and surprise acquittal.

As we settled in to witness the ceremony, Martha and I shared a long embrace. It was, both of us knew, the last grand occasion on which we'd be together for a very long time.

"Good luck," I whispered.

"You, too."

Archibald and Matilda were not the only young residents of Springfield bound for new adventures. Six weeks after I'd ridden back with the trunk full of gold, Martha and I had gone for a walk together out of town. The prairie was in full springtime bloom, the lush green grasses forming a beautiful contrast with the bright colors of a thousand flowers. A gentle, warm wind blew. We walked slowly through the fields, arm in arm, and I was happy to be able to enjoy nature's vibrant tapestry for once without being in a hurry to get from one place to another.

As we turned around to head back into town, Martha let go of my arm and put her hand to her mouth. I saw tears forming in her eyes.

"What?" I asked.

She started to speak, but then shook her head.

"What is it?" I repeated, more urgently this time.

"I don't know how to tell you this . . ."

"Just say it. You're making me worried."

"I'm leaving Springfield."

"I don't understand." All I could think in the moment was that Martha had agreed to marry a vagabond of some sort. Perhaps a traveling peddler selling patent remedies.

"Mary and I have been talking, for months now, and she encouraged me to do it." Martha looked me full in the face. The tears were gone; her fresh face shone with grit and determination, and I realized anew how much I treasured her. "It was her idea as much as mine. Oh, Joshua! I know how you admire Miss Todd. Please give me your full support. For her sake, if not for mine alone."

"Full support for what? What are you planning to do?"

"Go to school!"

"What?" I was sure I hadn't heard her properly.

"Go to school! To the Jacksonville Female Academy."

"But you're already good with the needle," I protested. "And I'm sure your quality at the hearth, with the saucepan, will improve over time, when you've had enough practice."

Martha flushed. "Neither cooking nor sewing is in the curriculum, I'll have you know. I'll be studying"—she took a deep breath—"reading, spelling, defining, writing, mental and written arithmetic, ancient and modern geography, history, natural philosophy, chemistry—"

"There aren't enough hours in the day," I protested.

"I'm not finished. Constitution of the United States and of Illinois, botany, astronomy, physiology, geometry, intellectual and moral philosophy, and algebra. Oh, and natural philosophy and evidences of Christianity. All the courses of instruction are listed in the catalog Mary got for me. I've been reading through it every night, before I say my prayers, to make sure I'm ready. I think I am."

What could I do but give her my support and blessing? And so I did.

After the wedding ceremony ended, there was much dancing on the lawn to the tunes played by a rump orchestra, several regular players on strings, supplemented by a changing cast of amateurs. Lincoln took his turn on the fiddle, playing up a lively tune while prancing about unevenly on his gangly legs, as the newlywed couple and the great throng of their guests twirled and laughed with delight. Even Stephen Douglas was coaxed out to take a turn on the floor, though he soon retreated to the side of Edwards's yard to intrigue with his fellow Democrats, no doubt planning their strategy for the fast-approaching presidential election.

The occasion was notable, too, for who was not present on

Quality Hill. Both of the bridegroom's brothers were absent. William and Henry Trailor, along with Big Red May, had been convicted of their many crimes. All three men would long remain in the state prison at Alton. Archibald had not attended any of his brothers' legal proceedings, and he'd told me he had no wish to see them ever again.

I caught sight of an aristocratic profile and went up to greet its possessor.

"Belmont! I was afraid you wouldn't make it back in time."

"Wouldn't have missed it," the banker returned. "I feel as if I'm almost a full-blown member of the community."

"For your services, we should make it official," I said.

The story of our successful rescue of the bank's gold had become well known in Springfield. Or, at least, a version of the story had become well known. In the public version, Belmont had fought off two banditti and rescued the bulk of the money. The banditti had not been captured, and Belmont admitted that in the confusion of the rescue operation he hadn't gotten a good look at either one. Nonetheless, for his services, Belmont was hailed as a hero.

Lincoln and Belmont were the only people in Springfield who knew the full story of the gold's recapture. One evening not long after my return with the treasure chest, I told them about how I had convinced Rose to let Lincoln have the gold to carry out his rescue plan for the state. Rose had taken enough coins to procure food in the meantime for the children dangerously near starvation. We'd shared a long embrace, one punctuated by kisses and tears on both sides. And promised each other we'd be together again, sometime.

The legislature had never replaced the crooked cashier at the State Bank in Chicago, the man whose failed attempts at pork speculation had begun the entire misadventure. Several weeks before Archibald's wedding, Lincoln told me the legislature had resolved to create a new position, that of president of the entire State Bank, to head off a repeat of the financial disaster that had befallen the state. The job would be based in the growing commercial center of Chicago.

"Sounds sensible enough," I said, distracted by the task of sorting through a crate of ladies' unmentionables that had just arrived at my store.

"I've been authorized to offer the position to you."

"What?"

Lincoln grinned at me. "The fellows in the legislature were mighty impressed by your calm dealings during the recent troubles. And of course by your reputation for probity in how you run your store. And *I* thought the location of the job in Chicago might be of particular interest."

I hadn't said yes yet, but I certainly hadn't said no. Indeed, I'd begun discussions with a few of the neighboring storekeepers on the square to find a buyer for my general store.

The wedding celebration carried on all day. Eventually it came time for Lincoln to make his remarks toasting the happy couple. Lincoln cleared his throat and, raising a glass, spoke eloquently about Archibald's lasting place in the hearts of the men and women of Springfield. "Hear! Hear!" called the crowd in return. Lincoln also praised the beauty of the bride with an enthusiasm that made her blush.

As Lincoln spoke, with the crowd gathered around him in a wide semicircle, I saw Archibald staring off into the distance. He had been the life of the party for most of the day, singing and drinking and dancing lustily with his new bride. But now, as I caught sight of him, there was an expression of faraway sadness on his face. I felt certain his emotion came from the knowledge he'd been betrayed by his two older brothers. Having depended all my life on the guidance of my older brother, James, I could scarcely imagine how Archibald felt.

At length the sun began to set. Below us at the foot of Quality Hill, in the town proper, tiny pinpricks of light began to wink on: hearths aglow, awaiting preparation of the evening meal; candles lit, ready for work to continue or leisure to commence.

I stood together with Lincoln, Mary, and Martha, gazing out at the beautiful vista. We all had our arms wrapped around each other. It had been a joyous day, a celebration of new beginnings and quickly approaching endings, and none of us wanted it to be over.

Belmont approached.

"I'm off for New York City in the morning," he said. "I've received word I'm to set up a banking operation for the family there. Wish me luck. I'll need it."

"I'm certain you'll be most successful," said Lincoln, "and that luck won't play any part."

"I hope so. I wanted to convey my sincere thanks for everything each of you has done while I've been in Springfield."

"Are you sure?" I asked, half drunk. "One of the things I've done is accused you of banditry."

"Well, everything but that," said Belmont. We all laughed. Lincoln and I shook his hand heartily, and Mary and Martha curtsied and accepted his gallant kisses.

Belmont took a few steps away before he turned back. "Say, Lincoln—" he began.

"Yes?"

"Do you want to come with me? To the East? New York City, or perhaps Washington. I know this country could use a determined voice like yours on a bigger stage. On the biggest stage there is."

One of Lincoln's arms was thrown around Mary's waist; the other hand rested on my shoulder. When Belmont made his proposal, Mary grabbed at Lincoln's arm, but whether to push him forward or hold him back, I could not tell. I thought I saw a look of temptation edge onto Lincoln's face. But before I could be certain, it had vanished.

Lincoln gazed out at Springfield and the vast prairie beyond. The setting sun lit up his blunt features as if he were a statue made of weathered copper.

"Someday," said Lincoln. "But there's more work to be done here. And more adventures to be had."

Historical Note

A House Divided is a work of imaginative fiction, but it is directly based on the actual life and times of Abraham Lincoln and Joshua Speed. Lincoln and Speed shared a room—and a bed—above Speed's general store in Springfield, Illinois, from April 1837 until early 1841, and Lincoln's contemporaries recognized Speed as his "most intimate" friend. In later years, Speed would serve as a bank president in his native Louisville.

The Trailor brothers' murder case is one of the great unsolved mysteries of Lincoln's actual law practice. (The brothers' name is also spelled "Trayler" or "Trailer" in various contemporaneous records, but I have adopted the spelling used by Lincoln himself.) Notably, one of the central primary source documents about the case is a long letter Lincoln wrote *to* Speed, as in real life Speed was absent from Springfield when the remarkable events took place.

"Dear Speed," begins Lincoln's letter of June 19, 1841, "We have had the highest state of excitement here for a week past that our community has ever witnessed; and, although the public feeling is now somewhat allayed, the curious affair which aroused it is very far from being, even yet, cleared of mystery."

The actual, known facts closely resemble those I have adopted for the novel. Archibald Trailor, the youngest of three Trailor brothers, was a carpenter living in Springfield. His older brothers, William and Henry, lived elsewhere in Illinois. An eccentric man named Archibald Fisher lived near William and was friendly with him. On the eventful occasion, the two older Trailor brothers, with Fisher in tow, came to Springfield to visit Archibald.

One evening, all four men went out together "looking about the town," but only the three brothers returned. The Trailors made preliminary searches for Fisher, but when they did not immediately locate him, William and Henry left Springfield and returned to their respective homes. None of this excited general interest until, several weeks later, the Springfield postmaster received a letter stating that William was suddenly spending great quantities of gold coins and bragging that Fisher had died and willed him $1,500.

The publication of this letter caused great tumult, and search parties were organized for the supposedly dead man. Cellars, wells, and pits were examined; recently dug graves were reopened; and Hickox's millpond was drained. Fisher's body was not found, but what appeared to be bloodstains were uncovered and officers were sent to arrest William and Henry. As a longtime peaceable resident of the community, Archibald Trailor was considered above suspicion.

Henry Trailor was detained first. After several days of questioning by the mayor and attorney general, Henry confessed that his brothers had killed Fisher and then, after the murder, enlisted Henry in concealing the body. Henry specified that he had seen Fisher's dead body and described the precise location of the murder and where the body was hidden; upon renewed searching, no body was recovered. Nonetheless, William and Archibald were brought before an examining court on the charge of murder. Lincoln and several colleagues defended the Trailors.

At this point, a Dr. Gilmore appeared in Springfield and

claimed that Fisher was alive and under his care. As Lincoln later recalled, "Gilmore's story was communicated to Henry Trailor who, without faltering, reaffirmed his own story about Fisher's murder." As a result, the townspeople concluded that Gilmore had fabricated his story and was in cahoots with the Trailors; many agitated that Gilmore ought to be arrested and thrown into jail, too.

A trial commenced. Henry testified to his brothers' guilt and "bore a rigid cross-examination without faltering or exposure." Further witnesses supported Henry's testimony with other evidence of the Trailors' guilt, including their suspicious actions on the night of Fisher's disappearance and evidence that William had suddenly come into an inexplicable fortune. These witnesses, reported an early historian, gave "a combination of testimony that seemed to weave a network of circumstances about the prisoners, from which it would appear to any other than a legal mind, to be utterly impossible to extricate them."

In response, the defense called Gilmore to testify that Fisher was actually alive and under his care. Gilmore explained that Fisher was "subject to temporary derangement of mind, owing to an injury about his head received early in life." And indeed, a few days later, Fisher himself, albeit "in bad health," was conducted back to Springfield. The Trailors were discharged by the court.

Both Archibald and William Trailor died within two years of their trial. One contemporary said, "If ever a man died of a broken heart it was Archibald Trailor." Neither man ever explained the suspicious circumstances that had led to the concerns of foul play in the first place. Henry Trailor lived for decades longer, but he never revealed why he had made the false charge of murder against his brothers. According to one early chronicler of the Trailors' story, "it is said that the three brothers never met after they passed out of the courtroom."

Lincoln himself foresaw that only fiction could make sense of the bizarre case. Recounting the history of the Trailor brothers' saga in the *Quincy Whig* in June 1846, Lincoln concluded by saying, "It may well be doubted whether a stranger affair ever really occurred." At the same time, Lincoln noted, "It is readily conceived that a writer of novels could bring [the] story to a more perfect climax."

While the gold shipment robbery scheme in the novel (my attempt at a 'more perfect climax') is my invention, many of the elements of that scheme actually did take place in Illinois in the tumultuous 1830s and 1840s. Crucially, in an era of "hard money," the amount of gold and silver coinage physically held by a bank in its vaults determined the amount of paper money or credit it could issue and therefore the economic activity the bank could foster. In one speech in the era, Lincoln complained about gold and silver coins "rusting in iron boxes" in bank vaults instead of being used in circulation.

The State Bank of Illinois was organized in the mid-1830s, with branches in several cities around the state, including Springfield and Chicago. From the start, the state banking system was riddled with mismanagement and corruption. The Chicago branch really did go broke when its cashier, W. H. Brown, lost $26,000 in bank funds in a scheme "to engage in pork speculation with two Chicago commission men." At one point in the late 1830s, the State Bank "suspended its discount [lending] business until it received a shipment of $280,000 in gold and silver from New York and New Orleans." And resourceful, armed banditti roamed the open Illinois prairies of the 1830s, searching for stagecoaches to rob. Gold and silver shipments destined for the State Bank were frequent targets.

Lincoln served on the joint select committee to investigate the State Bank in the Illinois legislature, and he gave several speeches on the banking turmoil that occasioned much excitement among his contemporaries, although they are notable to the modern reader mostly for their extreme length and nearly impenetrable subject matter.

The state of banking in Illinois did not improve quickly thereafter. An ardent spiritualist by the name of Seth Paine founded the Bank of Chicago in 1852. One of his first official actions was to hire a trance medium, a Mrs. Herrick, to give banking officers the advice of departed spirits. As one historian has recounted, "The spirit of Alexander Hamilton [the first secretary of the treasury] was, through Mrs. Herrick, to direct the policy of the bank. If a person came in to do business and Mrs. Herrick or the spirits did not approve of him, he was unceremoniously thrown out onto the street by some burly bouncers kept for that purpose."

Work on the Illinois and Michigan Canal, designed to link Lake Michigan to the Mississippi River, began in 1836 but ground to a halt when the state ran out of money from the combined effects of the nationwide Panic of '37 and the state's own financial mismanagement. Ironically, it was the failure of the State Bank in the early 1840s that spurred the state to fund renewed work on the canal, as the legislature realized that the only way out of the crisis was the revenue that the completed canal would produce.

The canal finally opened for navigation in April 1848. Almost immediately, it was overtaken by the emergent railroad as the primary means of passenger travel in the region. Nonetheless, the canal continued to play an important role in facilitating the shipment of goods throughout the 19th century. It remained in use until 1933.

Today, a system of rivers, lakes, canals, and gates termed the Illinois Waterway connects the Great Lakes to the Mississippi River. And the state's belief that the rude collection of hovels perched on the muddy ground beside Lake Michigan was destined to become a major hub for trade was soon realized. Chicago became one of the ten largest cities in the country by 1860 and the nation's second largest by 1890, a status it would hold for the following century.

The Ladies' Education Society was founded in Jacksonville, Illinois (about thirty miles west of Springfield) in October 1833. It is recognized as one of the oldest women's organizations in the United States. Shortly thereafter, the society created the Jacksonville Female Academy for the education of young women in the frontier state. The only qualifications for an applicant were that she desire education and be capable of benefiting from it. By the 1835–1836 term, the academy had sixty-eight pupils. It had a remarkably modern mission. As the 1836 catalog announced, "The object of the instruction imparted in this Institution is the cultivation of the physical, moral and intellectual facilities, in such a manner as that the pupils shall be prepared to perform well their part in the several relations of society to which they may be called."

The Sudden Change of December 1836, when a freak, sudden cold blast raced across the region, was one the most-recalled weather events in the early history of Springfield. At least four men who were caught out on the prairie froze to death, and countless livestock were lost. As one early historian related, "It has been told to me time and again that chickens and geese, also hogs and cows, were frozen in the slush as they stood, and unless they were extricated by cutting the ice from about their feet, remained there to perish."

In addition to the three Trailor brothers, many of the supporting characters in the novel are also drawn from life. As in the novel, the Trailor brothers' case was prosecuted unsuccessfully by Illinois attorney general Josiah Lamborn. Lamborn's legal career was characterized by ever greater failure. Shortly after he joined the bar, the Illinois Supreme Court found his conduct "highly censurable . . . undignified and degrading," but narrowly declined to disbar him. His most famous assignment was leading the prosecution of the five men accused of murdering Mormon founder Joseph Smith in Carthage, Illinois, in May 1844. All of the defendants were acquitted. When he was not renominated for the position of attorney general, Lamborn is said to have begun drinking heavily. He died of delirium tremens—alcohol withdrawal—several years after his term ended, at the age of thirty-eight.

Judge Samuel Treat presided over the Sangamon County Circuit Court from 1839 to 1848. He later served on the Illinois Supreme Court and Federal District Court for Illinois. In all, he served continuously in the judiciary for forty-eight years, during which time he presided in over 1,000 cases in which Lincoln appeared as attorney.

William "Big Red" May was the first mayor of Springfield, having previously served as an Illinois representative in Congress. He was replaced in Congress by Lincoln's law partner, John T. Stuart. After his mayoralty, Big Red was infected by Gold Rush fever and headed to California. He died in Sacramento in 1849.

Major Elijah Iles was a Springfield founder, businessman, and entrepreneur, who built the grand American House across from the new state capitol building in 1839. Major Iles had commanded the young Lincoln in the Black Hawk War of 1831–1832. Remarkably, the expedition in which Iles served included two future U.S. presidents (Lincoln and Zachary Taylor) as well as Lieutenant Jefferson Davis, future president of the Confederacy.

Other real-life members of Lincoln and Speed's circle of friends and rivals in 1840 Springfield included Democratic politician and long-time Lincoln rival Stephen Douglas (forever linked with Lincoln through his participation, two decades later, in the landmark Lincoln-Douglas Debates of 1858, as well as a presidential candidate against Lincoln in the 1860 election); the young, Princeton-educated lawyer James Conkling; Speed's store clerk Billy Herndon, later to become Lincoln's final law partner; Simeon Francis, publisher of the *Sangamo Journal*; the postmaster James Keyes; the court clerk James Matheny (later the best man at Lincoln's wedding); Lincoln's office boy Milton Hay; and the political scion (and Lincoln's future brother-in-law) Ninian Edwards. Ninian's niece Matilda Edwards was among the young women of Springfield who were courted by both Lincoln and Speed.

August Belmont was born in 1813 in Hesse, Germany, and grew up in the Free City of Frankfort. He was apprenticed to the Rothschild banking empire and sent to the New World to expand the empire in 1837, at age twenty-four. He quickly became a prominent banker, eventually settling in New York City. In later years, Belmont and Lincoln had a complex relationship. Belmont chaired the Democratic National Convention in Charleston, South Carolina, in 1860 that nominated Stephen Douglas to run against Lincoln. Still, Belmont strongly opposed Southern succession, and he supported the Union cause during the Civil War, although he wrote a steady stream of correspondence to Lincoln and his cabinet members, offering unsolicited (and, one imagines, unwelcome) advice on the prosecution of the war.

After the war, Belmont became one of the leading figures of the Gilded Age. He also found time for his interests as a sportsman. In 1867, he organized a horse race in New York City that survives to this day with his name. The Belmont Stakes is run every year in June as the final leg of horse racing's Triple Crown. Belmont died at his Fifth Avenue mansion in November 1890. It was front-page news in the following morning's *New York Times*.

As a young boy, the little "chief herdsman" Bill Davidson testified for Lincoln in a hotly disputed case. As Davidson would recall seven decades later, Lincoln "took my hand in his and talked to me in a kind and sympathetic way . . . Every time the lawyers on the other side tried to bully and frighten me, Lincoln appealed to the judge on my behalf. He so won my childish affections that he always held a warm place in my heart."

All of which brings us to Mary. Mary Todd was the subject of a highly spirited courting competition when she moved to Springfield in the fall of 1839 to live with her elder sister, Elizabeth (Todd) Edwards. One contemporary observer of Mary in Springfield wrote, "Miss Todd is flourishing largely. She has a great many beaux." The qualities Mary was seeking in a potential suitor are striking. She told her sister she sought "a good man, with a head for position, fame and power, a man of mind with a hope and bright prospects, rather than all of the houses and gold in the world."

Lincoln, Douglas, and Speed, among many others, all vied avidly for her hand. Speed had his moments—Mary complained good-naturedly in a letter to an intimate friend about "Mr. Speed's ever-changing heart, which he is about to offer to another shrine"—but in this field, as in so many others in their intertwined lives, the final battle came down to Lincoln and Douglas. Douglas is reputed to have proposed marriage; years later, Mary told a confidante that she had turned him down with a chillingly prescient statement: "'I can't consent to be your wife. I shall become Mrs. President, or I am the victim of false prophets, but it will not be as Mrs. Douglas.'"

That left Lincoln. As suggested in the novel, Lincoln faced opposition from the self-consciously aristocratic clutch of Todd sisters, who had grown up in one of the leading families in Lexington, Kentucky, before being sent, one after the other, to find husbands in Springfield. Mary's next older sister, Frances, considered Lincoln "the plainest man" in Springfield, and her eldest sister (and guardian), Elizabeth, later recalled that "Lincoln was unable to talk to women and was not sufficiently educated in the female line to do so." Nonetheless, sometime during 1840, Lincoln and Mary moved from friendship to courtship and wooing. As of the time the novel ends, in the late summer of 1840, it appeared to Springfield observers that the two ambitious young persons were on a smooth path to marriage and a lifetime of commitment and harmony.

The truth was very different, but that's a story best told at another time.

Acknowledgments

Like the other books in the Lincoln & Speed Mystery series, this novel is the product of substantial original historical research. In addition to those persons thanked in previous volumes, I want to thank the following for their assistance with my research efforts: Kathy L. Nichols, executive director of the Farmington Historic Plantation in Louisville, the Speed family home where Joshua grew up; Devin Payne Serke, assistant director at Farmington; Tom Wright of the Mary Todd Lincoln House in Lexington, Kentucky; and Tim Waits at the historic Cave Hill Cemetery in Louisville.

A House Divided benefited greatly from the careful reads and sympathetic notes of Joshua F. Thorpe, Christin Brecher, and Michael Bergmann. Initial drafts of certain chapters of the novel were developed as part of a writing group at the peerless New York Society Library. My colleagues at the NYSL included Lillian Clagett, Susan Dudley-Allen, Janet Gilman, Jane Murphy, Alan Siegel, Helena Sokoloff, Victoria Reiter, Carolyn Waters, and Mimi Wisebond. Writer and editor Patrick LoBrutto gave helpful input on an early sketch of the novel. Elena Hartwell generously lent me her equine expertise.

My publisher Matt Martz at Crooked Lane Books continues to provide fantastic support for my Lincoln & Speed series. I am grateful for the efforts of the entire Crooked Lane team, including Sarah Poppe, Jenny Chen, and Ashley Di Dio. My agent Scott Miller is a rock-solid guiding light and all-around good guy.

I have been fortunate in the past year to begin working with the tireless Kathie Bennett of Magic Time Literary on publicity matters. I am grateful for the continuing efforts of Kathie and her team, including Roy Bennett and Susie Zurenda.

My work on this book has been greatly aided by the support and encouragement of friends and family too numerous to list by name. I'll mention here only Roifield Brown, Shannon Campbell, Joel and Carla Campbell, Steven Everson, Donna Gest, Marc Goldman, Laura Kupillas, Atif Khawaja, C. Mark Pickrell, Bob and Rosemary Putnam, Joel Schneider, Mark Stein, David Thorpe, Alina Tugend, and Caroline Werner.

I could not have written the book without the love and support of my three sons, Gray, Noah, and Gideon Putnam, and of my wife, Christin Putnam. Christin is the first and last reader of every word I write, as well as an inexhaustible source of good cheer, keen editorial notes, and crucial plot points. You are my everything, Christin. I love you very much.

Finally, this book is dedicated to my sister, Lara Putnam. Lara was my first editor when we shared made-up stories with each other as children. (I think she has finally forgiven me for creating an imaginary friend, "Police-y," whose only apparent role in our make-believe land was to arrest *her* imaginary friend, "Ghosty.") She has since become an eminent historian and chair of the history department at the University of Pittsburgh. Lara was also present at the creation of this series, suggesting the essential insight that I could tell young Lincoln's stories through Speed's eyes. Since then, she has sent me a never-ending stream of historical ideas and tidbits to consider, as well as reading closely the draft manuscript of each of my books. I can never thank her enough.